The Road from
Cromer Pier

Follow the author on twitter: @authorgore
Facebook: Martin Gore
website: www.martingore.co.uk

The Road from Cromer Pier

Martin Gore

Dedication

When I wrote The Road to Cromer Pier, *it never occurred to me that there would be a sequel. Personally, I dislike books where the author leaves a cliff-hanger, forcing you to buy the next book to find out what happened. That I've written one at all is due to the touching feedback I've received from the first book, and a sense that while* Pier *was complete in its own right, my characters had a lot of unfinished business in their lives.*

I wrote it during the awful pandemic, but the action takes place before it. My heart goes out to the creatives across our land, deprived of their livelihoods, as we are of the joy their work brings us. As I write this, Cromer Pier Theatre stands empty, and the cast and crew are, as like as not, furloughed or worse. I can only repeat my dedication to them from the first book, and hope that they will be back to entertain us soon. In the words of Joni Mitchell:

'Don't it always seem to go, that you don't know what you've got 'till it's gone.'

My thanks to Claire Dyer and Juliet England as editors, and Simon Hartshorne for the graphics, including the splendid cover design. My thanks to the people of Cromer and its visitors who have taken the trouble to post those lovely reviews.

My thanks also, of course, to the staff of Cromer Pier Theatre who made me so welcome for the launch of the original Road to Cromer Pier *book, and to Jarrold's of Cromer for stocking it. I hope to see you all again soon.*

Although set in real places for much of the time, all of the characters are fictitious. The pier itself is owned by North Norfolk District Council and managed by Openwide Coastal Limited. Any similarity in name to any actual person is purely coincidental.

Martin Gore
March 2021

Also by Martin Gore:
Pen Pals – 2016
The Road to Cromer Pier – 2019

1.

April Showers

On stage at Cromer Pier Theatre, Amy Raven was doing a sound check with Judy, the theatre's sound technician, ready for the show that evening. It was sold out. Amy was the local girl made good, after all. West Runton born and bred. She'd had her first audition on this very stage more than ten years ago. She'd made her debut as a dancer in the 2009 show, when the international star Lauren Evans had been the headliner. It was Lauren who'd got her signed up by her agent, Frank Gilbert.

A capable singer and dancer, she'd appeared in various West End musicals and had had the lead in one for two years. She'd headlined in Cromer, and then Frank Gilbert had got her another leading role in the West End. She was the next big thing. Then, in 2018, her world fell to bits.

She was now picking up the pieces. This show was the first of her comeback, and she was nervous. But this was her hometown crowd; surely that would be easier? After all, she'd started her singing career busking on the promenade in front of this pier. She tried to think of tonight as just another gig.

Director Karen Wells sat impassively watching from the back of the raised seats. As someone with previous experience of the highs and lows of this business, she was interested in how

Amy was. She looked ridiculously thin, but her voice seemed as good as ever, if slightly rusty.

Could they take the risk? Frank Gilbert had contacted her a couple of months earlier to ask whether they'd consider a one-night show. They'd jumped at the opportunity. Not only did Karen want to help someone she considered a friend, but it also made excellent business sense.

But, of course, the big question that Frank Gilbert hadn't yet asked, but undoubtedly would, was about Amy headlining the Cromer Summertime Special once again. From his point of view, it would be a sensible next step. Karen knew Amy was now living at home with her family, but it was an uncompromisingly long season. Could the theatre take the risk?

Karen had asked her mother, Janet Wells, to come along that evening, and her boyfriend Bryn was playing guitar in Amy's backing band, so at least she wouldn't be short of advice.

*   *   *

Janet Wells sat in the garden of The Maples nursing home visiting Cyril Brown. Ordinarily, he'd have been performing his Punch and Judy show on the pier, but not this year. She'd wheeled him from his room on to the terrace, which had a nice sea view on a decent spring day.

She'd made sure that Cyril had plenty of layers on first, and a warm blanket around his lower half, but he always wanted to be outdoors. As much as he wanted to go home, Janet knew that a return from the nursing home looked increasingly unlikely as the weeks slipped by.

Cyril looked out and picked out the pier in the distance.

'I don't think I'll be doing my Punch and Judy show this summer, Janet,' he said sadly.

Janet nodded. 'Retirement comes to us all Cyril, even to me.'

She saw him looking at her quizzically. 'You hardly seem old enough, my dear,' he said kindly.

'Flatterer! I'm trying to take a step back from the theatre, but it's hard to do. I'm still pretty fit, and I have a mortgage to pay until next year. I'm planning to go down to four days a week when that's all done. I'm just worried that I'll be bored.'

'Seems sensible. How is young Karen these days?'

'Young? She's in her forties now, Cyril. But she's fine. She's got the directing role down to a fine art, and she seems so happy with Bryn. It's just wonderful to see. She may have found someone at last.'

As they paused a moment, she saw that he was nodding off. The prognosis wasn't good, and despite how well the home looked after him, he was now becoming frailer and more institutionalised. Cyril had no immediate family, so his visitors were older and they now came less frequently. But he was at least solvent enough to afford the fees of this rather upmarket establishment.

Janet felt sad that this immensely funny man, who had given his young audiences such enjoyment over the years, was now becoming burdened by worsening health. She reflected on her own life, given that she was now in her sixties, and what might lie in store in the future.

Karen had urged her mother to take things easy after running the theatre for so many years. But in truth Janet didn't really have much of a life beyond the place. As a compromise, she'd let Karen take over the production of many of the one-night shows. In fact, it meant she now found she had time on her hands most days, and it rather terrified her to realise that the theatre was increasingly running perfectly well without her.

*   *   *

Miriam Pemrose completed the thirtieth lap of her pool and relaxed with her head against the end of the pool, looking up at the sky through the glass roof she'd had installed after the divorce. She surveyed her tummy with annoyance. The trip to Venice had been pasta-laden and hideously alcoholic, and now she was paying the price. Her friends in Italy had treated her well once again, but she still regretted having to let ex-husband Lionel keep the villa they'd had together in Malaga.

She also regretted staying employed at Pemrose, even if it did provide her with a secure income. Her duties as a director were not onerous, but having to deal with Lionel on a continuing basis was a hassle. She had loved him once of course, before his many affairs started. They'd built a good business together. In the early days, he was shrewd with money, with a great eye for detail, and when they'd moved into the hotel industry, she'd enjoyed handling the refurbishments. Their last venture together, the Majestic, had been her favourite, and it was a big financial success.

She trusted the finance director, Jim Cameron, to be even-handed; after all, they'd been friends for years, and he had been helpful in brokering the divorce deal. She saw the accounts for their hotels regularly, and all was well.

But she'd seen a change at Friday's board meeting. Lionel had seemed more distant than ever. His demeanour suggested that there was something he wasn't telling her about, and when it came to Lionel, not knowing what was going on troubled her.

*   *   *

Lech Wojiek flew into Norwich that afternoon. The affable Polish comedian-come-hapless-magician had been hired as the compère for the season's Summertime Special show. As his flight landed, he removed the headphones from his ears and got ready to extract his six-foot-five frame from the lamentably small space in economy class. He could have afforded a seat with more legroom, but was not about to pay any more than necessary to Mr Ryanair, as he called the budget carrier.

He'd been reading some material Les Westley, a fellow comic and formerly the director of the show, had emailed to him. They were firm friends, although as Les was now Lauren's manager and partner, they didn't meet often.

Lauren had done three nights in Warsaw over the winter, and they had shared a lovely meal in Lech's favourite restaurant. Lech recalled that it was now ten years since he had first visited Cromer as a young and inexperienced magician with an unintended habit of bungling his tricks. Les had recalled a comprehensive dressing-down he'd given him in that first week.

Lech laughed at the memory. At the time, he hadn't understood more than half of what anyone said to him in English, but regular visits had made him pretty fluent in the language, although it was still very obviously not his native tongue. His wife Marina would be joining him in a couple of months with their daughter.

His career in England had been good. He now played the haplessly incompetent magician act for laughs, behaving as though he knew very little English. He'd come to enjoy British sitcoms too, and adopted Manuel of *Fawlty Towers* as a kind of role model. His ability to poke fun at the English had won him some comedy awards, and his one-man show at the Edinburgh Fringe had been particularly successful. He had no difficulty getting work in pantomime either, and enjoyed that particular piece of Britishness.

He had even thought about moving to Britain full-time. He loved the country which had given him a successful career doing what he loved. He was confused by this Brexit business, but knew it was off- limits in his act. Too many people had too many strong opinions to find jokes about it funny.

He walked through the main exit of the airport and out into the grey afternoon to collect the car he'd rented for the season, still a little confused by the right-hand drive. This time, he'd plumped for an automatic to avoid at least one of its complications.

He drove out of the gates of the airport and followed the signs for Cromer. He had rented Les Westley's old place for the season at mate's rates. It was rather more comfortable than that musty old mobile home he'd rented so cheaply when he had first visited all those years ago.

He had other offers now, of course. He had quite a following, and his agent had talked of television. His huge, shiny bald head and rubber comedian's face was so distinctive that he stood out from the crowd and could turn his hand to most things. But Lech still felt a loyalty to Cromer Pier Theatre that had taken a chance on him when he was a complete nobody. So now, having done other things in previous years, he'd been offered the compère role in the show.

He would shop for food the following morning. Karen would have helped by buying in a few basics for him. It was hard to think of Karen as his boss, because she had been in the show with him as dance captain when he first joined the cast. He was meeting her the following day to discuss plans for the show.

He would have the English fish and chips he loved tonight, washed down with warm beer. He parked the car and went into the first-floor flat he would call home for the next few months. The wind had got up and the tide was in, with waves crashing onto the promenade near the pier. He never tired of the view, with the little theatre on the end of the pier seeming to smile benignly at him in the teeth of the gale. He felt like he'd come home.

He showered and called Marina to say goodnight to the family before walking into town. He said hello to a couple of guys he recognised at the amusement arcade where he had worked some years before, when he was still scrabbling for every penny to send home. It still bore the name Pemrose Amusements. But Lech didn't find Lionel Pemrose amusing at all; he was the racist bigot who had fired him, simply for being a migrant.

He bought his fish and chips and, since the wind had abated somewhat, headed for the pier to eat them there. Sitting out of the wind in one of the shelters, he ate hungrily. He watched the fishermen as they tended their rods. He had tried his hand at fishing one time, thinking that he might save some money by catching his tea, but the fish had proved elusive.

As he binned his fish-and-chip paper, he saw a leaflet stuck to the wall advertising the previous night's Amy Raven concert. He remembered when they had both been new to the show, back in 2009. He recalled that Amy was a local girl, with jet-black hair, hence she'd adopted the stage name Raven.

He walked to the theatre, and as he walked in through the door, he saw a friendly face. Debbie was the bar manager, and he'd often enjoyed an after-show drink with her in the past, at a time when he'd had no other friends.

'Hi Lech, what are you doing here? Just before closing time as usual,' she said.

Lech smiled. 'I am looking for my favourite girl, and a pint of your Woodforde's Wherry please, Debbie.'

Debbie obliged, and as she handed it over, she asked the obvious question.

'You in the show, then?' she said.

Lech drank a third of his pint in one swallow and then paused, setting the glass down with a look of appreciation.

Debbie smiled. 'You don't get that in Warsaw,' she said.

Lech held the glass up in appreciation. 'Even worth flying with Mr Ryanair for,' he said.

He could see that she was vexed, hands on hips. 'You didn't answer my question,' she said.

Lech paused. It wasn't official yet.

He adopted a James Bond voice as he spoke in furtive tones. 'If I told you, I'd have to kill you, Miss Moneypenny.'

Debbie laughed. 'Like I'm shaken but not stirred. I know these things. There are no secrets from me.'

He left it there. Debbie tidied up, bid goodnight to her last two customers and locked the door.

Lech noticed that there was an open mic night on Saturday and made a note to come down. He had time to kill, after all. He'd even been known to sing something himself. He wasn't a celebrity as such, but some local people might recognise him. He enjoyed it when they did.

Les had taught him such a lot since their somewhat difficult start. He realised that Les earned a living not only because he was a good comedian, but also because he could turn his hand to different things. Lech had walked the same journey. He might not have been as good a comedian, but his hapless magician act made up for it, and he was both a better singer and a much better dancer than Les. He had the skills to make it in variety shows, a very British invention, and on cruise ships too.

He left the theatre as the light was fading, and the lights of the church glowed behind the Hotel de Paris at the front of the pier. He bid Debbie goodnight and walked back up the pier, the tide now receding, but the waves still audible in the darkness. He ventured up Jetty Street and saw the church lit up brightly. He wasn't especially religious, but he loved the Englishness of these places, and the beauty of the gardens when in full bloom.

He was far away from his family, but this place just felt like home to him. He was looking forward to the next day, and the season ahead. He slept soundly that night, tired by the flight and relaxed by the beer.

* * *

A few days after the one-night show, back at the Pier Theatre, Karen Wells was debating the future of Amy Raven. The Summertime Special show was really taking shape, but should they take a chance on Amy? They had delayed announcing the headliner too long already, and needed to make up their minds.

They were sitting in Janet's office, cluttered as usual with publicity materials and the assortment of paper which accumulated randomly on her desk. Janet was looking at an email proposal from Frank Gilbert.

'What do you think, Mum?' asked Karen.

Janet frowned. 'It's a good offer, but we've got to be practical, and she's a big risk.'

Karen nodded. 'That was Bryn's opinion, too. Her show was good musically, but she seemed washed out by the end. She did the signing afterwards, but she had to sit down. I thought she was going to pass out.'

Karen knew that, as director of the show, this was really her decision, but the theatre was still to all intents and purposes a family business. Karen could read her mother pretty well, though.

Janet seemed unconvinced. 'It's the intensity of the shows which bothers me. A variety show is so physically demanding she'd struggle to cope. If she flunks out, we've no cover at all.'

Karen knew this only too well herself. 'You spoke to her mother recently; what did she have to say?'

Janet sat back as she replied. 'She said Amy was stronger now, and that her last show had gone brilliantly.'

Karen could tell her mother wasn't convinced. 'It sounds like what Frank Gilbert told her to say.'

Janet shrugged. 'Exactly. She let people down and the industry doesn't forget easily. We're the best bet for her rehabilitation, living at home with her own family in a venue that she knows.'

Karen was fighting with her dilemma. 'But, Mum, it will be so hard to tell her no, won't it? I know we can't let sentiment get in the way, but, well …'

Janet nodded. 'Yes. It is hard, Karen. Do you remember when she first auditioned back in 2009? After Les saw her busking on the pier and bought the CD?'

Karen could still recall the young, skinny raven-haired schoolgirl.

'And even then, she only got into the show because one of the dancers got injured. She does work bloody hard, though. She was doing so well until, well …'

Janet nodded. 'Yes, she was. Look, I did have one idea. We could bring in an experienced understudy as a backup. The only problem is that folks coming to see Amy might be disappointed.'

Karen knew where this was heading and shrugged. 'I guess you could have some shows advertised as featuring the understudy too. Do you have anyone in mind? As the understudy, I mean?'

Janet smiled. 'Well, do you remember Hannah Masters? She's headlined the show a couple of times.'

Karen nodded. 'Yes; it was a long time ago, mind. She got pregnant and went away.'

'Well, she's in her forties now, and separated. Lives locally and her daughter has gone to university, leaving her with an empty nest.'

'What a waste of talent, Mum. She was really good. Better than me, if I'm honest. The audience loved her, too. She had real stage presence, and she's quite a dancer.'

'Yes. That's her. So, we could make her the understudy to the younger and less worldly-wise Amy?'

Karen thought that her mother was coming around, but she needed to push back a little.

'But Mum, surely she's a bigger risk than Amy? Has she worked much recently?'

'She's been doing dance and drama at a secondary school in Kent, but she's moved back here. She's singing in a pub in Holt tomorrow night if you're interested?'

Karen looked slightly sheepish and shook her head. 'Ah. Bryn's taking me away for the weekend. He's got tickets to *Hamilton*. I thought I'd get a break in before all the fun starts.'

'I see …'

Karen laughed at her mother's quizzical stare. 'Yes, OK. Let's be honest; living at home – well …'

'I cramp your style? Yes, OK. You have a lovely time. Bryn is absolutely lovely. Nice Welsh singing voice, too.'

'Yes, Mother dear. It's been a while since I've had a boyfriend. I'm too busy running your bloody theatre.'

Janet retaliated. 'Well OK, while you're enjoying your dirty weekend, I'll check out Hannah Masters.'

Karen stared at her reprovingly. 'Well at least I didn't have a quickie on the beach, as you did with my father!'

Janet enjoyed the banter. 'My God, that seems so long ago now. Have you seen him recently, by the way?'

Karen nodded. 'I'll see him with Carol and the boys in the school holidays. He's doing media stuff now. Carol's glad to be rid of that Saturday afternoon sulk when his team's lost.'

'I do lose touch. Let's fix a barbecue or something when they're down. The kids are at secondary school now, aren't they? It would be good to have some younger people around the place.'

Karen rebuked her. 'Meaning I'm over 40 now? OK, rub it in, why don't you?'

Karen left her mother to her paperwork, and both knew that neither of them had been particularly lucky in love. She headed down towards the Pier Theatre as the chilly April wind got up from the east. She thought the conversation had gone well.

Meanwhile, Janet reflected on the past. She still felt guilty and rather embarrassed that Karen was the result of a teenage one-night stand with Paul Warren all those years ago. But at least her daughter knew the truth, it having been kept from her as a dark secret for so long.

Janet wished Karen well with Bryn, while realising that if it led to a long-term relationship, she would be left alone in her impending retirement. She'd even played with those new-fangled dating apps on the sly, but just couldn't bring herself to take the plunge.

She'd tried one or two singles cultural holidays, but although she'd found the company pleasant, in general the males on offer were underwhelming. They tended to be retired teachers or accountants offering great wisdom whether it was required or not, or they tried to be funny without having any particular aptitude for comedy. Maybe after you'd hit 60, having any company at all was what mattered.

The next evening, she headed for Holt and sat at the back of the bar with an orange juice. She checked emails on her phone while she waited, then browsed the internet. Karen had at least imparted enough technological knowhow for her mother to join the twenty-first century.

It was a monthly music club, so the regulars filed in, and the place was full by showtime. A younger couple sat at her table, and they swapped some musical stories. They had no idea that Janet had met several of the bands they mentioned, and could have told many a story about them. In reality, though, people are just people, and what happened behind the scenes at Cromer Pier Theatre stayed private.

The host, presumably the landlord, came forward and took the microphone. A young woman dressed in black did the final tweaks and prods that people do ahead of a concert and then sat at the keyboard.

'Ladies and gentlemen, a real treat this evening. She's starting her comeback tour tonight after a spell away – our very own Hannah Masters!'

A slim woman of medium height with tinted blond hair wearing a black sequinned dress appeared from the back, walking confidently into the room, occasionally shaking the hand of an old friend as she made her way to the stage. The applause was warm and she immediately reeled off three covers in quick succession. It was apparent to Janet that Hannah had not lost any of her vocal power, and the sheer quality of the delivery was as impressive as ever.

Janet made one or two notes and even filmed one of the songs for Karen to see. Ms Masters might have been 20-plus years older than when she had last performed in Cromer, but if anything, her voice had matured and her self-confidence was there for all to see. Halfway through the set, she took to the piano herself, and Janet realised that the younger woman was in fact Hannah's daughter.

Mother and daughter did a duet of the Lauren Evans song *Maybe*. The resurgence of Lauren Evans as a household name had begun in 2009 when she had headlined in the Cromer Summertime Special show. As they sang it together, Janet remembered the turbulent events of that year, when Paul Warren had turned up out of the blue, and they had so nearly lost the theatre to the devious Lionel Pemrose. But everything had turned out all right in the end.

The standing ovation at the end of the performance rather confirmed Janet's overall impression; Hannah Masters was back. She allowed herself a glass of white wine as she checked her Facebook page. There was a picture of Karen and Bryn at the theatre, champagne flutes in hand. She hit the 'Like' icon and was preparing to comment when a voice spoke to her.

'Fancy you coming over tonight. Theatre royalty … I'm truly honoured.'

Janet looked up and saw Hannah's beaming smile. She'd aged of course, and had filled out a bit, but was still the bubbly effervescent Hannah she remembered.

'Hi, Hannah; hardly royalty! I'm not exactly Cameron Macintosh.'

'This is my daughter Gwen,' Hannah replied.

They were self-evidently mother and daughter, Janet decided as she shook her hand. 'I loved the duet, guys. I remember when Lauren first sang it to Les and me. It always brings me out in goose pimples.'

Gwen excused herself. She understood that Janet wasn't here for old time's sake. Hannah sat down beside Janet, sipping what looked like a large gin and tonic.

Hannah whispered, 'I'm glad to get the first one out of the way, Janet. Did I look as nervous as I felt?'

Janet shook her head. 'Not at all, Hannah. You seemed as self-confident as ever. You've a talented daughter, too.'

'Yes. She's at university now, but came home especially. She goes back in the morning.'

'You're an empty-nester then? What's all this about a tour?'

She noticed that Hannah looked rather embarrassed. 'Well, it's sort of true. Time to get back on the horse, I think. Trouble is that I'm wondering if I'm too old to have another go.'

Janet didn't want to build up her hopes, but Karen should at least see her. 'Well, I think you should come down to the pier to audition. We might be able to get you a slot in the Summertime Special show somewhere, but it's Karen's decision now, of course.

Hannah looked relieved at the suggestion. 'Really? That would be great. So, Karen is the director now?'

'That's right. Unfortunately, she's busy tonight, Hannah, otherwise she'd have come too. Why not drop her an email to arrange it? No promises, but nothing ventured and all that.'

Janet left shortly afterwards. She wondered what the underlying story of the lost years was, but, equally, knew that Hannah

Masters would make an ideal addition to the cast. The rest was up to Karen.

*   *   *

Karen and Bryn left the theatre straight after seeing *Hamilton*. Shortly afterwards, they reached their hotel and slumped into its bar, joining a couple of other late-night drinkers.

Bryn winced as he signed the bar receipt for two pints of lager, but decided not to mention the price of a pint of lager in his hometown of Port Talbot to Karen.

They'd met when Bryn played guitar for a one-night act at the pier. He was in the bar after the gig when Karen, on a night off, tripped on a piece of frayed carpet and deposited her pint of lager all over him.

Bryn wasn't given to much small talk, but having helped Karen up from the floor, he simply smiled and said, 'You'll be wanting another … lager, was it?'

The relationship started then, as randomly as that. Karen was taller than he was and did most of the talking. He was quiet, short and ginger-haired, but when he picked up his guitar and sang in his bass baritone Welsh voice, Karen just melted.

They were two slightly unusual individuals, but sometimes opposites attract.

She sat back and sighed. 'That was just fabulous, Bryn. You're right; I do need to get out more. I do miss London sometimes.'

'So, who's this Hannah Masters then?' he asked.

'Oh, she headlined for us before, back in the noughties. Gave it all up for love, didn't she, silly woman.'

'Is she any good then?' he said, before taking another sip of his beer.

Karen leaned forward, rather furtively. 'Oh, yes. To be honest, I'm playing a bit of a game. You see, I want to go with Amy, but Mum will never take a risk unless she's forced to. Bringing in Hannah will get me what I want. So, when she mentioned Hannah to me, I lied. I knew she was back in town. She's an obvious solution, but I just decided to let Mum think she'd thought of it herself.'

'Devious little minx you are,' he said.

Karen shrugged. 'Sometimes I have to be, love. Mum interferes in everything. Even the tiniest thing. Most directors wouldn't put up with it, but, well …'

' … She's your mum. Yeah, I get that,' he said.

Karen vented her frustration. 'I just want more responsibility, that's all. I keep trying to get her to cut her hours so she can't interfere so much, but she doesn't take the hint. Living with her doesn't make things any easier, especially with us. That bath sharing was embarrassing. I thought she was out for the evening.'

'Just as well I put some underpants on when I went down to get another bottle of prosecco, to be fair. Otherwise, she'd have seen me starkers.'

Karen giggled and finished her lager.

Bryn continued. 'Your bloody bed squeaks, too. Not exactly romantic, is it?'

Karen stood and pulled him up.

She kissed him and whispered, 'Well it's beddy-byes time now, babe, and tonight we can make as much noise as we like.'

2.

The Show Must Go On

It took a few days to arrange, but Hannah was looking forward to meeting Karen once again for her audition, and to seeing the old theatre where she'd experienced such happy times early on in her career. She wondered what exactly Karen had in mind. Although the house in Cromer had been left to her by her mother and was fully paid for, she still needed to work. She'd worked previously in a private secondary school near Tunbridge Wells, one with quite a strong reputation in the creative arts.

She'd been self-employed, and enjoyed the freedom. Her husband had a good job in the City, and they had enjoyed a great social life. Looking back, she didn't really know when it had started. But with hindsight, the signs were there. The counsellor had said it was quite a typical case.

But now it was over she was making a fresh start, however lowly. She'd got some shifts in a local supermarket, at least. She'd put her CV around the local schools to try to get some sessional teaching, but to no avail thus far. In her heart of hearts, what she really wanted to do was get back on stage.

She dressed in stage gear, closed the front door and unlocked the door of her car. As she drove down the road, she saw a car turn the corner rather slowly. A black BMW. A cold fear gripped her.

'Oh, please, no,' she said. But checking her rear-view mirror she was relieved that the car was nowhere to be seen. Perhaps she'd imagined it? It could have been anyone.

A while later she walked down the pier to meet Karen, who was sitting drinking coffee in the theatre foyer. It was typical April showers weather, but the earlier rain had cleared.

They hugged each other and drank coffee while exchanging a few stories, until Karen brought them to the point of their meeting.

'So, Hannah, to business,' Karen said, 'Mum was telling me that you were really good the other night.'

Yet Karen had an instinct that something wasn't as it seemed.

Hannah smiled. 'Well, that's nice of her to say so. I sang a lot down in Kent, of course. It was a girls' boarding school, so lots of drama groups, dancing and singing classes. I directed the student version of *Les Mis*, now that was quite an undertaking.'

Karen raised her eyebrows. 'I'll bet it was. Now, look, I have to ask. What's brought you back up here?'

Hannah hesitated. 'Oh. I'm separated. Mum died and Gwen's gone to uni, so I decided to make a fresh start back here.'

'What are your plans, then?' Karen asked, reasoning that asking something open-ended seemed the best way of extracting information in what was clearly quite a sensitive situation.

Hannah replied a little nervously. 'Well, I've got to get my voice back to concert standard first. I'm a voice coach, and I can teach piano and dance, too. But I'll admit I'd love to get back onstage again. I've never been afraid to get my hands dirty. You know that.'

Karen nodded. 'Good. Well, I think Mum's backstage already and I've got Gerald to play for you, so shall we go through and see what you've got for us?

*   *   *

Hannah belted out *River Deep, Mountain High* with Janet and Karen Wells sitting in the deep-red seats of the Pier Theatre. She'd done a couple of dance routines flawlessly. Karen had always liked the *Voulez Vous* dance routine from *Mama Mia*, and Hannah danced it with slickness and professionalism. She followed it with a tap routine of a similar standard.

Sitting there, Karen couldn't believe the transformation in the person now under the lights. This was not the hesitant woman she'd had coffee with.

Janet whispered, 'I wonder what's for the encore? Should be interesting.'

Hannah called down to her as she thought of replying. 'One more song, Karen? Is that OK?'

'Yes, of course, Hannah, take your time. Have a breather if you need one.'

The show needed to reach every member of the audience aged from eight to 80, meaning that the headline acts needed to sing material from any decade and any genre. Many headliners struggled with the variety of the challenge. But Hannah didn't disappoint.

Karen looked at her mother as Gerald played the introduction, a little concerned.

Her mother murmured 'Brave girl.'

She needn't have worried. Hannah sang *You'll Never Walk Alone* perfectly, as though she'd never been away.

They stood and applauded at the end and went up onto the stage. Hannah hugged them as they showed her out, and she was clearly emotional. Gerald was collecting his music and getting ready to leave.

'What do you think then, Gerald?' asked Janet nervously.

He replied in his deep Norfolk accent. 'I think she has an even better voice than when she was here before. More experience, I suppose.'

Karen smiled. Gerald was a one-man orchestra and as good a judge of talent as you would find. He was part of the bricks-and-mortar of the show; and in a world where brilliant is overused, he fitted the description as well as anyone.

'Are you thinking of her as a headliner?' he asked.

Karen knew that nothing got past Gerald. 'Yes, as Amy Raven's understudy. Doubling them up, perhaps?'

Gerald looked over his glasses at her. She still thought of him as her headmaster, given that he had known her since she was a child.

'Wise move, I think. Both troubled souls, though, I'd venture to suggest. Not without risk, but then great talents are often that way. I recall that Lauren Evans was a little, how shall I put it, highly strung.'

They smiled as he headed for the door. She talked over a few things with her mother. The detailed nuts and bolts of the show. But a few minutes later, Debbie shouted to them through the door.

'Karen! There's trouble outside.'

Karen looked at her mother and they both rushed out of the theatre.

*   *   *

Lech had been heading down the pier, making his way to a meeting with Karen. Some children were crabbing off the side of the pier, and a small girl was shrieking at her little brother, who was holding a large green specimen for her to inspect. Lech laughed at the childish interplay.

Hannah, meanwhile, was walking up the pier in the opposite direction, deep in thought and feeling contented after her performance. Adrenaline pumping, she basked in the realisation that she could still perform at concert standard. She'd worked on the dance routine relentlessly that morning, so that if they had a slot for a dancer, they wouldn't have any doubts.

She was barely aware of someone walking towards her, someone familiar.

'Hi, Hannah.'

She looked up to see her estranged husband Ian standing in front of her. She froze with shock, unable to speak.

'Time to come home, Hannah. Time to sort things out,' he said.

She couldn't speak. She didn't want this.

He smiled. 'Come on. Let's have dinner tonight. Posh frock time. I've booked that Majestic place. Let's get you home and out of that training gear.'

She shook her head and backed away. 'No. That's not happening, Ian. No way.'

She tried to push past him, but he grabbed her wrist tightly. She struggled, so he then grabbed her jaw with his other hand.

He put his face close to hers. 'I've told you before, Hannah, you know you need to do as I tell you, I've always known what's best for you.'

He turned slightly, pulling her towards him. Ian saw a large figure standing in his way.

'I think you need to let the lady go, my friend. This is not very polite,' Lech said.

But Ian didn't let Hannah go. He was about five foot eight but of a stocky build. Lech towered over him, but he still looked at Lech with disdain.

'Back off, mate. She's my wife. This is between us. Now bugger off and mind your own business.'

Hannah was shaking, but somehow couldn't speak. Lech wasn't about to go anywhere.

'Ah. Now I'm sorry, my friend, but you *Will* let her go. *Now*, if you please,' insisted Lech.

Ian spat out words of defiance. 'Oh, yes? Look, I said bugger off, so do me a favour and sling your hook.'

Lech smiled. 'Ah. Now, let me see. I'm six foot five and I did three years in the Polish army. You can try to make me, as you say, sling my hook, but I really would not advise it. Better for you to let her go, I think.'

Ian thought about it. Lech smiled again and took Hannah's other hand, pulling her away. The man released his grip. Lech put himself between Hannah and her assailant. He wasn't much concerned about being struck; after all, he'd been a boxer in the army. But in Poland he'd have been worried about a knife.

Instead, Ian snarled at his wife. 'You will come home, Hannah. I've told you before. You can't hide from me here, or anywhere else. Your Polish boyfriend can't follow you everywhere.'

He spat at Lech, but Lech deftly sidestepped it. With that, Ian turned and walked back up the pier at a leisurely pace. Lech was minded to follow him, but Hannah was hysterical. He put his arm around her shoulder and decided to walk her back to the theatre. He was wondering what to do next when Karen arrived, with Janet not far behind. A small group of tourists had gathered, and Gerald was there too now, taking charge.

'It's OK, folks. All sorted now. Show's over. Thanks for your help,' he said pleasantly.

Karen took Hannah into the small green room, and Debbie brought in some tea. Janet walked with Lech into the auditorium. He looked shaken. They sat in one of the rows of seats.

'Are you OK, Lech?' she asked.

'Yes. No problem. Bad guy. Her husband, I think?'

'Perhaps we should get the police involved?'

Lech thought for a minute. 'I'm not so sure. Sometimes the police don't like Polish people. I've seen this sometimes.'

Janet sighed. 'I'm sorry about that, Lech. It must be better now than when you first came here, though?'

'I guess. A little. People are getting used to us, I think. But with this Brexit thing, well ...'

Janet sympathised but moved on. 'What happened? She'd only just left us after her audition.'

'It was so quick. I think he was waiting for her. He grabbed hold of her arm. She looked terrified. I'm not sure if anyone really noticed. I was only ten metres or so away.'

Janet shrugged. 'Most people would have pretended not to notice. They don't want to get involved. You were brave enough to try to help.'

Lech was recovering somewhat. 'He was just a little guy. Lech is big guy. If he try again, I toss him off the end of the pier. If the tide is in, of course. He needs to cool off. North Sea is very cold, yes?'

Janet laughed. Lech the comedian was back.

'You're a good person, Lech. You stepped in when others wouldn't.'

He shrugged. 'I just see him holding her roughly. Then he grabbed her mouth. Not right. Not right at all.'

Janet nodded. She could see that Lech was actually quite shaken, under the comic facade. His face darkened as he spoke once more.

'When I was a child, we had bad police in Warsaw. They took people away. They took my aunt like that. In the street. I remembered that look. She was as terrified as the woman was today. I did not see her again.'

Janet took his hand. 'Well, at least things are better in your homeland now. As for Hannah, let's see what she has to say.'

In the green room, Hannah was sobbing quietly, with Karen sitting back hoping that she would become rational once more. Then she was hoping to piece together the rather confused jigsaw puzzle of Hannah's life. It accounted for her sudden return to the area, and her somewhat erratic mood.

It did of course give Karen a much bigger problem. She had envisaged supporting Amy with the more worldly-wise Hannah, but it had become clear that the older woman's problems were every bit as serious.

'OK, just take your time. Let's hear the full story, if you can. Might be best to start at the beginning,' said Karen kindly.

It was none of her business, of course. But over the years Karen had heard it all and she had her own backstory, too. Every business had its particular problems, she knew that. But showbusiness seemed to create more than most. The perpetual hand-to-mouth existence, the never really knowing where your next job was coming from. The travel and separation. The lack of anywhere you might call home. Relationships which came and went.

Karen had experienced all that during her time in London, and more besides. But strangely Hannah had quit right at the time where her career could have blossomed. Instead, she'd got pregnant and left the area with her new man. What a waste of someone so talented, Karen had thought at the time.

But then she found herself thinking about the sequence of broken relationships in her own life, and of her current boyfriend, Bryn. The idea that she could offer relationship counselling seemed laughable.

As they sat there Hannah seemed to be getting it together. The tears were becoming fewer, and her composure was returning.

She tried again. 'Your ex at a guess?'

Hannah nodded quietly.

'The one you left Cromer with?'

Hannah wiped the tears away. 'Yes. Been married 19 years. Couldn't take it anymore.'

Karen said nothing. One step at a time.

Hannah continued. 'At first it was fine. We were very much in love. Gwen arrived and it was great. Ian had a good job in the City, and we had a brand-new home in Kent. Money wasn't much of a problem. I was too busy to miss the theatre. I did all the mummy stuff. Looking back, I never really understood what was happening to me.'

As this story was going to take time to tell, Karen popped out to reschedule her meeting with Lech, who was by now rehearsing his new act on stage.

'Is the lady OK?' asked Lech.

'Yes, thanks to you. Must have been a bit scary.'

'Not as scary as Mister Les, I think. I remember he say, "In a normal magician's act in this country we take a rabbit out of the hat, not a mouse".'

Karen giggled and continued. '"We find that they tend to head for the exits, not that they need any encouragement after that performance." Yes, I do remember. I was backstage. I wasn't sure that you understood at the time.'

Lech grimaced his rubber-faced pout. 'Oh, yes. Lech understood. I was very worried. I could only afford a one-way ticket on Mr Ryanair.'

Karen realised she needed to get back to Hannah. 'Look, it will be great to catch up, but I'm afraid I need to reschedule our chat. I need to deal with this other matter first.'

'Of course. Is no problem. I want to try some new things anyway. OK if I use the stage for a while?'

'Of course. I'll be back in a while.'

She returned to Hannah, who now seemed more relaxed. She calmly and analytically laid out 19 years of coercion. The slow but sure undermining of her self-confidence. The decimation of her self-worth. The gradual closing down of relationships with female friends, and the blind jealousy of any link with the opposite sex. The sulks and the accusations of disloyalty. The refusal to engage.

Karen only knew what she'd read about such behaviour, but Hannah's words came out so calmly and clinically that it was compelling. She wasn't crying anymore. If anything, she seemed empowered, if rather bitter.

'But surely you sought help?' asked Karen.

Hannah shook her head. 'I should have, but I was too scared of what he might do. Just tried to manage it day by day. Then one day my neighbour found me with a black eye that I couldn't hide. Even then I didn't dare confront him, so with Gwen heading for university I just ran away. She's wise beyond her years. Said I should have done it years ago. Trouble is he's nice as pie with outsiders, life and soul of the party. Only Gwen and I saw Ian's dark side.'

'But why come back here? Didn't you think he'd follow you? Going to your mother's house was a bit obvious, wasn't it?'

'Well, yes. I guess it was. I wrote him a long note explaining why I was leaving and left my wedding ring, too. Mum died a few months ago, so it just seemed an opportunity.'

'Did Gwen know about it all?'

'Gwen actually suggested I left. She'd had enough of it as well. She saw what he'd become. Showed me online articles and stuff. He imposed strict curfews on her, too. Tried to restrict what she wore, who she went out with. She couldn't wait to get away.'

'So, what will you do now?'

Hannah looked up sadly. 'I haven't a clue. Go to the police, I suppose.'

*   *   *

Cyril dozed through the afternoons most of the time. His medication was making these naps more frequent. He was completely sound in mind, but his body had started to betray him. Sitting in his favourite armchair shipped in from home, he looked across at the pictures on his dressing table. There was one of his late wife of course, but it was the one next to it which triggered the memory this time.

It showed a smiling figure in a bright magenta-coloured suit, holding a silver trophy and shaking hands with the host, Bob somebody or other. He might not remember the guy's surname, but he could recall the rest of that night vividly, and he still had an old recording of the show, preserved on an ancient VHS recorder he had at home.

He'd not even been expected to win. The bookie's favourite was the singer, Cindy Valance. But this was before the era of phone-ins or online voting. Instead, the four judges had the final say. There had been five acts left in the final, but as they stood on stage for the finale, one by one the lights above the individuals went out, leaving only the surviving contestants illuminated.

'And now, in third place ... Cindy Valance!'

He remembered Cindy's feigned smile and cheerful wave as her light was extinguished, and the gasps of surprise from the audience. Maybe, just maybe, he thought.

The remaining contender was an impressionist. Cyril had laughed at the series of characters this guy had portrayed in his act. Even his impression of Margaret Thatcher had been good. But Cyril was a double act. His charming monkey, Felix, had been a big hit in the earlier rounds.

He felt the heat prickling his skin under the stage lights and was uncomfortable in his stifling stage costume. He thought he would melt if this went on much longer.

'But now ... who will be our winner tonight? I have the gold envelope here, which will make our winner a star. Ladies and gentlemen, who will it be?'

Cyril recalled that one audience member shouted for Felix, and he'd laughed. The impressionist had laughed, too.

'And our winner is ... Cyril Brown and Felix!'

He couldn't really remember much about what had happened afterwards. He vaguely recalled hugging the impressionist, but beyond that the whole thing had been a blur. It had unleashed a roller coaster which had seen him appearing at every major venue in the UK, including an appearance at the Royal Variety Show.

As he dozed, he remembered that year fondly. The success hadn't lasted, but no matter. He still had wonderful memories.

He knew that he now had limited life left. The unspoken words of visitors, the evasive half-truths people said to him, eyes not making contact. But of course, as his oncologist had once explained, incurable didn't mean unmanageable.

He had coped at home for a time, but now he was afraid that he would never see his home again. People avoided the topic when he raised it. The vague references to 'when you're stronger' didn't wash with him. He found the way people behaved annoying, but also sometimes amusing.

He tried to continue his writing, and his old laptop, keys worn so that the letters were invisible, sat on his desk. The staff found it amusing that this old codger had any understanding of computers. To them he was just the well-loved Punch and Judy man Cyril Brown. Most were too young to recall his years as a celebrity.

His meeting with Julia Maitland had completed the final changes that he needed to make. She had been his solicitor for many years, and was one of the few who knew the whole story. He took out a box from beside the bed and opened it. Inside he saw the bright smile of Felix the monkey looking back at him. He took him out and placed his hand inside the faded brown fur.

'What do you think, Felix old mate?' he asked the dummy who'd been his oldest friend and confidant.

He held the puppet to his ear. As he did so, Felix's mouth twitched in sync with the impishly high speaking voice that Cyril had given him over the years.

'Well, I think you're well buggered Cyril, me old mate, but it's been one hell of a show.'

*   *   *

In the early evening, Janet and Karen were sitting in the lounge at home.

'You can't just bury your head in the sand. It's simply too much of a risk,' said Janet.

Karen was becoming angry. 'So, you'd have us bail out on someone just because her husband's an abusive bastard? I've had previous myself, remember?'

Karen was close to tears as she spoke. Janet stared at her intently.

'You can't look at it that way, Karen. You're the director now. You're responsible for producing a successful show, not dealing with the performers' emotional baggage. Hannah was meant to balance the risk of Amy Raven not making it. Now she's a risk, too. One risk too many.'

'Thanks for telling me my job, Mum.'

There was silence. A mother and daughter stand-off. There had been a few of them over the years. Janet had inherited her father's tough-as-nails ruthless streak. Karen was a performer through and through and looked at things through a performer's lens.

They sat in silence for a while, Karen playing with her iPad as her mother tried to engage with a rather indifferent novel on her Kindle. Eventually Janet broke the silence. Karen could go quiet and sulk, just as her father could. But Janet couldn't leave a matter unresolved.

'Look, it's been a bloody difficult day, Karen. We're both exhausted. Let's look at it again in the morning, shall we?'

Karen nodded, 'I just can't stop thinking about her, not knowing what he might do next. If anything happened to her ... well, I ...'

Janet interrupted, 'You'd feel responsible? Yes, I've felt that

way many times. You know that I was going to fire Lech that
first year? I'm so glad I didn't.'

'Really, Mum? You never said. Mind you, he was really
terrible early on, wasn't he?'

Janet laughed. The ice was broken. 'Dreadful. But look at
him now.'

Karen set aside the iPad. 'So, what stopped you?'

Janet pondered. 'Well, he was cheap, I suppose, and that
year we all took a pay cut if you recall. But I steeled myself to
bite the bullet when I saw his second rehearsal. He was so bad
it was hilarious, but not in a good way. I was about to call him
in that morning when Les dropped in. He said he wanted to
give Lech another week, so I did.'

'So, you're a big softy too, aren't you Mum?'

Janet hadn't thought of herself in that way. She'd always
been hard as nails, like her father.

Janet shrugged. 'Well, I got used to putting on a tough
exterior many years ago. In a man's world you've got to be
prepared to be as macho as they pretend to be. For most of
them, it's all big girl's blouse stuff anyway.'

Karen knew that her mother had a point. You can't wear
your heart on your sleeve all the time.

'What about Amy? Where do you stand on her problems?'

Janet put down the Kindle and sat back in her chair. 'Well,
she got through the one-night show OK. But that was in front
of friends. How would she cope over a full season, in front of
strangers? That's a big unknown. And we won't know until
it's too late.'

Karen agreed. 'I've been thinking. Do you think that Uncle
Cyril would help? I mean I know he's very frail, but still ...'

Janet nodded. 'Yes, I've been thinking about that myself.

I'm sure that he'd want to help, but it doesn't seem a nice thing to do when he's so frail. It will involve him talking about stuff he hasn't talked about with anyone for years. He hasn't even talked about it with me, only my father when he was alive.'

'They've tried any number of things with Amy, I gather. But of course, you never know.'

'Well, if we are going to do it, then we need to do it soon.'

Karen nodded. 'Absolutely. I mean we need to get the headline acts sorted ASAP now. We're late as it is.'

'I didn't only mean that, Karen.'

'Then what, Mum?'

'Cyril has only months, possibly weeks to live. The cancer's spread. If I'm going to arrange it, I need to act fast.'

Karen nodded sadly. That Uncle Cyril was not in any way a blood relative didn't matter. He was everybody's uncle, yet he had no close family left in his last days.

*   *   *

A couple of days later, Amy Raven was sitting in her room at her parents' house in West Runton. Janet had phoned the previous day to suggest the meeting, but Amy still wasn't sure if this was a good idea. Everyone knew Cyril the Punch and Judy man, of course; indeed, she used to watch his show when she was little. But how could he possibly help her? The one-night show at the end of the pier had been a nightmare, although with her mother's help she'd got through it. But a full season in Cromer as Frank had suggested? Could she headline anymore? Perhaps she should just take a slot as a dancer? But Janet and Karen were trying to help, so when they suggested she met Cyril, how could she refuse?

She looked out over the garden, soaking wet in the rain. The old decking stage her parents had built for her to perform on when she was 12 looked old and worn now. They'd had parties where she performed for her friends and family, haltingly at first. At 15, she'd plucked up the courage to busk by the pier, earning a tidy sum from the tourists tipping coins into her faded cowboy hat. The hat was now on top of the wardrobe, she noticed, neglected and forlorn, a memory from when there was no pressure to perform. In the corner sat her old guitar, bought from a catalogue over the usual 38 weeks by her cash-strapped mother.

She recalled the day when Les Westley had bought her freshly minted CD, and she'd begun to nurse bigger ambitions. Those long sessions at the dance school, then the first talent night on the pier. Those nervous evenings at the Majestic Hotel with the creepy Lionel Pemrose. The phone call which dashed her hopes of being in the show, followed by the one which said that a chorus member had dropped out, followed by that heady first season. Night after night, show after show. The feeling of belonging and the sleep-depriving adrenaline rush after each performance. The ankle sprain and the ice bucket which got her through the final night. The roller coaster ride in the years that followed. Until that fateful night.

Thinking about it still terrified her, and she felt beads of cold sweat forming. She wiped them away, angry that it still tortured her so much. The anger stiffened her resolve. She stood on the bed and plucked the old hat from its resting place and put it on. She went downstairs and gave her long-suffering mother a big hug. She got into her car. On a fine day, she might have enjoyed the long walk to the nursing home, but not today. It was one of those Cromer days.

*   *   *

Janet Wells, meanwhile, was heading for Overstrand to meet Miriam Pemrose. Miriam was chair of the Cromer Pier Trust, and they met every so often to catch up. The Pier Theatre was an ongoing victim of Miriam's divorce. Lionel had never forgiven Miriam for snatching that particular prize from him by providing financial support to Janet Wells after the bank had pulled her overdraft. He was quick to forget that the actual reason for their divorce was his repeated infidelity, and seemed to blame his wife's disloyalty over the pier. His ability to rewrite history had at one time amused her, but frankly she was now just tired of the bickering.

Lionel seemed to delight in picking over the clauses in the very arcane tenancy agreement between him as landlord and the Pier Theatre as tenant, even resorting to overly frequent landlord's inspections to find more things which required attention.

For a business running on a shoestring, it bled the theatre trust of reserves of cash. Lionel took great delight in sending solicitor's letters at the slightest transgression, insisting that said transgression was remedied within the required 28 days. The quotes for the five-year redecoration Miriam had in front of her were frightening, but they would need to get that done over the winter, restricting the one- night shows they could put on. The petty vindictiveness from a person she had loved was unbearable, but business matters meant that their paths still had to cross. The more awkward he was, the more determined she became that he wouldn't win.

She was also worried about Jim Cameron. They'd met yesterday and he'd looked awfully downbeat. It wasn't what he'd said, exactly; it was that a generally plain-speaking man seemed to be picking his words very carefully indeed. It was as if there was much more going on than she'd appreciated. He was the meat in the Pemrose sandwich, she realised, trying to appease both sides, and he wasn't getting any younger.

The meeting gave Janet the chance to share the dilemma over their two headline acts. In many ways, Janet and Miriam had similar attitudes to life, yet rather different perspectives on the theatre. Janet was theatre through and through. It was her life and her livelihood. Miriam was really a punter who came along to shows from time to time, but having used her own money to save the theatre years ago she'd become chair of the Cromer Pier Theatre Trust rather by default.

'So, you have two local acts as headliners, but neither is exactly reliable?' she ventured.

Janet could not help but be embarrassed. 'Yes. That's about the size of it. Sometimes I think I'm mad.'

Miriam laughed. 'So, Janet Wells, the ice maiden of British theatre, has a heart after all? My word, I never thought I'd see the day.'

Janet shrugged. 'I have no idea how I got into this position. Probably because I know just how talented Amy is.'

Miriam sympathised. 'And you couldn't have known about Hannah's personal problems, could you?'

'No. That was a complete shock.'

Miriam thought for a moment, 'But you could just hire a headliner from one of the agencies? I guess there won't be so much choice now will there, though? Not at this stage.'

Janet nodded, albeit somewhat hesitantly.

Miriam smiled and continued. 'But you won't, will you?'

Miriam knew that, to many, Janet Wells was a tough cookie,

but there was also a softer side, eager to give people a second chance. Always prepared to see both sides of any story.

Janet shook her head, 'I think things will work out. I'm not going to change my plan because a bully-boy husband shows up. I don't believe in letting bullies win, do you?'

Miriam laughed. 'Including my ex-husband, of course. He came off second best, I recall. But what about Amy? What if, well, it happens again?'

Janet stared at her. 'That's why she's with Cyril Brown now.'

Miriam stopped and looked straight at Janet, suddenly understanding.

'My God. That's a bit, well ... nuclear.'

*   *   *

Cyril sat in his room, tapping away at his computer. Just another 20,000 words. He'd promised them, and he never forgot a promise.

His computer pinged to remind him of an impending visitor within the hour, so he needed to dress. He could just about manage that on a good day, and despite the torrential rain outside Cyril had decided that today was going to be a good day. He timed his medication so that he would be at his best, although Cyril's best times were now being measured in hours. He was rather nervous; not that he didn't want to help, but he wasn't sure that he could, and raking over the most traumatic period of his life still troubled him.

At the appointed time there was a knock at the door, and the nurse showed Amy in.

'Ah ... I am blessed by a visit from theatre royalty ... Miss Amy Raven, no less ... do sit down, my dear.'

'Theatre royalty? I think not,' said Amy, rather windswept and damp. She smiled as she sat opposite Cyril, who was wedged upright in his chair.

They spoke for a while about what she'd been doing in her career. Cyril was good at building relationships even with perfect strangers, and Amy was not unknown to him. He was simply trying to put her at ease. As the conversation briefly paused, Cyril decided that it was time to get down to it.

'Ah. I should introduce my partner. Felix, meet Amy Raven,' he said.

With that he brought out the bright yellow monkey with the beaming smile, and then placed the puppet to his ear, and seemed to listen to him.

'Ah, Felix says he was sorry that we missed your recent show on the pier. I'm afraid they don't let me out much these days. It was a great success, I understand.'

Amy was immediately at a loss for words. Cyril leaned forward and put his hand on hers. He smiled at her kindly.

His eyes were bright as he spoke. 'It was terrifying, at a guess?'

Amy looked down. She tried to reply, but the tears welled up and she just nodded.

Cyril continued. 'I imagine they gave you a shove for the last few yards on to the stage. They tried that with me, I recall, when all else failed.'

Amy nodded.

Cyril continued. 'I'm not sure how it is for a singer, but trying to deliver a ventriloquist's act after you've thrown up three times before going on is a bit of a challenge.'

Amy smiled thinly. 'Yes. Sipping water between each song helped.'

Cyril sat back. 'Well, Amy, I suspect stage fright is one of the few things we have in common.'

Amy nodded again. 'I guess. How did it, well, you know ...?'

Cyril interrupted, sensing her unease. 'How did it start, you mean? With me?'

'Yes. I'm sorry ... if you don't feel able to ... well ... '

Cyril sat back. 'At one time I'm not sure I could have, Amy. It was all too painful. But I'm so much older now. It was Batley Variety Club. Felix and I had been on the Royal Variety Show only a couple of weeks previously. I was fine ahead of the show. All seemed well. We bounced onstage after the introduction, and I remember I delivered the opening catchphrase, and a warm-up gag or two. Then some guy made some off-colour racist remark about monkeys. It threw me a bit, but I delivered the next line, and then looked at Felix. I knew the lines by heart, but the words wouldn't come out of Felix's mouth, or so it seemed. Then I lost the line entirely and dried completely. The more I looked at Felix, the more lost I became.'

He stopped, looking lovingly at his partner.

Amy interjected. 'That's awful. Whatever did you do?'

Cyril shrugged. 'Well, I was rescued by Brian Bassett, the comedian. He'd seen stage fright before and just ran on and cut into his routine. The audience would have noticed something was wrong, but he covered me until I'd got offstage.'

'So how did the theatre react?' she asked.

'Not too badly. It was 'just one of those things' they thought, and so did I. I just thought it was a theatrical dry caused by the racist bigot, so I moved on to my next engagement. It was a Rotary fundraiser back here in Cromer, and I was the star act after dinner. But when I came on, I couldn't get Felix to speak. I tried to use my larynx to throw my voice to him, but somehow no sound came out. I looked at him in complete terror and froze once again. I managed to get the band to cut to my closing song, and I bowed and got off at the end. Sat in the dressing room in a cold sweat.'

Amy nodded slowly. 'It's just dreadful, isn't it, standing there with an audience looking at you, when you can't find a single sound?'

Cyril smiled. 'Especially when the chair of the Rotary club was an ambitious young smart-arse called Lionel Pemrose.'

Amy looked aghast. 'Disaster. What happened?'

'He stormed into the dressing room and demanded to know what had happened. I'd messed up the timetable for the raffle, apparently. He said I was drunk, which of course I wasn't. I never drink before a show. I apologised but he was livid, called me an effing amateur, and similar pleasantries. It was quite ironic, as I'd done it for nothing anyway. I just wasn't in a fit state to explain.'

'I worked for Lionel for a while. Never again,' Amy said.

'Well, he does have a certain reputation. With the ladies, I mean,' he replied.

'Let's say he offered me dinner, but I didn't want to be his dessert.'

'Wise girl.'

The ice broken between them, he noticed that she seemed ready to open up now.

Amy continued. 'So, whatever did you do? You were a big star. You must have been terrified with so much to lose.'

'Jack Wells did everything he could to help.'

Amy recognised the name. 'Mrs Wells' father? Right. So how did you solve the problem?'

Cyril spread his arms in defeat. 'I'm sorry, my dear, but for me this story has no happy ending. Felix has never spoken in public from that day to this. Jack and I tried many things, but nothing seemed to work, and without Felix, well ...'

Amy looked crushed, rather as he feared she would. Cyril let the message sink in. He'd warned Janet that he couldn't produce a magic rabbit out of a hat, but had hoped that simply sharing the experience might help her in some way.

'Amy, I don't want to build up false hopes. I've read any number of books on the topic, and we're not alone. Bigger stars than you and I live with the problem. You've tried all the usual stuff, I assume?'

'Yes. Frank sent me to one or two people, but nothing has worked so far.'

'Janet tells me you fluffed a line in a show, then you lost the script completely.'

Amy nodded. 'It was completely out of the blue. Just as it was for you. But then I just couldn't go on the next night. I was terrified. It was simply awful. Now I can't even contemplate going onstage again. I only managed the show on the pier because I knew my friends and family were out front. Karen guided me onstage in total darkness, and as the band started the opening song, the lights came up. I just sang automatically. I tried not to look at the audience.'

Cyril nodded. 'A common solution. If you can see the audience as friends that is so very helpful.'

'But it didn't work for you?'

'With Felix no, alas not. But I took over my father's Punch and Judy show one weekend when he was ill, and I met the children ahead of the show, made little jokes with them, and did a few tricks. A sort of warm-up act, if you will. Then somehow doing the puppet show on the pier became easy after that. It

may have been because they were children, or because I was
speaking through the puppets.'

'But you never performed onstage again?'

Cyril smiled. 'Not as Cyril and Felix, no. I did a lot of
voiceover work to begin with, adverts and the like, to rebuild
my confidence. Then I appeared as a drop-in act in the pier
show. Just as a comic. Standard patter, no Felix to give a voice
to. Built a rapport with the audience, and they became my
friends. It seemed to help, but I was never a big star again.'

'But you did find your way back then? Conquered your fears?'

Cyril reflected on the question. She was looking for a rem-
edy, hope for her future which was hanging in the balance. He
dared not give her false hope, but wanted to give her something
to hold on to.

'Look, Amy, I saw you in the show for a couple of seasons
when you first appeared. You are an exceptionally talented
singer and a very professional dancer. Self-doubt is always with
us as performers, and I think we're all just one step away from
stage fright. Being in a West End production in a freestanding
acting and singing role is pretty scary, I would have thought.
Also, doing that one-person show must have been incredibly
tough. But Summertime Special is a variety show, so even if
you fluff something, your friends in the ensemble are such
professionals, they'll get you through it. So, whilst I said that
there was no happy ending for me, I see no reason why you
can't have a successful career here in Cromer.'

Amy sat weighing his words carefully. Cyril shifted uncom-
fortably as he felt the increasing need for his pain medication.
But he recalled one other conversation he'd had, which he saw
as relevant.

'Les Westley used to say that there was a 'Road to Cromer

Pier'. Sometimes, people go on to great things after they do the pier show. But sometimes it works the other way, too. When Lauren Evans joined us, her self-confidence was gone, and she had nowhere else to go. Frank Gilbert sent her here because it's a close-knit family of real professionals. The Wells family have seen it all, and if they believe in you then I say go with it. Karen and Gerald will build a show which minimises the risk of a repeat of the problem, as Jack Wells did with me to some extent. You must think of the audience as your friend, because in Cromer they are. You've been out front after the show, posing for selfies, having a joke with the punters. You know that if things went wrong for you your friends in the cast would rally around, and in any event your friends in the audience will understand.'

He picked up a glass of water unsteadily and took a drink. He knew only too well that the pain was coming back.

'Are you in pain, Cyril? Can I do anything to help?' Amy asked.

Cyril smiled, and patted her hand kindly. 'I rather doubt that you can, my dear. But then I'm not sure that I'm being of much help to you either, rambling on as we old people do sometimes.'

Amy shook her head. 'It's good to talk to someone who's been there. Experienced the cold sweats and the blind terror. At least you found a way out from it. That's reassuring at least.'

Cyril coughed a little, and took another sip of water, and set it down. 'Well yes, I suppose I did. What do you think, Felix?'

He reached for the puppet and put him to his ear. Having listened he gave the monkey an admonishing stare. 'Now that is not exactly politically correct, Felix. Referencing Miss Raven's stunning figure and good looks isn't allowed anymore. Oh?

What's that? Oh, yes, I agree with you there Felix, a season in the Summertime Special show is just what the doctor ordered.'

Amy looked up, close to tears. 'I'm not sure that I can do it, Cyril. I can't let anybody down.'

Cyril shook his head. 'But you must do it. By the time I'd learned to adapt, my chance had gone. There is a temptation to give it more time. But time doesn't heal this. Personally, I think it makes things worse, and this business doesn't give you time. Your time is now. My advice is to fight this fear and face it down for the lying, cheating, figment of your imagination that it is. Who are you actually afraid of, after all?'

It was a good question. Amy pondered it. Who was she actually afraid of indeed? Her colleagues? The audience?

She looked up and smiled. 'Yes. Who am I bloody afraid of? Just myself, I guess. Thanks, Cyril.'

She stood and leant forward to kiss the old man on the cheek, then did the same to Felix. Cyril shook her hand warmly as she left.

3.

Decisions, Decisions

Hannah was now in the middle of a long discussion with Janet and Karen Wells. She was incredibly surprised at the understudy offer that they had made to her. It was an amazing opportunity to rebuild her career and gave her potential headlining performances on certain dates, too.

The conversation with Miriam had reassured Janet. The Cromer Pier Theatre Trust was a charity, after all, and would back local performers. In Hannah's case they would not let intimidation or threats affect their decision.

In any event, Hannah had not seen her husband again after the incident, and it seemed likely that he gone home to Kent. The theatre had a volunteer, retired Detective Sergeant Graham Blakeley, who had agreed to keep a watching brief over her security in the meantime. Hannah's meeting with a local domestic violence charity had resulted in a short meeting with the police, but although they were sympathetic, the lack of any evidence rendered police action impossible. Even the altercation on the pier wasn't evidence enough on its own. They had taken her details and promised to keep notes on their database in case of a recurrence, but she felt less than reassured. The offer of support from Graham Blakeley was gratefully accepted.

* * *

Karen met Amy on her own later that day, although Janet had already spoken to Frank Gilbert. He was relieved to hear that Amy might find her way back in her hometown. He personally doubted that she would ever again make the West End, but at least she could earn a living in the business she loved.

'How did it go with Cyril?' said Karen, as she handed over a mug of coffee from the makeshift backstage kitchen.

Amy considered the question before answering, because she didn't really know how she felt.

'Well, he said that there wasn't any magic cure, but he learned to manage it later on, and he gave me one or two pointers to build on. Given that I'm in an ensemble variety show with support around me I think I'll get through it, but I can't give you any guarantees. It wouldn't be right to make a promise that I couldn't be certain of keeping.'

Karen was impressed at her honesty. 'The one-night solo show was a watershed for you, wasn't it? How did you think it went?'

'I thought my voice was good given that I'd not performed since, well, you know what. But I'll admit I was dead scared when you put me on stage and the lights went up. Picking *You've Got a Friend* was a good choice. I've been singing that since I was a child, but getting the band to play the intro in the darkness got me over a big hurdle.'

'You sang it at your first ever audition here, if you recall.'

Amy smiled. 'I was pretty scared then, too.'

Karen was keen to get her to open up on the topic. 'What did Cyril suggest?'

Amy thought for a moment, 'Well for one thing, at the point when I go on, I need to believe that I'm amongst friends, both in the cast and in the audience. He said that keeping that at the forefront of his mind helped him to keep the fear of failure at bay.'

Karen nodded. 'Well, yes. I've read that myself. It makes a lot of sense.'

'But I'm worried about going on to perform a solo alone with the audience. Crossing that threshold on my own still scares me, and you can't be expected to shove me on stage every night.'

'No, I'd rather not. But we can adapt the show to manage those entrances to minimise the risk. Has it ever happened mid-performance?'

Amy considered for a moment. 'Only the once when it first happened. After that, they covered it with my understudy a couple of times, before I bailed out entirely.'

Karen nodded. 'Yes, but our shows are fast-moving, and you don't have any lines to learn, do you? Just links to the next act, and the compère delivers most of those.'

'Yes. I guess.'

'So how would you feel about sharing the headlining role with Hannah Masters? She'd be your understudy, and do a number of shows as headliner to spread the load.'

Amy brightened. 'Hannah? So that's why she's back in town? I did wonder. I remember her from when I was a kid. She's terrific.'

Karen hesitated. Actors had personal lives too, so revealing Hannah's problems wasn't her place.

'She's recently separated, and living locally now. She's looking to come back into the business.'

Amy thought about what this might mean. This was about trying to keep her dream alive. It seemed an amazingly generous opportunity.

Karen smiled and looked at the painfully thin, pale figure in front of her, seemingly riddled with self-doubt.

Amy seemed to read her mind. 'What does Mrs Wells think, Karen? I mean I know you're the director and all, but has she discussed it with Mr Gilbert?'

Karen knew of her mother's reputation. She certainly took no prisoners in the world of commercial theatre. Yet if anything, it was her mother who was the more certain of the wisdom of the plan now.

'Yes. They both think it's a good solution. You're a quality headliner who's proved herself at a high level. Why wouldn't we hire you?'

Amy remained silent. Karen was becoming a little exasperated. She'd been where Amy had been; it was a tough business, and she knew what it took to get to the West End. Karen had had to give up on the dream, albeit for different reasons, and she didn't want to see Amy go the same way.

She tried again, keeping as calm as she could. 'Look, Amy, you need to decide what you want to do. I can take you on as a dancer if you'd prefer. You've proved yourself in that role years ago. Now, we think you're a lot better than that, but it's your decision.'

Amy wiped away a tear and spoke in a voice cracking with emotion. 'You've been there too, haven't you Karen? London, I mean? I remember you told us once.'

Karen nodded. 'Yes. A long time ago now. But I didn't have stage fright. And my family roots are in this theatre, remember? There was always a career here for me.'

Amy continued. 'So, then... if you don't mind me asking ...'

'Do I regret quitting London?' asked Karen.

'Yes. Look, if I'm being too ...'

'No ... it's fine. Could I have seen it through? Maybe. But everything had fallen to pieces personally and professionally, so I wasn't really in a fit state to recover. You have a specific problem to overcome, and we can help with that, I think.'

Amy nodded. Karen decided to end the discussion and give her time.

'Look, you've seen Cyril, and I've outlined the options as we see them. Talk to Frank and the family, of course. Let me know your decision by tomorrow morning, so I can make plans either way.'

* * *

It was at around 10.30pm that Lauren Evans came off stage in Manchester. It was the last of three nights there, at the end of a tour to launch her latest album. She took yet another mouthful of honey-infused hot water, unzipped her stage frock and put on a dressing gown, then sat down on a comfy settee, allowing herself to warm down.

There was a knock at the door and her husband, Les Westley, entered somewhat clumsily. In his hand he held a silver tray, waiter -style, with a single champagne flute, an open bottle of Moet & Chandon, and a glass of iced mineral water. Between his teeth there was a single red rose, matching the one in the buttonhole of his white dinner jacket.

'Loom slervice,' he said through his teeth. He looked ridiculous. Lauren laughed.

'You idiot,' she giggled, although she maintained a post-show whisper as instructed by the doctor.

'Well done. love,' he said, pouring the champagne and handing her the flute. He picked up his glass of mineral water, and they clinked glasses.

'Thank God that's all over, I'm knackered,' she said.

He sat next to her, leant over and kissed her full on the lips.

'Hungry?' he said.

'You bet. Bloody starving.'

He reached into the pocket and pulled out a cardboard box, handing it over.

'KFC. You star!' she whispered hoarsely.

She devoured the contents of the box, mayonnaise dripping down the front of the dressing gown.

Les leaned forward to open it and lick it off. Lauren pushed him away.

'Sod off, buster. You're getting nothing in that department. Not after extending this bloody tour.'

Les put up his hands in mock surrender. He took out his mobile, checking messages.

'Anything interesting?' she said, through a mouthful of KFC.

'Another one from Janet Wells.'

Lauren swallowed, then paused and looked at him sadly. 'Cyril?' she asked.

Les nodded. 'Janet says it's nearly time. Months, or maybe weeks, they reckon.'

Lauren said nothing. Just looked down.

Les read her mind. 'We're not going to Garda. We'll drive back to Cromer tomorrow. Have a few weeks back home?'

Karen nodded. 'Yes. I need to see him, Les. Look at us now. None of this … you … me … none of this … without Cyril.'

'I know, love. I know.'

He held her in his arms for a minute or two, just enjoying the quiet. She pulled away and wiped aside a tear. She cleared her throat and whispered.

'I had a chat with Amy this afternoon. She rang me in a right state. Couldn't work out what to do.'

'Yes. Janet emailed me for my opinion a couple of days ago. I told her it was too much of a risk, but she's gone ahead and offered it anyway.'

'Well, that's an ex-director talking and that's a fact,' she said tartly.

'She can't let sentiment get in the way, Lauren. It's her livelihood at stake, and Karen's. What did you say to Amy?'

'Well, I'm a performer, right? So as a performer I told her to grab the opportunity.'

Les laughed. 'Which is what I'd expect you to do. From her point of view, she has to do it.'

'Well, then. But I don't recall this Hannah Masters. Who is she?'

Les took off his dinner jacket and loosened his tie. 'An exceptionally talented lady who gave it all up for love.'

'Stupid cow. All men are bastards,' she said simply.

'Of course. But now she's back in town, so Janet's hired her to understudy Amy. Sort of a job share. Builds in a bit of resilience I guess.'

Lauren nodded. 'A second chance for her, then. The 'Road to Cromer Pier' rides again. Now tell me you wouldn't have done the same you old softy.'

Les shook his head. 'No, love. I'm not sure that I would. Some conquer stage fright and some don't. Cyril never did. What if she doesn't make it? And Hannah hasn't sung professionally for years.'

Lauren sipped her champagne. 'Is it money, do you think? I gather Pemrose is still being a bastard.'

'Yes, it probably plays a part,' he said, sipping the mineral water.

'Maybe I should do a one-night show while we're home? To make money for the trust?'

Les looked at her mockingly. 'What? The woman whose been sipping Manuka honey for weeks, praying that her voice would hold until tonight? No, Lauren. I think not.'

'But, well, it's only one more show,' she ventured.

'No Lauren. You need three weeks of rest. Recharge the old batteries and your voice.'

'OK. Just a thought. It will be lovely to be home.'

'Yes. We can have proper fish and chips at least.'

'You sure know how to treat a girl!'

He shrugged. 'But you get to write some stuff, too. Gerald's on standby.'

Lauren smiled, and kissed him, whispering into his ear. 'Take me home, Les. I'm knackered.'

4.

May Day, May Day

Just ahead of the May Day weekend, in the conference room on the top floor of Cromer's Majestic Hotel, Lionel Pemrose and Jim Cameron were sitting either side of the boardroom table, talking somewhat irritably. Cameron was reading a letter from the bank.

'I told you before, Lionel, but you wouldnae listen,' Jim Cameron said, as affably as the Scottish accountant could manage, given the situation.

But Lionel Pemrose wasn't in the mood. 'Bloody bank managers. That idiot Hodson hasn't got a clue.'

Cameron tossed the letter back across the table with a dismissive shrug.

'But all he can see is the overdraft going up, and us getting close to breaching our banking covenants. The casino refurbishment has gone way over budget and we're six months late opening. You cannae seriously expect him to wear that? This letter is a warning shot across the bows.'

Lionel looked up and snarled, 'After all the business I've done with him, I'd expect some give and take.'

Jim laughed, 'Now you surely have to be joking. You know the way their minds work. They dinnae like surprises.'

Lionel was having none of it. 'It's your job to you to put them back in their box and keep them there.'

Jim laughed, more sarcastically this time, as he often did when Lionel was going off on one.

'Well, if you can tell me what you predict the final costs will be and when we're going to open the damn casino, I'll do my best to do just that. I cannae make things up this time. I tried that before and see where it got us.'

He watched Lionel intently, and could see the rant slowly dissipating.

'All right, Jim. It's just that these bloody banks always hold all the cards. Freya says that she'll have a better idea when the conservation officer's been this week. It's tricky with listed buildings.'

'I still don't know why you want a bloody casino anyway. We've already piled up loads of debt by buying those chains of amusement arcades and betting shops. The interest charges are killing us. We're not the small family business that we were ten years ago; we've big assets and large debts to manage. All I'm saying is that we have to be careful.'

Lionel shook his head. 'Look, Jim, I got the building for a song, didn't I? And once we're open, we can get into online gambling, too. It's where the money is. It's not in tacky bingo halls and amusement arcades anymore. You're just stuck in a time warp.'

'Well, that's as maybe, but back then those tacky amusement arcades were making us decent profits. Now we're, well, heading over a cliff from what I can see.'

Lionel wasn't having any of it. 'Just you remind Hodson how many times he borrowed my villa in Malaga. He's been quite happy to share the fruits of our hard labour, hasn't he?'

Jim Cameron said nothing. Lionel stood to replenish his glass, and then his long-suffering finance director's. In the silence Jim could hear a distant fairground organ, the hubbub of tourists walking down the promenade and the ever-present seagull cacophony. Lionel poured two doubles of their favoured Glengoyne malt, threw two ice cubes into his glass, and handed the other one over, a grim smile indicating an end to the row.

Cameron pondered. Lionel would calm down, given time, and they would work things out as they always did. But matters were more complicated this time. There were personalities and loyalties involved. Lionel was besotted with Freya, whom he'd met only a year ago, and the feud with his ex-wife Miriam still flared up from time to time like an active volcano.

Freya Alcott-Palmer was a distant relative of the Queen's, or so she claimed. Very distant as far as Cameron had established so far. She was 15 years younger than Lionel, with no money and expensive tastes. Anyone could see she was taking Lionel for a ride. Anyone but Lionel, that is.

Lionel stood looking down towards Cromer Pier and the theatre beyond. An out-of-date billboard still advertised Amy Raven's one-night show. He thought for a moment. Now there was a blast from the past. She'd performed downstairs in the ballroom a few years back he recalled, just after the re-opening. Then she'd joined the Summertime Special show. The dark side.

The theatre was enemy territory with ex-wife Miriam in cahoots with Janet Wells and the Cromer Pier Theatre Trust. He'd made the situation as uncomfortable as he could, applying the terms of the lease to the letter, ensuring that the local council gave them nothing, his mates on it seeing to that. Yet they managed to survive somehow. Miriam had obviously used personal funds to prop it up, he thought.

Jim saw Lionel staring intently at his beloved pier, Lionel's biggest obsession after Miss Alcott-Palmer. If ever there was a lame-duck business in Pemrose Entertainment's empire it was the pier; well, at least until Lionel cooked up his hare-brained expansion project idea. At least the pier broke even most years, so it didn't really matter. Unlike Lionel's expansion project, it wasn't going to put the business into receivership, and Cameron out of a job.

*   *   *

Meanwhile, in the opulent boardroom of Schwarz, Stevens & Stanley in central London, Elena Schwarz was speaking in her cultured New England accent, relating eloquent anecdotes sourced from the personnel file of one of the partners, Tom Stanley. Anecdotes doubtless augmented by Jane Clark, his long-standing PA, who seemed embarrassed, trying to hide away at the back nearest the door. She was leaving too, in a few weeks' time. Corporate restructuring, they called it.

Tom Stanley was standing next to Ms Schwarz, and the gathering included a large contingent of his staff. Tom sensed that Elena was finishing up, thank goodness, by wishing him a long and happy retirement.

But I'm only 58, Tom thought. What should he say? He was tempted to tell Elena exactly what he thought, but one didn't do that, did one? One thanked people. People he'd work with a long time. Some he cared for, others less so.

There were gifts on the table in front of him, wrapped in glossy paper. One was obviously a bottle of champagne. There were flowers, too. Lilies, judging by their fragrance. He hated lilies. His late wife Maggie had loved them.

Tom did not feel inclined to celebrate, even though the payoff was extraordinary. The fewer partners there were, the more money each one made. Money was seemingly their only motivation.

He hadn't had long to plan his retirement do, so he'd pulled together a handful of his closest work colleagues for an early supper after work. Nothing too posh. Tom Stanley didn't really do posh. Then he'd splashed out on tickets for *Les Misérables* for them all. It suited his melancholy mood. The song of an angry man, his hopes and dreams dashed.

He realised that some might have seen his situation in an altogether more positive light. He was now extremely solvent, and in good health as far as he knew, so he felt he had a lot left to give. But that was the point, really. It was all too soon.

The obligatory card and presents were handed over to warm applause. He kept his remarks and words of thanks brief. Tom was no great orator. He had a dry Yorkshire wit, not often understood by his southern colleagues, and certainly not appreciated by the Americans. So much of his working life had been spent with troubled organisations, and he relied on his instincts about people and relationships. He'd made his career in turning round failing businesses, but it was their people who had mattered to Tom.

But after the US partners had taken his company over, things had changed. Increasingly, he found their sausage-machine approach to insolvency distasteful, given that companies that might have been saved were not given the opportunity. Looking back, he realised he'd been naive.

He shook Elena's hand, whilst deftly escaping her hug and the peck on the cheek. He moved on to the others swiftly, then escaped the boardroom with its expensive hardwood furniture and contemporary soft furnishings. He had cleared his desk yesterday, and had the box sent home by company courier. One more expense that they could stand. He simply had to return to his office, put the unopened presents and card in his briefcase and he was good to go.

Jane appeared in the doorway. 'You forgot the flowers, Tom,' she said knowingly.

Tom looked at her reprovingly, as a teacher might look at an errant pupil.

'If I want a second career as a florist, I'll take a college course. You have them.'

Jane smiled. 'All set then?'

'Seems like it. At least Elena kept it fairly brief. Rather shorter than her usual death by PowerPoint.'

Jane shook her head and grinned as she placed a mug of tea in front of him. She sat down opposite him, and then produced a sandwich box from a plastic bag on the side table.

'The last supper, albeit at lunchtime?' she said, as she placed the box in front of him.

He smiled. 'Orlando's hot pork and stuffing? You're an absolute star.'

She took out her own less calorific lunch and they ate in silence for a while.

'I'll miss Orlando's,' he said, as he licked his fingers, and extracted the obligatory crackling.

'As will I,' Jane said.

They fell silent again. Two work colleagues, and sort-of friends. Jane was 15 years younger and lived in Notting Hill. He had the elegant flat on the river near Canary Wharf. They had worked together for ten years, and knew that, after the theatre this evening, this was probably goodbye. Tom sat back for a moment and sipped his tea.

'So, what's next for you, Jane?'

He saw her thin smile. 'Interview tomorrow. Can't say I'm looking forward to it. Haven't had an interview in years.'

'You'll be great. You *are* great.'

'Thanks, Tom. I'll get fixed up. Plenty of jobs about. I'll just miss this place.'

'And me, of course?' he asked, looking at her over the rim of his spectacles.

'Even you, sarcastic old sod that you are.'

Tom laughed. 'Less of the old. I'm not ready for this. Too young to retire.'

He saw her pause for a moment, as if picking her words carefully.

'It is too soon, especially after Maggie.'

He nodded sadly. 'Yes, it is. Less than 12 months.'

He still couldn't really talk about it. He was pleased when she broke the silence.

'So, what will you do now? Have you had time to think?'

'Not really. I need more time to assimilate it all. They call it decompression, or so that outplacement consultant called it. Return to real life. I got Elena to pay for my professional indemnity insurance for three years, just to keep my options open.'

He noticed that she was toying with her earring, as she was apt to do when she was thinking. 'That won't be easy for you after all those 60-hour weeks.'

'No. It won't.'

With that he tossed the sandwich wrapper into the bin some distance away, noting with satisfaction that his aim was true. He then stood and walked to the window, taking in the familiar view across the Thames in silence. Eventually he spoke and, unusually for Tom, his words came from the heart.

'It's weird, you know, Jane. A sudden stop. Suddenly it's all over. After all these years. Like you're on a computer game and it comes up with 'game over'; just like that. I should be happy I suppose but ...'

He stopped abruptly. Eyes fixed on the river, he saw a tourist boat heading upstream.

He sensed that she might be about to reply, but sometimes you just can't put yourself where someone else is. She sipped her tea and listened to the background hum of the city beyond the double-glazed, hermetically sealed world of Schwarz, Stevens & Stanley. She too was leaving the bubble in a week's time. She'd not taken any holiday that year, so she had plenty to use up. Working with Tom, you never asked to take any.

He'd always been that way. Totally driven, with his eye constantly on the prize. Get a result then tidy up afterwards. Most of the time it worked, but just occasionally he got caught out. Tom always went the extra mile to secure a deal, even if that meant spending hours of his own time on it. There were any number of businesses he'd help to save over the years. Any number of livelihoods secured.

He shook his head slowly, then snapped out of it. 'OK, that's that. Onwards and upwards.'

Jane smiled. He could be stubborn, but when Tom lost a battle, he moved on without looking back. The exception was Maggie. He'd never seemed able to move on from that.

He hugged her, and she looked up into his brown eyes suddenly glistening with sadness. Suddenly he looked rather old, she thought. He gathered himself and coughed a little.

'Thanks for everything, Jane. I apologise for all the late nights and early mornings, my irritability when things got lost and I blamed you. I'm sorry that you never seemed to use all your holiday. Thanks for your tireless organisation of a chaotic diary, for the correcting of my dreadful grammar in reports … oh, and thanks for all the hot pork and stuffing butties.'

She laughed as she saw him briefly wipe away a tear while feigning another cough.

'Not to mention the tea,' she said warmly.

'Of course. Mustn't forget the tea.'

With that, he headed out into the May afternoon. It was warm in the sun, but a biting east wind cut through it, and he pulled his dark-blue coat around him. For once, he had time on his hands. He would not meet his colleagues at Rules until 5pm, ahead of the show.

He'd weighed up his options and decided to take the Thames Clipper back home and return on the Jubilee line later that evening. He loved the river, and joined the queue at the pier, along with a few early-season tourists who were probably heading for the Tower of London downstream.

He stood looking upstream for a while and realised that in future he would have no work-related reason to come into the centre of London. He suddenly had a deep feeling of regret that it was all over, and bitterness welled up within him.

He chided himself. 'Stop it, Tom, right now,' he muttered. Then he realised he had said it out loud.

'I'm sorry?'

A short American man in front of him turned. He wore a Pittsburgh Pirates baseball cap and held a *London A to Z* in his hand. Tom shook his head.

'My apologies. I was just thinking out loud.'

The American smiled and motioned towards two bored children standing nearby.

'That's OK. I do that a lot with these guys. I cuss a bit

for sure. Kids get bored easy. Figured we'd go to the Tower of London this afternoon. See the Crown Jewels. Keep 'em busy.'

'Enjoy. If they get too much you could always get the Beefeaters to stick them in the dungeons. There's plenty of room these days.'

The American laughed as the boat pulled in, and they separated as they boarded. Tom stood at the back breathing deeply as the sense of freedom washed over him. It felt good for a moment. He was relieved of the back-to-back meetings, the constant giving of half-truths to his boss and, more recently, the queues for late-night takeaways. He wouldn't miss some of that, he conceded.

As the catamaran headed downstream towards Docklands, he looked back at the London skyline receding into the distance. He moved inside into the warm after the bulk of the passengers got off at the Tower of London. He waved to the American family as they disembarked, envying the bubbly uncontrollability of the kids and the company they offered. Tom was heading home to an empty flat, albeit a comfortable one with a nice view of the river. He became irritable once more as he found he was feeling sorry for himself. As they went past Traitors' Gate, he decided there were one or two people he'd like to send on a one-way trip through that particular aperture.

5.

Publicity Day

One afternoon the following week, Hannah travelled home. She'd enjoyed the photoshoot she'd done on the pier with Amy and the cast that day, and rehearsals were going well. They'd worn their stage costumes for the first time, a special moment for any performer. The press releases were ready for publication, and a number of publicity appearances had been booked.

She'd enjoyed the cast social night too, a pier tradition for which the cast and crew got together, doing turns and building a team bond which would last throughout the season. These people were now her friends. In addition to Lech and Amy there were six dancers, two of them male. There was a young Welsh tenor, an Australian juggling impressionist and a magician who was rather better at his tricks than Lech had been all those years ago.

She could feel her self-confidence returning. She had not appeared in public for so long, but having broken the spell by appearing in pubs at Gwen's suggestion, she was convinced that she could sing better now than she could as a youngster. She had learned voice-coaching skills which had given her a better understanding of the underlying physiology, so she was going to grab the opportunity that the full season at Cromer offered.

She had started to cover some of Amy's pieces in the show, which wasn't easy, as Amy had written them for her own voice. She was a little scared, but at the same time she felt alive, for the first time in years. Being a housewife and bringing up her child had brought its own rewards of course, but this was her time.

She'd not seen Ian since that day on the pier, and after a couple of weeks of being escorted by Graham they decided she no longer needed his protection.

Her feelings for Ian were still complex. Despite events, she still loved him, or at least she thought she did. There had been some great times while Gwen was growing up. To the outsider, Hannah had wanted for nothing. Nice home, nice lifestyle, nice holidays. She missed her career of course, but enjoyed bringing up Gwen, and was friends with her circle of playgroup mums. They had a good social life, and Ian was earning plenty of money at the bank.

But as she looked back, she realised that he'd been late most evenings, meeting his chums after work in the pub as some commuters did, and played golf on Saturday mornings. Then he began playing on Sundays, too. When they moved to a bigger house to reduce his commute, she became cut off from her friends. Meanwhile, her husband dismissed any new ones she made as irrelevant. Indeed, her whole life became irrelevant, limited to bringing up Gwen and keeping house. She had taken the job at the school as it gave her a musical outlet.

Although Ian worked in the City, and they had the West End so near, they never went there. She loved musical theatre, but Ian hated it. She'd wanted to go with friends at the weekend, but of course Ian's golf came first, and there was nobody to look after Gwen. When her mother had a stroke, Hannah went back to Cromer to look after her. She gradually began to realise that she was more relaxed in her hometown than in her Kent commuter bubble, and as Gwen grew older and became more worldly-wise, she began to rebel against her father's attempts to manage her behaviour. Her mother tried to play peacemaker, but that only seemed to make things worse. Hannah always got the blame.

Now, arriving home, Hannah went into the house through the kitchen door to put away some shopping. She boiled the kettle for tea. Something felt wrong, but she couldn't think what. She stirred the tea bag and added milk, before absent-mindedly wandering through to the lounge.

'Home at last, Hannah?' came a familiar voice.

She stopped abruptly. Ian was sitting on her settee, a mug of tea in his hand. It was then that she realised; the kettle had been warm.

She struggled to find any words.

'Surprised to see me?' he asked.

Hannah recovered herself a little. 'Yes. How did you ... '

' ... Get in? Oh, that was easy. I just remembered where your dear mother left her spare key. Simple, really,' he said.

Hannah summoned up her reserves of resolve. 'Please leave ... now.'

Ian laughed. 'No. I don't think so. After all, this is just as much my home as yours. Our country retreat.'

Hannah couldn't believe that this was happening. 'No. It's not, Ian. Mother left it to me.'

He shrugged. 'But you're my wife, remember? What's mine is yours and so on.'

'Only until the divorce comes through. It's over, Ian. I wrote to you,' she insisted.

'Yes. I got your silly little note. You've had your break now.

I know Gwen leaving for uni took a bit of getting used to, but she seems settled now. It's time to come home, babe.'

He got up and took the mug from her hand. Before she could respond, he pulled her close and kissed her, or at least tried to. She recoiled, moving her head back.

'No, Ian. Look ... look; I made it clear.'

She extracted herself from his arms, shoving him away. 'Please leave, now,' she said.

Ian shook his head. 'I don't think so. Look, you're going through a funny time of life. It plays tricks on the brain. We need to get you some medical help. Probably a menopause thing. We'll go on holiday. Nashville, if you want. Time to take us seriously now.'

He sat once more. She couldn't think what to do. He motioned her to sit too. She ignored him.

'Ian, I've made it clear that it's over. I'm living here now, and I'm picking up my showbiz career up again.'

He laughed. 'Showbiz career? You don't call that theatre showbiz? Full of old farts on Zimmer frames.'

She shook her head. She was frightened and furious at the same time. She was trying to work out how to get him out of the house. *Her* house. The brass-necked arrogance of the man. She was about to respond when he got up and headed for the kitchen.

'Just sit down and drink your tea,' he said affably. 'I've got some steaks for dinner. They don't seem to have an M & S in this shit-heap of a town, but I found some half-decent ones from Morrisons and a decent red Barossa. I'll just light the oven.'

She couldn't believe this. He was taking charge again. Setting the agenda. *His* agenda. Years of avoiding confrontation welled up.

She wasn't having this. 'No, Ian. You're not staying. I want you to leave now, please. *Now.*'

He hesitated only momentarily, then continued into the kitchen. She heard him switch the oven on. He clearly had no intention of leaving. Nervously, she turned away and took out her mobile phone, and frantically searched for Graham Blakeley's number.

'Calling someone?' he asked, returning from the kitchen.

She dropped the phone in shock, but as she bent down towards it, he put his foot on it, the cracking of the screen quite audible in the silence. He stooped and picked it up.

'Useful things, phones,' he said. 'Tell you what people have been up to. Photos, too, and videos, of course.'

She couldn't move. Her powers of speech had deserted her. She felt completely paralysed.

Ian flicked through her messages, and then looked at her. 'Your boyfriend isn't watching over you anymore, then? He didn't last long, did he? Dipped his wick and dumped you, I shouldn't wonder.'

She remained silent, thinking about how she could get out of this.

Ian stared at her. 'Was he any good in bed, Hannah? I mean he looked about 60, but you always did have an eye for older blokes, and what with Viagra, who knows?'

She shook her head. 'You were always paranoid, Ian. I've never played away.'

He was becoming angry now. 'Don't lie to me. He stayed over two nights running. I was watching.'

She tried to stay calm. 'For your information, he slept in the spare bedroom. He's a retired police officer who offered to help. I was frightened.'

He mocked her. 'You really expect me to believe that? Is that the best you can do?'

'Believe it or not, I've never played away. Unlike you, of course.'

He sneered. 'Well, I wasn't getting much at home, was I? You were pretty hot when I first met you, but look at you now. I told you to keep at it in the gym like I do, but you wouldn't listen.'

She stayed silent. She didn't want to inflame him, but needed to stand her ground. He pocketed the mobile, and smiled, rather forcibly taking her hands in his.

'But I want to give us a second chance, Hannah. I mean, it was only a fling, and you were as much to blame. I've always loved you and I've given you everything you could want. Nice home, great lifestyle, plenty of posh dresses and facials. Nice holidays.'

She stared at him icily. 'No. We're done. I'll pay my own way from now on, thank you.'

He scoffed. 'In that fleapit of a theatre in front of a few near-dead punters? I doubt that would keep you in fancy underwear, let alone shoes.'

She was angry now. 'For your information, I'm a headliner in the show. It's a full season in a West End-standard show which sells out most nights. Then I'll probably do cruise ships through the winter. I don't need you anymore. Now please leave.'

His face formed an evil stare. It was a stare she'd seen before, as had Gwen. She expected to feel his hand crack at the side of her face, and steeled herself, but then he relaxed and smiled.

'Headliner, eh? Wow. My Hannah a great big star. You'll be on *Britain's Got Talent* next.'

Hannah remained calm. 'It's a start. It's where I was when I first met you.'

'Since when I've earned £100,000 a year and you've earned peanuts.'

'So?'

'Well, I'm not having you flashing your knickers every night to a bunch of old perverts. You might as well work at a strip club. No chance. I'm not having it. Do you understand me?'

She thought about running to the door, but decided that she wouldn't make it. She'd tried that before at home, but the last time he'd dragged her into the downstairs bedroom. She didn't want to risk that at any price. She decided to try to take control of the conversation.

'It's all announced next week, Ian. I've done the publicity shoot today, as a matter of fact.'

'Ooh … a publicity shoot, eh? So that's why you're wearing those hold-em in knickers, is it? Mind you, they can do wonders with Photoshop these days.'

She decided to ignore the slur. He'd been doing this for years, but it wouldn't work anymore.

He took out his own phone. 'Well, if it's publicity shots you want, you should have asked me. I have plenty of you, if you recall. Videos, too.'

He smiled. She *had* forgotten.

He saw the look of fear and continued. 'If you like, we could go and make some more videos together? We can eat later if you like?'

She realised that she was now in an impossible place. She couldn't get away, but she knew how this would end. As luck would have it, her phone rang.

He took it out of his pocket and looked at it. 'Ah. Probably your policeman friend. You won't be needing him anymore.'

He dismissed the call but was distracted in doing so,

dropping his own phone. As he leant down to pick it up, she grabbed a cut-crystal vase, her mother's favourite, and wheeled around, catching him on the side of the head with it. Although it was only a glancing blow, he was knocked off-balance, and she kicked him in the backside as she fled. He tripped over the coffee table and fell to the floor. It gave her a few precious seconds to reach the front door and fling it open. She had no keys and no phone, but she ran as fast as she could towards the parade of shops. Anywhere public, she reasoned. Reaching the newsagent's, she begged to use their phone, and Mrs Gupta agreed without question.

Fifteen minutes later, Graham Blakeley appeared. Ian was nowhere to be seen.

6.

Money Troubles

A week or so later, in the boardroom of the Majestic Hotel, Jim Cameron was sitting alone in front of his laptop, trying to create a silk purse from the proverbial casino-based pig's ear. He'd come in on a Saturday morning to try to work things out, annoying his wife by doing so. But play with the spreadsheet as he might, he couldn't see how to convince the bank that Pemrose Entertainments could possibly sustain the investment involved on top of their existing debt. Even if you could actually call it an investment.

He knew that the latest set of monthly accounts would make the bank uneasy, so he had included a note saying that he would provide fresh forecasts to the bank, ready for when Hodson returned from his imminent holiday. In doing so he'd at least managed to buy them some time.

Lionel had furnished him with estimates as to the remaining costs and timescale to complete the refurbishment of the first-ever Pemrose Casino. Even using the figures provided, the additional overdraft required seemed impossible to secure through the existing banking arrangements, and Cameron knew that the figures Lionel had quoted were pie in the sky.

Sensing that Freya Alcott-Palmer's estimated costs were a work of fantasy fiction, Cameron had bullied Lionel into securing a second opinion from a trusted source. The second set of figures confirmed his worst fears.

While the traditional Pemrose amusement arcades on the east coast would show their usual respectable profit, the spending spree of recent years had left the organisation laden with debt. Not only had Lionel overspent in acquiring chains of rundown coastal amusement arcades, but he'd also bought some betting shops in the north of England which now seemed to be failing. The interest on that debt was looking increasingly unsustainable.

The remaining profits could in no way pay for the hideous costs still to be incurred on the casino, and it was now less likely that it would ever make money, especially in the rather downmarket area where it was situated. All in all, betting on a casino in the current climate seemed like backing a three-legged donkey in the Grand National, but when he'd said as much to Lionel, he had received a typically icy retort.

Cameron stood up and sighed. He couldn't see any way he could convince the bank to continue with this lunacy and the business was going to go under very soon as things stood. Lionel was playing roulette all right, and he was going to lose his shirt, along with a chunk of Jim's pension.

Jim did, however, congratulate himself in one important respect. Following the highly acrimonious divorce proceedings involving Lionel and his ex-wife Miriam, he had taken the opportunity to restructure the group, segregating the hotels business from the arcades. The hotels were doing very nicely thank you, and as Miriam only had shares in these, it meant that he didn't need to tell her about this mess.

Lionel would doubtless blame Peter Hodson and the bank, and then Jim. Then it would, by some fanciful construction of facts, be Miriam's fault. But the reality would dawn when the bank called in the overdraft.

He was looking out at one Victorian relic of little value to Pemrose Entertainments, Cromer Pier, and then he had a thought, about the bizarre lease arrangements between Pemrose and the Pier Theatre. Many years previously, the wealthy Collingworth clan who owned the pier had decided to sell some assets, presumably to pay death duties or the like. They offered the pier to their long-standing theatre director, Jack Wells, but he had been worried about the financial risk involved, so they gave him a long-term lease on the theatre only, as a reward for his long service to the family.

A young but successful businessman called Lionel Pemrose had jumped at the chance to buy what he saw as the jewel in the town's crown. He thought that in time he could build an entertainments complex on the pier, only realising later that the pier's Grade II listing made any redevelopment virtually impossible. Worse still, the ongoing maintenance costs required were reflected in the low price that he had paid. He had always maintained that the pier was a long-term investment, and in Lionel's twisted mind nothing was trivial where the bloody pier was concerned, so Jim picked up the telephone and rang the solicitors, just to be sure of the facts about the lease.

*   *   *

Bank manager Peter Hodson wasn't really enjoying his Saturday either. He'd read the management accounts for Pemrose Entertainments the previous day, and didn't like what he was seeing. Peter was an experienced banker, well thought of by his superiors, and he was looking forward to a long and happy retirement in a couple of years.

He and his lovely wife Angela lived in a suitably large house outside the picturesque town of Holt. Their two daughters were now married, leaving a sizeable empty nest and a burgeoning disposable income.

He'd run a tight ship, with only one or two insolvencies on his watch, and the bank had come through from the 2008 recession largely unscathed. He could see what was unfolding at Pemrose and would ordinarily simply have foreclosed on them without a second thought, now that they'd breached the bank covenants.

But instead guilt and a deep foreboding surged through his gut. It had been just one mistake. One bloody silly mistake he'd made years ago. But it meant that he needed to find a way to sort this mess out. Because to fail would most likely leave his life in ruins.

He was going on holiday the following day, a fortnight in a private villa in Tenerife, so he was trying to be in a position to switch off. He crafted an email back to Jim Cameron saying that he 'looked forward' to reviewing the revised forecasts on his return. But he'd certainly keep access to his work emails while he was away.

In the afternoon, Hodson headed for the golf course. The benign sunshine earlier on disappeared as the wind got up, making the links rather more difficult. He had a lot on his mind as he tried to focus on his game, but following an indifferent round he was glad to reach the clubhouse just as it started to rain.

He went inside and ordered a black coffee, joining his golfing partners for a snack before returning home. As he was finishing, he saw a red Jaguar pull into the car park. The registration plate revealed its owner; PEM1. Lionel Pemrose. The last person he wanted a conversation with before his holiday.

He finished his coffee and pretended to look at his watch. 'Sorry, gents, I need to get off. Thanks for the game. See you in a couple of weeks.'

He headed for the door, but he was too late. 'Afternoon, Peter, going so soon?' said Lionel, holding the door open for him.

'Afternoon, Lionel,' he said.

'Can I buy you a coffee? Things to discuss,' asked Lionel.

Peter hesitated.

The older man continued, 'It won't take a moment. I'll walk you to your car.'

Unable to escape, Peter walked to his car with Lionel by his side.

'So, Jim supplied you with the management accounts? Anything more else you need?'

Peter replied, 'I've been a bit busy, Lionel, but I gather Jim's got some forecasts, so I'll review them when I get back from holiday.'

Lionel nodded. 'Of course. If you want Jim and I to talk things over on your return, that would be fine. There've been some problems with the building, but it's going to be fantastic when it opens. It'll make a bomb, that casino.'

Having reached his black BMW, Hodson pressed the remote to open the car door. He decided that he needed to prepare the ground, but didn't want to have the row there and then.

He looked at Lionel directly. 'Well, as I say, I'll need to review things when I get the revised forecasts. The management accounts don't look great, I have to say. I see you've broken some covenants.'

It was clear to Lionel that Hodson knew exactly what the figures were.

'Well, we've done a lot of business together, and I don't think I've let you down yet.'

Except for the disastrous acquisition of those bingo halls which were riddled with asbestos and are still losing money, and those betting shops as well, thought Hodson. He opened the car door, but Lionel continued the conversation.

'Goodness, it looks like a squall's coming in,' said Lionel. 'Perhaps I need to get some sunshine, too. Might go off to my villa in Malaga sometime myself. Where are you headed? Somewhere warm, no doubt?'

'Tenerife. Get some sun and hopefully play a bit of golf,' Peter replied. 'I'll give Jim a call on my return when I've looked at his forecasts. I'll see you later.'

Lionel smiled, but just as Hodson moved to close the door, the other man spoke once more.

'Of course, well enjoy your holiday. Oh and by the way, Lizzie sends her love.'

Hodson waved and started the car. There it was. His worst nightmare. Lizzie.

*   *   *

Tom Stanley sat on the terrace of the Trafalgar, a popular Greenwich watering hole. He was sipping a pint of London Pride while waiting for his steak pie and chips. Maggie would doubtless have chided him for having two lots of chips in the same week, he noted sadly. It was Saturday, and he'd walked through the tunnel to Greenwich. He'd tipped the busker who played *Streets of London* rather better than many did, wandered by the Cutty Sark, and around the shops, rather aimlessly. To be honest, he only knew it was Saturday because there were more people about. Fortunately, May had been rather warm and sunny, which had kept his mood a couple of notches north of sombre.

He had reached the same unpleasant realisation of many retired professionals, that the world goes on perfectly well without you. He had agreed to stay in contact with the business for three months, to sort out odds and ends. But there had been no contact. Elena obviously doesn't need me, he thought.

For someone who had worked long hours for most of his life, as Tom had, it was hard to reconcile himself to the fact that he now had no real purpose. For many, that is entirely fine; they can dig their allotment, play a daily round of golf, travel wherever and whenever they please, or rant on social media should they so desire.

But for Tom Stanley his work had largely been his life. He had enjoyed the cut and thrust of the business. The celebration when a deal was done, the consolatory late-night double whisky when something you'd worked on for months had fallen through. It was a roller coaster of highs and lows, and he had loved it. Maggie understood that. She had created their social life around, amongst other things, their mutual love of London theatre and her amateur dramatics group in Greenwich. She was tolerant of her husband's late nights and early mornings, of the dinner parties he cried off from at the last minute.

As he wrestled to come to terms with his sudden return to what, for many, was normal life, he sought whatever distractions he could find. As he sat there alone, he read the newspaper, which was full of the latest Brexit news. He then turned swiftly to the back pages. An upcoming Cricket World Cup offered him some potential entertainment, and he had some tickets courtesy of his former colleagues.

He had met Jane for lunch in Covent Garden the previous day, as his treat for all of her hard work over the years. She had been offered two jobs that week, and he tried valiantly to be interested, offering observations, since she was clearly seeking them. It was nothing personal; he cared about Jane a good deal, but quite simply Tom wasn't interested in anything. The food was very good, but he wasn't really hungry. The place was full of suited-and-booted City types on an extended lunch break, a bleak reminder of his old world, or tourists from various parts of the globe.

Jane asked what he'd been up to, suddenly aware that her job hunt had monopolised the conversation.

Tom thought for a while, having speared and chewed a piece of rare fillet steak.

'Bugger all, to be honest.'

Jane laughed. 'Sounds like paradise to me.'

Tom grimaced. 'Sod that for a game of soldiers. I expected some calls from the office. The Swanson deal was still ongoing, for a start. I expect young Cookson will need my guidance on some aspects of that for starters.'

He noticed that Jane had stopped eating momentarily. She hesitated then sipped from her perfectly chilled glass of St Clair Sauvignon Blanc. Tom paused too. Jane knew she'd been rumbled. He read body language too well.

'Yes. Well, I think you'll find that 'young' Cookson left the same day as me,' she said.

Tom stopped eating now and set down his knife. 'I see, so ...'

Jane set her knife and fork down too. 'Look, Tom, I didn't want to tell you. It will only annoy you.'

Tom shrugged. 'Well thanks, but what, pray, have Elena and her Yankee Doodle Dandies been up to now?'

Jane shrugged too. 'Whatever. I guess the grapevine will kick in anyway. They've closed the business recovery division entirely. They've made the whole team redundant.'

Tom leaned forward a little and stared at her intently for a moment. She ignored him and sliced a nice piece of salmon en-croute. They ate silently for a while. Tom sensed that she was wondering if she had done the right thing in telling him. He took a rather hearty glug of red before finally speaking.

'I've known some of those guys since they started as students. I'm surprised they haven't been in touch.'

'They will be I expect, but they're still processing what happened. Elena just called them all into the boardroom and told the whole team in one go. It was a terrible shock. Some were in tears.'

Tom sighed, but then reflected on her news. 'Well, we didn't really fit with their core business, did we? Still made them plenty of money, though.'

Jane frowned a little. He seemed to be taking it better than she thought he would.

Tom looked at her over the rim of his brown tortoiseshell glasses, as he picked up his knife once more.

'Don't think I'm anything but bloody furious, Jane.'

She frowned in surprise. 'Didn't you know about their plan then, Tom? I thought you might have.'

'No. They didn't tell me anything. In hindsight, I should have seen it coming way back when they bought us.'

'Don't start feeling guilty. Nobody blames you.'

Tom shook his head, resumed eating and gesticulated with his fork. 'Well, I do seem to have been wallowing in self-pity of late. It's time I stopped being so pathetic, really.'

Jane shook her head and smiled. 'Why not go it alone once again? I'm sure some of the guys would join you. They really do respect you, even if you're a little … well … challenging at times.'

It was Tom's turn to smile. Jane was ever the diplomat.

'Well, I thought about it. But the truth is that I did make a few mistakes of late. We'd have barely broken even this year. Elena wasn't happy. But when you're working at a risk if the deals don't happen, well … '

'But you still won more than you lost, though.'

'*We* did, Jane. A team effort. But Elena likes nice steady upward growth, and we're not that sort of business. They'll float the group on the stock market next year, I suspect. Meanwhile I've had a lot of time to think, and this is a young man's game and I'm tired. I love it, but I'll kill myself in the end.'

Jane looked up reprovingly.

Tom nodded. 'Yes, I know you've said that to me a number of times before. So did Maggie. But now I realise that I need to find a new direction.'

'And what might that be?'

'Therein lies the problem, Jane. Frankly, my dear, I haven't the slightest idea.'

* * *

A couple of weeks later, with Whitsun approaching, Tom Stanley was going stir-crazy. He looked out over the Thames from his balcony as he sat at his small table. Maggie's empty chair was a constant reminder of her absence, and yet he couldn't bring himself to remove it.

In a fit of abject boredom, he'd collected a pile of assorted holiday brochures from a local travel agent. Jane had suggested it at lunch. After all, when one is retired it's what one does, doesn't one?

He went inside, and switched off the television, bored with the relentless Brexit coverage. He leafed through the glossy brochures wondering how these organisations could afford to fund this mountain of full-colour printing. He'd travelled to some faraway places with Maggie, of course. Now he could afford any holiday he wanted, yet it all seemed rather pointless without her to share it with.

He picked up an Italian brochure and saw Lake Como. They'd honeymooned there, in a stunning hotel right on the lake. Where was it now? Bellagio. That's it, he thought. He thumbed the pages and found the hotel. Not the biggest, but right on the lake, with a nice little loggia.

But without Maggie this was all a waste of time. He'd thrown himself into his work after she'd died only months after being diagnosed. They had planned to buy a place somewhere new. They liked Tuscany and Brittany, but Maggie wanted somewhere nearer, on the English coast. Then it all fell to pieces. He'd been with her, of course, when they had been given the bad news. A brain tumour. She'd been so matter-of-fact about it, accepting of her fate in a way that he never could.

He regarded it as theft. Theft of their life together. Maggie, on the other hand, had had quite a strong religious faith, which helped her to deal with things. She'd smiled as he brought her in some tea on that particular morning, along with a lovely bouquet of flowers. He'd hugged her, choking back tears as he did so. Then as he set her back on her pillow she smiled briefly and drifted off. A few moments later, she stopped breathing. The end of a 25-year marriage, cut short so brutally.

He snapped out of his self-pity. It was Maggie who had

been cheated. He was still very much alive. He was the lucky one, but now it all seemed completely pointless. He desperately needed a purpose. But what could he do? Some voluntary work? Become a non-executive director even though he didn't need the money? Take up golf? Try as he might, nothing appealed to him at all.

*   *   *

Late that afternoon, Jim was in the conference room at the Majestic, which doubled as the Pemrose headquarters. Lionel came in breezily, went to the coffee pot and poured himself a black coffee, adding two sugars.

'Afternoon, Lionel,' said Jim, surprised at the other man's lack of greeting.

'Good afternoon. We've things to discuss, Jim.'

Lionel sat opposite him and Jim saw that he had a handful of documents. Experienced at reading upside down, Jim noticed a solicitor's letterhead. Lionel despised solicitors, and generally left legal matters to him. Strange.

Lionel was brisk and to the point. 'I've decided to let Hodson take a legal charge over the Pemrose Hotels assets. I didn't want to do it, but if that's what it takes to shut the idiot up then so be it. I've had the bank send over the documents while he's on holiday, so you won't need to give him those projections. I've shown them to the solicitors, and they've tweaked the wording. They're happy for us to sign them.'

Jim was stunned by this turn of events. 'Well. That is a turn-up for the books. I think I'll need time to go through things. Let me see the documents.'

Lionel shook his head. 'No time, old son. I said we'd get

them back for Hodson's return. I'm fed up with cashflow constraints. The boys at the golf club are whispering about us not paying our bills on time. I can't have that.'

Jim responded calmly. 'But these people aren't the company solicitors. They don't know the implications.'

'What implications? It's a standard bank guarantee form. Just needs two signatures; yours and mine.'

Cameron didn't want a blazing row, but now he had no choice.

'Well, they need the minutes of a board meeting to approve it, for one thing,' he said.

Lionel nodded, 'Yes, it's in here. All done and dusted. Just needs signing.'

Cameron shook his head. 'But the meeting does actually need to have taken place. I need to give seven days' notice to the directors, including Miriam.'

'No time for that, Jim. Let's just bung him the forms and shut him up. Miriam won't be any the wiser.'

Cameron closed his eyes and rocked back in his chair. Lionel was clearly desperate. When Jim spoke, he was angry, but his voice was icily calm.

'I can't do as you ask, Lionel. We'd be in breach of the Companies Act. It would be fraud as well, most likely. I can't let you break the law. If you had discussed this with me first, I could have told you as much.'

Lionel threw the papers across the table. 'Just do as you're bloody told for once and sign those damn documents. We haven't time to mess about.'

Cameron calmly pushed them back across the table. 'No, Lionel. I'm not going to let you put us both in jail. Do you want me to resign?'

Lionel stood, eyes blazing, but said nothing.

Jim let a few moments pass, and then spoke. 'If you want to do this, then Hodson will be fully aware of what we need to do. You know full well that under the articles any charge on the assets needs the approval of all the directors, and that includes Miriam. You cannae wish that inconvenient truth away. I cannae and willnae have it.'

Lionel was simmering now. But Jim continued calmly. 'Come on, Lionel. This isn't good for the blood pressure at our age. Let's sit down and talk this out. You've never tried to put me in a corner before and trust me, I will nae have it.'

Lionel thought about it and then seemed calmer. He hadn't thought that Jim would dig his heels in like this, and wouldn't dare fire him. He and Hodson were too close to risk it. Jim poured them both a Scotch in the heavy lead-crystal glasses and set one down in front of Lionel. He initially ignored it, but as Jim sat down, he reached across and took it.

'Look, Lionel, there is no way that Miriam will agree a bank charge over the hotels she part-owns. Why should she? She has the accounts for Pemrose Hotels and doesn't give you any problems with those. Just a simple quarterly board meeting. But trust me, if you try to pull a fast one on her like this, she'll dig her designer heels in like you've never seen before.'

Lionel simmered, drinking the Scotch as Jim continued. 'You'd be mad to put the hotels at risk just to save entertainments. If it goes wrong, you'll lose everything. Hodson would flog this place off at a knockdown price and leave us with bugger all.'

Jim noticed that Lionel seemed calmer now, so he continued. 'If I show him the projections, he'll like as not require a bank review. Getting the bank review done buys us some time without any risk to us whatsoever. With a bit of luck, he'll bankroll the higher overdraft while it proceeds, giving us another month at least. By then you can see how things are going with the casino. Frankly, I've no idea why he's being so generous. If he pulled the plug now, he'd get his money back'

Lionel snapped. 'I don't want some kid from a Big Six firm telling me how to run my business, Jim. It'd cost a bomb as well.'

Jim nodded. 'A few thousand yes, but we'll fix the fee and I'll make sure he appoints someone with experience who will add some value. Hodson will understand.'

Lionel glared at him. 'And Miriam?'

'Well, it's just a consultant helping out. They'd look at the group, hotels included, but Miriam doesn't need to know that the bank put them in. If you want to put the charge on the assets, she'll have to know. You don't have any legal way of avoiding it.'

He looked across at Lionel. His face was devoid of colour, and even his staff had remarked that he seemed distant recently. They were surprisingly loyal to Lionel, because he could be completely charming. He cared about their families and had a great recall of names. He was good with the customers as well; particularly the older guests who liked to meet the proprietor.

But the group was so much bigger now, with more hotels, the block of amusement arcades and the betting shops. Lionel couldn't attend to all the detail personally, and neither of them was getting any younger.

Jim had talked about floating the group off, allowing both Lionel and Miriam to contemplate retirement, but Lionel had roundly rejected the idea. Cameron had come to understand why; Lionel was scared of retiring. He simply loved the cut and thrust of business and would die of boredom if he ever retired.

Lionel was looking at his phone now. He'd got quite nifty with the technology, although one of the backroom staff at the Majestic had set it up, of course. Jim brought him back to the discussion.

'Lionel?'

'Yes, what? Oh, well, if you think that's best, I'll go along with you. Just make sure we get the money.'

Jim smiled with relief. Lionel could switch moods so quickly. Now all he had to do was to negotiate a change of plan with Hodson, who must have thought all his problems were over when Lionel offered to give him an asset charge. The Majestic had been an absolute bargain. Bought for next to nothing from the administrators at the height of the banking crisis and beautifully refurbished with Miriam's creative eye, it was the jewel in the crown of the Pemrose empire. But Jim wasn't about to let it be put down as security for Lionel's crackpot casino.

7.

Meetings

It had taken rather too long to arrange this meeting, but Hannah was now sitting with Graham Blakeley at Cromer Police Station. He was dressed in civilian clothes and sitting on the opposite side of the table now. He found his ex-colleague Detective Inspector Brent rather annoying. One of a new breed of policemen, Graham thought. Everything process-led, and the process required evidence, of which there was none to speak of.

Hannah had filed a complaint, but nothing had been seen of her husband, and enquiries suggested that he was taking an extended holiday abroad. The house in Kent was deserted, and the neighbours knew nothing.

'Well, at least your husband hasn't filed a complaint of assault, Mrs Castle. Whatever your domestic difficulties, by your own admission he would have grounds, you know. Your statement says as much.'

Blakeley was incensed at the insensitivity of the man, but knew that he could only really act as a friend, rather than as a policeman.

Hannah stared back at Brent. 'But he was threatening me. Trying to control me. He had no right to be in my mother's house anyway.'

The officer looked at the blue-highlighted line in his file. 'But you left a key; it says so here.'

'Well, yes, we had it under a pot outside in case we lost one.'

Brent continued, 'To a house which, although it was your mother's, is actually an asset of the marriage. Look, I can't arrest him for accessing a property which you gave him a key to, and in which he has a legitimate interest. Surely you can see it from my point of view, Mrs Castle?'

'Masters. Hannah Masters. I'm separated.'

'My apologies, Ms Masters. Look, I do sympathise, but we don't know where he is, and even if I manage to find him, what grounds do I have for detaining him? From your statement, he didn't assault you, and he seems to have visited to try to mend your marriage. I can't charge him for that.'

Graham had expected this of this particular officer. He decided to try one particular line of attack.

'Look, I know it's hard to prove, but her husband's behaviour bears all the hallmarks of coercive control. You've seen the interview notes with the counsellor. And what about the incident on the pier?'

The officer nodded, turning to the document in the file.

'Yes, but you know as well as I do that these things are difficult to prove and there is just not enough evidence to do more than we already have. Kent Police will keep the file open, but until Mr Castle returns there isn't much I can do. When he does, they'll interview him. That in itself will tell him that he's crossed the line. I really doubt that he'll show up here again, Ms Masters.'

Hannah shook her head in dismay. 'But what about his threats? The videos?' she said, sobs mixed with embarrassment in her voice.

The officer nodded. 'Well, it *was* just a threat, and it would of course be a criminal offence to share them. In my experience, many people might make threats, but few carry them out.'

'You don't know Ian,' she said coldly.

Graham interjected calmly. 'You should know that Hannah is appearing in the Cromer Pier show starting at the end of June, so the publication of those videos would destroy her career. This is a serious risk.'

'Well, I acknowledge that, but Ms Masters consented to the recording of the videos in question. There is nothing to suggest he recorded them without her consent.'

They had reached an impasse. Leaving the police station, they walked together in silence. Blakeley was not completely surprised by the outcome. They didn't have the staff to follow up on things like this, and ideally a female officer would have interviewed Hannah, but one simply hadn't been available.

Graham judged Ian Castle as a real risk to Hannah's safety, given her demeanour when the incident had concluded. He had seen enough in his career to judge the body language of the Hannah he had seen in the newsagent's that day. She wasn't making it up; she was quite simply terrified.

* * *

Peter Hodson wasn't sleeping well, and thus wasn't really enjoying Tenerife that much, stunning though the villa was. He couldn't get the Pemrose problem out of his mind, and he kept hearing Lionel's voice.

'Lizzie sends her love.'

He got up quietly at 3am, stomach churning with a cold fear. He made himself some tea and sat down in the lounge.

He wanted to sleep, but his guilt denied him any rest. In the cold light of day, he might wonder if he was over-analysing things, but there isn't much rational thought at 3am.

Was Lionel marking his card? Or was it just a follow-on reference to Malaga? Maybe he was over- thinking it? Peter's wife often said that he was given to over-reaction and seeing hidden meanings in things.

He relaxed at the thought, but then fear took hold once again. Lionel didn't waste time on chit-chat. No, everything that Lionel did or said had a purpose, Peter decided. He had received Jim's projections and they didn't look good. He had tried to ignore the problem while he was on holiday, but in only a few days he'd have to face up to it.

He had seen an initial email from his assistant the previous week saying that Lionel had agreed to a charge on the hotels, which would have been an ideal solution, but early the previous day he'd received word that Lionel had backed out, for what he said were 'legal complications,' whatever that meant.

So, what could he do? Well, the obvious tactic was a bank review. The customer had to pay for it, and it gave the manager cover from accountability. He could, of course, get any accountant to do a bog-standard bank review, but he needed someone who might just have to know the full story; and why conventional solutions weren't available. He needed a people person who could broker a deal that let everybody think that they had got what they wanted. He put his head back and drifted off momentarily. Then the words came back.

'Lizzie sends her love.'

He pondered further and drank his tea. He thought about the deals he'd done over the years, and the people he'd met. There were many capable people out there who could do this job with perfect competence. But there was one thing he needed above all other. He needed to be able to trust the person he hired.

Then his memory stirred. It must be at least 10 years ago now. A plain-spoken Yorkshireman not afraid to give it straight. He had expected to wind a business up and take a loss, but this guy offered another option. The business had been saved and the managers who had bought it were now doing very nicely, thank you.

Tom Stanley. The name just popped into his head. Old enough and tough enough to cross swords with Lionel Pemrose, and he'd get on well with the blunt Jim Cameron. But the trust question? Well, he had to trust someone, and Tom Stanley was as straight as they came.

He felt better now. Yes. Tom Stanley was his man. He had a list of contacts in the office, so he would call him as soon as he was back from holiday. He could only hope that he was still in the business.

* * *

Cyril Brown was sitting in his room, although it was warm and his patio door was open. He had got up early, dressed himself as much as much as he could, and was making the most of what was his best time of day. He had another couple of hours before his guests arrived, and he had just completed the final edit. He saved the file on his ancient laptop and attached the file to an email. Selecting the name, he pondered a moment and then hit the Send key.

'There. It's done,' he whispered to himself. He just about managed to lever himself up from his desk, then used his frame to manoeuvre himself into his armchair. The effort of his work, coupled with the physical effort expended in that simplest of movements, tired him greatly, and he fell asleep almost immediately.

Later that morning, Janet Wells, Amy Raven and Lech Wojiek arrived at the nursing home. Janet had spoken with the manager the previous day to arrange the visit, and although the limit was usually two visitors, they had allowed three on this occasion as a one-off. Amy was keen to join Janet, as was Lech, who well remembered Cyril's help over the years.

The nurse said that Cyril was awake and on reasonable form that morning. As they entered, Janet was shocked that he seemed to look weaker than ever. His face was devoid of colour, although it lit up at their arrival. They sat and had tea with him, although Cyril was now struggling to hold his Pier Theatre mug straight, and Amy had to help him at one point.

'Well, Janet, are things going well with the show?' he asked.

Janet interjected, 'Very well, Cyril. Karen sends her best. As you'll imagine, she's rather busy.'

Cyril nodded, 'Of course. And how is Lech getting on? Still releasing mice into the audience?'

Lech laughed at the memory of his first disastrous rehearsal on the pier all those years ago. That Cyril's mind was so sharp only made his physical condition seem all the sadder.

'I try not to, Mr Cyril. My family are with me this year, so no mistakes this time. Here, I have a picture.'

He showed Cyril the picture, and they talked about his growing family. The Cyril of old was rising above his illness for a while.

'Amy, could you just hand me that box, my dear? I have something that Lech might make good use of.'

Amy was puzzled, as she knew what the box contained. She handed it over to Cyril, who in turn passed it to Lech.

'Now, I know you've become something of a ventriloquist these days Lech, and I rather think this chap might find his voice again in your hands.'

Lech opened the lid and saw the genial face of Felix looking up at him benignly. He immediately realised what an amazingly symbolic gift this was. Cyril smiled, although there seemed to be a sadness behind the smile. Lech said nothing, but simply took the old man's hands in his own before hugging him.

Cyril sniffed, wiped his nose with a handkerchief, and smiled again. Now he looked at Amy and took out a small jewellery box.

'You've come a long way from busking on the pier haven't you, Amy? Now, when we last met, I said that you needed to see the audience as a friend, but I didn't leave things to chance. Just before the final that night, my wife gave me a set of lucky cufflinks, to wear on stage. Clearly, they brought me luck that day, so I think you should have them now. A good luck charm for the season, if you will.'

Amy opened the box and saw two cufflinks, each one a tiny dice. A double six for luck. She leaned forward and kissed him on the cheek.

'You simply lovely man,' she whispered.

'We'll get them sewn into your costume,' said Janet.

Cyril nodded. 'The show must go on.'

'Indeed, it must,' she replied.

They talked a little more, but it was apparent that Cyril's body was exacting revenge for his half-hour of normality. The girls kissed the old man but left him sleeping. They kept their silence as they walked towards the car. The sun came out as they drove back along the seafront.

'Drop me off here please, Mrs Janet,' said Lech, as they reached the corner near the pier.

Lech got out, with Felix in his box. 'I must start new material right away.'

*   *   *

It was now Tuesday, and Jim Cameron had expected a phone call. He knew that Peter Hodson was back at work that day, and doubtless would want to review the projections he'd sent to him. But he hadn't expected him to ring at 11am that same morning.

'Jim, good morning. Peter Hodson.'

'Peter, good morning. Did you have a good holiday?' Jim asked, rather more cheerfully than he felt.

'Fine. I looked at the projections while I was on leave, and I'd like to meet as soon as possible. This afternoon, if you can?'

Jim had cleared his diary deliberately, so they agreed to meet at the bank at 2pm. He emailed Lionel telling him that Peter Hodson had been in touch. Fortunately, he knew that Lionel was playing golf. He was relieved when he received a simple email reply, clearly from Lionel's phone. It read simply 'Keep me informed.'

Jim Cameron knew he could do little to satisfy Peter Hodson. There was a time when Lionel Pemrose had a reputation as a sound businessman with a shrewd business brain. But the ill-judged acquisitions had bled the group of cash, and the casino project was heading for disaster. Jim had also only recently found out that Lionel had signed several contracts for further building work.

They had worked together for many years, but respect is based on trust, and increasingly Jim didn't trust Lionel anymore.

As he walked the short distance through the town to the bank, Jim reviewed his approach. Peter Hodson was an experienced manager with a nose for danger, and as the previous projections had failed to come anywhere close to reality, he saw little to be gained from spinning more fairy tales.

He entered the branch and was greeted at reception by Charlotte, a former Pemrose employee.

'Afternoon, Charlotte,' he said warmly.

'Good afternoon, Jim. I'll take you through. Black coffee?' she said.

As they entered a smartly decorated conference room, Peter Hodson shook Jim's hand warmly, and they made small talk until the coffee arrived. Charlotte departed and shut the door.

Hodson looked over his spectacles at Cameron. 'OK, Jim. What the hell are we going to do about Lionel?'

Cameron shrugged. 'Well, I could give more optimistic projections, but they'd likely be just as flaky as those that I've given you before.'

Hodson grimaced, 'Yes, those amusement arcades he bought were a frigging disaster, and as for those betting shops … and what on earth is this bloody casino project? I can't think that Miriam would have allowed that when they were married.'

Jim smiled grimly. 'It might not be a good idea to point that out to Lionel.'

Hodson looked across at him intently. 'You know you've blown the covenants and I've no security to justify an increased facility. Nothing works.'

Jim met his stare. 'I know. I'm not going to lie to you, Peter. We've done too much business together for that. The hotels business is doing really well. If we expand further, we'll need your support, so I'm not about to sell you short.'

Peter was becoming exasperated now. 'The obvious solution is to take a charge on the hotel assets. There's more asset cover there. I thought Lionel agreed that with my assistant while I was away?'

Jim countered immediately. 'I knew you'd say that, but Miriam has shares in Pemrose Hotels, and he'd need her permission. There is no chance whatsoever that she'll agree.'

Hodson wasn't too surprised. 'Well, I thought that when Lionel offered it. I assumed she'd agreed. Do they still hate each other?'

Cameron grimaced. 'Huh. More than ever. The board meetings are strained, to say the least. I make sure we have as few of them as possible and get things done and dusted in an hour max.'

'You can't run a business that way, Jim.'

'Well, it's not ideal. But the hotels business is fine, you've seen the accounts.'

'Yes. It was a smart move to split the business from your point of view. It hasn't been so good from my point of view, mind.'

Cameron remained silent. Something was troubling Hodson. He seemed rather nervous for someone who could simply pull the plug and walk away. What was his problem?

Hodson stood and tweaked the blind to shut out the afternoon sun. 'Would Lionel take personal guarantees? On his house? The place in Malaga, perhaps?'

Cameron expected this suggestion. 'I rather doubt he would. He's never done that before.'

Hodson looked up sharply. 'He wasn't going bust before. He needs to listen for once.'

'True.'

Hodson continued. 'Well, if he won't, we need to see some assets being sold, to get the exposure down.'

Cameron nodded. 'That would take time, of course. Can you give us three months?'

Hodson was in two minds. He was using the standard banking ploys, but Jim had all the answers ready.

'We seem to be going round in circles Jim. Come on, what have you got by way of a solution?'

Jim remained impassive. 'Sorry Peter. I don't have one. Pull the overdraft if you must. I don't have a magic wand to sort this out.'

Peter looked at him. 'You've done the sums, Jim. The bank gets out pretty clean, doesn't it? We won't lose much money if I act now.'

Cameron thought for a moment. 'Maybe. Who really knows with an insolvent business?'

Hodson continued. 'You could probably sell most of the arcades off, except the turkeys that Lionel bought recently. What else?'

Jim was finding the conversation unlike any that he'd had with Hodson before. He tried humour.

'The pier might be an interesting challenge to sell, Peter.'

Hodson rolled his eyes and laughed. 'I'm glad I don't have to deal with Janet Wells, not after last time.'

Cameron smiled back. 'To Lionel that is the biggest asset of the lot. Not in monetary terms, of course.'

Hodson shook his head. 'He's not still holding a candle for that bloody pier, is he?'

'You're forgetting that Miriam is chair of the Cromer Pier Theatre Trust, just to add to the witches' brew.'

Hodson dropped the fountain pen he'd been toying with.

'All in all, a bloody mess,' he said.

An ice cream van cruised outside the bank, playing *Beside the Seaside* as if mocking him. He stood to close the window as it started to rain. He just needed to buy time. He was dealing with a long-standing customer, a businessman with a strong presence locally. Yes; this he could justify to his head office if the chips were down. He sat again.

'OK, Jim, we've talked enough. It's clear that Lionel won't listen to you, so I need to show him who's boss. I'm going to appoint a consultant to do a business review. Lionel can pick up the bill and I'll extend the facility to meet your overdraft for the next month. Hopefully, this guy will talk some sense into him.'

Cameron was puzzled. Why hold back? But OK; Lionel would have no choice but to accept.

'Well, that seems fair. Do you have someone in mind? I'd rather it wasn't one of those Big Six auditors with sharp suits and no business sense.'

Hodson shook his head. 'Oh, no, I don't think that would work with Lionel, do you? Let me think about it. I'll let you know shortly.'

They shook hands. Both were uneasy, yet they realised that it was the best that they could do.

*   *   *

When Jim had gone, Peter looked at the mobile number on the card. He'd last spoken to Tom Stanley probably five years ago, when he'd been looking for assistance on some deal or other. Peter had looked at so many proposals that he'd forgotten the details. Now he rather needed this man to be available. He'd looked for a Plan B, but couldn't think of one. Any rational analyst would tell him to put Pemrose under, because the bank would get out without taking much of a hit.

His thoughts went back to that sunny day back in 2009. It was to be a golfing trip, followed by a family holiday. Lionel was flying out the following day, and Hodson's wife and children a couple of days later. The golf event was a business trip, giving Hodson the chance to meet influential people, or so he could argue if required. Lizzie, Lionel's PA, who he'd met once before, was there to greet him at the airport.

She drove them up to the secluded villa high in the hills and showed him to a splendid guest annexe. He'd expected the others to be there, but apparently some late change of plan meant that they weren't there until the next day. With hindsight, he might have smelt a rat, but actually he hadn't.

Lizzie suggested he might like a swim after his flight, and the sumptuous private pool did look inviting. He changed into his swimming trunks, and by the time he reached the pool Lizzie was swimming. She wore a plain white bikini and had clearly spent a few days topping up her tan. Yes, she looked gorgeous, yes, he should have smelt a rat, but he either didn't realise or didn't care.

They had dinner in a small local restaurant, and she talked about her career aspirations. She was young and very naive, he recalled. But she also had a delicious sense of humour and seemed to be genuinely interested in banking and finance, which some people of her age might have found dull. The wine flowed, and they took a taxi back. She made coffee, and they each had a brandy.

They watched a film. He sat at one end of the settee, she at the other. He felt very relaxed, something that he'd always found difficult to achieve. As the film ended, he got up, and she followed. She seemed to stumble slightly, and he reached out to steady her, taking her arm. They were suddenly rather close, and he found himself looking down at this diminutive girl.

'Thanks for a lovely evening, Lizzie. It's been great fun.'

She smiled and seemed to try a mock curtsy. 'No problem. I had a lovely time.'

She raised her head and kissed him full on the lips. 'Nighty night, Peter,' she whispered.

With that they went their separate ways. He was both relieved but ever so slightly disappointed that the evening was over. He hauled himself over to his room by the pool and stripped off his clothes. He tumbled into bed, tired from the day, and somewhat the worse from the alcohol.

It seemed a long time later, although it couldn't have been that long, before he felt a draught from the door which opened on to the pool area. He wasn't aware of his surroundings, and more than half asleep, as he felt a naked body cuddle up to his back.

He turned to see her smiling face illuminated by the outside light of the pool.

'Hi, Peter.'

He should have turned her away, of course. It was a set-up for sure. But he didn't.

They made love and awoke together and made love again. She showered as he dozed peacefully. He awoke sometime later, as she returned with breakfast, now fully dressed.

'Things to do. Enjoy your breakfast,' she said, setting down the tray.

As she headed for the door, he got up to hold her. She kissed him once more, just fleetingly. He moved to say something, but she put her finger to his lips.

'Don't say something you don't mean, Peter. It was thoroughly lovely. Our secret.'

With that she headed out of the door without another word.

Peter showered and tidied the bed clothes strewn across the king-sized bed.

He padded into the main part of the villa, expecting her to be in the lounge or the kitchen, but she wasn't. Then he looked on the drive and the car had gone. As the other guests started arriving, including Lionel, he suddenly realised that Lizzie wasn't coming back. He wanted to ask Lionel where she was, but decided against it. He played in the golf competition later that afternoon, an appalling feeling of guilt and foreboding in his gut.

Lionel moved from guest to guest, and servants appeared as if from nowhere. It was a jolly evening, but there were no female guests; it was a stag golf affair. The next day followed the same format, but on two different courses. By evening, he was physically exhausted after two rounds of golf and went to bed early after yet another substantial dinner.

Some of the guests were English residents, and he swapped cards with several of them, thus justifying the trip to himself. Lionel picked Peter's wife and children up from the airport the following morning, and he hugged them all warmly. He took their cases to their bedrooms and put his wife's case in their room. He felt guilty that he would be sharing the bed in which he had made love to Lizzie with his wife, but had no choice.

Lionel shook his hand as he left for the airport. If Lionel was intending to make anything of Lizzie's presence, he gave no indication of it. He had been the perfect host, and Peter's wife commented on it as they settled in later that evening.

He'd lived with his guilt, although it had receded a little over the years and he had just about learned to live with it. Even now, he couldn't be sure that Lionel had actually meant the reference to Lizzie as a threat, given the context of the remark, but Peter couldn't take the risk.

He yanked himself back to the present, punching in the number. After several rings, the phone was answered.

'Tom Stanley.'

*   *   *

At the time of receiving the call, Tom was drinking tea and reading the Times. He'd had lunch with one of his erstwhile colleagues earlier, and had finally found a holiday, although he hadn't actually booked it because, as much as he liked the itinerary, he just couldn't see the point in going. Life seemed just as pointless as ever. No Maggie to enjoy it with, and no work to make a difference to the world in which he lived.

He heard the ringtone and looked at it suspiciously. Only nuisance callers rang him these days, and he was minded to decline it until he saw a mobile number which seemed somehow familiar. In the end he picked it up.

'Tom Stanley.'

'Good afternoon, Tom, It's Peter Hodson here. Remember me?'

Tom thought for a moment. 'Ah, Peter. Yes, I do remember. Good lord. It's been a long time.'

Hodson continued. 'Well, I need your help with a client of mine. An entertainments group in Cromer. A family business. Need a bank review doing urgently. Any chance you might do it for me?'

Tom was puzzled. He'd never really done bank reviews as such. He'd just made his name as a guy who could fix broken companies. Any big-ticket accountancy firm could do this very easily. Why him?

He mentioned his semi-retirement but had to admit he was intrigued. More than intrigued, actually, he was pretty desperate for something to do, he conceded to himself.

Peter was certainly keen. 'You'd be doing me a favour. This is a sensitive matter. Pemrose is a high-profile client locally, and to be honest I'm as much worried about how we might keep the business going as the bank's exposure.'

Tom frowned. A bank manager not worrying about their exposure. Very strange.

'Well, I was planning a holiday, but I can pop up this week and we can talk things through if you like.'

'Yes. How are you fixed tomorrow? As I said, the sooner the better.'

Gosh, he is keen, Tom thought. 'Well, yes. Why not send some figures over? I'll study them this evening, so I can get a picture in my mind.'

And so it was agreed. An email duly arrived with a sheaf of attachments. He spent most of the evening reading. He decided to go by train to give himself more preparation time, and agreed to meet Peter Hodson at 2pm the following day. He was booked into one of the group hotels, the Majestic, which was also the company headquarters. As he was likely to be there for the duration of the project he googled it, wary of faded seafront hotels, but it seemed fine. He felt re-energised. Besides, he liked the seaside.

He contacted Miles Blackthorn, one of his ex-colleagues, to assist in the review. He was of course already fixed up with one their former competitors. But he suggested a younger member of staff, Tara Reddy. He contacted her, and although she'd decided to go travelling in the autumn, she was quite happy to earn some quick cash. Tom had hired her on the apprenticeship scheme when she was 16, but she'd risen through the ranks at amazing speed. She was determined, highly numerate and, to the unwary, seemed completely harmless.

Tom recalled how, on one occasion, after a rather dismissive comment by a director of a company they'd been looking to acquire, it was Tara who had found a black hole in the accounts. From what he'd heard about Pemrose, such skills might come in useful. They agreed a fee, but Tara knew the drill with Tom. The fee was for all the hours the job required. She didn't mind at all. Numbers were her friend, and to be honest she didn't have many of the human variety. Tom said he'd call her once he'd got the assignment signed up with the bank.

*   *   *

The full run-through of the show had gone very well that day, and Hannah was feeling extremely relieved. This was one of few opportunities for her, as understudy to Amy Raven, to perform the headliner role ahead of opening night, now just weeks away.

Amy was in the audience with Karen and Janet as Hannah sang, and it was particularly strange to perform Amy's two big hits with her sitting in front of her. But all three came backstage at the end to congratulate her.

Being back onstage was such a big part of the process of healing after Ian. She was her own woman once again, and as she drove back home, she felt that she'd really turned a corner. She was still worried that Ian might appear once more, but she'd changed her car and developed a series of different routes home so that she could see if he were stalking her.

As she drove up to the house, she initially thought she'd miscounted, since the houses looked much the same, but on turning onto what she thought was her drive, she pulled up short. For there, stuck into her lawn, was a For Sale board.

She got out and tried to work things out. It must be a mistake. Someone had got their wires crossed. She took out her key and pushed it to the keyhole. It wouldn't go in. Then as she looked more closely, it was clear that the locks had been changed. In panic, she went to the kitchen door at the rear. This time, the change was more obvious. She looked through the patio window and saw that nothing was out of place in her lounge. Except that the patio door had been fitted with an additional security bar.

She went back to the front and noticed that the garage door had been left unlocked. She lifted it and found piles of her possessions in the middle of the floor. Clothes, shoes, cosmetics. On top were the contents of her underwear drawer, and on top of one of her bras was a DVD case, with a ribbon around it.

She picked it up but didn't want to open it. She knew what was inside, of course. There was no note. Nothing to indicate who had done this, but she knew. She opened the boot and piled in as much of her stuff as she could. She thought that Ian might appear at any moment, so she was desperate to get away. She slammed the garage door shut and got into the car. Starting the engine, she burst into tears, but reversed out at speed, then drove off, not having a clue where she was going.

She doubted if Karen would be home, so she headed for Graham Blakeley's house near Sheringham. A pretty little bungalow with an immaculate front garden, as she recalled.

As she drove, she tried to work out how Ian could sell a house belonging to her. It was unthinkable. Then the awful truth began to dawn on her. She'd been in such a state when her mother died; he had taken care of everything. How many forms had she signed without reading them? He'd been so kind at the time, so very thoughtful. He'd even read a poem at the funeral. Now she had a nasty feeling that she was facing the ultimate humiliation that her husband could inflict; he was making her homeless.

It was becoming a fine afternoon, and as she pulled into the driveway, she saw Graham tending the garden. Getting out of the car she dissolved into tears. Graham stood, and she ran into his arms.

'Hannah, whatever's happened?'

'He's selling my house, Graham. He's selling my flipping home!'

He took her inside and sat her down. He made some tea, and as she calmed down, he extracted the story from her as best as he could. He'd had an uneasy feeling that more was to come, but in spite of a further conversation with his ex-colleagues, he'd been completely unable to get them to understand the threat.

His initial thought was that this latest escalation would provoke more urgent police action, but as he pieced together what had actually happened, he realised that on the face of it the police would regard this as just another aspect of a domestic dispute.

But then Hannah mentioned something more sinister. She took the DVD out of her handbag and handed it over. Graham immediately realised that this was significant and asked her simply to put it on the coffee table. He saw the red ribbon on it and was appalled. He went to the kitchen and returned with a plastic freezer bag. Using the bag to avoid touching it he unclipped the case. He checked for a note or any markings on the DVD, but there wasn't anything.

He put it in the bag as he explained. 'I don't want to touch it. If it contains what we think it does, your husband has just made a mistake. It was placed on top of the pile you said, not just in with the rest of the stuff?'

Hannah nodded. She was staring blankly into space, still trying to absorb the sheer horror of what her husband had done. Graham sat next to her and put an arm around her shoulders.

'You can stay here tonight, if you wish to that is. I'll do what needs to be done. You'll be safe here.'

Hannah nodded and mumbled her thanks. He held her for a while, and she seemed to welcome the reassurance it gave her.

Eventually, she gathered herself. 'Thanks, Graham. I'll stay here if I may. I just need to feel safe tonight.'

It was later that afternoon when Graham Blakeley finally got in touch with Janet Wells. Hannah simply wasn't up to a telephone call, and Graham had agreed that he'd give Janet the latest.

Janet was stunned. 'But surely he can't sell her home without her permission? There must be an explanation. Have you spoken to the agents at all?'

'Well, as luck would have it, I know the agent personally, otherwise he wouldn't have discussed it. His son got into a bit of a scrape a while back when I was on duty. He owed me one.'

'That was a stroke of luck. Did he agree to stop the sale? With the state of the property market now, it could sell very quickly.'

Graham replied, 'Well, from what he said Hannah's husband has already sold it to one of these 'sell in seven days' merchants, and he's selling it on their behalf. If I'm right, Hannah doesn't own the house anymore. He's sold it beneath her. I haven't dared tell her, and I may have got my facts wrong.'

'My God. But that must be fraud. He can't do that, can he?' she said, incredulous.

'Well, I'm not so sure. I googled it, and if in the transfer from her mother to Hannah he got it registered in his name at the Land Registry, then apparently, he can.'

Janet was at a loss. 'What on earth can we do? It goes without saying that the theatre will stand by her. What do you suggest?'

Graham could only think of one thing. 'Look, I know it's after 5pm, but we need to get her to a solicitor urgently. I gather that you can file what they call a Home Rights Notice to prevent a sale if you are living at the property. She doesn't know a solicitor locally. Do you have someone you can ring tonight? Bit of a long shot, but she is obviously desperate.'

Janet could get in touch with the theatre's solicitors, but doubted that they would be able to do anything at short notice. Then she had a thought.

'Well, I can try Julia Maitland. She's a close friend of Miriam Pemrose, and I do know her socially. Let me ring her immediately. Where is Hannah staying tonight?'

'With me,' Graham replied. 'I'm making up the spare room. She's frightened out of her wits. Oh, and one more thing. On top of her pile of clothes in the garage there was a DVD case with a ribbon on it.'

Janet was horrified. 'My God. You don't think?'

Graham replied calmly, 'I haven't watched it, and I won't. I couldn't do that to her. I've just bagged it as evidence. I'll get in touch with the police first thing in the morning. I'll leave

Hannah here, but I don't think our friend will come looking for her. He's a vindictive controlling bastard, but a coward, of course. They all are.'

'Oh. That's just awful. OK. Let me think. Thanks for all you've done, Graham. It's above and beyond. Let me sort something out right now.'

8.

Next Day

Tom Stanley arrived in Cromer by train at lunchtime, into the austere two-platform station, which seemed to be wedged between a large supermarket and a small retail park with the usual suspects. It felt as if the railway was now an inconvenience to the town, although once it had been its lifeblood. It was as if the town's rich Victorian heritage was being airbrushed away.

A young lady in a dark-blue suit of corporate design beckoned to him. They shook hands, and he deposited his case in the back of her smart VW hatchback.

Tom was still puzzled as to why Hodson had come to him. They'd got on well in their previous dealings, shared a love of cricket and had attended a corporate do at the Oval together. But they hadn't really stayed in touch. Of all the accountants available, why had Hodson bothered with him?

As they drew up outside the bank, Peter Hodson opened the car door for him, shaking Tom's hand warmly. The wind was getting up, and the plentiful seagull population seemed to sense that a storm was approaching.

They went into Peter's very corporate-looking office on the top floor, which was obviously now a multi-use conference venue. Tom was grateful for a strong black coffee, as the catering on the train had been non-existent. He took out his tablet and an A4 pad on which he'd written a number of headings.

They made small talk about family, although they had forgotten the names of each other's wives, and Hodson obviously didn't know anything about Maggie's valiant fight for life. He seemed nervous, Tom thought, and reluctant to get to the substance of the meeting, but he was the client after all, and Tom wasn't under any time pressure.

Eventually, Hodson steadied himself, smiled nervously and coughed briefly.

'Now then, Tom. Pemrose Entertainments. Hopefully, you've had a chance to read the documents?'

He had, of course, and the next hour was spent talking about the business. Tom already knew most of the salient facts. The business was going bust. He'd seen it all before. Successful local businessman over-expands, makes a couple of bad deals but can't bring himself to admit it.

The end game was always pretty much the same. The bank did a review, pulled the overdraft and the business went into administration or receivership. Given that the bank had a charge over the assets, they could get out largely unscathed, leaving the owner and the creditors to carry the can.

It was obvious that in this case Hodgson was relatively safe. If he had bailed out a couple of months ago the bank would have got out clean. Now it wasn't so clear. Why was he waiting? This wasn't likely to get any better. Why even bother with the cost of a review?

He let Hodson ramble on for a while, laying out the standard bank review process, with which Tom was already completely familiar. The terms were fine, of course. Tom tried to look interested, but was frankly bored by the formality. This was a charade. Hodson seemed to be at the end of his spiel, and he finally got to cut through the bullshit.

'Well thank you, Peter. Clearly, we can meet the requirements, and I'd be pleased to help. I just have one or two things I need to clarify.'

Peter smiled. 'Of course.'

Tom leaned back in his chair. 'Well, any accountant from any top firm could do this job. Now don't get me wrong; I'm flattered that you rang. But why me?'

Peter became almost conspiratorial in demeanour. 'It's sensitive locally. Lionel is a local bigwig and I need to make sure I explore every opportunity to retain the business.'

Tom thought for a moment. Had he misread the numbers somewhere? Maybe he should take another look at the figures? But no. The brief conversation he'd had that morning with the finance director would have corrected any misapprehension as to the facts, and it hadn't.

He decided to have it out. 'Forgive me, but this doesn't add up.'

'Oh ... er ... in what way?'

'Well, unless I've missed something, and I don't think I have, Pemrose is going bust, and your exposure is increasing by the day. You don't need a bank review to tell you that. You know it, and so do I.'

Hodson looked momentarily annoyed, but then slumped back, eyes closed. Tom was just the man he thought he was. Recovering his composure, he then spoke quite calmly.

'Pemrose isn't going under, Tom. Nothing you've said is in any way inaccurate, but in the next two weeks or so, I need you to come up with a way out which satisfies all parties, including Lionel Pemrose.'

Tom looked into Hodson's steely gaze, and now knew why he'd been hired. Behind the steely-eyed gaze, he saw something else; Hodson was frightened.

*   *   *

Hannah was lost in thought. It was 2pm the following day, and she was sitting in a conference room at Julia Maitland's offices, with Graham by her side.

At 2am that morning, the nightmare had kept returning to her in all its horror. Eventually she'd given up, made some tea, and had sat in Graham's lounge reading a trashy novel.

'Couldn't sleep?' a voice asked quietly.

She looked around as Graham entered the room. 'Oh. I'm sorry, did I wake you?'

'No, not really. An inability to sleep seems to be an affliction of the retired. I quite often find myself awake in the early hours of the morning.'

'Bad dreams? About your job, perhaps?' she ventured.

'No, not really. Wel,l once in a while, maybe. Met some weird people in my time, I'll admit.'

'Weirder than my husband?' she said darkly.

He thought for a moment. 'Well, sadly, yes. Some plain bad, some weird and bad. Met all sorts.'

'Was there ever a Mrs Blakeley, Graham?'

'Yep. We divorced 10 years ago. She said I'd rather be married to the police than to her. I can't complain. She had a point.'

'I'm sorry.'

'Don't be. I bear her no ill will. She remarried and we're still friends.'

'Great.'

They sat in silence for a while, and then Hannah changed the subject.

'I was wondering, Graham. Have you come across many people in my position?'

He thought for a moment. 'A few. Before we gave it the label of coercive control, of course. It's more prevalent than people think. The problem for the police is who to believe, and the lack of evidence. It can make us ... I mean them, slow to react.'

'Tell me about it,' she said sadly.

Having Graham to support her was a godsend. He at least understood what she was going through.

Now she was suddenly yanked back to the present, as Julia Maitland breezed into the room, having spent the morning piecing together what had happened to the house which Hannah had called home. With the introductions completed Julia sat, opened the file and put on her reading glasses.

'So, Hannah. Look, I've made some enquiries this morning and I'm deeply sorry to have to tell you that as Ian managed to register himself as the owner at the Land Registry, he can in fact sell the property without your permission. He has actually already sold it to a sort of finance-house property company. The agent is in fact now selling it on their behalf. I'm so sorry, Hannah, but you need to be clear as to what Ian seems to have done.'

Hannah dissolved into tears as she spoke. 'But that's just not legal, surely? It was Mum's house and she left it to me.'

Graham put his arm around her shoulder.

Julia explained. 'I understand that entirely, Hannah, but somehow a document has been signed which allowed it to be registered in his name, not yours. Could he have forged your signature, perhaps? If so, he's committed fraud.'

Hannah was distraught, but couldn't find anything to say. Just as she thought she had put the past behind her and was breathing fresh life into her old career. A career which she had sacrificed for her husband, who had now cheated her out of her inheritance.

Eventually, choking back her tears she coughed, and spoke calmly and rationally, 'Look, I can't guarantee I didn't sign something. When Mum died, Ian handled everything. He was so kind and understanding, and my mind was all over the place.'

Julia nodded. 'Quite understandable. Your husband's behaviour has all the signs of coercive control, so the manipulation in respect of the property follows a pattern. Irrespective of the ownership matter, I'd advise you to file for divorce immediately, so we can secure as many of the marital assets for you as we can.'

Hannah shook her head. 'I doubt that it will amount to as much as you think it will.'

Julia and Graham looked at each other in surprise. Graham spoke first.

'But he has a good job in the City. He must earn six figures. You own a big house in Kent?'

She nodded sadly. 'Yes. But he could have taken out a second mortgage to pay off his gambling debts. And I have suspicions about his job, too. He never takes time off. Now suddenly he's got all the time in the world.'

There was silence. Some marriages are just one big illusion, and you had no idea what went on beyond the facade. It was beginning to make more sense to Graham.

He spoke quietly. 'So, are you saying that he might have been fired? If he'd been suspended, even, then his employers wouldn't be keen to discuss it, even with the police.'

Julia nodded. 'Banks don't like staff with money problems. It leads to temptation.'

She continued. 'But let's be practical and do what we can to stop things. I'm going to file a Marital Home Rights Notice with the Land Registry. If they agree, it will prevent a further sale, and gives you the right to reoccupy. Then I'll prepare divorce papers to force him to disclose the financial position.'

Hannah nodded, but then became distressed. 'But what about the DVD? If he publishes that ...'

Julia responded. 'Well, that's a criminal matter, isn't it, Graham?'

'Potentially. I'm seeing the police later, and as I have written authority from Hannah we'll pursue a case for harassment and coercive control. There is a strong implied threat with the DVD. I bagged it as evidence, and his fingerprints are doubtless on the box, so the evidence that he has done this is strong. I think he's crossed the line now.'

Julia interjected,' I think we need to file for an injunction preventing disclosure. It's a civil process and not my area of expertise. I'll speak with the partner concerned and we'll file today if we can.'

Hannah sat motionless. The world was rotating on its axis, and she just wanted to stop it turning. How could he sell her house without her consent? This was incredible but apparently true. And then there was the DVD. Embarrassing and highly invasive.

She spoke quietly. 'I just fear that he will publish the DVDs on social media. I'm not really into Facebook and stuff, but well ...' She stopped, becoming tearful and embarrassed.

Graham spoke to her calmly. 'The platform concerned

will take down any obscene material quickly, and if he tries it, he will have committed a criminal offence. I actually don't think he's that stupid, Hannah. But I'll get onto that as quickly as I can.'

The meeting ended there, but Janet arrived to look after Hannah, while Graham headed to the police station. Julia left them in the conference room to put into action what they had discussed.

'Gosh Hannah, you've been to hell and back in the last 24 hours haven't you, love?' said Janet.

Hannah managed a thin smile. 'Just a bit.'

Janet continued, 'Well, I've spoken with our chair, Miriam Pemrose, this morning. She's the co-owner of Pemrose Hotels. We've secured a flat at the Seaview Hotel, part of the Pemrose Group. You can stay there until this all blows over.'

Hannah looked up, surprised. 'Oh, well, that's very kind, but I'm not sure I can afford the rent. This is all just so awful.'

'There's no charge, Hannah. Miriam owns the hotels and she's happy to help. But what worries me is your state of mind with the opening night not so very far away. I've spoken to Karen, and if you'd like to take a leave of absence to sort things out, we'll completely understand.'

Hannah wiped a tear away and smiled. She shook her mind straight and looked intently at Janet.

'No way, Janet. If I don't do this, then he wins. Trust me, that's so not going to happen.'

*   *   *

Amy Raven was rather disconcerted that Hannah was not at rehearsals that morning, and the stand-in dancer was in her place. At the break she cornered Karen in the tiny green room tucked away behind the stage.

Karen did her best. 'Hannah's got a problem, Amy. She'll hopefully be in later.'

Amy shook her head. 'Look Karen, she told me about her husband, and what he did. And I thought I was the one with all of the problems.'

Karen sympathised. 'Well, I can't say too much, but we can cope without her if we have to. We made contingency plans, as you saw this morning.'

'But what if I can't ... well ... if I have a recurrence?'

'You won't. This is not a solo show, it's an ensemble. We're confident that you're going to be fantastic.'

Amy shook her head. 'Well, I'm not. You don't know how absolutely terrifying it is Karen. Your mouth won't move. Your body goes numb, as if paralysed. It's just, well ...'

Karen smiled. 'As a matter of fact, I do know. It happened to me a couple of times in London, but someone kicked me up the arse and I almost flew on stage. I was so terrified I seemed to find a different gear. I promise you I won't do that with you, mind. They say it traumatises people too much.'

'So how did you get out of it?'

'Well, it's a bit like Cyril said to you, actually. There was a person who loved the show so much she'd booked a front row seat for every performance. I met her after the show one time, and she paid me so many compliments I blushed. We sometimes don't realise how much what we do matters to the audience. They all have their ups and downs, but music sticks in the mind. I had a solo about a little girl in the show, and it turned out that this lady had lost a daughter just three months old. The song resonated with her so much.'

'Goodness. What did you do?'

'Well, she was there every night and I simply couldn't let her down after that, could I?'

'Well, no. I guess not.'

'So, as I went on every night, I looked directly at her and sang to her alone. That broke the spell, I think. It's the same as Cyril told you. If the audience is your friend, then what is there to be frightened about?'

'Well, I'll sing to Cyril if and when he comes down, but he won't make every performance, will he?'

'No, but Celia Stanwell will.'

'Who?'

'Celia Stanwell is one of our biggest fans. She attends every performance. She books seat A10 for every show. She's coming along at noon today for some PR photographs with the local paper. She'll meet you and Lech, and you can get to know her. She's a real character.'

'So, she's the friend I sing to?'

'Yep. Except on that Thursday. We do hope that Cyril will make it, but he's very frail, as you know.'

Amy seemed reassured at least. 'It seems that you have a plan, then.'

'I'm a director. I'm paid to have plans. And don't worry about Hannah. She's a very tough cookie. She'll be here for the pre-shows, come what may.'

*   *   *

Tom took room service in his nice sea-view room at the Majestic, which included a decent desk area and a good-sized table on which he'd laid out the files that Jim Cameron had provided.

One of the things he couldn't stand was dining alone in restaurants. He missed Maggie's company more desperately than he ever cared to admit, and sitting opposite an empty chair only made his mood worse.

He had a bottle of red wine for company, along with the box files. He'd discarded the room-service tray outside the door before getting down to work.

He thought about his conversation with Jim Cameron that afternoon. Often in these situations, the finance director presented pretty spreadsheets showing that all would be well, that salvation was just around the corner if the bank would only hold its nerve. Instead, Cameron had been brutally candid about the state of affairs. Yet it was he who had agreed to the bank review.

Tom liked Cameron. There was no attempt to spin the situation as anything but terminal, and as Peter Hodson seemed to be of similar mind, he remained unsure as to why he was sitting in this very pleasant suite with a lovely view of a Victorian seaside town and its iconic pier.

He'd read a ten-page summary that Cameron had supplied and couldn't argue with any of it from what he'd seen of the figures. He'd encountered people like Lionel many times in his career; a local businessman who makes some money, so he gets the idea he has the Midas touch. He expands into other parts of the country, then goes into bookmaking, an industry he doesn't know well, and worse still he buys an owner-managed chain based far away.

Then, of course, the scourge of any family-run business; an acrimonious divorce. Cameron had been quite clear that Miriam Pemrose had kept Lionel in check. She had been sensible to keep her stake in the hotels group as part of the settlement, he thought. Shrewd lady.

And, of course, he'd spotted another aberration. Why on earth did they own a pier with a bar and restaurant, but not the theatre at the end of it? Cameron had attempted to explain but had rather given up. It was clearly a Lionel Pemrose vanity project. Worse still, his wife appeared to have gone over to the dark side.

Tom took a sip of his quite reasonable house red in the stupidly oversized glasses favoured by posh hotels. Pemrose was a basket case quite unlike any he'd seen before, with the bank not wanting to pull the rug, and the finance director seemingly not seeing any alternative.

But something rang alarm bells in the figures, and one comment that Jim had made came back to him. He took out his mobile phone and dialled. A sleepy voice answered.

'Tara Reddy.'

'Tara, it's Tom Stanley.'

'Oh. Tom. Sorry, just let me put my glasses on. Sorry. One minute.'

'I hope I'm not disturbing you.'

There was a brief silence. 'OK, Tom. I'm with it now.'

'I'm so sorry, Tara. Were you asleep?'

She yawned then laughed. 'Most people are at half-past midnight, Tom.'

Tom looked at the clock. 'Oh, I'm so sorry. I lost track of time. I'll call back.'

'No, it's OK. I'm awake now. What's up?'

'Pemrose. Change of plan. Instead of coming here, will you go straight to Crewe in the morning, to Brewster's head office?'

'Crewe? You sure know how to treat a girl, Tom.'

'What?'

'Never mind. Something stinks at the bookmakers, doesn't it? I was looking earlier on. I was going to ring you.'

'Good girl.'

'Inappropriate, Tom. But I'll let it pass,' she said evenly.

'Ah. Sorry, Tara. But you're on it, then.'

'Yes, Tom. I'll get the first train I can in the morning. Assuming I can get at least some sleep *right now* that is …'

Half an hour later, Tara Reddy finally put the light out. Tom was pleased.

9.

The Review

Tom spent much of the next week and a half visiting the various businesses down the coast using a pool car provided by Pemrose. He knew that you could only get a feel for a business by being physically present and meeting the local management. He could see that certain parts of the business were sustainable, while others, notably the casino and the bookmakers, were not.

As it was the nearly the weekend and Tom had done a lot of travelling, Jim Cameron had suggested that he visit the Pier Theatre and take in a show in the evening. The work was going pretty well, so Tom agreed. The numerous visits that he had undertaken had helped him to understand the business, and many hours of poring over spreadsheets had helped to give him the evidence to support his gut feeling. He'd agreed to meet Tara on Monday to get her initial findings on the northern bookmaking concern. It was clear that sending her to the bookies had been a good idea. Tom could have done the digging himself, of course, but Tara was more likely to find things. She appeared disarmingly young, female and very naive. In fact she was anything but, as many misogynistic males had discovered to their cost.

Tom meandered down from the hotel towards the pier after breakfast. It was a day of unpredictable weather. In the sunshine, and out of the wind, it was really quite warm. He'd dressed accordingly, but suddenly the biting wind got up as he reached the front, walking in the shade of the terrace of buildings. The smell of fish and chips mingled with the salty air wafting in off the North Sea, and he could see a hardy family seeking to position their windbreak in a way that would mitigate the biting north-easterly wind. The man was deploying a large stone as a mallet, while the mother debated whether sunscreen was necessary for her two young children, who were clearly oblivious to the weather. She gave up, and instead helped her husband to secure the windbreak. Tom felt the sadness he always experienced when he saw a typical family doing ordinary family things. Grief was never far from the surface with him these days, with its vindictive sibling loneliness not far behind.

Reaching the pier, he realised that he was a little early, and in spite of the hearty breakfast he'd taken in his room, he decided to have some tea, along with a quite enticing-looking muffin. He found an empty table outside and allowed his thoughts to drift back. The sunshine broke through, bathing the pier in bright sunlight. The warmth on his face was really very pleasant. The tide was going out, but the waves made a relaxing swishing noise as they broke over the pebbles on the shore. It was very peaceful save for the odd seagull cry, or the sound of excitable children crabbing nearby. It was as if the world was at peace with itself for once, carrying Tom along with it.

The tea was good, and the muffin decadently delicious. He'd put on weight since Maggie died, and in recent times more still. This assignment, with its fine dining, recurring full English breakfasts and decadent treats like the muffin, not to mention the ever-present lure of fish and chips, were unlikely to help.

He yawned contentedly, although not really because he was tired. He tended to stay up late working, but then never really slept well. In the dark hours of the early morning, he found himself reaching out for a sleeping Maggie, only for the awful realisation to bite him as he awoke. If time healed as they said it did, then it ought to get its finger out as far as Tom was concerned.

He snapped himself out of this negative thought process. This pier was, of course, a part of the Pemrose empire, but it was clear that it was a most illogical, if quite delightful, anachronism. The restaurant and bar generated a decent income, and the theatre leased the rest. But when you looked at the maintenance costs of this Victorian relic, it struggled to break even.

It would be much better to flog it off and generate some cash to get the overdraft down, but Cameron had already given him the heads-up. The mutual hatred of Lionel Pemrose for Jack Wells. The botched-up deal under which Pemrose got the pier, but with Jack Wells as his tenant in the theatre. The hiatus of 2009, when Pemrose tried to bankrupt the theatre so as to take it over, only to be thwarted by his now ex-wife.

He was here to meet Janet Wells, and Cameron had warned that she was not to be underestimated. He'd agreed the cover story. He'd been brought in by Lionel to recommend improvements to the business, and even if Janet was savvy enough to see through the cover story, Tom should just stick to the remit. Stay on receive mode, thought Tom. He had an appointment with Miriam Pemrose later that week, and Lionel was back from Malaga shortly, so Tom could meet the man himself.

He entered the box office, which was at the front of the pier, far away from the theatre itself, standing proudly at the far end of the pier. He was greeted by a cheerful lady in a smart Pier Theatre uniform. As he stood waiting, he looked at the assorted memorabilia on sale, while other people came in to buy tickets for a Simon & Garfunkel tribute act. He was looking forward to it, having been a fan since childhood. He'd seen the real thing with Maggie in Hyde Park a few years ago, and he remembered a very warm summer's evening, and the sun setting late into the concert. Another beautiful memory of the good times long gone.

A voice interrupted his nostalgia trip. 'Tom Stanley?'

He turned and saw an older woman dressed in a smart black top and designer jeans. She had a cheerful and engaging smile.

'Janet Wells? Glad to meet you,' said Tom.

'I thought we'd start in the theatre. After all, it's what we're here for,' she said brightly.

'That would be fine, Mrs Wells.'

'Janet, please, no need for formality,' she said, opening the door which caught ever so slightly as she opened it, making the bell jangle.

They walked down the pier to the theatre side by side.

'Do you know Cromer well, Tom?'

'No, somehow, I've never been this way before. My first time.'

'So, from your accent you're from Yorkshire?'

'Yes. Leeds. Although I've lived in London for many years.'

'And you're staying at the Majestic, I understand? Good choice.'

'Well, if you're working for Pemrose it does make sense. A very well-run hotel. Comfortable.'

'Yes. My chair, Miriam Pemrose, did the interior design work when they bought it. Very stylish.'

'Indeed. I've always been an art deco fan. My wife was, too.'

'Jim told me of your bereavement. I'm so sorry.'

Tom thought for a moment. He found sympathy the most difficult thing to deal with.

'Thanks. Some time ago now. Gosh, it's still a bit cold in this wind, isn't it?'

Janet laughed. 'And if the wind changes direction we'll be the warmest place in Britain. Welcome to Cromer.'

They reached the end of the pier, and Tom noticed that the large posters advertising the Summertime Special show were being put up.

'Amy Raven? Now, where do I remember that name?' he said.

Janet was a little surprised. 'Well, she's one of our own, but she did some West End shows. Are you a theatre fan, then?'

'Oh, yes. Maggie and I are ... were ... massive fans of theatre, musicals in particular. Yes, that's where I remember her from. She had the leading role, as I recall.'

'Well, if you're a fan then you should enjoy this. They're rehearsing this morning, so we can sneak a peek during our tour. We open in three weeks.'

They walked into the foyer of the theatre itself, and a woman smiled as she polished glasses behind the bar, recognising Janet.

'Sounding good, Mrs Wells,' she said, nodding towards the theatre.

'It better had be by now, Debbie,' Janet replied, as they went through the right-hand side door leading from the bar to the theatre itself. Janet took a moment to pause and explain.

'So, just to explain the layout. Up to this door is Pemrose Entertainments; Debbie works for Lionel. From this door onwards is ours. The toilets are a bit like no-man's-land. We clean them, but Lionel is supposed to maintain them.'

Tom smiled grimly. 'No-man's-land. You make it sound like World War One.'

Janet stared at him darkly. 'Trust me. It feels that way sometimes.'

As he entered, he took in the plush red seats of the auditorium. The stage was fully lit, but the house lights were half up, so he could make out the mass of iron girders and red oxide paint of the fabric of the building.

Janet beckoned him to sit. 'That's the director of the show, my daughter Karen, in the front row,' she whispered.

The music struck up and the dancers, in sweatpants and hoodies, swung into action. Then Amy and a male singer entered from each side of the stage picking up the melody.

Tom seemed genuinely fascinated, Janet thought. Could this be an accountant who sees beyond spreadsheets?

They reached the end of the number, and Tom applauded warmly. 'She's terrific, isn't she? Actually, they all are. Such a slick routine,' he murmured.

'We like to think so.'

Karen thanked the ensemble, referred to a few notes, and ended the rehearsal. They needed to clear out so that the set for the one-night show could be built. Karen came back to greet them.

'Hi, Mum. What do you think?'

'Sounded fine to me. Let me Introduce Tom Stanley. Tom's doing some work for Lionel.'

'Oh ... hi, Tom. Hope you liked the sneak preview. It's still a work in progress at this stage.'

Tom shook her hand. 'I thought it was quite stunning. Well done to you. At that standard, this show must have a pretty big budget.'

Janet smiled. 'Not as big a budget as Karen would like, but yes. We're the only full-season variety show left in the world.'

'But you'll need a lot of bums on seats to turn a buck, won't you?' he asked.

Janet realised that Tom might like theatre, but the accountant inside him couldn't help itself.

'Yes, we do,' said Karen. 'But we sell out more often than most and have a big regular following. It's not easy, but we get by.'

Tom sensed he'd gone too far. 'I'm sorry. I didn't mean to talk it down. I'm a trustee of a theatre in Greenwich, nowhere near as big as this one, of course, but I'm not unfamiliar with how difficult it can be.'

Karen saw that the discussion was turning to business, so she excused herself and left them alone. Debbie arrived with coffee, and Janet sensed it was time to dig a little deeper. She looked at him and smiled.

'So, what cunning little plan is Lionel hatching now then?'

Tom was a bit taken aback, but he had been well briefed.

'No cunning plan. Jim just brought me in to take a look at what is a very much bigger group these days. Make some recommendations.'

'Good luck with that. How have you found Lionel so far?'

'I've not met him as yet. He's away this week. My colleague and I will finish up in a week or so and I'll meet him with my findings.'

Janet nodded, and sipped her coffee.

Tom sensed an elephant in the room. 'Jim gave me the history lesson, so I know about 2009. It must have been an awful time.'

Janet nodded. 'Yes. The bloody bank pulled the rug at the same time as Lionel's rent fell due. A bit too much of a coincidence, in my view. I think Lionel was pulling Mr Hodson's strings, but fortunately Miriam Pemrose stepped in at the last minute.'

'I'm seeing Miriam shortly. Judging by what Jim told me, you must make quite the dynamic duo.'

'We like to think so.'

Tom thought for a minute. The idea of collusion between Lionel Pemrose and Peter Hodson was news to him and might give a clue as to why Hodson was so uneasy. Tom didn't have time to mess around. This pier thing was a distraction that was barely worth bothering with, but he sensed that the resulting feud between Miriam and Lionel was not serving anybody well, and that fresh hostilities were possible at any time.

He'd pulled out the Cromer Pier Theatre Trust's accounts, of course. It was bobbing along, but clearly never far from a cash flow problem. A couple of decent bequests kept it ticking over, although it was manifestly a struggle.

He sat upright; his brow furrowed as he spoke. 'Now forgive me, Janet, but I do tend to be pretty blunt. Anyone can see that this current arrangement serves nobody well. You need the income from the bar and restaurant, but that all goes to Lionel, and the lease cost is a big millstone round your neck.'

Janet nodded. 'It was the botched-up compromise I inherited from my father. This theatre has been my life. I was in the show myself at 15, and took it over when he died. We've muddled on ever since. It's Karen's livelihood too, of course.'

Tom nodded. 'Have you ever thought about retiring? Running this must be a strain. All these one-night shows to arrange, then the Summertime Special and Christmas shows ...'

'Have *you* ever thought of retiring?' she enquired politely. He wasn't sure if he'd been rude. And her reply was so uncannily relevant to his own situation.

'I'm sorry. This must mean so much more to you than just a career,' he said.

'Yes. It certainly does.'

He backtracked. 'If it's any consolation, I do know how you feel, to an extent. I was made redundant from my own company a while ago. Been bored stiff ever since. Frankly, I'm enjoying this assignment. At least I'm hopefully doing something constructive for a while.'

Janet nodded. 'I'm sorry to hear that, Tom. Tough on top of … well, everything else.'

'Yes. Retirement is my worst nightmare; I'd certainly struggle to recommend it.'

They drank their coffee without saying any more. Then Tom continued, 'Look, if as part of this review I can ease the tensions, I'll try. I've a soft spot for theatre, and this stand-off isn't helping either business. Jim knows that, and Lionel can't be that stupid.'

Janet decided that earlier on in the conversation she'd been a little tetchy. 'Well, I'd sleep easier at night if our future were more secure. But the pier is iconic to this town, and Lionel seemingly wants it irrespective of the cost. Getting the theatre would be the final victory over my father, and now over Miriam. I can assure you that Miriam and I would like to resolve things, I'm not sure we need an accountant to help us, more likely a marriage guidance counsellor.'

Tom laughed. 'Oh, I don't think I'd be suited to that. I'll stick to numbers; they're much less complicated than people. Let's leave it there. I'll do what I can.'

Seeing Karen coming out of a side door to the stage, Janet led him down through the seats to meet her.

'Good. Now let's do the backstage tour, shall we? I'll let Karen do this bit. Now, up to this door is my job, but what happens behind it is Karen's isn't it, Karen?' said Janet.

Karen smiled. 'It sure is. Come on through, Tom.'

'I'll see you this evening, Tom. Over to you, Karen.'

Karen showed Tom through the side-door by the stage, and into a little rabbit warren of backstage rooms. Amy Raven was on her way out.

'Amy. Good job today. Sounded great,' said Karen.

'Thanks, Karen. Getting there, I think.'

'Miss Raven? Tom Stanley. We saw you in London. Terrific.'

Amy blushed. 'Oh, thanks. Seems a world away now.'

'It must be exciting, a new show only weeks away?' he suggested.

Amy seemed to struggle to form a reply.

Karen stepped in. 'Amy's going to be great. We've got Hannah Masters understudying her, too. Should be a great season.'

'Yes. I'm looking forward to it,' said Amy, recovering a little.

They continued the tour, ending up on the stage. Tom looked out across the rows of empty seats.

'Have you ever been tempted, Tom? To perform I mean?' asked Karen.

Tom laughed. 'No. I think not. Maggie did some am-dram, but I just enjoyed the pub afterwards. The shared experience. Good times.'

'I first appeared on this stage at 14. Loved it ever since.'

'It's in your blood then, Karen, your mother's, too. I quite envy you; I've never really had that creative spark, somehow.'

'Probably just as well. There's not much money in it. I wouldn't change it for the world, mind.'

'But you had a spell in the West End, I gather. That must have been fantastic.'

Karen dodged the question. 'Oh, that was long ago now. I've been the director here for 10 years.'

'So where do you see yourself in five years' time? I suppose it would be difficult to move on from a family business.'

Karen thought for a moment, surprised that she'd not thought to ask herself that.

'Yes. I guess I'd like to do more here but, well, working for Mum ... she's a force of nature.'

Tom nodded, 'Ah. Yes. It's not easy working with family. Normal business rules don't seem to apply.'

'No, they don't. I love her to bits but, well ... you know how it is.'

They stood in silence for a while. Karen picked up some bits of paper from the stage and put them in a bin. Then she spoke once again. 'So, about tonight. If you come to the box office at 6.15pm, I'll walk down to the theatre with you. These guys really know their stuff, and I've always loved the music.'

'Good. Yes, me too. It'll be good to go out for once. I've not been out much of late, and I've been looking at so many numbers this week, it'll make a real change.'

With that they walked back up the pier, the sun having fully broken through. He could see the charm of this place from this vantage point; the Victorian seafront buildings with the church behind them, the pier oozing the charms of a bygone age.

They parted with a handshake, and he realised something as he walked up the slope towards town. For the first time in a while, he had enjoyed himself, and now he was looking forward to an evening out.

10.

Malaga

Lionel Pemrose awoke to the warmth of sunshine beaming through the blinds. He was at his villa in Malaga, but he was now alone. Freya had left yesterday morning, while he was asleep. He'd had no warning that she intended to leave, although they'd had words the previous evening. He dragged himself out of bed, went into the kitchen to put the kettle on and absentmindedly turned on the news.

He looked at his phone for any sort of message. Text, email, WhatsApp, Messenger … but there was nothing more from her. He looked at the email she'd sent from the airport yesterday morning. The feeling of betrayal welled up.

Dear Lionel, I'm sorry that you will get this message in such an impersonal way, but I'm not good at confronting emotional issues. You know that I've put so many hours of my time into our London project, and as we are now so close to opening, your decision to make drastic cuts to the budget at this time jeopardises the delivery of my vision for a venue which is exclusive and will attract high-net-worth individuals. Saving a few thousand now is trivial in the context of the overall plan, and it saddens me that you have lost confidence in me at the eleventh hour.

Rather than get into a row with you, I'd rather just take some time to think things over, so I'm flying back to London to reflect. Perhaps, given time, you'll reconsider your decision and come around. I do hope so. Relationships depend on trust, and I fear your decision means that we cannot build a life together given that your trust in me is gone.'

Best regards
Freya

Lionel shook his head and laughed. Drastic cuts? Close to opening? No, darling. You just asked me for another bundle of money for 'unforeseen expenditure' that I don't have the capacity to fund. When I explained the position that the company was in, you developed an immediate migraine and headed for the spare room. Emotional blackmail won't work this time.

He poured the hot water into the mug, stirred in milk, and stirred the tea bag until it became builder's tea. He noted that the box of teabags he always brought over from England was nearly empty. He'd have to bring some the next time he came out, whenever that might be.

He suddenly felt very alone. When he was married, he and Miriam always had friends and business associates over, and he would come over for golfing trips, nominally on his own but sometimes with female company other than his wife. He remembered a few nice days, and nights, with Lizzie, among others. The villa, beautiful though it was, seemed so empty these days, when once it had been filled with people and laughter. Not much to laugh about now, Lionel reflected ruefully.

He slipped his phone into his pocket and opened the blinds.

The brilliant sunshine glistened on the sea as he went out onto the terrace and sat down on his comfortable patio suite.

He sipped his tea and lay down, closing his eyes against the strong sunlight. He felt suddenly calm, with the stormy seas of business, and his relationship with Freya, put to one side for a moment.

He was sad, of course, but not really surprised. She had lied repeatedly, feeding her posh consultant friends with his money. Now he had no choice. He simply didn't have any more to spend. The bank review was a sham. This Tom Stanley chap would reach the expected conclusions to justify his fee. Lionel had thought about meeting him before his Malaga trip, but decided that there was no point. Hodson was a banker so he knew all of the tricks, but Lionel had him under control. He recalled the cold fear in his eyes at the mention of Lizzie. Lionel might have his problems, but Hodson had a bigger one.

Lionel had always had an unyielding determination to succeed. But, at the point of no return, he could cut and run. He had already decided to end it with Freya before they flew out, but now he had managed to do it without lots of tears and rows. He'd simply cut off the blood supply to the leech that she was, and the leech had gone off to find some other mug.

She no doubt expected an immediate reply, pleading for her return, but he hadn't replied at all. Instead, he'd contacted the bank to say that Freya had lost her Pemrose Entertainments credit card and could they put a stop on it immediately. She was also unaware that he had just put the casino subsidiary into administration, and that her salary as project director would therefore cease immediately.

He didn't like losing money. But at least this way he had stemmed the bleeding. And Freya's friends who had subscribed to preference shares in the casino project would find that their investment was worthless. Trivial sums to the wealthy but embarrassing for Freya to explain to her rich friends. He didn't need Jim Cameron to do the maths for him. His loans to the casino company were secured on the building itself, and in a rising London commercial market might minimise his loss, horrific though it still was.

The phone rang. Freya. He declined the call, having already decided that there would be no conversation at all. Instead, he rang Jim Cameron. Lionel knew that Jim would just about resist saying, 'I told you so'.

'Oh. I see. Look, I'm sorry about Freya, Lionel. I apologise if I said some unkind things,' said Cameron.

Jim was trying to find the right emotionally supportive words, while feverishly evaluating the implications for the business.

'No, you were right, Jim. But I've cut off the leech now. I'll fly home in the morning and meet this Stanley chap. Who knows, he might have found a creative solution to the rest of the mess.'

Cameron was thinking on his feet now. Putting the casino company under had implications which he'd need to discuss with the bank, and of course with Tom Stanley. He played for time.

'If you need a day or two to sort things out, Lionel, there's no need to come back so soon. Tom's still unravelling the goings-on at Brewster's, and I'll need time to work out the implications of the administration of the casino subsidiary. Go and play a bit of golf if you like. Get your mind straight.'

Lionel was happy enough to stay in the sun a while longer. He had of, course, thought of selling the villa, or at least letting the bank have a mortgage on it, but it would mean burning his bridges since it was the only home he owned now that Miriam had the house in Norfolk.

Cameron put down the telephone and grimaced. Although he was pleased that Lionel had seen the light, he knew that all it did was crystallise losses in the loans Pemrose had made to the casino, and things elsewhere were dreadful. The monthly figures from the bookmaker's group in the north were worse than ever. He could only hope that Tom Stanley might shed some light on the problem.

*   *   *

That same morning, Tom Stanley was meeting Tara in London, and he too had found the figures disturbing. How could a bookmaker lose so much money? He rented a meeting room near Euston for the meeting, lamenting that the logistics of travelling from east to west in England meant that meeting in London was sensible.

Tara arrived shortly afterwards, having travelled back on Saturday afternoon, so that she'd at least had Sunday off. She was pleased that she'd been able to produce an eight-page summary of her findings on the train. It had been a tough assignment, but she had thoroughly enjoyed it. Bernie Brewster, the previous owner of Brewster's Bookmakers, had treated her like an office junior. A big mistake.

She had installed herself in an office above the biggest branch of the chain and watched the punters come and go. She found the whole business model distasteful. The same punters each day, ramming money in the slot machines, moaning that the high-stakes ones had gone, and betting on the horses or dogs, or the football, at all times of the day. The town was grim, bedevilled by high unemployment and increasing poverty, empty shops littering the High Street. Two major factories had closed in the area in recent times, and the region was reeling from repeated blows to its economy. Bernie had sold up at the right time.

But it took a bit of detective work to establish another problem. Tara had booked into a Premier Travel Inn off the High Street and visited the King's Arms, a fairly nondescript pub a few doors up from the bookmakers. She'd taken a book to read while sipping her mineral water, and watched some of the punters. They were watching Sky Sports and one man, referred to by his mates as Pete, collected some bets, but instead of turning left as he exited the pub and heading to Brewster's, he went right instead.

The landlady brought her food and Tara engaged her in a bit of banter about 'the lads'. She learned that Pete Landis was a local welder who took bets down to the bookies for the others ahead of kick-off. When she left, after a vegetarian meal that was at best pretty average, she ventured 50 yards down the High Street, but saw nothing of interest. Then as she turned, and looked up a side street, there it was. Dan Rooney's Bookmakers.

Walking past the front door it was apparent that the paintwork was rather fresher than that of the surrounding buildings. Interesting, she thought. Back at the hotel she searched the Companies House website for Dan Rooney's Bookmakers. She found nothing. After googling the name, she came across a local newspaper clip. Rooney's was sponsoring a youth football team, and in the picture was Mr Rooney himself. He was standing next to Bernie Brewster. She went on the firm's website and found that the organisation was only two years old. Checking further, she spotted a company name which appeared in the small print. Revisiting Companies House, she found the name she was looking for, Phoenix Betting Limited. She read through the director's details and smiled as she found what she was looking for.

She needed to be careful with her next step, so as not to arouse suspicion, but trawling through the account records at Brewster's, she found that Pete Landis had been a regular up until two years ago. Bingo! She then smiled at her own inadvertent joke.

She typed up her findings on the way down to London and emailed her summary to Tom so that he could think about the contents before they met on the Monday.

Tom helped himself to a coffee in the rented conference room, situated in a well-kept if rather old building. After spending time in the slower-paced Cromer, he found the buzz of the city outside disconcerting. He was surprised at his own feelings, given that he'd not been away from London that long.

He'd read Tara's paper and smiled. She had done both the financial legwork and the forensic stuff well. The problem was what to do with the findings. Doubtless Lionel would go ballistic. He'd want to sue Brewster for sure, but litigation would take years, and the more Tom thought things over, the less likely it was to succeed. Tara had given him the ammunition, but Tom needed to be careful how he decided to use it.

He then reflected on the rather hasty email he'd had from Jim Cameron earlier, advising him of the latest news on the casino. He decided to speak to him while he was waiting for Tara.

'Jim? Tom Stanley.'

'Ah. How goes it?'

'Well, I'm meeting Tara this morning to review Brewster's.'

'Has she found anything interesting?'

'Well, it's early days, although I think we've got something we can work with. But we need a bit more time to evaluate things. When is Lionel back?'

'End of this week. I've had him stay out of my way a while longer while I think about the casino mess. If he'd told me, I could maybe have managed things better, but that's Lionel for you.'

'I shouldn't worry. You're the biggest secured creditor with those loans, so the liquidator will need your say-so on things.'

'I hope so. Do you want to reschedule your meeting with Lionel in any case?'

'Yes. I suggest we meet on Friday, then we'll see Lionel together ... maybe on Monday? I think from what we've said previously we need to be on the same page before we see him.'

'What about Peter Hodson?'

'Well, I always present a draft report to the company for an accuracy check before I submit it, so I'm not being pressured by him yet.'

'Good. So, we'll meet Friday then?'

Tom rang off, pleased to have bought more time. Tara arrived half an hour later. She carried a small computer case containing a slim high-specification laptop, along with her tiny Mulberry handbag. In contrast Tom had a flight case full of files and his battered old briefcase with an equally battered Dell laptop with keys worn away through heavy use. He'd never quite bought into the paperless office idea.

'So, how was the north of our fair land?' he asked lightly.

Tara looked at him over her dark-rimmed spectacles as she booted up the laptop.

'Oh, OK in general. They all insisted they weren't racist as they all had best friends who were Asian.'

Tom shook his head. 'I'm sorry. In hindsight sending you up there wasn't a nice thing to do. Good job, though.'

Tara shrugged. 'You get used to it. Mr Brewster treated me as an office junior. Worked a treat.'

Tom laughed. 'I thought he might. Bit of a dinosaur from what I've heard. Sharp businessman, though?'

'Yes. Well, I think he's got a bit of a shock coming.'

'He saw Lionel coming, didn't he?'

'Yes. Did you look into the rents on the properties as I suggested?'

'Yes. They're as absurd as you said. Mostly in High Streets which were prime locations at one time.'

'But I counted the empty shops in the High Street there. Over 30 per cent are unoccupied. Brewster couldn't know that my family owns shops across the north of England, could he?'

Tom laughed. 'Of course not. So, Brewster is charging Pemrose top dollar for the sites. No wonder he's in trouble. Signed up for stupidly high rents, to pay for Brewster's pension, no doubt.'

Tara continued, 'While at the same time the income has plummeted. Brewster's former business partner is Dan Rooney, isn't he?'

'Yes, and my spies tell me he's … erm, shall we say, romantically involved with Brewster's sister,' Tom replied.

'And all the while Brewster draws a director's salary for the business he sold to Lionel.'

'Yes. I'm not sure Lionel's going to be impressed with our Mr Brewster.'

Tara was intrigued. 'Can he sue him? Is that how this matter ends? In court?'

Tom pondered for a moment. 'Actually, I don't think so. The

law doesn't protect businessmen from doing stupid deals, and Brewster hasn't set up in competition in his own right, has he?'

'It's suspicious that Rooney has opened up in most of the same places though, surely?'

'Suspicious, yes, but he'd have to prove that Brewster was involved in the business, and that won't be easy. He's not a director or anything. Not that he'd be that stupid.'

'It's pathetic, though. The whole business. Sad people giving away money that they can't afford. Most of them on benefits. It shouldn't be allowed.'

'As a Muslim you would be rather opposed to gambling, I would guess?'

'Like Muslims don't gamble? My cousin was a Muslim, but he still bankrupted himself gambling. Committed suicide last year.'

Tom looked up into her sad eyes. 'I'm sorry ... if I'd known I wouldn't ...'

' ... Have sent me?' she interrupted. 'Well, I wanted to go. To see what possessed him to be so stupid.'

'So, did you find out?'

'Perhaps. They always think they'll win it back, don't they?'

'I guess, Tara. I don't really know. The most I've ever done are office sweepstakes.'

They sat quietly for a moment.

Tara changed the subject. 'Do you miss it, Tom? The company I mean?'

Tom thought for a moment. 'Our American friends and the politics, no. But I do miss the people, oh, and the buzz of London, I suppose.'

'So, you'd find Cromer a little quiet, then?'

'Just a bit. Some nice people, though, and at least this has given me something to focus on.'

'So, what's next?'

Tom passed over some A3 sheets bearing his calculations. 'Well, let's go through these for an hour or so, then I'll treat you to lunch if you don't have a better offer. There's a good vegetarian down the street I went to with Maggie.'

'Yes. Sure. To be honest they weren't big on vegetarian menus up there, either.'

They sat poring over the figures for a while. Tara, much less experienced, still seemed to have a really good grasp of the issues. Tom went to lunch satisfied that he'd got the building blocks of his report. He doubted that either Lionel or Peter would be impressed, but he had a bit of time to refine things.

After lunch, they headed for the tube. They were about to part when Tom paused.

'Look, you've done a great job on this. If you're free, would you like to come up to Cromer to help present the findings? Only if you've nothing else on, of course. Good experience and I'll pay. It's quite a pretty place, actually. In a quaint old English sort of way.'

Tara adjusted her hijab and looked at her phone. 'I'm going to a friend's wedding on Saturday, but I could come up for the meeting on Friday if it would be helpful? I could travel back that evening.'

'OK, that's fine. Thanks once again, Tara. I'll see you on Friday, then.'

*　*　*

Arriving back in Cromer later that afternoon, Tom felt rather tired. He'd noticed that he seemed to tire more easily these days, and although he wanted to crack on with the presentation that he was planning to share with Jim Cameron on Friday, he found himself nodding off. Rather than fight it, he threw off some of his clothes and lay down on the rather comfortable king-size bed, falling into a heavier sleep than he had intended.

When he awoke later that evening, needing to eat, he decided to go out for a change, and found the aroma of fish and chips compelling. He sat out on the pier as evening set in, and the light began to fade. As he ate, he witnessed the strange phenomenon of the sun going down over the sea on what was after all the east coast, and the glorious cloud formations playing extraordinary tricks with the light.

He strolled to the end of the pier and saw that there was some sort of event on in the theatre bar. It was an open mic night. He wandered in, and Debbie pulled him a pint of Woodforde's. She never forgot a face.

'You going to take part then, sir?' she asked.

Tom stopped midway through his first sip. 'Oh, I rather think you'd find my singing underwhelming. Expecting any of the cast in tonight?'

Debbie pointed across to the far side of the room. 'Karen's in. You've probably met her. And the lady next to her is Amy Raven, she's headlining this year.'

'Oh, yes. Well, they should be worth a listen at the very least.'

He took a seat tucked away in a corner. He looked out at the coastline, and suddenly felt relaxed. Maggie would have loved this. He tried to tell himself that life was getting better, but there wasn't an hour, leave alone a day, when he didn't miss her. And it was impromptu things like this which they both loved.

He remembered Washington Square in New York, where at dusk they had witnessed a most amazing impromptu gathering of musicians of all races playing all genres of music. They played because they loved it, and he and Maggie had loved it too.

He was a long way from New York here in Cromer, yet the people were friendly, the fish and chips had been perfect, and now he had a pint of particularly nice beer. Only Maggie was missing, and in spite of himself he conceded that he felt lonely.

A few young singers went first, one girl tweaking her guitar to get it in tune, wrestling with an obdurate microphone, clearly nervous. She was only about 20, if that. The same age as his daughter would have been had she lived. The girl started rather haltingly, but he could see her confidence building as she got into the song, leading to warm applause at the end. An older couple sat next to him as the place filled up. Then he felt a hand on his shoulder. He turned to see Janet Wells smiling at him.

'Hi, Tom. Would you like to join us?'

'Oh ... yes, of course. That's ... yes ... most welcome ... thanks.'

He excused himself to the older couple and moved across to where Karen was sitting. Another pint of Woodforde's arrived, as another act took to the stage.

'So, are you singing tonight, Karen?' he asked.

'Well, sometimes I do. We let everyone have a turn. Are you going to have a go then, Tom?' she said.

The friendly smile was just like her mother's, he thought.

'Ah ... perhaps not. I'd rather hear you guys. Leave it to the pros,' he said.

'Well, we just fill up any empty spaces. It's really about encouraging young talent.'

'Like Amy? She's local, isn't she?' he asked.

'Yes. She was busking by the pier when my predecessor Les Westley spotted her back in 2008. She's come a long way since then.'

'Goodness, yes. But you're a dancer by profession, aren't you?'

'Yes. But as you've seen, for the Summertime Special you need to be a complete all-rounder.'

'Being appointed director was a big step for you, then? But I guess you'd seen the show come together so often it helped'.

'Well, when Les moved on it seemed like a big deal, but it's getting pretty routine now, if I'm honest.'

'Oh. Itchy feet, then? Every job gets easy after a few years.'

'I guess it does. I've never really thought about it. I could never leave here, though,' she said.

The next act was ready, ending the conversation, but Tom found the dynamic between mother and daughter interesting. A deep fondness for each other, and yet not without some tension.

There was an intermission, and Karen's boyfriend Bryn arrived to join the group. Tom bought a round, and as he handed Janet her glass, she whispered to him.

'So, how is it going? Have you met Miriam yet?'

'Ah ... Well, yes, we're nearly done. I'm seeing Miriam tomorrow so everything should be done by next weekend, I think. How's the show going? Are bookings going OK?'

'Yes, very promising. Opening night's not far off. You should come along before you head off. We have some pre-shows too.'

'Well, I suppose I've no reason to rush off. Might have outstayed my welcome at the Majestic, mind. I might have to start paying.'

Janet laughed. 'Spoken like a true Yorkshireman. Mind you, you won't find Lionel offering discounts.'

Tom smiled. 'Well to be honest I've always found hotel prices in this country pretty high. Nice place, the Majestic, so I'll stay on there, I suppose. But I just miss having my own space, and I find hotel food a bit too sophisticated and repetitive. Had fish and chips from the chippy tonight, just for a change.'

'Eating in a hotel on your own isn't much fun, is it?'

'No. I often take room service just to avoid it, if I'm honest.'

'As do I, not that I go away often. This place takes up most of my time.'

'Time is not something I'm short of now, since I ... well, I suppose you might call it retired.'

'Ah. Well, I can't see me retiring anytime soon.'

'I shouldn't, if I were you. Personally, I find retirement rather underwhelming thus far. Much better to have something worthwhile to do.'

Janet was sipping her white wine, but paused and looked at him, an impish smile on her face.

'So, working for Lionel is worthwhile, then? Forgive me if I find that a little difficult to believe.'

Tom was caught out momentarily but stopped himself reacting. Not having met Lionel yet, he was trying to take as he found, but the evidence increasingly suggested that he wasn't a terribly nice man.

'Well, I find every business employing people worthwhile. I don't judge a man until I've actually met him.'

Janet looked embarrassed. 'I'm sorry. That was a cheap remark. I've just lived with the problem that is Lionel for some time. What he did to me in 2009 was underhand, and he continues to do everything he can to sabotage my business.'

'No worries. I'm not surprised you take that view. Now, tell me, what are you going to sing this evening?'

'Me? Oh, no, I don't usually bother. Leave that to the youngsters.'

'Why ever not? I spotted your picture on one of the posters earlier. You must have been a bit special.'

Janet paused. 'It's been a while, for sure. Karen is the better singer, and as a dancer she was West End standard. But I was in the show as a singer when my father ran it. Hence the picture.'

Tom wanted to ask more about the family but thought better of it. Karen's father obviously wasn't anywhere on the scene. Was Janet a widow or divorced? But at that moment Karen got up, and he noticed that Bryn was plugging in his guitar as the second half seemed to be imminent.

'So, you love musical theatre, then? What are your favourites?'

'Oh, well I guess there a quite a few. *Les Misérables* would be in there, of course. *Hamilton*, we loved. Maggie's favourite song was *Climb Every Mountain* from *The Sound of Music*. We saw it together years ago in London. Such an inspirational number.'

'Ah. Good choice. I don't think we've had that one in a show for a while. Although I'm not sure that dancing nuns would work too well in a variety show.'

At that point, there was a ripple of applause as Amy Raven picked up the microphone. She seemed nervous, thought Tom. It seemed strange to see a show headliner so ill at ease at close quarters, but she sang her two numbers flawlessly before sitting down to huge applause, hugged first by Karen and then Janet. Did they seem relieved, or was he imagining it?

In any event, it was a privilege to hear an amazing talent sing, especially as she was only ten feet away from him. Another round of drinks arrived, as Karen did a couple of songs. As she sang, Tom felt relaxed by the alcohol and the sociability of the gathering. It seemed a long away from the bitterness of the struggle between Lionel and Janet over the theatre.

Karen completed her set, and Janet stood to join her. Karen looked a little puzzled but shrugged as her mother took the microphone.

'Good evening, folks. Thanks to all of the acts who have

performed here tonight. The Cromer Pier Theatre open mic night has seen any number of talented singers over the years, and in two weeks' time our latest graduate, Amy Raven, will start a headline season in the Summertime Special show. We're also delighted to welcome back another local girl, Hannah Masters. As always, it's great to see the town come alive at this time of year, and if you're a visitor we welcome you to Cromer and hopefully you will return to this very special theatre. Karen and I will close proceedings with a song that is special to one of our visitors here tonight. I seem to remember I sang this in a school production once, only this time we have no backing track. Are you ready, Karen?'

Karen shrugged, took a swig of her lager, and put it down. She smiled at Janet, and they stood side by side, sharing the microphone. Self-evidently mother and daughter, singing together as they had sung so often, in the perfect vocal harmony of family.

Tom was touched. They were singing *Climb Every Mountain.*

11.

A Week Later

Tom Stanley waited to meet Lionel Pemrose on the other side of town from the pier.

He had met both Jim Cameron and Tara the previous Friday, and the full extent of what had been going on at Brewster's surprised the usually unflappable Cameron. Tara left to head back to London, but the meeting continued between the two men, as they debated how best to proceed in the meeting with Lionel.

A PowerPoint presentation was unlikely to play well, given Lionel's limited attention span. Cameron was also concerned that anything that he said would feel like 'I told you so'.

The situation at Brewster's was so much worse than Cameron had thought. He and Lionel had fundamentally disagreed over the move into betting shops, so he'd been left entirely on the side-lines. It was clear that the whole structure of the deal had made the business unsustainable. Brewster and Lionel had been mates for years, with Brewster a slightly older mentor to the younger man.

But was what Brewster had done a provable breach of contract? Tom thought not, and Cameron agreed. Lionel would want to sue for sure, but that could take years, and had a limited chance of success.

Cameron was relieved that he was dealing with a world-ly-wise operator in Tom Stanley. Other accountants would simply have written the report and given it to management to fact-check. But there was no report at this stage. Stanley was clearly trying to find an outcome with which all parties were happy.

What Stanley didn't know was that in Cameron's suit pocket he had his signed letter of resignation. He planned to resign on the Monday. He was tired of being blind-sided and ignored by Lionel, and increasingly disliked him. He'd retire contentedly on a decent pension, and still had his shares in Pemrose hotels.

In the end, Tom had decided to meet Lionel alone, so that he could be as blunt as he liked. He arrived early that morning and went into the Majestic conference room, poured himself a coffee and waited.

After ten minutes, he gave up on his notes and looked out of the window towards the pier. The weather was warm, but the day was overcast. He planned to stay on for a few days. The opening night of the show was Friday, and he planned to be there to see it.

Suddenly, the conference room door opened and in walked Lionel Pemrose, bronzed from his stay in Malaga. They shook hands and made the usual small talk. They sat facing each other, with Lionel at the head of the table and Tom down the side.

Tom was content to let Lionel lead the discussion, because in the final analysis he was actually paying the bill for this.

'Well, Tom, I think I've rendered your little study rather irrelevant now' said a smiling Lionel.

Tom decided to underreact. 'How so?'

'Well, I assume Jim briefed you that I've closed the casino project down? As Mr Hodson wanted. A great shame as with his support I think it would have been a success, but banks are banks, I suppose.'

Tom smiled. Lionel was as big a bullshitter as he'd expected. Say nothing. Let him continue.

Lionel seemed surprised by the lack of response. 'Well?' he said.

Tom looked down at his notes, then looked at Lionel, and maintained a level tone as he spoke.

'Yes, Jim did advise me. To be honest, that may not have been the best route to follow from your point of view. It renders the loans you made to the casino company virtually worthless, and with those debts written off you have now broken all of the banking covenants, although frankly you'd breached most of them already.'

Lionel looked slightly winded. Tom's face, on the other hand, betrayed no emotion.

Lionel rallied. 'Well, I think that sometimes decisive management action is needed to sort a problem out. With the casino project terminated, the business is back in profit. A short-term cash flow problem maybe, but nothing we can't handle.'

Again, Tom made some notes on his pad, worked out some figures on his calculator, and let an infuriatingly long period of silence elapse. He then slid a piece of paper across the table and continued calmly.

'An interesting perspective given the position at Brewster's. Take a look.'

Lionel studied the paper, frowned and shrugged. 'I'm not sure what you've been told, but your girl has got her figures all wrong. Short-term cash flow problem. You can't lose money as a bookie.'

Tom looked across, with a rather more fixed stare. 'That girl, as you call her, is an extremely competent accountant.

Your Mr Brewster isn't, however, a great judge of people. He underestimated her, rather as you appear to be doing. It only took her a few days' work to ascertain the full facts.'

'What facts? Look, Bernie Brewster is a personal friend.'

'Well, that's as may be, but I'm afraid the deal you've struck gives him a nice salary for which he is doing extraordinarily little, and you are paying him a fortune to rent these betting shops in High Street locations which are dying on their feet. Add in the loss of the fixed-odds betting terminals and small wonder they're losing money.'

'Look, I ...'

'Perhaps if I go through the details, you'll see things more clearly.'

It took Tom 15 minutes or so to explain. Takings were falling not because of factory closures, but because so many ex-customers were now betting at the new bookies set up nearby in several towns. As final proof, he handed over pictures of Bernie Brewster in one of the shops, talking to the owner.

Lionel was suddenly rather quiet. He poured a glass of water and swallowed it down. His face seemed to have lost its bronzed glow.

Tom continued. 'I'm afraid that Tara's figures make grim reading. There is no way you can make money with the deal as it is currently structured.'

Lionel was now very pale indeed. 'Then I'll sack him immediately for gross misconduct and take him to court for breach of contract. I'm not standing for this.'

Tom shook his head slowly. 'Well, I'm not at all sure you'd win, since you can't prove he is linked to the rival business. He's not listed as a director, and in any event, you don't have any money to fight with.'

Lionel flared. 'I don't have the money. What are you talking about?'

Tom stared at him directly. 'The business is insolvent, Lionel.'

'What do you mean?'

Tom chose his words with care. 'Well, the official meaning of insolvency is being unable to meet your obligations as and when they fall due. To meet the test, you would need bank support. Support I doubt you can rely on. If you wish to sue Mr Brewster at your own expense, then that's up to you.'

Lionel shook his head. 'The hotels group is doing fine. I'll just sign the cross-guarantees with the rest of the group.'

Tom nodded. 'I do agree that the hotels business is sound. A good business and very well run. But I'm afraid that the bank will require the agreement of all shareholders, and that won't be forthcoming.'

'How do you know that? I can be very persuasive,' insisted Lionel.

'I asked Mrs Pemrose last week. She declined.'

Lionel looked intently at him. 'Who gave you permission to disclose my financial affairs to my ex-wife? That's not within your brief.'

Tom stared at him. 'You did.'

Lionel was becoming angry now. 'I did no such thing.'

Tom reached for the briefing letter, glanced at it briefly and pushed the relevant page across the table.

'If you look at paragraph 14a, you'll see I was given access to all directors and shareholders, and the brief includes the hotels group and entertainments.'

Lionel pushed it back but remained silent. Tom decided to sit things out. Lionel got up and poured more coffee. He offered Tom a refill, which he accepted. Lionel sat down and smiled, albeit grimly.

'OK, Tom. So, have you any good news this morning? Or am I to walk down there and throw myself off the end of the pier? Assuming I do still own it, of course.'

Tom laughed. 'Well, as you say, the hotels group is sound, and I think that the arcades down the coast seem to be doing OK, and with the revamps and new machines they should do well in season.'

'Yes. Cost a fortune, that bloody asbestos, but things should start looking up this year.'

Tom sensed that Lionel was becoming more pragmatic, so he let him lead, hoping that he would realise his predicament, and begin to seek solutions.

'So, Tom, I'm clearly in a spot of bother, what do I need to do to placate our Mr Hodson?'

Tom picked out another paper. This one had scribbled figures and some bullet points he'd prepared the previous evening.

'Well, as I say, the Brewster's deal is quite simply unsustainable. The quarterly rents fall due next week, so I'd tell Mr Brewster that you aren't going to pay. I'd stop his salary, too. And, of course, the final consideration for the business is due next month, so we stop that, too.'

'But he'll lock the shops and sue us. The losses will get still worse then.'

'Well, they would, but I'd send him a legal letter alleging breach of contract and put the business into administration straight away. You are the biggest creditor, so you'll call the shots. Worst case you lose the lot, best case you get a deal worked out by the administrators which allows you to continue trading.'

'But there will be a legal battle. He'll claim he's a creditor too.'

Tom smiled. 'Which you won't need to worry about. You let the administrator handle it and see if he can construct a viable business, by getting the shop rents down, for example.

'But why would Brewster agree to that?'

'Because, as we say in Yorkshire, he'll get next to nowt if it goes under, and he'll have a load of empty shops in towns where there are already plenty. Sometimes it's better to get *summat than nowt.*'

Lionel was weighing his words. Tom noted that the bluff and bluster were gone.

'All right, Tom. Let's just park that for a minute. Are you saying that if I do this, having closed down the casino project already, Mr Hodson will get off my back?'

'No, I'm not. The losses built up are too big, the debt is too high, and the bank is still overexposed.'

'Then what's the point?' said Lionel, his hands splayed for emphasis.

'Because at least the remaining business makes money, rather than losing it. Then you can rebuild. It's always difficult to make the first pound of profit. It gets easier after that.'

'True. But what more do I have to do to put Hodson back in his box? Frankly, I might as well put the lot under. I might at least sleep at night then.'

Tom found it interesting that he was beginning to glimpse the person under the facade. Lionel was a typical small businessman who runs a really good business when he's hands on, but can't cope when things get bigger, or if he goes into a business sector he doesn't understand.

Tom continued, 'Well, I don't have great options. The bank

will ask for personal guarantees, which I'm quite sure you won't want to give.'

'Too right.'

Tom was puzzled. 'Yet you'd be prepared to give him a charge over the hotels?'

'Yes. I have the documents ready. At least with the charge over the hotels Miriam shares the risk.'

'Well tear them up, Lionel. That's not going to happen. Frankly, why would she agree? She's doing very nicely from the arrangement.'

Lionel banged his cup a little too hard. 'You can say that again, that gold-digging cow.'

Tom knew the drill. The businessman in trouble was always looking for someone else to blame. In this case, Miriam was a convenient scapegoat.

He shrugged, 'Whether that is true or not doesn't help you, Lionel. The alternatives include selling assets off. Some of the arcades perhaps? Consolidate your position?'

'I'm not sure there would be any takers, and Hodson has them as security already.'

Tom nodded. 'Yes, he does. But not the pier. He's never taken a charge over that for some reason. Probably because of its age. Frankly, it makes no sense to keep it now. It barely breaks even and one unexpected maintenance bill puts it the red. I know it's dear to your heart, but it could do the trick …'

'No.'

Tom had expected this reaction, but it offered a way out of sorts. Getting rid of two loss-making ventures stopped things getting worse, but the bank was still horribly exposed.

'Well, then I'm rather out of options.'

Lionel leaned back and shrugged. 'So, what would you recommend?'

Tom thought for a moment before responding. 'Well, I certainly couldn't recommend allowing any further increase in the bank's exposure, could I? I think you should discuss the Brewster's situation with Jim and then your solicitors. Then get revised projections for the next three months across the summer when trading is good. I'll speak to the bank and see if they'll give us another week or so to reach a conclusion.'

'But what about the payroll? It's due next weekend.'

'Then Jim will need to get busy. I'll stay on here if you wish. Then if you decide about Brewster's, and Jim gives me the projections, I'll see if I can get the bank to meet the payroll. But don't misunderstand me, if they meet the payroll this month it only buys you a week or two more to figure out what else to do. Give them personal guarantees, pledge your hotel group shares or flog a few assets, logically the pier; those seem to be your choices.'

Lionel sat stony-faced. 'It doesn't matter to people like you, does it?'

'Meaning?'

'You people always get paid for doing the bank's dirty work.'

Tom found the remark offensive. This was Lionel's fault, yet he had the nerve to blame everyone else.

He replied rather tartly, 'If you don't wish me to continue, Lionel, I'll happily hand the file back. If you'd had one of the Big Six accountancy firms on this job, you'd have been in receivership by now. I'm trying to get something to work for all parties, but, equally, I'm perfectly happy to head for home if you want me to.'

Lionel had nothing he could say in response, and Tom

knew it. He collected up his things and packed them in his battered old briefcase. Your move, Lionel old son.

Lionel smiled thinly. 'Ok Tom. I'll go along with you. You'll talk to Hodson in the meantime, and I'll brief Jim immediately.'

With that, Lionel got up and spoke once more while moving towards the door.

'Oh and when you see Mr Hodson, be sure to tell him that Lizzie sends her regards, will you? A mutual friend of ours. Will you do that for me?'

Tom was puzzled. 'Lizzie? OK, yes, I'll be sure to mention it.'

With that they parted company with a firm handshake and Tom was left alone in the conference room, wondering what he still didn't know about this whole affair. He decided to ring the bank and, to his surprise, not only did Hodson take his call straight away, but he invited Tom to come over immediately.

It was going to be an interesting meeting, Tom thought. It was obvious he'd been picked by Peter Hodson because normal rules didn't apply in this case. He took out his pen and wrote down 'remember to tell Hodson that Lizzie sends her love'.

*   *   *

Tom went back to his room and shed his jacket since the sun was bathing the town in its warmth. He walked to the bank, where Peter Hodson showed him straight up to a conference room. It took the next 40 minutes or so for Tom to articulate his findings. Hodson spoke little, merely scribbling the odd note.

'So, to summarise, I've left it with Lionel to talk to Jim Cameron. If he puts Brewster's into administration now, I can at least see how the rest of the core business will make money again, but the payroll needs paying, so in the short-term the overdraft will get worse.'

Hodson shook his head. 'I can't let the payroll go, Tom. Red lights are flashing at head office. I don't have the latitude I used to.'

Tom paused. He'd figured that if the numbers were convincing enough the bank would meet the payroll. But if Pemrose was on the regional radar, Hodson would have to justify every decision he made.

Hodson shook his head wearily. 'I'm between a rock and a hard place. What did Lionel say?'

Tom thought about it. 'Well, it was a difficult conversation. He's out of his depth and there's nobody to blame but himself. He seemed to understand the options. He knows Brewster screwed him, so I think he'll do what is needed there. Oh, and he insisted I told you that ... now what was it ... ah, yes ... Lizzie sends her love. I've no idea what that means, but presumably you do?'

Hodson closed his eyes and put his head back. Tom decided to wait. In the silence the air conditioning whirred, mingling with the ever-present cries of seagulls. The church clock chimed, but still Hodson stared at the ceiling.

Tom broke the silence, 'Want to tell me about it, Peter? What is said in this office stays in this office.'

Hodson breathed deeply and shrugged.

Tom decided to continue. 'So, you ring me out of the blue, for a bog-standard bank review any accountant could do, and you know that the figures say to pull the rug, so why hesitate?'

Hodson nodded but said nothing. He looked desperately tired. Tom knew the feeling. The body craved sleep, but the brain wouldn't oblige. Life was on hold as the black cloud hung over your life, but one that wouldn't ever move on.

He speculated, 'At a guess this you know this Lizzie, er, rather too well?'

Hodson nodded. 'I've been a fool, Tom. I needed someone I can trust to find me a way out. I'm sorry.'

Tom nodded. 'He's said this to you before, at a guess?'

'Only once, so I wasn't certain that this was his game. As he has repeated it to you, now I am.'

Tom shrugged. 'OK. So now we need to evaluate the risk.'

Hodson looked up sharply. 'Evaluate the bloody risk? No shit, Sherlock. My job, my marriage, not to mention my bloody pension.'

'Well, yes. I get all that. But when did you last see the lady? What job did she do?'

'She was Lionel's PA. I haven't seen her since the ... well, I guess about ten years ago.'

Tom frowned. 'And did she make any claims at the time? Try to blackmail you I mean?'

'No. We parted on good terms.'

Tom shrugged. 'Well, I can't say I've met anyone called Lizzie during my lap around the business. It seems as if someone called Christine is his PA now. Is Lizzie even working there now?'

'I don't know. But that doesn't mean anything. One phone call and I'm screwed. You need to find a way out that I can sell to head office. I'm struggling to justify the continuing support.'

Tom looked at him in astonishment. 'No shit, Sherlock! Had you foreclosed a couple of months back, the bank might have got out clean.'

'I know, but I didn't dare.'

Tom sighed. He was really struggling now. His own credibility was at stake, and he still had a strong sense of honesty and integrity. Hodson stood and poured himself a coffee. Tom declined. He was looking at his notes and thinking on his feet. What should he do now? Should he just walk away?

But then he thought of the people he'd met in the business, including people like Debbie. He'd never forgotten his working-class roots, and it was always the little people who suffered the most.

'OK. Let's think this through. Jim will show that with the casino and Brewster's gone the business will make money over the summer, and by the end of the season the bank's exposure will be less than it is now. Amusement arcades make their money in the summer; surely even your head office will see that?'

Hodson sat and seemed more rational having shared the dilemma. 'But then what? It would be simpler if he agreed a cross-charge on the hotel group's assets. That's what he agreed to do only a few weeks ago.'

'Miriam Pemrose would have to agree too, but she won't. And Lionel thinks you wouldn't dare put him under, remember? Are you going to call his bluff?'

Hodson seemed distracted. Tom understood. Once you are in that mindset, your brain stops functioning rationally and you can't think your way out of a problem.

Tom continued, 'My other suggestion is that he sells off assets. But of course, that would take some time and the only assets that are saleable are the arcades which are profitable. Except of course the pier. You've never had a charge over that, have you?'

Hodson shook his head. 'Head office would never agree. How do you value a Grade II-listed pier that could be blown away in the next storm?'

Tom smiled. 'Well, I see the argument, but it's survived for more than a century, after all. I've asked Lionel to consider selling it. That would help with the debt.'

'Good luck with that. There's no chance he'll sell it. That pier is the jewel in Lionel's crown.'

Tom was rather irritated. 'A stupid feud with the Wells family, and now of course Miriam Pemrose and Janet Wells are partners in crime. Formidable adversaries indeed.'

They talked some more, but Tom sensed that they were going round in circles. Hodson had no constructive options to offer. He excused himself to take a phone call in his office, returning ten minutes later.

'Sorry about that, Tom. You were saying?'

'Well, all I can think of now is to get that payroll paid, which buys us time. Cameron's projections will show the business making money and your exposure coming down somewhat by September. You can sell that to head office pending a review of which parts of the business can be sold to negate the exposure. You can demonstrate that the loss-making bits are being got rid of. I can write that up for you pretty quickly.'

Hodson was weighing his options when Tom's phone rang. It was Tara. He decided to take it. Tara didn't waste his time.

'Hi, Tara. I'm just in a meeting. Is it urgent?'

'Hi, Tom. Yes, I'll be quick. I rang Jim Cameron about some of the final details for the report, but the woman I contacted said that Jim was no longer an employee of Pemrose. She seemed rather upset. He resigned this morning, I gather. You may have heard already, but I thought I'd better check.'

Tom looked up at Hodson as he spoke. 'No, I hadn't heard. So, Cameron's resigned then? Let me think now. Just give me a minute, will you?'

Hodson looked concerned at the news but said nothing.

Tom continued, 'Look, I'll tell you what. Drop what you're doing and look at Jim's financial model through to September only, assuming that Brewster's is in administration by Friday, and the rest of the business continues. Let's see what the bank exposure looks like in September. I need to get the payroll met by the bank to buy us time. Can you get them to me by tonight, please? Just make some sensible assumptions that we can tweak in the model.'

'Well, yes, I guess that's not too tricky. It's a decent model, not too complex. I'm on it.'

'That's great, Tara. Thanks for the call. Good work.'

Tom rang off. Hodson spoke more calmly than he felt.

'So, even Jim's had enough, then?'

Tom nodded. 'Seems like it. If Lionel had listened to him, he wouldn't be in this mess.'

'This is a disaster, Tom. At least I could trust Jim. Now it's a rudderless ship.'

'Well, yes, but Tara will come through with the figures, and I'll write you a report by the morning, which will give you something to sell to head office so that Pemrose survives in the short term at least.'

'Thanks, Tom. Is there anything you need from me?'

'No, I don't think so. Ah ... but if Lionel gets in touch, just duck the call. I'll track Jim down. The more help we get from him the better.'

* * *

By 2pm, Jim Cameron was standing on the clifftop at Royal Cromer Golf Club. He was playing on his own that afternoon, as he sometimes did when he wanted to think. It was a fine afternoon with little wind, and he was wearing a polo shirt bearing the club's crest, with tailored shorts. He attempted a long putt, and was content when it went close enough for him to tap in for his par.

He decided to have a break before playing the next hole. It was pretty quiet this late on, and it had been quite a day, after all. He had a cool drink in his bag and took a long swig as he sat on a bench looking out to sea. He felt relaxed, as if the weight of the world had been lifted from his shoulders.

Lionel had accused him of disloyalty, and of being a rat deserting a sinking ship. He replied that If the ship hit an iceberg, the skipper was to blame, not the poor sod who had pointed out the iceberg long ago. Tyler, the hotels group's chief executive, heard the shouting match and interrupted them. He tried to calm the situation, but Lionel was adamant, insisting that Tyler escort Cameron off the premises.

There had been any number of calls to his mobile since he'd departed, including two from Lionel. Jim did feel a bit guilty about avoiding the calls from Tom Stanley, but he just needed time.

He stirred to get up and resume his round, but then his phone rang again; this time it was Miriam Pemrose. He hesitated, but then accepted the call.

'Miriam. Good afternoon,' he said politely.

'I've just heard the news, Jim. Tyler rang me. You can't do this. Lionel will drive the business over the cliff-edge. You have to reconsider. Tyler says the same.'

Jim wasn't inclined to change his mind. 'Well, I rather think Lionel fired me after I resigned, in any case. He's not listening to me. Casinos? Bookmakers? What was the man thinking of?'

'I don't want it to go under, Jim. Lionel will never cope with that. And the people. Some of them are friends. Actually, I consider that all of them are.'

'The hotels are fine; you needn't worry about that. Tyler will look after them.'

'But a lot of our longest-serving staff members work in the arcades and on the pier. I went to school with some of them. I know I'm being sentimental but, damn it, I couldn't live with myself if I didn't try to stop this madness.'

Jim wasn't surprised at Miriam's response. 'Look, Miriam, Tom Stanley is working for Hodson, but he knows what needs to be done and Lionel will have to listen to him, even if he won't listen to me. Lionel even tried to give the bank a legal charge over the hotels until I warned him that you and I could sue him if he did. He's that desperate.'

'That's what I'm afraid of. When Lionel's cornered like this, he just lashes out. He needs someone who can help him reach rational decisions.'

'Aye, he does. And that used to be me, but not anymore.'

'So you wouldn't reconsider if I asked you to come back?'

Cameron thought about it for a moment as Miriam continued.

'Lionel will have to ask you to come back, of course. I get that.'

Cameron hesitated. The three went back to the early days. He'd always liked Miriam for her no-nonsense way of dealing with people. While she was around, Lionel had someone to restrain him, keep him doing what he was good at. Without her, Lionel had become more and more difficult to work with. But this was the first time that she had hinted that she still in any way cared about the man.

The divorce had been painful, but she hadn't been able to accept yet another affair; a private detective had caught Lionel in flagrante with Lizzie. Yet Lionel still despised her for saving Janet Wells and the Pier Theatre. That was ten years ago, but it might as well have been yesterday.

Jim relented. 'I'm prepared to think again, but you need to sort out your differences out with Lionel, too. He's acting like a wee boy.'

'All right, Jim. I'll try to be flexible where I can, but I'm not about to jeopardise the hotels. No chance.'

'Tom has the data he needs anyway, but if he wants any help, I'll give it from outside the business. I'm prepared to do that much for you, but not for bloody Lionel.'

'Right. Good. That's helpful. Will you ring Tom, then?'

'Yes. I'll do that. I'm playing golf, but I'll ring him when I'm done here.'

'Thanks Jim. Much appreciated. I know Lionel's being an arse.'

They rang off. Jim smiled and shook his head. He stood and took out his driver. He walked onto the tee and set up his ball. He looked back towards Cromer and Lionel's beloved pier. They had one thing in common; they were both very fond of this place, their adopted home. Jim was looking forward to having his freedom. He set himself and watched with pleasure as his drive flew reassuringly straight down the middle of the fairway, bisecting the bunkers intended to catch the errant drive.

*   *   *

Tara completed the financial models by early evening and sent them to Tom. He had no time to review things in detail, so he checked the bottom-line figures and sent them on immediately to Jim Cameron. The two men spoke briefly and agreed to meet at a quiet pub in Overstrand. It was early evening, and relatively quiet, so they could talk freely.

Jim was casually dressed and reddening nicely after his afternoon on the golf course. Tom still had a tie on, but his collar was undone. He had never quite made the journey to casual workwear, but at least he had shed the jacket, and the shirt had short sleeves.

'Have you been here before? To Overstrand, I mean?'

'Only on foot. The coastal path. A nice walk last weekend. You're a member of the golf club on the clifftop, then? The Royal Cromer?'

'Yes. Played this afternoon to clear my head.'

Tom sipped his beer and smiled. 'You'll be planning to play a lot more now, then? Assuming you *have* actually retired today.'

Jim laughed. 'Maybe. We'll have to see. Miriam seemed keen that I change my mind. Let's see what happens.'

'Well, Tara's just re-jigging your models and doing the sensitivities that the bank will expect. I sent you the base figures a little earlier, but I doubt you've read them as yet.'

Jim looked at him quizzically. 'And what will be the outcome, do you think?'

It was Tom's turn to laugh this time. 'Well, according to the report I've already written, the bank should agree to bankroll the business through to the end of August, pending the outcome of the restructuring, conditional on Brewster's going into administration, of course.'

'And the figures will bear that out, will they?' Jim smiled knowingly.

'Well, we've just used your projections, so they better had. But when I get Tara's final figures, I'll send them over. If you can't make money from the arcades in season, God help you.'

'True. Your Tara did a good job on our Mr Brewster. Sucked him in and spat him out, by all accounts.'

'He's not very bright and he doesn't rate young women, particularly young Asian women.' Tom replied.

'There's still some dinosaurs left, then. Big mistake. She's a class act.'

'Well, I imagine he's licking his wounds tonight. His friendship with Lionel is over, it seems.'

Jim sat back, wincing a little as his body responded to its earlier exertions. 'Do you think Hodson will go for it?'

Tom set down his glass, 'Well, he will, but will the funding committee? With Hodson you're dealing with a human being, whereas with a funding committee ...'

'... You're dealing with faceless shiny-arsed bookkeepers,' Cameron interjected.

'Exactly.'

Jim finished his pint. 'The report should do the job. Then we have a bit of time to sort this shambles out once and for all.'

Tom finished his drink too. 'What would you do if you were Lionel?'

Jim thought for a moment. 'Well, I think I'd go and get some cash from somewhere.'

*   *   *

Lionel wasn't having a good day. He'd spoken to his lawyers, of course. Dispiritingly, the solicitor had agreed with Tom Stanley. The chances of successfully suing Brewster seemed remote. He might win, but it would take months, if not years, and cost a lot of money in legal fees.

He realised that he'd made a mistake over Jim Cameron. He was now extremely nervous. Cameron had been the bedrock of the group from the start. More recently, as the group had expanded, Tyler had taken over running the hotels for him, making up for the loss of Miriam.

The Majestic had been an amazing success, but it was the last project that he and Miriam had done together. A beautiful building, which he'd bought for a bargain price from the receivers in the 2008 recession, and which Miriam had transformed into an art deco-styled hotel of great beauty and quality. They had always been a great team. He with the eye for making money, she with an eye for style, and for knowing what customers really wanted.

But he now had to face up to the fact that this diversification strategy had been a disastrous failure. Reflecting alone in his flat on the top floor of the Majestic, while consuming several whiskies, he was forced to accept that as little as he innately liked people like Tom Stanley, his analysis was objective, clinical and devoid of any preconceptions.

He was getting old, and with Freya gone, and Miriam no longer his wife, he was alone in the world. He could of course call on his Rotary pals, or his mates at the golf club. But close allies were few and far between, and the bitter row with Jim Cameron had cost him one of his few remaining friendships.

He'd also been played for a fool by another so-called friend, Bernie Brewster, which hurt too, of course. Then Tyler, the man who he'd mentored, had told him exactly what he thought about his treatment of Jim Cameron. The man he'd recruited as a raw youngster had grown into a seasoned businessman and was now his heir apparent. Lionel was forced to concede that these people couldn't all be wrong, and he'd acted impetuously, as he was apt to when he felt the need for it.

He'd stopped all payments to Brewster and instructed that the payroll transactions be stopped too. He'd also called the number of an insolvency firm given to him by Tom Stanley. The Grim Reaper would visit the business tomorrow.

He'd tried to reach Jim Cameron, but without success. He had spoken briefly to Tom Stanley that evening, who had assured him that he had all the information required, and would send him the initial report by early tomorrow.

Lionel found it ironic that Stanley would be sweating over his spreadsheets in his room on the floor below. He'd not been seen much in the restaurant or the bar. A rather sad and typical accountant, he thought.

But in spite of how bad things were, he was confident that he still had Hodson under control. The bank would meet the payroll because Tom Stanley's report would do the trick and buy him some time. A lot could happen between now and the autumn. He felt a little more cheerful.

Lionel looked at his mobile and noticed a third missed call from Bernie Brewster. He smiled. No doubt he'd received the solicitor's letter. Time for you to sweat Mr Brewster, he thought.

He finished his glass of whisky and set it down. Putting on his white jacket and tie, he headed down to the bar. A young singer was doing a set in the restaurant after dinner, and he wanted some company. He'd always enjoyed the banter with the hotel guests, and they were the only friends he had right now.

Meanwhile, oblivious to Lionel's depressed state, Tom populated the report with the numbers from Tara's model, and sent that to Jim Cameron at around 10.30pm, expecting a reply by early morning. He was watching some documentary or other on TV, when his tablet notified him that an email had arrived.

Hi Tom

Looked through figures and report. Talented lady, your Tara! Happy with both documents. As you say, we are in our best trading period now, so the bank's position will only improve over the summer.

   I'm playing at Sheringham early tomorrow, but available after lunch if you need anything further.

Cheers for now, and good luck!
Jim

Tom smiled. He reread the report the report one more time and forwarded it to Lionel. His mind was too active for sleep, so he took a brief walk out along the promenade. He saw Lionel in the bar, but decided he'd rather not debate things further. He stood looking out to sea, which looked flat calm. The sun had only recently gone down, and there were still quite a few people out. He walked back past one of the amusement arcades, the staff working on, blissfully unaware that their fate hung in the balance.

Returning to his room, he was surprised that Lionel had already replied; a simple thank you and his OK to publish. He couldn't really have read the figures in the time available, Tom thought. Probably just skimmed the report and conclusions. He forwarded the report to Peter Hodson, satisfied with his day's work. He slept soundly, his brain obligingly switching off. For once, no thoughts about Maggie interrupted his sleep.

12.

Thursday

Tom spent the next couple of days relaxing, and visiting the stunning stately homes at Felbrigg and Holkham. On Thursday morning, he was woken both by the early light, and the seagulls perched on the balcony above his room. He looked at his clock and groaned. He tried to go back to sleep, but failed. Eventually he gave in and took a long shower, having plenty of time on his hands.

He made himself a mug of coffee, using the Pier Theatre mug Janet had given him rather than the stupidly undersized cup and saucer the hotel supplied. He turned on the news and found that his Times had been slipped under the door as usual.

He had a meeting with Peter Hodson later, at which he expected to hear that the funding committee had signed off on the proposal. Hodson had felt confident, and he had no reason to doubt him.

Then he was going to have a nice sociable lunch at the golf club with Jim Cameron, who appeared to be relishing his freedom. Assuming that all went well today, his assignment was complete, too, and he could let Tara go off on her travels. He was staying on until Sunday at least, as he was planning to see the show on Saturday night as Janet's guest.

He planned to go to Lord's the following week, otherwise

his diary was clear. The empty Docklands flat beckoned. Back to square one. He thought about Maggie, feeling slightly guilty that he'd thought less about her of late, albeit because he was getting on with life. She'd have loved the stately homes, he thought ruefully.

But she'd also have chided him for feeling sorry for himself. They'd had the conversation, of course. The conversation that no married couple ever wants to have, and for which he was woefully underprepared. It had been pretty obvious early on that however good modern medicine had become, it could only postpone the inevitable. She was stoic to the end, and had never expressed bitterness or self-pity. She had even managed to go to the theatre days before she died, determined to squeeze the last drop out of life.

He'd abandoned their bedroom only in the final few days, when the nurse was there so often that she might as well have lived in. But it was Tom who had been with Maggie that last morning. She had looked serene and at peace in death, with even the slightest hint of a smile, he'd thought.

She had said that she was worried about leaving him, a thought which seemed to resonate at times like this. He could look after himself and exist as a person. But living … could he call this living? With Maggie the social diary was always popping up with surprises. A visit to friends one weekend, a theatre trip the next. The coffee table was always strewn with holiday brochures, as Maggie beavered away on the tablet looking for the best hotel deals. The ridiculous last-minute weekend away to Sussex, Suffolk or Somerset, courtesy of some special offer she'd seen.

He'd moaned and complained at the time of course, as these things invariably conflicted with his all-consuming passion for work, but it was Maggie's way of living their lives, since he couldn't be bothered to organise things. Now he so much wished that he had taken the trouble.

He dozed off for a while and had a mixture of weird dreams and memories of happier times. He awoke a while later, and dressed for breakfast. He looked outside and opened the window. The sun was already pretty warm, so he wondered what to wear. The meeting at the bank surely required a suit, while the lunch required casual dress. But then he recalled that Hodson had worn an open collar at the last meeting, so he abandoned the tie. He recalled that Maggie found his stiff-upper-lip approach laughable, so he put on some light-coloured chinos and a patterned short-sleeved shirt. He felt slightly under-dressed but laughed at himself. The last thing that Hodson would be worried about was Tom's attire.

* * *

Lech was up early, too. It was the first pre-show that afternoon, and he had carried on Les Westley's policy of getting down to the theatre early. Early to people like Lech was of course around 10am, since he was used to late, adrenaline-fuelled nights. He carried the box Cyril had given him and was going to rehearse his act once more. He was now the compère, as Les had been, and he enjoyed the loosely scripted interaction with the audience.

Debbie saw him enter and smiled. 'Showtime, Mr Lech?' she asked.

'Mr Lech is always rehearsing. Mr Les says so. I learn much from Mr Les.'

'Mr Les is like as not relaxing somewhere much warmer

than here, Lech. I imagine Lauren is relieved her tour is over. I doubt she's up yet, either.'

Lech entered the auditorium still smiling. Actually, Les and Lauren were only a few miles away at their hideaway on the clifftop near Overstrand, but that was a secret. Lauren was suffering throat problems and wouldn't be singing anytime soon, although they would both see the show in the coming weeks.

He'd spoken to Les about Felix, as he hadn't been able to find out much online about Cyril Brown and his partner, just one short clip from the talent show which had made them famous. Les had come up with a really old VHS tape which he had converted to a DVD. Lech had watched it so much he could almost recall the whole routine, not that he needed to.

The two men had come to know each other quite well over the years. Cyril had kept up his Punch and Judy show on the pier until last season. Lech would walk by and talk to him about all sorts of things. Not only did Cyril have an encyclopaedic knowledge of his hometown, but he also seemed to know the entertainment industry almost as well as Les did.

Lech had been shocked by the sight of the gaunt figure at the nursing home, apparently wasting away. But Cyril's intellect was clearly a sharp as ever, and as always Cyril remained so forward-looking and positive. His decision to hand over one of his most treasured possessions, Felix, had touched Lech very deeply. Cyril and Felix had briefly been household names, and handing over the dummy was an amazing gesture.

But it was also confirmation, if any were needed, that the end was near. Although they had reserved Cyril and a carer front-row seats for that day's show, it was far from certain that he would make it. But if he did, Lech was determined that

Felix would speak once again, and he headed for the stage to work on the high-pitched accent required.

*　*　*

Lauren had invited Amy Raven to visit her that morning ahead of the show. Les had a meeting he needed to go to, and Lauren wanted the company, although she was under strict instructions to rest her throat.

She'd had tests at a specialist clinic the previous day and was waiting for the results. The nodules identified were like as not benign, and quite typical of those professional singers tend to get, but she knew surgery might be necessary. And, at the back of her mind, she understood that, in a worst-case scenario, she might never sing again.

She was sitting outside on the roof terrace, enjoying the fine weather. The house had a lovely view of the sea, and on such a day she couldn't help but feel blessed. It had all been such a roller coaster, after all. Ten years ago, she had been virtually bankrupt. The record company had declined to renew her contract and headlining in the Summertime Special show was the only way of earning money and retaining some self-respect.

Riddled with self-doubt in a town she didn't know at all, she had rebuilt her career, thanks mainly to Les and, of course, Janet Wells. Now when she came back here it felt more like home than her native Wales.

She'd been incredibly lucky. Les had become her manager and partner. He was the first to recognise Lauren as a songwriter as well as a performer. Together, they had now written five best-selling albums. The latest tour had been an amazing success, including five European dates, which had allowed them to visit stunning cities such as Vienna, Rome and Barcelona.

Much as she'd loved the tour, she now felt drained, and was enjoying the rest, even if her voice was a major worry at this time. She had begun to write again, picking out chords on a guitar propped up by her sunbed, or on the piano in one of the bedrooms downstairs, which doubled as a makeshift studio.

Coming here took her away from the London bubble, which was a mixed blessing. On the one hand she missed the creative buzz of the capital, and some of her close friends. She couldn't even speak to them on the phone at present, with her voice restricted to a hoarse whisper. On the other, she could write when she chose and relax when she pleased.

Lech had brought the family around the previous Sunday for a barbecue, which she'd enjoyed in spite of resorting to sign language at times. They could also go out for a walk or a meal without being recognised too often, courtesy of a change of hair colouring and dark glasses. Her Welsh voice would normally have been a bit of a giveaway, but not at the moment.

She sipped her hot lemon and Manuka honey drink and, as she set it down, the doorbell rang. Les had suggested that she got Amy around that morning while he was away. She would be company for Lauren, but it would also kill time for Amy before the first show that afternoon. Les believed that the stage fright problem was beatable in what was a fast-moving ensemble show. Even her solos were accompanied by the chorus, so she was never onstage on her own. But in the end, who knew for certain?

Lauren answered and Amy, dressed in a light summer top and shorts, hugged her warmly. Lauren whispered her welcome and produced a tumbler of iced orange juice as they went out onto the terrace.

'My God, this place is stunning,' said Amy.

'Yes. Les found it. He said it was time to have a hideaway here,' Lauren whispered.

'So, this is how the other half lives.'

'Until you knacker your voice, of course,' said Lauren.

'I'm sorry Lauren, are you OK?'

'Probably. I'm not sure. Waiting for test results. Until then, no singing for me.'

'If my stage fright returns this afternoon then I won't be singing any more either.'

Lauren flared. 'Don't be silly, Amy; that's not going to happen. They love you here. It's ideal for you, playing at home, amongst friends. Holidaymakers who just want a good time, not London posers half- watching Facebook while you're working your socks off.'

'I hope you're right. My chat with Cyril was helpful, although he never really overcame it.'

'I need to see him. I've just been busy having these tests and stuff. How is he?'

'Not good. They're bringing him to the show this afternoon from the nursing home. Well, at least they're hoping to, but he's fading fast now.'

Lauren suddenly looked deeply sorrowful. 'Oh, I hadn't realised he was that bad. Well, then, I'd better get in to see him tomorrow if I can, voice or no voice. I'll get Les to come along, too. He can talk for England. Lovely man, our Cyril. I just owe him so much.'

'I'm sure he'd like that. He told me his own story, but he absolutely adored talking about you.'

'Well, everything he said would have been true. Cyril has always told it the way it was.'

'It must have been hard for him to taste the fame he did, then have it all snatched away by stage fright, just when he'd made it.'

'Well, that's what drove him to stop me leaving that day, I think. He could see I was giving it all away. Full of the high and mighty, and yet actually without any self-confidence whatsoever.'

Amy shrugged, and looked up. She was close to tears.

'I know the feeling, Lauren. There've been times recently when ...'

' ... When you want to just pack it all in?'

'Yes.'

'I've felt like that, too. But neither of us has lost our talent; it just went away somewhere for a while. You'll get it all back, just like I did. You've sold the Summertime Special show out for several weeks, as I did. Cyril showed me the paper that day, and I realised that all of those fans were my friends, and you just can't run away from your friends, can you?'

'I guess. That first season was such a dream, the one I did as a dancer. I was so young and naive then. I even threw up before the audition. I only got the role because one of the other girls broke her ankle. I was totally starstruck when they introduced you as the headliner. I'd only ever seen you on TV.'

'You were starstruck? I was bloody terrified. They told me I had to dance, but I didn't have a clue. You guys were awesome. I was just relieved when Les told me I only needed to do the basics steps. Isobel must have been in despair. She had the patience of a saint.'

Amy laughed, but Lauren had a coughing fit and reached for her drink.

'Are you OK, Lauren?'

'Yes. I just can't talk beyond a whisper at the moment; when I forget, my vocal cords lose the plot.'

'I'd better go then, so you can give them a rest.'

'Oh, no. Don't go yet. All I've got is the latest Celia Braun or, failing that, daytime TV. Anything but that. Tell me about the show, the set list and stuff, then I'll keep quiet.'

So, Amy did, and when they parted, they hugged warmly. Amy was touched that Lauren had kept in contact with her for ten years now, in spite of her spiralling fame. She was just as ordinary as ever underneath the glitzy facade, and of course she had introduced her to Frank Gilbert, the agent who had built her career to date. There was much at stake that afternoon, she realised, but she felt pretty confident that she could pull it off. It was time to go to the theatre and find out.

*   *   *

Peter Hodson shook Tom's hand as he showed him through to the conference room. Once inside, the pleasantries and coffee done and dusted, Hodson pushed a copy of an email he'd received that morning across the table. Tom read it, but it didn't take long. He looked up at a sombre-faced Hodson.

'Shit. That's a turn-up. I thought they'd give it time. It's a seasonal business, after all.'

Hodson nodded. 'As did I, but they simply didn't buy into the future prospects. Too big an exposure over next winter. They've lost all confidence in Lionel, and I didn't dare tell them that Jim Cameron had gone.'

'Well, I guess the whiff of legal action over Brewster's won't have helped, either. They may think that the administrators can run the business better over the summer and secure some form of sale.'

Hodson sat back in his chair. Tom knew that he was

dreading the move that he was now required to make, and was genuinely surprised at the decision. He'd seen worse situations where the bank had held its nerve. There was more to this than met the eye. Bank politics, perhaps.

Tom handed the email back. 'He won't put anything like as much in as they want him to in that email. He'd be putting his whole life on the line. No chance.'

'I know. It's not even worth bothering with. I've dealt with Lionel for years. I was surprised when he volunteered a charge over the hotel assets.'

'Well, at that time, he was besotted with the casino idea. At least he's put that one to bed.'

'He'll have to meet the payroll from his own funds now. Will he do it, do you think?'

'I'm not sure what he'll do. From what I know of Lionel, he'll probably blame me, actually.'

Hodson remained silent. Neither wanted to mention the other problem. Eventually Tom decided that they needed to deal with that taboo. Lizzie.

'Well, I imagine you're now contemplating how you will deal with Lionel's nuclear option?'

Hodson nodded sadly. 'I've tried googling her, but I can't find her. I tried LinkedIn, too. No go.'

'She could've changed her name. Or got married? I did drop her name into a social conversation with Jim Cameron, but he just said that she'd left the group a long time ago. I didn't dig any further. I mentioned it to Tara as well, without giving her the background. She's a social media type. I'll chase that up with her.'

'I'd be grateful. There just isn't much more I can do for now.'

Tom nodded. 'When is Lionel expecting an answer? I didn't commit to a time.'

'Tomorrow. The payroll needs to go over the weekend,' Peter replied.

'Then we don't have much time. I'll ring Tara now. She's had a few days, and she knew that it was important, although not why. Can I use this room for a while? I don't want to run into Lionel at the Majestic.'

'Of course. I understand entirely. I'll craft something to send in the meantime. I'll need to ring him by noon tomorrow. I may just have to call his bluff. But I don't think he's bluffing.'

Hodson left Tom alone, who sighed to himself. Things had suddenly turned ugly, but frankly in his line of work Tom was used to things changing quickly, both for better and for worse. He rang Tara.

'Morning, Tom,' she said. She was in the bath, but no matter.

'Morning, Tara, thanks again for the figures, by the way. Unfortunately, the bank didn't buy it I'm afraid. I'm thinking through other options.'

'Oh, my. That's torn it. Mind you, I wasn't completely convinced myself, if I'm honest.'

Tom smiled. 'Well, we did our best, but there's another matter I needed to follow up with you. Lizzie Stack? Any joy?'

'Oh, well, no, not really. I tried Facebook, Instagram and Twitter; oh, and LinkedIn, obviously. But you didn't give me much to go on. At the age she was then, she could have married, emigrated or anything. I did think I could try Ancestry. com; you never know.'

'Ancestry.com? Whatever's that?' Tom asked.

'Oh, it's a family history site. You never know what you'll find on there. Got to be worth a try. People post stuff on the forums when they're looking for a relative. It's fascinating. You should try it.'

'I'm not sure there is anything much in my ancestry worth finding. Most of my lot went down the pit. I was lucky to escape that particular fate.'

'Most of my history is in India, of course. Look, I'll have a try with this Lizzie person this afternoon, but there's not much to go on. Did you have a picture at all? Anything more you can find will help. It's a bit of a needle in a haystack otherwise, to be honest.'

'OK, Tara. Do what you can for me, will you? I can't tell you what it's about, but it's really important. I need to find her in the next 24 hours if at all possible.'

'Crikey, Tom. You don't want much, do you? But leave it with me. I'll do my best.'

Tom rang off. There was only one other option. Hopefully, he wasn't on the golf course.

'Jim Cameron,' the voice responded on the third ring.

'Jim. It's Tom. Are you OK to speak or are you hitting golf balls this morning?'

'Not today. Bit stiff. How's it going? Are we still OK for lunch?'

'I'm not sure we'll feel like eating, to be honest. The bank turned us down. Big problem.'

'Jesus, that's a disaster. If he cannae meet the payroll, well ...'

' ... Yes. Look, Jim, I need some more information. I can't tell you why, but I need to track down that Lizzie person urgently. Is there anything else you can think of?'

'Lizzie? Well, as I said, she left us years ago. After Miriam found out about her dalliance with Lionel, she couldnae stay on. It just got embarrassing for both her and Miriam. She'd be mid-thirties now, I suppose. Let me think. The HR department should have more on her. Why not get it from them?'

'Well, it's rather sensitive.'

'Ah. Yes, OK. Look, give me half an hour. I'm still a director, so Margaret in HR will give us the information. We've worked together for years. Leave it with me.'

And Tom did. He popped out for a coffee, choosing to sit outside by the church to get some air. There was nothing he could do unless either Tara or Jim came up with something.

About an hour later, he was sitting back in the conference room when an email came in from Cameron's personal account. He had forwarded a message with Lizzie's details appended, along with a picture taken for her ID card.

Tom examined the information carefully and forwarded it to Tara straight away. Then he saw something which puzzled him. He rang Jim immediately.

'Hi Tom. You're on a mission today! Am I still going to get my lunch? A man's gotta eat.'

Tom laughed. 'Yes, indeed. But look, it says here she started in the company as Lizzie Honeywell, but later changed it to Lizzie Stack. Did she get married or something? It doesn't say.'

'I noticed that. As I recall, her parents split that year, and she changed her name to her mother's maiden name. Does that help?'

'Well, it might, and you've included her new employer too. Thanks for your help. I'll see you shortly.'

'No problem. Look, this is obviously something confidential you're dealing with, but if you tell me more, I might be able to help you. No pressure, though.'

'Thanks. Maybe when this is all over.'

With that he concluded the call and rang Tara immediately.

'Tara, I've got you looking for the wrong girl. I forwarded an email a few minutes ago.'

'Of course. With a new employer and her date of birth it was a doddle.'

'What? You've already found her?'

'Yes. If her LinkedIn profile is up to date, she's working as marketing director for a small hotel chain based in Southwold. From her Facebook profile, she's got a partner but isn't married. She's on Twitter, too. A doddle when you gave me the right name. Oh, and she's registered as a director on Companies House, too, with a home address. I've copied and pasted the stuff into an email which I'll send you now.'

Sure enough, the email that came through gave him the detail needed. Then he tried a simple google search which found her immediately. He was comparing the picture on the website when Peter Hodson came in with a draft letter he planned to send in the morning.

'Any joy?' he asked.

Tom turned the laptop around and pointed at the picture. 'Is this your Lizzie Honeywell, then? It looks like her from the picture Jim Cameron gave me. Look.'

Hodson looked intently at both pictures. He put his face close to the screen.

'That's her. If you look closely, she has a mole on her neck in both pictures. She's aged a bit, of course, and the hair is different, but that's her. How on earth did you find her?'

'Tara came up trumps when we got her name right. She changed her surname.'

'Thank God. I suppose the question is, what do we ... I mean I ... do now?'

Tom hadn't thought that through, of course. But it looked a fairly small group from the website, so a simple telephone call might be all it took. If he was prepared to make it.

Hodson was still looking at the picture. 'I just don't know what to do for the best.'

'Frankly, neither do I. It's a gamble and a deeply personal matter.'

'Yes. I'm going to have to ring her. At least you found her for me. Thank you both for that.'

Tom offered an opinion. 'I'm not convinced that you have a problem with her. There is no evidence that she and Lionel are in any form of contact. I think he's bluffing because he's desperate. If Lionel's going to blackmail you, she will either duck the call, or else tell you straight.'

Hodson wrote down the number and hesitated. Tom collected up his papers to leave, but Hodson motioned to him to stay. 'Let's get it done. As you say we'll know what we're up against, and you can at least be a witness if she tries to blackmail me. Are you OK with that?'

Tom nodded. 'Blackmail is a criminal offence. I'll record the call if you like.'

Hodson dialled, while Tom hit record on his mobile, and placed it next to the speaker.

'Randle Hotels Group,' a friendly, professional-sounding voice intoned.

'Good afternoon, my name is Peter Hodson. Could I speak with Lizzie Stack please?'

'Let me try her number for you. Which company are you with, please?'

'No company, I'm an old friend looking her up.'

'Oh, I see, Mr Hodson. I can see that she's on the telephone right now, but if I can take a number, I'll get her to ring you back when she's finished.'

Hodson hesitated, but then gave her his mobile number and rang off. He looked at Tom.

'We'll see if she rings back. If get a call from Lionel, we'll know the truth.'

'I guess. I'll give it ten minutes, but then I must leave you to it. Is that the letter you brought in?'

Hodson handed over the letter that he'd drafted to go to Lionel in the morning. It was a typically blunt bank letter, with quite a number of 'the bank requires' in it. The upshot was that payments would no longer be honoured, and that the overdraft facility was withdrawn with immediate effect. The only olive branch was that Lionel could provide additional security for the debt such as to minimise the bank's exposure, but he only had three business days in which to do it.

Tom was pondering how Lionel might react when Peter's mobile rang.

He answered it, and hit the intercom button. 'Good afternoon, Peter Hodson.'

'Hi, Peter. It's Lizzie Stack here. How are you? It's been a long time since we last spoke, hasn't it?'

She sounded genuinely pleased that Peter had called, thought Tom.

Peter kept it light. 'I'm good, Lizzie. You've moved on and up I see. Marketing director now. Congratulations.'

'Yes. Took me a while. I didn't have any experience of the industry until I joined Pemrose, so I had an awful lot to learn. Are you still at the bank?'

'Oh, yes. Retiring soon, I hope. Kids are at university now. Empty nest.'

'I'm not far away from you down here, but I don't really get up your way at all.'

'Oh, nothing changes here, Lizzie. Seen much of Lionel at all?'

Tom winced at the question.

Lizzie pondered before replying. 'Oh, no. It must be five years since I bumped into him at a conference. Give him my regards, will you?'

'I will,' said Peter, smiling at Tom.

Lizzie continued, 'So, what can I do for you, Peter? I'm due in another meeting in a few minutes, but happy to help you if I can.'

Hodson hesitated. 'Well, look Lizzie, this is all pretty awkward. I just wanted to apologise about Malaga. I behaved shamefully. I'm so sorry. I've never had the opportunity to say it to you.'

There was a momentary silence. 'Well, it was a long time ago, Peter, and I was just as much to blame. After all, I knew you were married, and I made the first move. Don't worry about it. We were both adults. I did a lot of things I regretted at Pemrose. I'm a big girl now, and I don't look back. Lionel taught me that if nothing else.'

'Yes. I still feel guilty, though.'

Lizzie sensed something more. 'But why raise it now? Has something happened?'

Hodson had been put on the spot. 'Well, it's just that Lionel keeps saying to me "Lizzie sends her love", and I wasn't sure whether he was in touch with you. Seemed a funny thing to say. He's said it several times now.'

Lizzie laughed. 'Oh, he doesn't change, does he, old Lionel? Is he in a tight spot then? Only we were offered that crap building in London where he's building his casino, and he paid way over the odds.'

'Well, I can't really comment, you know how it is.'

There was a pause, and it was clear that Lizzie was weighing her words.

'Yes, I do. I know exactly how it is with Lionel. Look, I'll admit he asked me to seduce you at the time. He figured that having a hold on you was going to be useful to him. It's me who should apologise to you. I behaved like a cheap hooker, so I bear full responsibility.'

* * *

The people carrier pulled up at the front of the pier, and the nurse got out. She eased Cyril out of the large side-door, while Janet unfolded the wheelchair. He gasped a little as they manoeuvred him and wrapped a blanket around his midriff. He looked desperately thin, Janet thought, but the old man beamed as she kissed him on the cheek.

They wheeled him down the pier, avoiding the Punch and Judy stand which sat forlornly under its dark tarpaulin. Cyril waved to one or two locals and noted that little had changed. Generations of children had bought crab nets and were casting their lines optimistically over the side of the pier, hoping that the little creatures would have a nibble on the bait. The latest cohort was having a fine old time in the sunshine.

Janet was relieved that at least the weather had obliged, and it was pleasantly warm for the old man as they trundled his wheelchair down the boardwalk. In the end, the GP had simply shrugged and said that an afternoon at the theatre might be good for him. He would probably only last until the interval, by which time his medication would be wearing off, and in any event he usually had an afternoon nap.

As they entered the bar, Debbie came across and hugged him and the staff applauded as they wheeled him in. They'd timed it so that the rest of the audience were in, so Cyril was wheeled in last.

Cyril smiled and sat back contentedly. He was home, at least for this afternoon.

As Janet sat beside him, he whispered to her, 'Now let's be realistic about this. I can only really do the first half, I'm afraid, and much as I'd like to see the rest and meet the cast afterwards, it's not going to be possible, so please give them all my love.'

Janet nodded and the house lights dimmed as the stage lights came up and the overture started.

Backstage the dancers were ready, with Amy sandwiched between them and Hannah by her side. The dresses were identical, a tactical ploy by Karen in case something went wrong. Karen stood in the wings. She was always nervous at the time of the first pre-show. In theory, she could stop the show for technical reasons, since the ticketholders accepted that this was a pre-show. In reality, she never had and had no intention of starting now. But this was the first moment of truth for Amy.

Amy felt fear rear up in her stomach. She focused on what Cyril, Lauren and so many others had told her. The audience is your friend, remember that. But this was the moment, and she felt scared. What song was it again? What on earth was the first line? Panic welled up, and her flight instinct grew with it.

When the moment came, the two dancers in front stormed on stage, but Amy momentarily hesitated. She felt a hand on her shoulder, and Hannah behind her, her voice nearly drowned by the overture.

'Don't you bloody dare,' she said.

With that, she gave Amy a gentle push, and they joined the others onstage. Once she started singing, Amy powered through the opening number with the dancers providing the harmonies. The lights flashed in time, and as they hit the final note the audience roared their appreciation.

Amy moved to stage front, where Cyril was applauding warmly. She bowed, smiled and tossed a red carnation to him, then blew him a kiss. Janet caught the flower and put it in his buttonhole.

Towards the end of the first half, Lech appeared, holding something under a black cloak.

'Ladies and gentlemen, we are privileged to have with us today what we in the trade call theatre royalty. He was an icon of his era, winning the BBC smash hit show *Talent Spotters* and appearing on the Royal Variety show. He is our very own Mr ... Cyril ... Brown!'

The spotlight was on Cyril, and local audience members who knew him stood to applaud, causing others to stand, too. Cyril waved and smiled cheerfully.

'But Cyril was one half of a wonderful double-act, and his better half hasn't spoken for over 20 years. But, today ... that better half will have his say. Ladies and gentlemen, I give you the one and only Felix the monkey!'

With that, he removed the cloak and Felix was there, looking up at him as the audience applauded.

'Don't you lot look funny?' said Felix, Lech manipulating his mouth.

'Look, Felix, these people didn't pay good money to be insulted!' said Lech.

'What? They paid to watch this rubbish? Amazing. Hey, look at that woman in the front row. My word she's ugly.'

'Felix! That's not nice. Now I want you to apologise right away!'

'All right, all right, Mr Lech. Look, madam, I'm sorry you're ugly ... OK?'

'Personally, I think she's a bit of all right. You speak for yourself!'

'I wish I could, but in case you haven't noticed I'm just a dummy with your hand up me bum.'

'Did you make Cyril Brown look as stupid as you're doing with me?'

'He never needed my help with that, and nothing changes.'

The gags were a bit feeble, but there were plenty of them and Cyril laughed along, his eyes drawn to his dear friend Felix, who had found his voice once again. The tears were never far away as he thought back to his own performances on this very stage. He'd started as a young comedian, before acquiring Felix for the princely sum of four pounds and ten shillings. He learned the ventriloquist's skill at a stage school in London, courtesy of a veteran of the art. It had taken months to get it right, and it was Jack Wells who had let him add Felix to the bill at the end of one season. It was an instant hit with the audience, so it was here that it had all begun.

He was drawn back to the present by Felix's voice chirping once again. A stagehand had handed Lech a fake message.

'I've just had message for a Mr Cyril Brown,' said Felix.

'Is there a Cyril Brown in the audience?' asked Lech.

Cyril smiled and raised his hand.

Felix seemed to be staring. 'Ah, Mr Brown. Message from HM Revenue and Customs. Apparently, you tried to register me as your spouse for tax purposes. Now, I'm not saying he's tight ladies and gentlemen, but have I had so much as an engagement ring? No, I have not. Now I've got news for you, sunshine, if you think I'm washing your undies you've got another thing coming.'

Lech interjected smoothly. 'It sounds like you're already married, Felix. Now maybe we should sing a song for this lovely audience?'

'Do I have a choice with your hand up my bum?'

'Probably not. Now, Felix, what did you and Cyril close your act with then?'

'We never got that far, mate. The audience were asking for their money back by then.'

'Maybe we'll quit while we're ahead, then. Ladies and gentlemen, singing her latest single, the fabulous Amy Raven!'

With that, they exited stage right. Amy was in the wings stage left, waiting to go on. She seemed icy calm, but Hannah and Karen were immediately behind her, in case she faltered. She did not.

As expected, Cyril left at the interval, visibly tired. He kissed Janet on the cheek as they exited into the sunshine.

'A wonderful show, Janet. Thank them all so much for me. Sorry I can't stay for the second half. Past my bedtime, I think. Oh, and thank Lech for his sketch with Felix. It was very, very special.'

With that, they trundled down the boardwalk together, Cyril smiling to locals and holidaymakers alike. By the time he reached the car, he was dozing but the two carers managed to get him back into the people carrier for the return journey.

Janet wiped away a tear at the realisation that it was unlikely that Cyril would ever see the pier and his beloved theatre again.

13.

Friday

Lionel was sitting in his office at the Majestic when Peter Hodson rang him with the news. As soon as Lionel answered, however, he clicked the Send button on the email containing the letter spelling out the bank's position.

'I'm sorry to be the bearer of such bad news, Lionel. The funding committee won't buy it, I'm afraid. The casino administration and the situation at Brewster's have eroded their confidence in the business. There's nothing I can do now, other than send you the letter of confirmation, which I've just forwarded by email.'

There was a silence as Lionel tried to frame a response. 'Well, that's obviously most disappointing for my employees who won't get paid and will most probably be out of work soon.'

'Of course, I'm really sorry. But you can of course put in the extra funds yourself to meet the payroll or offer us a charge on personal assets. You can bring forward further proposals at any time.'

'Well, time was when an area manager's word was his bond, Peter, but obviously not anymore.'

'I'm sorry that you take that view. I have sought to find a solution, hence I brought in Tom Stanley who is a turnaround specialist. I'm sure that he would still be prepared to lend a hand should you need it, given Jim Cameron's untimely departure.'

'Well, thank you for your advice. I may just walk away entirely. After all, your loss in administration now will be significantly higher than if your funding committee had showed some bottle. I'm in touch with a number of interested parties. I'm sure even Lizzie will have a view.'

So, there it was, in a single contrived and nakedly threatening sentence. Peter decided that it was time to take that card away from his hand once and for all.

'Well, good luck with that. I'm open to further discussions right up until Tuesday evening's deadline. It's interesting you mentioned Lizzie. I spoke with her yesterday as a matter of fact. She asked to be remembered to you. Marketing director of a hotel group now. You must be so immensely proud.'

The silence at the end of the line made it clear that his message was very much received. He only hoped that a vindictive Lionel had no further mud to sling.

'Yes, well, I'm glad she's progressed. It's just such a pity that this decision will blight a few people's careers. I'm sure the bank's reputation will suffer when our local businesspeople learn that it won't support a business with a strong track record, but no matter. I'll let you know my course of action.'

'Of course, Lionel. I'll await your response.'

With that he put down the phone and looked across the table at a smiling Tom Stanley.

'Well, that went well, Peter. You'll be drummed out of the Rotary and blackballed at the golf club for this.'

Peter responded rather indignantly. 'The bloody cheek of the man. Somehow none of this is his bad management. Of all the nerve. So, what do you think he'll do, then? Let it go under or find some cash to keep it going?'

Tom toyed with his Mont Blanc pen as he thought about it.

'I think he's too proud to let it go under. No, I think he'll find some cash to meet the payroll, but how he gets the overdraft, I've no idea. He won't put his place in Malaga on the line, and Miriam won't let him sign a charge over the hotels.'

Tom packed his briefcase ready to leave, and Peter stood too.

'We'll see, then. My thanks for your work and Tara's, too. Are you heading back to London?'

'No, I'm spending the weekend here. I'm going to see the show. Guest of Janet Wells. Then I might do a spot of walking this weekend; the weather's looking good.'

'The Summertime Special show with Janet Wells. Well, I'm afraid that Mrs Wells and I, er ...'

'Yes, well, I didn't get the impression you were the best of pals with her when I mentioned your name.'

'No. Probably not. Look, it would be useful if you could stay until next Wednesday to see how this plays out. We'll pick up the hotel bill if Lionel kicks off. Have a break on us and come in on Wednesday for a chat?'

'Well yes, OK then, I'll do that, provided Lionel doesn't evict me.'

*   *   *

Graham Blakeley walked into Cromer Police Station and rang the desk bell. A familiar face greeted him.

'Hello, Graham, how's retirement, mate? The weather's been good for that allotment of yours.'

'Indeed, it has. I've an appointment. Has DI Brent arrived yet?'

'Yes, he arrived a while back. Let me see if he's available.'

The desk sergeant headed back into the office behind

reception, and presently DI Brent came out to meet him. It felt strange signing in and going back into the interview room in which he'd spent so much time.

Brent took out a file and a ballpoint pen. He read a few notes, and then wrote the date on an A4 pad before continuing.

'Well, first of all good work with that DVD, Graham. It had several fingerprints on it, although we can't match them as Mr Castle has no criminal record, and we don't have Mrs Castle's prints for elimination. But doubtless they'll be helpful when we do track him down.'

'I didn't think he had a criminal record. Hannah didn't know of one.'

'Kent Police have visited the house once again, but he's nowhere to be seen. It's in a very private close but neighbours haven't seen him, and there's no car on the drive either.'

'He's done a runner, then.'

'We've drawn a blank on the vehicle registration you supplied, too. Nothing's tripped the cameras, so if he has a car, it's a hired one. He could have come up by train, I guess, but it's a bit remote here, and we've asked around local car hire places. Nothing doing.'

'Probably hired in Kent.'

'Yes. But we're still really short of hard evidence against him. The act of dumping his wife's clothes is only a civil matter, as is selling her home from under her. Nasty and plainly vindictive, but not coercive control as such; they could just be signs of an acrimonious divorce.'

'Well, yes, but you do have a statement from Lech, the guy from the theatre, about Castle's aggressive behaviour towards both him and Mrs Castle on the pier. That's independent corroboration of what was actually a physical assault.'

'Yes, I agree that is helpful. But I think the thing that tips the scales is the ribbon on the DVD, and its positioning. The ribbon is clearly new, whereas the DVD is in an old, cracked case. A clear sign that the ribbon is a definite threat. Shame she didn't take a picture of the pile it was on.'

'She was dumbstruck at the time. Who wouldn't be, coming home to that? She's still scared stiff. I took her down to the pier for the show yesterday, and it looks like I'll have to do that indefinitely, unless or until you arrest him, of course.'

'Look, I know this is really difficult for her as the victim. I hope PC Edwards' visit reassured her that we are taking the matter seriously.'

'Have you viewed the DVD?'

'Yes. With PC Edwards. It's what Mrs Castle said it was. Apparently completely consensual. Nothing perverted as such, and of course taken with her consent, by her own admission. Not helpful in that sense, but the positioning and the ribbon do constitute clear threats.'

'And he knows where she is going to be and at what time every single day. From a personal security point of view, I'm genuinely concerned for her safety. I said that in my statement.'

'Yes, you did.'

DI Brent looked at the file again, then at Graham. 'Well, I've spoken to the specialist domestic violence unit we have in Norwich, and they agree that we need to find our Mr Castle as soon as we can. They've filed a warrant to enter the house, by force if required, to search the place. They will also meet his employers to see if Mr Castle is really on holiday, or if there's something more behind it.'

'Good. That will reassure Hannah a great deal.'

'You never know what we'll find in a search, do you? A

bloke who wants to take videos of his wife might have other stuff on his computer, too.'

Graham nodded. 'Yep. We've seen that before a few times, haven't we?'

* * *

Lionel was reading a letter from a company called Latchmores. They had approached him the previous year, but at that time he hadn't been interested. He had no idea who they represented at the time, other than they were a larger group in the same line of business. A few months ago, recognising that there was a growing problem with the business, Lionel had been lining up a Plan B. He'd arranged some visits to group locations, ostensibly with the clients acting as property surveyors. Latchmores said that their client was interested and would come back to him.

The letter was marked in capitals 'subject to contract', and it contained an offer to buy Pemrose Entertainments Limited. Had they offered back then what they were offering now, he would have turned it down. But in his current predicament it seemed to be a very decent offer. If his sums were correct, the bank would still take a hit, but much less of a nosebleed than in a forced sale through an administrator.

But to go down this route he needed to find the cash to meet the payroll due on Monday. If Jim's figures were correct, then the business would then more than pay its way through the peak season. At one time it would have been easy, he'd just have lent the business the money. But after a hideously expensive divorce and his rather lavish expenditure on Freya, it wasn't that simple. And it was also a real risk.

What if he put the money in now and the bank still pulled the overdraft? Suppose the sale fell through subsequently? If that happened, he'd have poured in good money after bad. But could he really bring himself to let the first-ever business that he'd created go under? For all his faults, Lionel still cared for his people.

Take Debbie, for example. Now the bar manager in the theatre bar, who had joined him straight from school. Could he look her in the eye when she didn't get paid and lost her job? In spite of his love of Malaga, Cromer was still his home, even though it now only consisted of the penthouse above the Majestic. Then, of course, there was his position in the community to consider. He had always been the big shot in the town. Pemrose sponsored any number of things, and he was the go-to guy when you wanted something done.

He really needed to talk this out with someone, but his choices were limited with Jim Cameron gone. He didn't want to worry Tyler. He was doing a fine job in the hotels chain and had already been unsettled by Jim's departure. The logical choice might be Tom Stanley, still a resident at the Majestic, but whose side was he on? He could go to Cameron, of course, but the words he'd said that morning were harsh and unfair, and he'd have to reveal his Plan B, which was a further deception.

He found himself thinking back to the good old days when the group was so much smaller, and it was a family business run by himself and his wife, with Jim always keeping things right in the engine room. He looked at the decor in the penthouse around him. He recalled the work that Miriam had done in this very room. He saw two stylish fifties chairs she'd spotted during a furniture hunt that spring. Where was that antique-come bric-à-brac place that they'd got them from? Miriam would remember both that and the price they'd paid, too.

The affairs had just been the result of opportunity. Too much alcohol and too many solo nights away from home. Some were after his money, like Freya; others, like Lizzie, were bright young things using him as a stepping stone. Not that he blamed them. Both had got what they wanted from the rather tawdry deal. His attempt to use her name to blackmail Hodson was a pretty crude bluff, and, with hindsight, a mistake.

The affair with Lizzie had been the final straw for Miriam, as was his deception over the pier project, a concept to transform it into a larger entertainment complex. Tom had made a random comment recently which had stuck with Lionel.

'In my experience, it's much better to build friendships for the future than focus on old enemies from the past.'

He came to a decision and picked up the telephone, dialling a number that still he had on speed dial.

*   *   *

Tom was just about to leave for the theatre. He was dressed casually for a balmy early summer's evening when it gets dark around 10pm and it's still warm. He felt very relaxed. His assignment was over for the moment and there was nothing further he could do.

He'd acted rather spontaneously earlier, unusually for a person given to meticulous evaluation. His ability to prevaricate had driven Maggie to distraction.

He'd found himself looking at property in a local estate agent's window. Houses weren't cheap, but compared to London they seemed so. He rather despaired of the pitiful returns that his investments achieved these days, and had thought about a buy-to-let. But he didn't want the hassle of tenants or paying the high service charges that agents might demand.

He liked the idea of a place by the sea, and this looked very much cheaper than Kent, where he and Maggie had looked previously. There weren't great commutable options from Cromer to London he thought, not that that was going to be a problem to him. If he'd learned anything of late, it was that an office could be anywhere.

He'd picked up a few details in one estate agent's and then, not being in any hurry for once, had decided to do a trawl of the others. Returning to the hotel, he decided to view four properties over the weekend, just to get a feel for the market. He was quite undecided whether he'd run it as a holiday let, or just rent it to close friends, or just let it appreciate in value over time. Maggie would have laughed, he knew. Talk about spontaneous decisiveness!

As he walked down to the pier, he could sense the season coming alive. Lots of families were enjoying the warm evening sunshine and the aroma of fish and chips hung in the air. There would be no discussion tonight of Pemrose Entertainments, who owned the very pier he was now walking on.

Every staff member wore a polo shirt bearing the Pemrose crest, blissfully unaware that they might not get paid on Monday. Tom chided himself for having failed to convince the bank to keep the faith, but his practical side told him that he'd done everything he could.

As he reached the bar and went inside, he couldn't see Janet, so he queued up for a beer in what was becoming a quite crowded bar. As he ordered, he spotted the black-clad theatre owner coming through from the auditorium and waved.

She smiled, and he gestured to offer her a drink.

'Gin and tonic,' she mouthed, and he handed over his card to the woman behind the bar. There was no sign of Debbie tonight and, in the circumstances, he was happy that there wasn't. He'd never been comfortable keeping bad news from people. Pushing through the throng, he reached Janet, handed over her drink and, to his surprise, found himself giving her a peck on the cheek.

'Good evening, Janet. You've certainly sold some tickets tonight.'

'Good evening to you, Tom. Yes, we're sold out for the next three weeks. Young Amy is quite a draw.'

They moved into a corner, and Janet removed a reserved sign from a small table in a tight little nook.

'Perk of the job,' she said as they sat down.

'Has it gone OK thus far? The show, I mean' he asked.

'Yes. No cock-ups so far, or at least none that the audience would notice.'

'But *you* would, no doubt.'

She laughed. 'Not so much these days. It's Karen who spots the fine details.'

'I wonder where she gets that from?' he replied mischievously.

He sipped his beer with satisfaction.

She continued the small talk. 'So, you're staying the weekend, then?'

'Yes, actually until Wednesday now. Some loose ends to tie up.'

'So, what are you planning to do? You have a whole weekend to explore the gem that is the Norfolk coast.'

'Well, actually, I'm planning to do some viewings; I'm thinking of buying a holiday place here. Just looking to see what's about.'

'Really? Well, that does sounds like fun,' she said.

'Does it? Well, I guess it could be. Maggie would have been all over it.'

'I'll bet she would. Personally, I enjoy looking at houses and spending other people's money. Particularly a Yorkshireman's.'

She laughed, and he found himself looking at her reprovingly.

'Really? Then for your cheek you can come too. If you'd like to, that is?'

She thought for a moment. 'You know what, that does sound like fun. I do know the area and you don't. It would have to be Sunday, though. I'm busy here tomorrow.'

He was rather taken back. It appeared that, without intending to, he'd asked a woman out.

'Well, that would be great. I've not booked any viewings yet, so I can arrange them for Sunday. Three of them are with the same agent.'

'Well, that's fine. Yes. You know, thinking about it, I don't get out to see the local area all that much considering I live here,' she replied.

'Good. Actually, would you like to join me for breakfast to see what I've picked? Or is that enemy territory?'

Janet nodded. 'Oh, that would be fine. Miriam still part-owns it, so we do meet there from time to time.'

'Good. 9.30am OK?'

'Yes. Right, that's fine. Let's go in, we'll be ahead of the crowd.'

14.

Saturday

Lionel walked to his Jaguar in it's reserved space behind the Majestic. The staff had cleaned it yesterday, as they did pretty much every week. Bright red with cream upholstery, it bore personal number plates, of course. He'd had it a long time, and she was getting older now, but Lionel loved the old-style Jaguar. The new ones just didn't have the sheer class of the older models, and it meant that he always stood out from the crowd.

But this morning was not a good morning for him. It involved delicate negotiations with an adversary who knew him better than anyone. But there could be no bullshit, and no hidden agendas. This person could see right through him.

He eased the Jaguar out of its space and cruised along the seafront, then through the town towards Overstrand. Without knowing it, he passed the gates of Lauren and Les' home, and then pulled into another driveway somewhat closer to the sea. It was built originally in the fifties, and retained many of its original features, but it had been extensively extended on the coastal side.

He got out and almost walked straight in through the front door through force of habit but remembered to ring the doorbell just in time. A few moments later the door opened.

'Lionel. Good morning. Come on in,' said Miriam, politely if slightly overly formally. There were no hugs or polite pecks on the cheek as she escorted him through to a sun lounge at the back. Its bi-fold doors opened wide on to the expanse of lawn and the well-maintained hedge, beyond which was the sea, somewhat hazy that morning.

Lionel nearly sat in what had been his favourite chair, but thought better of it, and elected to sit on the settee instead.

'Coffee?' Miriam asked politely, before disappearing into the kitchen.

Lionel looked further around the far side of the house, and saw the new glass annexe, with its smart grey UPVC frames and the swimming pool within. He knew that she'd had it done, but hadn't seen it, not having visited for some years.

Miriam returned with a cafetière of coffee and poured it into a tasteful china mug. Lionel took a sip as she sat down opposite him.

'Now then, Lionel, to business,' she said briskly. 'From the tone of your call the other day, the departure of Jim Cameron and the shenanigans of the Grim Reaper Mr Stanley, I'd venture to suggest you're in a bit of a pickle. Would I be correct? A simple yes or no will do, none of your usual bullshit. I know you too well.'

Lionel stopped, his cup halfway to his mouth. He set the mug down and smiled.

'Then I think yes is the only possible answer, but I'm sure that …'

Miriam raised the palm of her side and stared at him. ' … Hold the sales pitch right there, Lionel. I want to say something first.'

Lionel shrugged and sat back, gesturing her to continue.

Miriam began, 'That's fine. Now, I'm going to say here and now that if you've come to ask for cross-guarantees from the hotels group to prop up your entertainments company, nothing doing. I'll also make it clear that I am sick to death of the petty backbiting about me behind my back, and your lack of transparency in matters which affect me. I'm also disgusted at your treatment of a loyal employee like Jim Cameron, someone without whom I strongly doubt there would have been a Pemrose Group at all. Now I want to know once and for all where things stand, and what you want of me.'

Lionel was minded to fire some shots back, but instead calmly went through the position, and handed over a copy of the Stanley report to the bank, the letter from Hodson and the email containing the Latchmores offer.

Miriam took the documents and briefly read them as Lionel outlined the contents of each one. This was a Lionel stripped bare of the usual facade, and rather more like the younger Lionel from the early days of their marriage, she thought. He freely admitted that the casino project had been a disaster, and that Brewster had mugged him. Most unusually, he didn't seek to blame anyone else, indeed he acknowledged that Cameron had opposed both projects.

'Well, thank you, Lionel. At least you've given me the unvarnished truth for once. So, what are the options? I gather that you need to respond to Hodson by Tuesday.'

Lionel spoke again, calmly and factually. 'Well, unless I can meet the payroll, the whole thing goes into receivership on Tuesday. Without the bank facility, I'll have to do that, because I'd be trading while insolvent if I didn't.'

'Right. So, none of the staff would get paid, including those in the arcades and on the pier?'

'That's the case, sadly, yes. Many of them will probably be let go to get the cost base down while the receiver flogs it off, probably for a much lower figure than Latchmores would pay for a going concern.'

'An offer which the bank might find attractive?' Miriam asked.

'Yes, but they won't meet the payroll. You can see that from their letter. The bank's funding committee rejected Tom Stanley's recommendations.'

'Then fund it yourself. Why ever not?' she said, rather dismissively.

'Because even if I do that and the bank play ball, the proceeds of the Latchmores sale won't cover the losses we've already made, and although the streamlined business should make money in future, they've lost confidence and I lose the money I put in to meet the payroll too. In administration the bank calls the shots as the biggest creditor of the business.'

'But no impact on the hotels group?'

'No. It's a separate facility. We're trading profitably and meeting the banking covenants.'

'Then what do you want from me?'

Lionel looked at her and smiled.

'Absolutely nothing, Mim. I simply thought that I owed it to you to tell you the situation face-to-face, and that I'm likely to call in the administrators early next week. I'm afraid that there will be some adverse publicity and reputational damage, and I've no control over what the administrator does. For all I know he might shut the pier, for example. It doesn't make much money as you know, and it does need some maintenance work which they certainly won't pay for.'

There was silence, save for an antique clock which ticked

away, as if counting down to judgement day. Lionel sipped his coffee. She shook her head as the full impact of the news sank in.

'Many of our long-servicing people will suffer badly. Some of them have been with us since the start.'

'Yes, I know, love, although the new owners will keep some of them on, of course, and we might find some others work in the hotels if needs be,' he said.

'Yes. Good thinking. What's your Plan B, Lionel? You always have one.'

'Well, unless we did a cross-guarantee involving the hotels, then I don't have one, and you are right to refuse that. Neither of us should be taking too many chances at our age.'

'Unless it involves buying a chain of bookmakers and a casino of course,' she said sharply.

Lionel smiled thinly. 'Point taken. Frankly, I'm just really tired, and although I hate the impact on the staff, I've decided that I'd rather get rid of entertainments, let Tyler run the hotels and semi-retire, I think.'

It was the first time that Lionel had ever mentioned the 'R' word. This was a different Lionel, but Miriam needed some time to think. After all, he could be laying a trap for her. Was he trying to con her into putting the hotels up as security? If so, he was deluding himself. But she didn't want to see the business that they'd had since the early days go under. Her own reputation mattered.

'All right. I think I understand the picture clearly now, so now I'll think things over. I'll ring you tomorrow morning. Payday is Monday, but one day later won't matter too much,' she said.

'No. That's fine.'

He got up and looked across to the pool house. 'That looks nice. Very stylish, as always.'

'Yes. I like it. I try to swim most days, so it's very handy.'

They walked to the front door.

She spoke one more. 'How's your golf?'

'Not great. Difficult to focus on it right now. My putting's a bloody disaster.'

She laughed as she opened the door. 'Let's face it, Lionel, your putting's always been a bloody disaster. Remember that pairs tournament at Hunstanton? I left you a three-footer for the cup, and you missed.'

Lionel nodded and smiled. 'Yes. I do recall. Well, thanks for hearing me out. I'm sorry to spring this on you, I really am.'

'Well, thanks for telling me face-to-face, and sharing the documents. If I want to speak with Tom Stanley or Peter Hodson, I assume that you wouldn't object.'

Lionel shook his head. 'Not at all. Tom is still staying at the Majestic. I'll text his mobile number to you.'

'OK, thanks. I found him to be quite down-to-earth and practical. He didn't give your game away, mind.'

'Yes. He's from Yorkshire; he tends to tell it like it is.'

'OK. Why don't you go and get some rest? You look knackered.'

She reached out and kissed him on the cheek. He smiled and waved to her as he got in the Jaguar.

She shut the door and went back through to the lounge. She decided that she needed advice, so she rang Jim Cameron, and he agreed to get hold of Tom Stanley. They agreed to meet at 6.30pm, with or without him there. Time was clearly of the essence.

Lionel whistled contentedly as he drove back towards the Majestic. Miriam hadn't kissed him in years. She was obviously convinced by his display of sincerity. Interesting.

* * *

PC Carla Edwards arrived at Hannah's temporary serviced apartment at around 10am. Hannah was coping, just about, and being in the show gave her both an escape from reality and hope for the future.

She'd asked Graham to come along, too. His work with the police seemed to have ratcheted the investigation up somewhat. Hannah showed Carla through to her small sitting room, where Graham was already sitting. Edwards took out a file from her briefcase and looked again at the notes.

'Hannah, firstly let me give you an update of the latest developments in your complaint, then perhaps we can discuss next steps?'

'Yes. That's fine,' responded Hannah.

'Well, following the conversation with Graham, we obtained a search warrant for your property in Kent. Two officers visited, but found nobody at home, and no car was visible on the drive. Surprisingly, in view of his previous behaviour, the key you supplied still worked, and they cancelled the alarm without difficulty. We conducted a brief initial search, and it seemed that all was fine. The place was clean and tidy, but it appeared that the house had not been recently inhabited.'

'Well, at least that's something,' said Hannah.

'They did a brief search of each room. Nothing too invasive, but looking for any sign of things which might be unusual. Nothing seemed untoward, but when we reached the upstairs study, we did find two further unmarked DVDs, so these were bagged and taken away as evidence. Then we tried to access the hard drive of a desktop computer, but found it encrypted. We removed that for further analysis.'

'That's his work computer,' said Hannah. 'The bank might help with that.'

'I'll come on to that. We found no passports or driving licences anywhere. The officers secured the premises and confirmed that the garage was empty. They then spoke to neighbours who confirmed that to their knowledge there hadn't been any comings or goings of late.'

'I see.'

Carla continued, 'Kent Police then reviewed the items collected, including bypassing the limited encryption on the hard drive. The DVDs contained two videos of you and Mr Castle, and I think you know the rest concerning those items, so I'll leave that there.'

'Thank you.'

'No evidence of any further copying?' said Graham.

'No. Not that was visible in the search. They only checked the obvious places, of course.'

'Yes, of course.'

Carla Edwards then looked at Hannah and spoke slowly and carefully.

'It's the hard drive that's the difficult bit. Images and videos, not of you I may add, but of concern to child protection investigators.'

'My God,' said Hannah.

Carla put her hand on Hannah's. 'Yes. I know it's tough. Did he use the study often?'

'Well, yes, he worked a lot of evenings. International banking is a 24/7 business, so he was often talking to Singapore or Tokyo at those times.'

Carla hesitated momentarily. 'Except that there were no work files on that computer. In fact, it didn't belong to the bank at all.'

Hannah just stared. Graham put his arm around her. 'Go on, Carla,' he said.

'Well, we then went to Mr Castle's employers, who were obliged to talk to us as part of our live police investigation. Their HR director advised that Mr Castle was suspended several weeks ago, pending investigation of what they called irregular transactions. It also appears that he had failed to report his worsening financial situation, which he is required to do under bank regulations.'

Hannah broke down at this point and put her head on Graham's chest.

'Keep going, let's get it over with,' he said grimly.

'Yes. Let me cut to the chase. As a result of what we've found we have a warrant for your husband's arrest, so that we can interview him, both in respect of your complaint for coercive control, and possible offences involving the material on his computer. We've also sent a forensic team to the house, and they will carry out an intensive search, collecting fingerprint and DNA samples for comparison.'

Hannah recovered her composure. 'So, where does that leave me? As it stands now, I have nowhere to live and I'm appearing every day in a publicly advertised show, so at any time he can show up again. What are you going to do about that?'

'She has a point, Carla. Kent Police will focus on the child protection offences, but Hannah has legitimate safety concerns which must be addressed. I can't be everywhere.'

Carla nodded. 'Yes, we do acknowledge that, so we have local officers actively looking for Mr Castle and have increased our presence on the pier. He is now a very much wanted man, and when he is caught he is likely to serve a significant prison sentence for what he's done.'

Hannah looked up at her sharply. 'Not for what he's done to me, though? Those videos could be on the internet right now. He could have shared them, too. You have no idea how it feels. No idea whatsoever!'

*   *   *

Tom was about to board a boat trip to Blakeney Point when his mobile rang. He'd decided to do some touristy things, having arranged four property viewings for the following day. Fortunately, he could move out of the queue to take the call, although the signal was a bit patchy.

Jim kept it brief, although even then Tom only understood about half of what he was saying. Something about an offer for the business. But the place and time of the meeting were clear, and he agreed to attend. He wondered about confidentiality, but as both Miriam and Jim were directors, he didn't really see a problem, and Peter Hodson had asked him to assist.

But he didn't trust Lionel one bit. There was never complete transparency. However, at least they had finessed the one ace that Lionel had pretended to have in Lizzie, and the bank's position was now in no doubt at all. Tom wondered how much extra rope Hodson had granted Lionel over the years. It had increased the bank's exposure and been highly unprofessional. Ironically, in an era of spreadsheets galore, what had ultimately done for the business was Lionel's recent track record. In the end, business still depended on honesty and trust, which Tom found reassuringly old-school.

He re-joined the queue now boarding the boat on a pleasant Saturday afternoon, and tried to put the meeting out of his mind. He was going to see the seals. He knew that

Maggie would have laughed out loud at the sight of Tom engaging with wildlife, since he was given to switching off the TV whenever anything animal-related came on. She'd have loved this place, he thought. He sat down at the back of the open clinker-built boat, helping a young mother to steady her little girl as they came aboard. They chatted briefly as the boat set off, Tom glad of the simple human engagement that he missed so much.

*   *   *

Lauren and Les drove back from the nursing home in silence, and not because Lauren was protecting her voice. When they had left the nursing home, and got into the car, Lauren had broken down, and Les had held her in his arms as she sobbed.

'He's just wasting away. There's hardly anything left of him.'

'I know, love,' said Les, his own voice cracking with emotion.

'I'm glad we did it, though. Visited him. One last time.'

'A special man, and as lively a wit as ever inside that shell of a body that's giving up on him.'

'Makes my medical stuff look trivial.'

'But you've got your whole life ahead of you, now you've had the all-clear.'

'Seems unfair when you see Cyril in such a state.'

'Nonsense. Cyril's had his life, and I'll bet he wouldn't change a thing, stage fright or not.'

'He seemed pleased to see us, anyway. His smile hasn't changed a bit.'

'And the nursing home staff loved meeting you. Those pictures will be all over Facebook tonight. They don't meet many national treasures.'

'National treasure, my arse. I'm not that flipping old yet, Mr Westley.'

Les laughed as they drove back. 'Showtime this afternoon. Hope Amy's doing OK,' he said.

'I spoke to Janet yesterday, she said it had gone well so far,' she replied.

'Typical of Lech to build Felix into his act at the last minute. He's surprisingly good at throwing his voice. Is there nothing that bloke can't do?'

'You've never fancied being a ventriloquist, then?'

'Me? No fear. I'll stick to stand-up. It's much easier.'

'I wonder if he'll find a woman to saw in half this year. Do you remember that fracas?'

Les laughed. 'Don't remind me. We nearly had a strike on our hands.'

'Well, I was bloody nearly starkers when he came into my dressing room. He did at least knock, I suppose.'

'He saw your tattoo, I gather,' said Les.

'I think he probably saw more than my tattoo, Les.'

'He'd have got fired but for you. The first time you really joined the team. You talked them all down.'

'Well, he was even further from home than I was, and he didn't even speak much English. I felt sorry for him. You were being a total bastard, I recall.'

'Yes, I was. Not only did I have him to worry about, but also a truculent Welsh diva with delusions of grandeur, and the theatre going bust around me.'

'I wasn't that bad really,' Lauren protested.

'Yes, you were. You went AWOL twice, remember? I had hair before I met you.'

'Yeah. I was a right bitch, wasn't I?' she said.

'Yes. But you had a lovely bum.'

'Meaning I don't anymore? Watch your step, Mr Wesley.'

'Your rear is fine by me, Miss Evans, as is your tattoo!'

Cyril meanwhile had nodded off in his chair, still holding the signed picture, and the card in which it was enclosed. Les had taken it the day before at the station, with Lauren sitting on a utilitarian railway bench, smiling to the camera. The card had a handwritten message.

You will bounce back, you know.
The great talents always do.
Well thanks to you I did.
All my love
Lauren xxx

*   *   *

Tom and Jim arrived at Miriam's house at the same time, Tom's hired Ford Focus looking rather understated against Cameron's blue Mercedes soft-top. They shook hands and Jim rang the doorbell.

Miriam opened the door dressed in a red and white top with white jeans, which even Tom, with his untrained eyes, knew were certainly not from Matalan or Primark. Jim hugged her warmly; clearly, they were old friends. Tom shook Miriam's hand rather more formally.

They went out into the sun lounge, and Jim admired two huge art prints which were recent acquisitions. Looking out towards the swimming pool, it was apparent to Tom that this lady had both taste and the funds to indulge it. The divorce had been good to her, he thought. Lionel's fortune was predominantly held within the businesses, one of which was essentially worthless.

They sat down and, and although this might have been seen as a business meeting, Miriam produced a bottle of red wine. As Jim sorted that out, Miriam briefed Tom about her meeting with Lionel, and gave him the opportunity to review the document from Latchmores.

'Have you had any dealing with Latchmores, Tom?' asked Jim, setting down his glass on a nearby coffee table.

'Yes, I have. They're very reputable. No issues there. Were you not aware of this approach, then?'

'No. One of Lionel's Plan Bs. I did have my suspicions, mind. One too many surveyors looking at the sites, and not just asking about the buildings.'

Miriam was vexed. 'Why can he not trust those close to him with the facts? Why the Machiavellian schemes all the time?'

Jim laughed. 'Well, you were married to him, Miriam. If you don't know, why are you asking us?'

Tom read the letter. 'It looks a decent indicative offer. Any idea who the client is?' he asked, ignoring the banter.

'Could be Bailey's. Or Ingram's, perhaps. Both are expanding and have the funds.'

Miriam nodded. 'I'm a bit out of touch these days, but I've certainly heard of them. I'm keen to hear how you think that the bank would respond to this offer. Surely they would have agreed to meet the payroll if they had known that this offer was on the table?'

Tom considered this and jotted some numbers down before responding.

'Well, not necessarily. This doesn't mean that the deal will come off at that figure, if at all, and Hodson has given Lionel far too much rope already. The reference in the letter to their lack of confidence in future viability is basically banking speak for we don't trust the bloke, I'm afraid.'

Jim chipped in. 'I agree with Tom. Lionel's run out of road, and I'm not sure Peter Hodson will be there much longer. He's close to retirement and this hasn't covered him with glory. Even on these figures, the bank won't get out without a loss, so it doesn't change things as much as you might think.'

Miriam shook her head in dismay. 'And the bloody staff get the shitty end of the stick for his stupidity.'

Tom shook his head. 'Well, I think we need to clarify that a little. The staff are preferential creditors, and if the administrator takes them on, they will like as not get their money. They may have to wait a while. The question would be whether the administrator carries on the business as is. There may be some redundancies, but the government would pick up the tab for the redundancy pay if the company can't.'

'Well, I guess that's something. But is there no way that the organisation can be saved from going under? The bits that are left are viable, surely?'

Tom shook his head again. 'Not with this bank. They want their money back as soon as possible. The only way to save it would be to put more money in from somewhere. That's where the cross-guarantee with the hotels group comes in.'

Miriam glared. 'No chance. I've made that clear.'

'As have I,' said Jim.

'Then unless you find a new investor, or you put in fresh investment, administration is the only answer.'

Miriam looked puzzled. 'Then why would I put the money in for the payroll, assuming the staff are at least partially protected?'

Tom shrugged. 'Well, financially you wouldn't. You don't

even have any shares in Pemrose Entertainments, which is good because Lionel's shares are worthless. In saying that, I'm assuming that the casino venture is a complete loss. That wasn't in my review, because Lionel had already put it under.'

'But a sensible assumption, sadly,' said Jim.

Miriam picked up on something. 'Tom, you said that financially you wouldn't get involved. But are there any other reasons?'

Tom nodded slowly. 'Well, only that the business bears the Pemrose name, and although Pemrose Hotels is entirely separate, there may be some reputational impact on that business. It's very manageable, mind. But it's a family business with a family name, and you have to live here. Lionel is very conscious of his reputation in the town, and I guess that you have some skin in that particular game.'

Miriam nodded. 'Yes, I do. So suppose I agreed to put in half of the payroll, and Lionel does the same, what will Mr Hodson do then?'

Jim interjected. 'It doesn't save the business, and arguably you've just thrown good money after bad.'

Tom was more analytical. 'Well, that's right to a point, although I think the bank would allow more time for the sale to go through, and the business would certainly realise more money out of administration than in it. An administrator just wants to flog it off quick and grab the fee. The moment it's in administration, Latchmores' client will cut their offer substantially. At least we can now demonstrate we have interest in buying the group and have shown faith by meeting the payroll.

Miriam nodded. 'OK. But how much of the business will survive? I mean the jobs. Some of the staff have been with us for years.'

Tom considered for a moment. 'Well, any head office jobs will go, and probably almost immediately, but I think most of the arcades will be OK, even the more recent acquisitions down south. Lionel spent a lot of money refurbishing them and getting rid of the asbestos risks, and they seem to be making money now. What do you think, Jim?'

'Yes, I agree. It's been a long journey and the costs were pretty crippling, but they should make money. The only business that they might not want is the pier. If it's Bailey's or Ingram's, that isn't their game and maintaining that Grade II-listed structure would be a real drain. Not worth the risk for the rather pitiful return unless they reheated Lionel's gin palace project of 2009, of course.'

Miriam grimaced. 'Don't remind me. But could the administrator decide to shut the pier? That would be a disaster for the theatre, not to mention the town in general. Without this season's income, we'd go under as well.'

Tom hadn't really thought that aspect through. 'Well, if it's making money, and with the theatre paying the rent it should, then they'll probably keep it open. But that is up to them, and if an unexpected cost cropped up, they could just lock the doors one day. In no circumstances will they take any risks.'

Jim nodded. 'It's a vanity project that has never made sense financially. But we should discuss clause 3c.'

Tom looked puzzled, as did Miriam.

'Clause 3c? I'm sorry, I don't follow,' she said.

'Neither do I,' said Tom.

Jim smiled. He was glad that he'd got hold of a copy a month or two back.

'It's from the original agreement under which Lionel bought the pier, and Jack Wells retained the lease on the theatre. Clause

3c gives Cromer Pier Theatre the right to buy the pier at 10% below market value should it ever been put up for sale.'

Miriam looked somewhat astonished.

Tom laughed. 'Oh, that's going to complicate things for the administrators.'

Miriam was puzzled. 'Is Lionel aware of that clause? He didn't mention it, but I wouldn't be at all surprised if he had some sort of cunning plan. It's always been an obsession.'

Jim mulled it over. 'Well, he signed the agreement, of course. He may have forgotten, but somehow I doubt it.'

Miriam sat back and closed her eyes. The two men looked at each other. It was Miriam's decision at the end of the day. Jim knew that as chair of the Cromer Pier Theatre Trust, she would potentially have divided loyalties, hence he thought that he should remind of her clause 3c.

Tom was trying to get his mind around how you would put a market value on a Victorian pier, and of course he knew that the bank didn't even regard it as a chargeable asset for security purposes.

Miriam looked at them both and spoke calmly. 'I'm inclined to meet half of the payroll from my own funds, provided that Lionel does the same, but only if the bank agrees to keep the facility open until say the end of September, so that we can sell the business in an orderly fashion. It will also give us a chance to see if the trust can raise the funds to buy the pier, and whether the other party is even interested.'

Tom said nothing. It was her money, and she'd had all the relevant information. It was really none of his business. But Jim took a harder line, as an old friend could.

'I think that's rather generous, Miriam. But why should you lose money through Lionel' mis-management? The end game for the staff is likely to be the same, in any event.'

Miriam nodded and smiled at him. 'But this town is my home, and it's given Lionel and me a good life. Neither of us is getting any younger. Some of the staff are my friends, too. At least this way they'll get paid on Monday, and with the time available we can see if there are vacancies in the hotels.'

There was a pause. Neither Tom nor Jim had anything further to say

Miriam continued, 'That's settled, then. If that's my decision, what's next? Tom, what do you suggest?'

Tom replied. 'Well, time is short. I can at least try to contact Peter Hodson tonight. Could you email me that letter please?'

'Will he have the authority though? With the funding committee on his tail?' asked Jim.

Tom nodded. 'Yes. He's secured additional funds from the shareholders, there's an interested buyer, and the business can fund itself through to September. Yes, I think he can sell that.'

Miriam nodded. 'Good. You do that and I'll email the Latchmores letter. I'll speak to Lionel first thing in the morning. If he won't put up his share then I'm done with this, but at least I'll have tried.'

'Getting hold of a bank manager on a Saturday night? Good luck with that,' said Jim.

Tom put him right. 'If I leave him a message, he'll come back within an hour. That much I can guarantee.'

What Jim didn't know was that Tom had Hodson's home number, and an instruction to ring him day or night. He dialled it there and then, but it went to voicemail.

'Peter, it's Tom Stanley. I'm with Miriam Pemrose and Jim Cameron, and I think we have a route forward which we'd like to discuss. Could you call me back urgently please?'

*   *   *

Amy finished another performance and dashed out to the theatre foyer. By tradition, the cast of the Summertime Special meet the audience after the show. Janet had never understood why more theatres didn't follow suit, as it went down so well with the audience.

She found herself surrounded by her fans as she signed CDs and posed for selfies. The children posed with her as their parents took pictures of them with the local celebrity made good. Janet smiled as she saw Amy apparently loving every moment. Had the spell been broken? She could but hope so.

Lech was just as popular, having built up a big following over the years. But this time he had someone with him. A smiling Felix.

Janet walked back up the hill through the town with Karen. The show was going well in spite of the worries with both Hannah and Amy. Bookings looked strong for the coming weeks, and the weather wasn't bad, either. What could possibly go wrong?

15.

Sunday

Cyril was awake at around sunrise that morning. He hadn't always been an early riser, but that now seemed to be the pattern. He was in pain but managed to ease himself out of bed and onto his walking frame. He completed a somewhat tortuous and time-consuming trip to the loo, before slumping back into his chair, quite exhausted by the exertion required for even this simplest of tasks.

He clicked on the TV, then drowsed for a while, until the nurse came in with his medication. He was pleased to see her, as he really did need pain relief. His body was giving him serious discomfort this morning, and he could feel his heart pumping away inside him.

The young nurse was cheerful as always. 'Everyone's talking about Lauren Evans this morning, Cyril. I was sorry to miss her visit. Is she really glamourous, then?'

She took his blood pressure and gave him his various medications.

Cyril chuckled. 'Every inch a star, my dear. Sadly, she's not singing right now or doubtless she'd have joined in the residents' sing-song. She's just the girl next door, really. Very down to earth.'

He showed her the signed picture, and the attached card.

'Wow, that's lovely, isn't it? Said right from the heart. What's the story behind it?'

'Oh, I think that's a longer story for another day, my dear. I know you have lots to do now. Pop back when you have more time.'

'Well, I must admit we're a bit short-handed this morning, so I'll be back later,' she said, wheeling the trolley out of the door.

Cyril looked again at the picture of Lauren, a high-gloss photo of the smiling star, posing with a gold disc for her latest album. She looked absolutely on top of the world, he thought. A far cry from the timid creature waiting for the train back to Wales that day, he thought.

'Yes, Lauren, the great talents do bounce back, and you most certainly did,' he murmured, before drifting off into a place where the pain couldn't hurt him anymore.

*   *   *

Tom awoke at around 7.30am that morning. He'd returned to the Majestic after the meeting, had dinner, and then emailed Peter Hodson attaching the Latchmores offer letter Miriam had forwarded. He was hoping that Hodson would have seen the email and would return the call immediately.

At 8am precisely, his mobile rang.

'Tom, it's Peter Hodson. Sorry, I know it's early, but I didn't get back last night until it was too late to return your call. I've read your email. I've heard of Latchmores, but what do you make of them?'

'They're certainly reputable. So any client will be a credible bidder. They wouldn't waste their time with people who haven't got the money to do the deal. But I don't know what information they've had from Lionel. Probably much like what you've seen from Jim, I suspect.'

'But if they were to buy the business at that price, how does the bank look?' Peter asked.

'It rather depends on whether Pemrose recovers any money from the casino debacle. I attached my crude estimate. You'll do a lot better through this route than in a forced sale, though, that much is certain.'

'I agree. I'm happy to take this back. We've secured more investment from the owners, after all, and there is interest in a trade sale through a reputable broker. Yes, I think they'll give it a three-month extension of facilities on that basis.'

Ton agreed. 'It seems good to me. If you wish, I'll let Miriam and Lionel know that you are supportive provided they meet the payroll between them. Do you want me to do that, or would you prefer to do it yourself?'

'No, that's fine, Tom. Just drop me a line confirming that they will put the money in, and an addendum to your report based on the email you sent me so I can forward it on.'

'Right. Will do.'

'We'll need someone to see the sale over the line, unless Jim will come back to do it ... '

'Well, you could ask him, but I don't think he will,' Tom replied.

'Well, could you stay on to see it through for us? Bringing the Pemrose clan to the table is a considerable achievement on your part. I'm most grateful.'

'Well, let's get this interim arrangement done first, then we can work something out.'

Tom rang off, then contacted Miriam and Jim to confirm.

Miriam was pleased. 'Thanks Tom. Now just leave Lionel to me.'

*   *   *

Karen had been surprised that Janet had agreed to go out with Tom for the day. She'd never really known her mother to date anyone, much as Janet denied that a date was what this was. As far as Janet was concerned, Tom was looking for a property and she knew the area. She was simply helping out.

Nevertheless, Karen couldn't help remarking that her mother was dressed to impress; the designer-label white jeans and burgundy top were in marked contrast to the normal theatre-manager black, a work uniform which seemed to prevail irrespective of the occasion.

'Wow! I hope he's worth it, Mum,' she joked as her mother gathered her handbag.

'Very funny, Karen. I haven't noticed you at the pinnacle of fashion very often.'

'Miaow ... well, at least if he's buying a second home, he must be solvent at least.'

'Well, we'll see about that. I'm not sure if we're seeing caravans, chalets or something from *Grand Designs* to be honest, and I'll admit I have an ulterior motive.'

'Oh?'

'Well, any friend of Hodson's is unlikely to be a friend of ours. Tom's working for Lionel too. I want to find out what he's up to.'

Karen's jaw dropped, 'God, you don't trust anyone, do you?'

'Not where Lionel's concerned, no. But Tom does seem to be good fun, I'll admit, and I might need some company when gorgeous Bryn whisks you up the aisle.'

Karen shook her head, 'Fat chance. On what we both earn, we'd be the ones looking at chalets. House prices here are just going berserk.'

'True. Is he going touring soon? After Glastonbury?'

'Possibly. He's talking about going to Nashville in October to peddle some of his songs.'

'Will you go with him? That sounds like a lot of fun.'

'Doubt it. Not unless you're cancelling the Christmas show.'

'Well, of course I'm not, but if you're not careful you'll become just another 60-plus woman who's never travelled anywhere.'

'Well, I'll admit he suggested I come along. I'll give it some thought.'

'Book tickets, Lauren. We need to live a bit, you and I. Right, I'm off. I'll see you later.'

'You will be careful, Mum? I mean, I know what you're like after a bottle of cider and fish and chips.'

'I'm hoping that I'll do rather better than that, Karen. Starting with a nice breakfast at the Majestic. Now, I must away.'

'Your hot date awaits. Enjoy!'

With that, she kissed her mother on the cheek, ignoring the admonishing stare.

Fortunately, the weather looked fine, so Janet walked down through the town to the Majestic, stopping on the way to chat to a number of locals who knew her. The church was busy with the bells summoning the faithful.

She entered the Majestic through the stylish foyer which, although not original, Miriam Pemrose had cleverly incorporated with the building's original features. Tom was sitting in a comfy chair by reception, reading the Sunday Times when she entered. He smiled and gave her a polite peck on the cheek.

'Hungry?' he asked.

'Yes. I normally have a bowl of muesli if I'm lucky.'

'Well, I hope we'll do a bit better than that. Shall we go in?'

He escorted her through, towards the restaurant, but a voice behind him made him pause.

'Morning, Tom,' said Lionel cheerfully.

'Good morning, Lionel,' replied Tom as he turned in response to the greeting.

'Oh, and good morning Janet Wells, too. Good to see you this fine morning.'

He hugged Janet and kissed her politely, although Tom couldn't help but notice that Janet stiffened as he did so.

'Good morning, Lionel. I'm taking Tom on a property hunt this morning, so he's treating me to breakfast.'

'Ah. Well, we all fall in love with this place, don't we? Enjoy, both of you. Oh, Tom, just to let you know that Miriam rang this morning. We're all agreed, so you can tell Peter, if you would.'

'Oh. Yes, that's fine. I'll do that later.'

Janet did a double-take. What did that mean? She was too polite to ask, and in any event, they were quickly shown to a nice table near the doors which opened onto the terrace looking out over the sea.

'Miriam did this so beautifully,' said Janet.

'Yes, It's lovely. I used to hate staying away overnight, but this has been a real home from home. I've got one of the executive rooms. It has windows on two sides and a sea view. Fantastic.'

'I knew it under the former owner, Jim Collins. He went bust in 2008. Lionel bought it at a knockdown price, and Miriam did the redesign.'

'Yes. And now it does very nicely. Sadly, in my line of work I was rather busy during the 2008 banking crisis. A close friend of mine committed suicide, too. Bad times indeed.'

'Oh, that's just awful. I nearly went under, too. But that's probably not a story we should discuss since it involves both

Lionel and Peter Hodson. I wouldn't want to speak ill of your employers.'

Tom hesitated. He knew most of the story anyway, but wanted to keep off the subject of his work. The revelation about the sale of the business and the impact of clause 3c had to be off-limits today. His friendship, if this was what it was with Janet, mustn't impact on his work.

'Let's keep off the topic of work today, Janet; it's Sunday, and a beautiful day for a house hunt.'

'Oh. So, you're one of those few men who actually enjoy house hunting, then?'

He shrugged rather evasively as the waiter arrived to take their order, getting him off the hook.

'So, I've booked to see four properties. One here and the others up the coast. A lot of different prices, just to get a feel for what's around. The first one is right near the seafront overlooking the pier in fact. Here, have a look at the details.'

She took the glossy sheet, and immediately realised that there would be no chalets on this trip today. She knew the town so well that the location was immediately recognisable. A stylish one-bedroomed apartment with a stunning sea view over the pier. A big lounge area, a nicely sized bedroom and bathroom adjoining it, and a big dining room/kitchen. It had clearly been the subject of a very high-quality refurbishment, with a selling price to match.

'Not exactly in the first-time buyer bracket, is it? Beautifully done up, though,' she ventured.

'Yes. Gorgeous sea view. You don't get views like that In Leeds.'

'But only one bedroom? Don't you need space for guests?'

'Well, ideally I'd like two bedrooms, yes. I have tried to keep up the friendships we had as a couple, so it would be good to have two,' he replied.

'And there's no parking in the middle of Cromer, particularly in season. You can get a resident's permit, but would one want to park one's Rolls Royce in a public car park? Perish the thought.'

Tom laughed. 'Rolls Royce? A five-year-old Focus, more like. I've never splashed the cash on cars. Second-hand is much better value.'

'Spoken like a true accountant.'

Tom was enjoying the banter. 'Well, that's what I am. I could have done worse. My brother went down the pit.'

'Is he still around? I guess he must have retired, one way or another?'

'He took early retirement. Got a bad knee injury when a pit prop fell on him. Lives near Selby now. I visit him from time to time.'

'Are your parents still alive?'

'No, Mum died three years back. My Dad long before her. Pits aren't exactly healthy places.'

Breakfast arrived, and they ate in silence for a while. After Lionel's comment, Tom knew that Janet would know that something was up but was probably too polite to ask. He didn't feel good about keeping it a secret from her, but that was the way it went sometimes.

There were a lot of things he didn't know about Janet, of course. For example, who was Karen's father? Where was he now? But those answers would either emerge in good time, or they wouldn't. But at least she was good company at breakfast.

'That was very good indeed,' said Janet, finishing up.

'Glad you enjoyed it. It's good to have company for breakfast for once, I must say.'

'I imagine so. However good the hotel, being a solo resident is never great.'

'No, indeed. In fairness, Lionel knows how to run a good hotel.'

'Yes, he does. Jim Tyler does most of the work now, of course,' she said.

'*Jim* Tyler? Everyone calls him Tyler?' he asked.

Janet explained. 'Well, there were two Jims, and Jim Cameron was here the longest, so Lionel just called him Tyler and it stuck. Having met him now, how do you find Lionel to work with? I'm intrigued.'

Tom thought for a moment. 'He's quite typical of a self-made man. Driven, determined. Good eye for detail. But prone to believe that as he's run a couple of businesses successfully, he has the Midas touch. Which of course he doesn't.'

'That feels about right. He can be very generous, caring and kind one minute, then manipulative, devious and ruthless the next,' she replied.

It was obvious that Janet knew the man very well indeed.

'Right. If you're ready, let's go and see this place.'

'Right-oh. Thanks for breakfast.'

'My pleasure.'

*　　*　　*

Lionel was back up in the penthouse. As genial as he'd been with Tom, the phone call with Miriam had angered him. He did not appreciate the lecture he'd been given, but at least she'd agreed to put in half of the money. He had hoped that she might have stumped up the lot after his brilliant theatrical performance, but half the payroll would do, he decided.

What Miriam didn't realise, though, was that Lionel was very much in the mindset of Mr Micawber, as in 'something will turn up', and wasn't about to sell the business that he'd created just to appease the bank if he could avoid it. He'd had every intention of meeting the payroll, in any event. He had yet to work out how he would make Hodson pay for bailing out on him, but give it time.

He had also been amused to receive a letter from Bernie Brewster's solicitors threatening all sorts of legal action against him. Nice try old son, but the subsidiary he'd created to buy Brewster's was now in the hands of the administrators. They could deal with the legal claim, in return for their fat fee.

But he did still need to find a big lump of cash somehow. He had thought of getting Tom to assist; after all, he was a turnaround specialist. But seeing him having breakfast with Janet Wells, he'd decided against it. He judged a man by the company he kept, and would never forgive Janet for double-crossing him in 2009. Sooner or later, he would make her pay for that too.

In the meantime, he'd booked a tee at Royal Cromer Golf Club for 1pm that day. He was playing golf with Jim Cameron, conceding that he needed to get him back on board. To secure the money, having someone to reassure a potential investor was important, and most people found Jim reassuring.

He'd also had contact from Freya, saying how much she missed him. Doubtless somewhere in their romantic reconciliation, the subject of her rich friends' worthless shareholdings in the casino would come up. As the major secured creditor, he believed that he would sweat some cash back out, although the building was in a parlous state. It really needed knocking down, but the Grade II listing rendered that unlikely.

He decided to invite Freya to come to Cromer next week

for a couple of nights. She wasn't worth the posh London hotel and Savoy dinner to him anymore, but he only really wanted her in bed, and he liked the idea of using her for once and on the cheap. He might even get the engagement ring back. It would be a shame if it got lost while she was in Cromer.

But there was one other idea that he'd had. One asset that he could sell, over which the bank had no security. He didn't want to do it, but if that's what it took, then so be it. The previously isolated and deflated Lionel had reinvented himself. The cunning, vengeful and vindictive Lionel was back.

*   *   *

Hannah got up rather late; the punishing dance routines had left her limbs sore. Today was a bigger test still. As advertised in the programme, she was the headliner for that day's matinee. It was a long time since she had headlined, and although nervous, she was exhilarated.

She made a mug of tea and then sifted through the post which the hotel kept for her each day for her to collect. It was mainly the usual rubbish redirected from her Cromer property. A redirect made necessary since she could no longer access the house.

She was about to throw them in the bin when she spotted a white envelope. It was addressed to her at the hotel. Feeling the edges, it was obvious what was inside, but there was something else, too. She put on some rubber gloves and used a kitchen knife to slit the envelope open carefully.

She looked inside and burst into tears. She rang Graham straight away, and he answered just as it was going to his answerphone.

'Hi, Hannah. What's up?'

She tried to stay calm. 'He's sent me another DVD, addressed to the hotel. He knows I'm here. And he's included something else of mine too.'

'Keep calm. I'll be over right away.'

*   *   *

Karen was having a quiet morning when the phone rang at home. It was a call they had been expecting for a while. In Janet's absence, Julia Maitland told Karen that Cyril Brown had passed away that morning.

'Oh, that is such sad news. To be honest we've rather been expecting it, though. He looked so weak. I know Lauren Evans dropped in yesterday, and he'd have loved that at least.'

'Yes, indeed he would. Well, I'm his executor, so I'll set to work with my staff on things tomorrow.'

'Well, if you need anything let me know. I'm sure we'll all come to the funeral. It'll be a big event, I'll bet.'

'Thanks, Karen. Can you tell Janet for me? And pass the word around at the theatre? We can talk about the funeral later next week.'

Karen did the round of phone calls, including one to her mother, giving everybody the sad news . She was about to take a leisurely walk down to the pier to have a late breakfast with Bryn when the phone rang again.

'Yes, Graham?'

She listened with dismay as she heard about the turn of events. It was Sunday, so the likelihood of an immediate police response was not great.

'How is she feeling? She must be in shock.'

'Bit shaken but holding up. She's getting showered and is ready to come down to the theatre. I said I'd ring you to let you know what's happened.'

'Do you think she's up to it? I can't imagine how she must be feeling.'

'Well, she says she is, but I'm no performer, so I really wouldn't know how it all feels.'

'All right. Bring her down and let's play it by ear. Would you be OK to sit in during the show to give her extra assurance? I know it's a lot to ask on a nice Sunday afternoon.'

'Of course. Will do. They need to catch this guy. This isn't going to end well. He's pretty desperate. Wife gone, job gone, wanted by the police.'

'Yes. I'll ring Amy, so we have some options. Thanks, Graham.'

Amy was having a relaxing bath when the phone rang, but her mother handed her the receiver after Karen said it was urgent.

'OK, Karen. I'm on my way. No worries.'

Karen headed down to meet Bryn at the cafe on the pier. He got up as she arrived, and she kissed him.

'Sorry, love, I can't stop. Bit of a crisis with Hannah. I need to get down to the theatre. Can you get me a coffee and a bacon butty and bring it down for me?'

'Of course. Just go,' he said.

She met Lech in the theatre and brought him up to date with events. Lech didn't like what he heard.

'He's a bad guy, Karen. I don't like the way he held Hannah. Not safe. I tell the police this.'

They had a brief discussion, but in honesty they couldn't do anything until Hannah arrived. Bryn came in with her sandwich, and she munched it quickly while bringing him up to date.

'I can stick around if you want. If you show me a picture of the guy, like?' said Bryn.

'Thanks, love. To be honest, I've not seen a picture either. I need to sort that out,' she said.

She was thinking about ringing her mother, but knew if she did it would ruin her day out. In any event, what would she bring to the decision anyway? If Hannah was up to it, she'd headline; if not, poor old Amy wouldn't get a break, but so be it.

Hannah came in a few minutes later, and Karen took her into the green room for a chat, leaving Graham, Bryn and Lech outside in the foyer.

Karen sat her down. 'How are you feeling? A dreadful thing to happen. I'm so sorry.'

'It was a shock, as it proves he knows where I am. That's spooked me a bit, I'll admit.'

'Well, look, I've asked Amy to come down as backup. Your decision, I just don't want you to feel pressured.'

Hannah shook her head. 'Thanks, but I'm fine. I'm headlining this show this afternoon. I just can't let him win. He's had his way for too many years. He's not stopping me this time. I need to prove I can do this.'

She was breaking down now, and Karen put her arm around her shoulder.

'Brave girl. That's absolutely fine, Hannah. Your decision entirely.'

At that moment, there was a knock at the door and Amy came in. She sat the other side of Hannah and extended her arm around the other shoulder. Hannah sat with her head down and her eyes closed.

Amy was incensed. 'That cowardly bastard. They'll surely catch him now. He's going down for this.'

'I hope you're right, but nothing would surprise me now,' said Hannah.

'Well, if you want me to …' Amy replied.

Hannah shook her head. ' … No, it's fine, Amy. I want to do this. For me. I have to.'

Amy hesitated, looking at Karen who shook her head.

Amy continued. 'Of course you have to. You show him. He mustn't win.'

They sat for a while as other cast members arrived.

Hannah wiped her eyes and stood up. 'Right. I need to warm up. I'll go and get dressed. Thanks, guys.'

Karen wasn't completely convinced, but had to let it go. 'Graham and Bryn are staying just in case. Graham's out front and Lech and Bryn are your minders backstage. I'll be there, too. Have you got a picture of him, by the way?'

'Graham has, so he can share it with the ushers,' Hannah replied.

'Good. Fine. OK.'

Hannah left to get dressed, and Amy followed, but Karen stopped her. 'Stick around, Amy. I'm not sure that I could do this after what she's been through. Use your discretion. Try to stay in the background, but be ready to dress quickly if necessary.'

'Yep. Understood. We can't let him win.'

'No. We can't and we won't.

*   *   *

Tom drove into the driveway of the final property, at Weybourne. This was the most expensive one, and it looked it from the outside. A recently completed barn conversion, it looked absolutely stunning. Janet had read the details and noted the eye-watering price tag.

They got out and Tom shook the estate agent's hand. Her lack of knowledge about the property suggested she was a part-timer doing the Sunday viewings, but Tom was quite happy to wander at leisure without the sales patter. The lady pretty much stayed outside enjoying the sunshine while Tom and Janet looked around.

The ground floor featured a dining room with a kitchen and bedroom off to one side. They climbed the stairs to a first-floor lounge, complete with a wood-burning stove built into an open brick fireplace.

'Wow,' said Janet, looking approvingly at the vaulted ceiling with exposed oak beams, and a mezzanine above.

'Yes. Wow indeed,' said Tom.

'But could you live in an upside-down house? It would take a bit of getting used to.'

'Well, yes, but the lounge is just fabulous. I love the beams.'

Janet nodded, 'Me too. Cosy wood burner as well. All this and a nice walk to the beach.'

'Two good-looking pubs, too. I feel a pint and Sunday lunch coming on.'

'It's lovely, Tom. Really lovely,' she said.

'Bloody pricey, though,' he said ruefully.

'Typical Yorkie. It's the best we've seen by a mile though, don't you think?'

'Well, I'll admit I could feel at home here. I'm not sure about the others.'

'Yes, I could too ... oh, sorry I didn't mean ... well, you know ...'

Janet was embarrassed, but Tom laughed. '...It's OK, Janet. I know what you meant.'

They went outside, and Janet remarked that there wasn't much in the way of a garden.

'I'm not sure I'd be here enough for that to matter.'

They thanked the agent and left the car in the drive as she left.

'Time for Sunday lunch now, I believe? The Ship Inn looked good, so I booked it.'

Janet was surprised, but was content for someone just to organise her for once.

They arrived at the pub, and although Janet offered to pay, Tom declined.

'No, no, after all you've given up your day off to help, so the least you can do is let me buy you lunch.'

Janet acquiesced, and they sat for a while checking their respective phones. Nothing of consequence.

'So, which one should I buy, then'

'Are you serious? Are any of these contenders?' she said in reply.

'Meaning can I afford them?' he laughed and took a swallow from his pint glass.

'Well, no. Well, yes, I suppose. Well ... I'm not sure what your plan is. Do you want to run it as a holiday let? If only just to friends? If it's just a bolthole, then the apartment in Cromer was very quaint and had that view. I don't really know.'

Tom paused. He gathered his thoughts before he spoke.

'Well, I've bought and sold a few businesses in my time, and our only real indulgences were the West End theatre and travel. Maggie was an only child, and her parents died a few years back, leaving us their place in Kent. The savings don't earn much, so why not have a place somewhere? We were about to start looking when Maggie was diagnosed, so it didn't happen.'

'Oh ... I see. That's really so awfully sad,' she said.

There was a bit of an awkward silence.

Tom looked a little morose as he continued. 'To be honest, I've been floundering a bit of late. First losing Maggie, and then my career. I'm just drifting through life now, not sure what I want anymore. This project has at least got me away from an empty flat in London and given me some sort of purpose.'

'Ever think of going back to Yorkshire?' she asked.

'Oh, no. There's nothing much there for me now' he replied.

Janet realised that there were similarities in their respective positions. 'Well, at times I wonder if my life is just drifting, too. I do love the theatre. But I do sometimes wonder where it ends. Like you, I don't want to be retired and bored stiff, and I've also got Karen to consider, but when do I get off the merry-go-round?'

The food arrived, and they debated their respective menu choices for a while. Tom was impressed, setting his knife and fork down at the end and sitting back contentedly.

'Well, that was excellent, wasn't it Janet? So, back to the future. Surely Karen will take over from you one day? That's the obvious succession plan, surely?'

Janet sipped her wine and thought before responding.

'Well, I'm not sure whether she would want to run the theatre. Karen's happy as a creative. I only took it on because my father died so suddenly. She has Bryn now, as well, her first serious boyfriend in years. I've never seen her so happy, if I'm honest. So, who knows where that will lead?'

Tom nodded. 'Succession is always difficult with family businesses. Selling them on is tricky as the entrepreneur is part of the DNA if you're buying it. You'd be tricky to replace. The arts sector isn't known to pay well. I was the trustee of a theatre at one time. I was shocked at the salary that theatre management get paid.'

Janet smiled. 'Well, I'm not likely to be buying a second home anytime soon. It was fun looking though, I must admit.'

'I'm glad you enjoyed it. Thanks for coming along. It's been fun. I do like it here, and I'm not given to indulging in frivolous exercises, so I'm seriously thinking about what we've seen today.'

Janet was intrigued. 'Which one? The last one was just so homely with the oak beams and the wood burner.'

'Yes. But I'm not sure it isn't a bit *too* quiet. I've got used to having the buzz on my doorstep in London, and I'm not sure I want to lose that entirely. That flat in Cromer was brilliant for the view. If you've been brought up inland as I was, having that sea view never loses its magic. The trouble is, as you say, I need a second bedroom, and parking would be a right pain.'

'I agree. Having been born here we take the seaside for granted, although walking up that pier to the theatre in a force eight gale tends to remind you of the forces of nature at times.'

They declined pudding but had coffee, and Janet suddenly realised that the matinee would have finished by now. She looked at her phone. Nothing. It most have gone off without incident, she thought.

'So, Tom, what happens with you now? At the end of the assignment? Back to London?'

'Well, I'm not sure. Things are a bit fluid right now. I'm off to London on Wednesday. Then I'm meeting some friends at Lord's on Friday. Nice bit of corporate hospitality. Beyond that, well we'll see.'

He hesitated a little, but then spoke slowly, and rather nervously. 'Well, there was one thing I was going to mention. I have a friend with some useful theatre contacts, and wondered if you'd seen *Hamilton*. I can get a couple of tickets if you can break free one evening. It's just a thought, mind; you might be too busy in high season.'

Janet thought for a moment. 'Well, Karen is always telling me to break free of the theatre more, so, yes, I'd love to. She saw it with Bryn and raved about it.'

'Well, that's grand. Give me some dates when you're free. I'm not terribly likely to be that busy myself.'

With that they headed back to Cromer and, as he dropped her off, he shook her hand with both of his, thanking her so much for coming. He suddenly seemed tongue-tied. She got out of the car and waved him goodbye.

*   *   *

In a rather dingy hired caravan within walking distance from the village, a lone figure looked at his pay-as-you-go mobile and checked his emails. He sensed that he was running out of options. The bank had retracted the sale proceeds of the house. Something about a legal problem with the transaction. He had heard about it on Friday, but it had been too late to do anything.

There was also an emailed letter from his employer, stating that as he had failed to attend the disciplinary hearing on Friday, they had adjourned it until the following Friday, but that if he failed to attend, they would hear the case in his absence.

More worrying still was that he knew from a friend in the bank that the police had been to see them. He placed a call to a female friend in Kent, who lived near his home. She drove by the house and saw police cars in the driveway.

He looked at the video playing on the computer screen. Him and Hannah in happier times. Before she'd betrayed him by leaving. Because of her, he now stood to lose everything.

He couldn't even pay off his gambling debt because, somehow, she'd blocked the house sale.

That policeman lover she'd taken up with was getting in the way. He needed to see her soon so he could talk some sense into her. Tell her how much he loved her. How much she owed him for the lifestyle he'd given her. How could she betray him and go off with some old fart of a policeman?

He'd got lucky with her address. He had followed her and her lover back from the theatre the other night and seen the hotel where she was staying. He saw them go up a corridor leading to a serviced flat in the hotel, so he simply wrote the address on the envelope and dropped it in the letter box.

But even now she hadn't contacted him. Surely, she must see the damage she was doing to him? While she was enjoying herself appearing in her deadbeat end-of-the-pier show, he was hurting. How cruel was that?

He finished his can of lager and cast it aside. He went to the fridge for another, but found it empty. He cursed his luck.

*   *   *

Janet sat drinking tea as Karen brought her up to date on her own day.

'But why on earth didn't you ring me, love? I could have come straight back.'

Karen had been expecting this. 'Because frankly there wasn't time, and what extra things could you have done that I didn't do?'

'Well, I don't know …' said Janet.

Karen gestured in frustration. 'Exactly. You need to switch off and let me handle stuff. I'm not a novice anymore.'

'All's well that ends well, I suppose. How on earth did Hannah get through it?'

Karen shrugged. 'She's a true pro with everything to prove to herself. She won't let him win.'

Janet nodded. 'But you had Amy on standby, too? That was a wise move.'

'She was there at every costume change to help her though it. Great to see. There were lots of hugs at the end. Graham took her home afterwards, and we've all got pictures of the guy on our phones now.'

'So presumably Graham is in touch with the police? He has the envelope now?' asked Janet.

'Yes. It contained another DVD and an item of her underwear, apparently torn to pieces.'

Janet was disgusted. 'Sick. How on earth does she cope?'

'Surely she can't for much longer. She's gone back to the hotel now, but we can't keep moving her and giving her round-the-clock security. We need the police to do something. He has to have found out where she was living by following her from the theatre. He must be staying locally. I had Graham out front this afternoon and Bryn on the stage doors. But I think we need to hire security guards for each show until this resolves itself.'

'Yes. You're right. I'll fix that in the morning. I know it's expensive, but we have a duty of care. I'll make sure that we search bags thoroughly on entry, too.'

'But look on the bright side, Mum. We proved that Hannah could headline the show if anything happened with Amy, and the backup dancer also did well. The audience was great. Good feedback.'

'Did Hannah go out front afterwards?'

'Yes; she insisted. Graham and Bryn acted as minders.'

Janet laughed. 'Bryn? As a minder? Not exactly Tyson Fury, is he?'

Karen pouted. 'Well, he's *my* Tyson Fury, even if he is only five foot six.'

'I know. He's thoroughly lovely. You are blessed.'

'How about your date, Mum? Did you drag him onto the beach for a quickie as usual?'

Her mother allowed the standing joke about Karen's conception on Cromer beach to pass her by.

'Well, we had a really nice day, followed by a lovely late Sunday lunch at The Ship at Weybourne.'

Karen indicated her approval. 'Good choice. He knows how to treat a girl, at least. So how many static caravans and seedy chalets did one view on this property hunt?'

Janet shook her head. 'None at all. Four houses, with this one being the favourite. Let's see now.'

Janet thumbed through her phone pictures, found a couple of the Weybourne house, and showed them to her.

'Crumbs, Mum. That's posh. There must be some money in insolvency, then?'

'Well, yes. Buying and flogging businesses. But his wife died only last year, and they still have the money from her parents' place, apparently.'

'Oh, how sad. Is he OK?'

Janet considered. 'No, not really. He recently got made redundant from his own company. He freely admits to being a bit lost at the minute. This project with Lionel has been a bit of a lifeline.'

'Well, it sounds like you had a really nice day. Will you see him again, do you think?'

'I might,' said Janet. 'He's invited me to see *Hamilton* with him in London when I can get away.'

Karen chuckled. 'Oh, yes ... then back to his London pad to look at his spreadsheets?'

'Well, I hadn't got that far actually. I'll need to sort out a date first.'

Karen looked at her quizzically. 'But do you trust him now, then?'

Janet frowned. 'I don't trust so easily, Karen. When I prodded and probed about what he's up to with Lionel, he rather dodged the subject. Something's going on and he's not telling me anything. So, no, not entirely, if I'm completely honest.'

16.

Friday

Jim Cameron was catching up with things, restored to his old office in the Majestic.

The golf had been pleasant the previous weekend, and Lionel had been at his affable best, Jim thought. Apparently without a care in the world.

Lionel had, albeit it in his own way, apologised for recent events. He appealed to Jim to reconsider his decision and asked him just to stay on until the sale was completed. They had worked together for so many years that Jim decided to see things through to the end, if only out of loyalty to the staff.

The payroll had been paid, and Jim was studying a letter from the bank outlining the terms under which facilities had been temporarily restored. The bank had reserved the right to withdraw the facility at any time, but in any event the facility must be paid by August 31st without fail.

He'd met Peter Hodson earlier in the week, and although he was made very welcome, it was clear that any trust in Lionel had now gone, and that the deadline would not be extended.

Lionel appeared more concerned about the arrival of Freya the previous night. Jim was also concerned; having seen at first hand the poisonous influence she could wield. He'd expected to meet Lionel that morning, but was now advised he'd left early to take Freya out for the day.

*   *   *

Tom, meanwhile, was having a really enjoyable day at the cricket. The match itself, a World Cup game, was played on a perfect English summer's day, and he'd been royally entertained by the corporate sponsors of the box. But it was during lunch, while idly flicking through the complimentary paraphernalia on the table, that he came across a guest list. To his surprise, he saw a name he recognised, Paul Jennings, a senior partner at none other than Latchmores.

Small world, he thought. But then the corporate finance industry wasn't that big. They had done a deal together some years previously, although Tom was so poor with faces he would never recognise him again.

Tom was relieved that Jim was back. It made doing the deal easier, and how much due diligence the client had done was rather hidden by Lionel's cloak-and-dagger approach.

He'd agreed to review things with Jim the following Monday. But as he stood there watching the crowds enjoying their Lord's picnics, he realised that he'd heard nothing from Jim about the sale. It had only been a few days, but eight weeks to close a deal required some urgency. He rang Jim to get an update.

Jim's Scottish voice came on the line, 'Hi, Tom, how's the cricket? Enjoying the sunshine at Lord's?'

'Indeed I am, Jim. Picture-perfect ground on a picture-perfect day. How go things with the due diligence?'

'Nothing to report as yet. I've been trying to pin Lionel

down, but he's not around today. Unfortunately, Freya's back on the scene, so he's out for the day.'

Tom smelt a rat. 'Oh, that's not good. Hodson will be expecting an update from me on Monday.'

'Yes, I know. Should I ring Latchmores myself? I'm concerned, but I don't know this guy at all.'

'Well, as luck would have it Latchmores are guests in one of the boxes, and one of the partners is here today, so let me ask him first.'

'Fair enough. I don't want to rock the boat, but time's moving on,' said Jim.

They left it there and Tom got his friend to make the relevant introduction.

'Hello, Tom, I think we've met before, haven't we?' said Paul Jennings, the Latchmores partner, sipping what was clearly not his first red wine of the day.

Tom shook his hand. 'Yes, we have. I just couldn't remember what the deal was, though. An age thing, I guess.'

Jennings knew immediately. 'It was the Gerson deal. A few twists and turns, but we made it in the end.'

Tom remembered. 'Ah, yes. I remember now, Paul. Gosh, that was a long time ago, wasn't it?'

'It was. So, I gather you retired back in the spring. Bit of freedom at last?'

'Well, yes, but I've been doing some work with Pemrose Entertainments up in Norfolk. The owner's retiring. A soon-to-be acquisition for a client of yours, I'm told?'

Jennings looked puzzled. 'Oh. That's interesting. Who's the manager handling it for us? I'm not sure I'm familiar with it.'

Tom thought for a moment, 'Well, Mark Fieldhouse signed

the letter, I think. We don't seem to have progressed with due diligence yet. Probably just some glitch or other.'

The partner seemed a little embarrassed now. Tom found his hesitation troubling.

'Oh, that's not good enough. Look, let me make a couple of calls and I'll see what's going on. I'd have expected us to be on site by now. As you know, if you snooze you lose in this business.'

They left it there. Tom went back to the cricket, enjoying the company and feeling quite mellow as the chilled white wine gave way to best bitter. It was during the tea interval when the partner took him to one side. It was not good news. He rang Jim Cameron immediately.

Cameron was just heading off. 'Hi, Tom, tea interval, is it? You retired people have all the luck,' he said.

Tom had no time for niceties. 'We have a problem, Jim. Mark Fieldhouse left Latchmores last Friday. I gather Lionel rang him up to chase him for that letter before he left. It's an indicative bid for Pemrose, not really a formal bid. Worse still, the client pulled out on Tuesday after they got some reports from their property people. Something about the asbestos work not being properly certified.'

There was silence for a moment, as Jim absorbed the news. 'Good grief. I wonder if Lionel knows about this. It might not have been communicated due to the change of personnel.'

Tom replied rather negatively, 'That's what I wondered. But I'm told that Latchmores emailed Lionel on Tuesday, but they sent it to his personal email address. I've asked for a copy of it so I can forward it on.'

'Good. If it's not on the company server I can't get to it,' said Jim.

'Exactly. Where's Lionel now? Is he back yet?'

'I'm not sure. Freya came over a day earlier than expected and they went off for the day.'

Tom was suspicious. 'Are you sure about that, Jim? It wouldn't surprise me if he and his girlfriend are in Malaga by now.'

Jim wasn't sure either way, 'Well, they left before I got in this morning. A bit unusual for Lionel to get up early, I'll admit. Leave it to me. I'll make some enquiries.'

'OK. I hardly need to tell you what this means.'

'No. I guess it's a question of when you or I tell Peter Hodson the news.'

Tom certainly wasn't looking forward to it. 'Let's check the facts first. See if you can get hold of Lionel .'

Jim was terse in his reply. 'Huh. If I get hold of Lionel first there won't be much left of him. He's lied to the lot of us again.'

'Well, he's certainly been selective with the facts.'

'I prefer my version, Tom. Leave it with me.'

*   *   *

Julia Maitland put aside the file relating to Cyril Brown's estate and took out the one relating to Hannah Masters. As far as she knew, the police had not yet tracked down the estranged husband, but as her solicitor, she had applied to court to have a restraining order put in place to exclude him from a ten-mile radius of Cromer. Not very enforceable, but better than nothing.

She went through to the conference room, where Hannah was sitting with Graham Blakeley.

'Good morning. I saw the show the other night, Hannah. Really terrific. Pass on my congratulations to the cast, and to Karen, would you?'

'Oh, yes. Thanks. Thanks a lot. I will,' Hannah replied haltingly.

She was hollow-eyed from lack of sleep, and not far from tears.

'I was sorry to hear about your estranged husband's latest contact, Hannah. I hope that the police are taking the matter as seriously as they should. I did contact a senior police officer in Norwich to formally express our concerns. Is there anything to update on police matters, Graham?'

'Well, the envelope wasn't franked, so it was hand-delivered. Almost certainly he's living somewhere locally. I've done what I can with some contacts I still have, but I don't have the badge anymore. PC Edwards has been out with some community support officers, and they're visiting holiday accommodation, showing his picture. It's that sort of foot slogging which gets results. I have an assurance that three officers are on it this weekend. They're also visiting local car hire places, too. We know from DVLA that he sold his BMW.'

Julia nodded. 'Let's hope they get a result. You did so well, Hannah, getting through that show on Sunday. I don't know how you did it.'

'Neither do I, frankly,' said Hannah rather miserably, staring straight ahead.

'Well, I do at least have some positive news. The court has set aside the sale of your property after it became clear that you didn't in fact sign it over to your husband.'

Hannah looked up. 'I didn't? Then who did?'

Julia shrugged. 'I can only assume that he did. The signatures on the documents are not yours at all. He's clearly tried to fake your signature on multiple documents, but they don't really pass any close scrutiny. The court accepted that there is strong evidence of fraud. They've set aside the property transfer, and the property is legally yours once again.'

'Thank God,' said Hannah, visibly brightening.

Julia smiled. 'I'll be getting the keys back to you as soon as I can. So at least you've got your home back.'

Graham hugged Hannah, who was dabbing her eyes with a tissue.

'A great result, Julia,' said Graham. 'We've actually been wondering what to do next about Hannah's accommodation.'

Hannah gathered herself. 'Well, thinking about it, he knows where I am, so I'd far rather be at home. At least something has gone my way for once. That's brilliant news. Thanks, Julia.'

'Glad to be able to help. Actually, I officially retire today, but I'm working part-time to run out my remaining cases, so I will keep in touch.'

*   *   *

It was late afternoon by the time Lionel and Freya arrived at the villa in Malaga, having dropped the Jaguar off near Stansted at the house of a friend who had a couple of big barns and would store it under cover for the time being. Freya wasted no time in settling in. She appeared in the doorway, naked except for a loose see-through wrap. She headed out to the secluded pool area, shedding the wrap as she lay on a sun lounger. It was still very warm in the bright sunshine.

'You're so incredibly slow, Lionel. Get the champagne and join me, darling. Do get your priorities right.'

Lionel laughed. He felt like a train robber running away from the law, but knew that he'd done nothing illegal. Having received Latchmores' latest email, he had replied with a number of queries, so as far as he was concerned, there was still a deal to be done. Depending on the response, he would advise the bank in due course.

Meanwhile, he had every intention of enjoying Freya's stupidly carefree love of life, even if it came at a price. He enjoyed the prim and proper demeanour belying a darker side which would make a prostitute blush. He'd missed her, whatever her flaws, and he wanted her back in his life.

Barring a miracle, he would now have to let Pemrose Entertainments go under. Miriam could deal with the small-minded backstabbers in the local community, because he intended to stay here in the sunshine with Freya.

He took the chilled champagne and two flutes to the patio, where Freya was now applying sunscreen to her lower body. She invited him to help with her upper half, and he readily agreed.

17.

Monday

Jim had spent the weekend trying to find Lionel, but the calls went to voicemail and emails went unanswered. Tyler confirmed that he'd seen Lionel leave with Freya early on Friday morning, and one of the porters recalled loading suitcases into the boot of the Jaguar. This was more than just a day out with Freya.

Jim Cameron had spoken to Latchmores that morning, after Tom had forwarded a copy of their latest email. Apparently, they'd received a further request for clarification from Lionel on Thursday. Having taken advice from their client, though, they would be writing to Lionel today. The issues with the botched clearance of asbestos were so serious that they would not move forward on any basis unless that was remedied. All Cameron could do was to get copied into their reply. He felt professionally embarrassed, but something needed to be done.

He rang Tom, now back at his flat in London. 'So, it looks like he's scuttled off to Malaga as you feared.'

'Seems like it. We'll need to wait for that reply, because that formally closes off the possibility of a deal being concluded in the timescale the bank requires.'

'Will you ring Hodson in the meantime?' asked Jim.

'Well, if there are no other options. I certainly don't see any other possibilities,' Tom replied.

'Me neither. Presumably, I can expect a letter requiring the immediate paying off of the bank's overdraft almost immediately. Then what?'

Tom thought for a moment. 'Well, I'd call an emergency board meeting of the directors for tomorrow, requiring Lionel's attendance. I'd get your solicitors involved, too, so that you get appropriate insolvency advice. Don't make any payments or place any orders. Stop any credit cards, as well.'

'OK. Understood. The only thing which springs to mind is the supplies to the pier. Beer and foodstuffs …'

'There's nothing you can do there. I did give details of an administrator to Lionel a while back, so I'll let you have that, too. Once they're appointed, you are in their hands. They may want your help or not, as they see fit. Sorry to say it, but you're just another employee.'

'I might be back on the golf course sooner than I thought,' said Jim, more than a little sarcastically.

Tom could only sympathise. 'Yes. I'm sorry that Lionel's treated a friend so shabbily. Will you talk to Miriam in the meantime? There are things you can say to her that I can't.'

'Like clause 3c?'

'Yes. I have to say that I didn't feel at all comfortable keeping that quiet when I was with Janet last Sunday. Now the balloon is going up, she needs to know urgently. She's going to need some time to come to terms with things.'

'OK, leave that to me, Tom.'

'Fine. I'll let you know how Hodson reacts. Speak to you later, Jim.'

Tom poured himself a coffee, frustrated that he'd not seen

this coming. With hindsight, it was all a bit too good to be true, but in fairness the letter wasn't a fake and events could always derail a deal. He'd seen plenty of that over the years.

He'd been thinking about Janet as well, and her comments about retirement. Raising the money to buy the pier would be virtually impossible in the time available, but in any event would she want the extra responsibility that went with it?

To succeed, they would need some major donors or a lottery donation, and they couldn't do that in 30 days, but then again who would want to buy a Victorian pier?

He picked up the phone and rang Peter Hodson. It went to voicemail. He left a message. So, in the absence of anything better to do now, he began to think how he would raise the money to buy it himself.

Peter Hodson returned his call about an hour later and was obviously dismayed by the news.

'I should have known that we couldn't trust Pemrose. He's a nasty piece of work.'

'Well, yes, although you're actually in a slightly better position as at least they met the payroll. That's one creditor that the administrator won't have to pay.'

'True. Presumably I just send the termination letter? I imagine poor Jim is expecting it.'

'Well, yes, subject to him receiving the letter from Latchmores. I've advised him as to what to do and gave him a recommendation for the administrator.'

'Good. Is there anything else? You know, I'm actually really sorry about this, especially as it's a local business. You certainly did your best.'

'Yes, thanks, but I'd like to share something with you, if I may. Were you aware that the Pier Theatre lease has a purchase clause allowing them first option to buy it? Market value less 10%?'

Hodson paused. 'Well, actually I do recall something now you mention it. It's a long time ago. But why do you ask? Are you thinking of buying it? Or of advising the Pier Theatre to?'

'Possibly. Unless you'd object to my being involved. Bringing the ownership under a single entity is only logical, surely?'

'Well, no, I wouldn't object at all. To be honest, I guess I owe Mrs Wells something after 2008. She isn't likely to sing my praises. Feel free to try. I mean it's a hell of a long shot, but good luck to you.'

After terminating the call, he decided that he would be needed in Cromer that week, if only to offer support to a person he now thought of as a friend. He went into the bedroom to put some clothes in a suitcase. A piece of him thought he was being stupid, but what else would he do that week? He also admitted to himself that he wanted to see Janet again.

*   *   *

Janet was sitting in Miriam's sunroom. It was cloudy, with rain forecast, and Janet seemed surprisingly downbeat at the news.

Miriam smiled. 'I thought you'd see it as the opportunity we've always wanted. To get the whole pier at last …'

Janet seemed unconvinced. 'Yes, I suppose it is. It's just that Tom didn't give me any inkling that anything was wrong last Sunday, and I was with him most of the day.'

Miriam was unimpressed. 'Well, he couldn't really, could he? I was going to tell you once the sale process was under way, but the deal fell through and it's going into administration now, triggering clause 3c.'

'Poor Jim must be devastated after he agreed to put off his retirement to handle the sale.'

Miriam agreed. 'Lionel has shafted all of us. Most likely he's fled to Malaga with that floozy who caused most of the problems.'

'It'll send shockwaves through the town as well. The pier staff will be really upset, for a start.'

Miriam was becoming angry now. 'Yes, and everyone will assume our hotels have gone bust, too, so I'll have to deal with that as well, while Lionel suns himself by the pool. Only last weekend he mugged me into feeling sorry for him.'

Janet sighed. 'It's not what I need right now. I'm still worried about Hannah. That husband of hers is in town somewhere, they reckon. He might do anything at any time.'

Janet's phone pinged, and she clicked on the message. 'Ah. Mr Stanley is on his way. Apparently, he thinks that I might need to talk. Huh. I just hope he's brought his bloody chequebook.'

Miriam was vexed. 'It's not Tom's fault, Janet. This is about what you and Karen want. If you want us to have a go at raising the money, I'll back you 100%. But if you'd rather leave it as is and take your chances with the new owners of the pier, then so be it.'

'Yes, I know. I'll talk to Karen after the show tonight when it's quiet.'

Miriam couldn't help but think that back in 2009 Janet would have been only too happy to get a hold of the pier. But I guess we're all a bit older now and less accepting of change, she thought.

Janet changed the subject. 'Oh, it's Cyril's funeral on Wednesday. Are you coming?'

Miriam hedged a little. 'Well, there was bad blood between

him and Lionel, but I always loved the old boy, so, yes, I do plan to attend. Mind you, if Pemrose goes into administration tomorrow, we'll have to see.'

'Do you really think we could raise the money?' Janet asked.

Miriam thought about it. 'Honestly? Well, maybe in three months, but not in 30 days. To be honest, I don't think it's feasible, but who knows?'

*   *   *

The formal notice from the bank arrived at about 3pm and Jim sent out the notice of an emergency board meeting, amending it to read 3pm the following day. He had spoken to the solicitors, putting them on standby. The only question then was whether Lionel would attend.

Having sent the email and tried Lionel one more time, he realised that there was absolutely nothing more he could do. He packed up his briefcase and decided to call it a day. He stopped by Tyler's office to let him know about the bank letter.

Tyler nodded and shrugged. 'He's in Malaga. I emailed him about a fundraising event he was meant to be compèring here next week, and he replied saying that he was staying in Malaga for a while. Sorry. He seems to be replying to me, but not to you. Classic Lionel head-in-the-sand stuff. Is there anything I can do to help?'

Jim remembered one thing. 'Well, I can't order any supplies for the pier. Can you have a word with Debbie and ship some beer and wine down there if they need it? I don't want them running out and smelling a rat.'

Tyler nodded. 'Yeah, will do. It's been known to happen before. I'll just say there was a delivery stuff-up.'

Jim smiled. 'Many thanks, I'd appreciate it. You know, I really didn't think it would come to this.'

Tyler stood, and shook his hand. 'We all owe you a lot, Jim. All the crap you've taken over the years. Lionel's always been very fair with me, but dumping you in all this mess after he begged you to come back. Well, frankly that's just disgusting.'

Jim headed for the lift.

*   *   *

Tom arrived in Cromer in the early evening, not really sure what he'd do next. The rain was coming down heavily and Janet had not replied to his earlier text. Maybe she was upset that he'd kept the situation to himself. Perhaps she just needed time to think.

He pulled into the car park of the Majestic and dragged his suitcase from the car in the pouring rain. Hurrying into reception, he almost bumped into Tyler, who was heading off for the evening.

'Oh, hi Tom, back with us again? Jim went off early this afternoon. Did you need anything?'

'Well, this is sort of a social visit, I guess. I came along to be around in case I'm needed. Have you managed to track down Lionel down yet?'

'Yes. It's as we thought. He's in Malaga.'

Tom was unimpressed. 'Where I'd imagine the weather is a little better than here.'

'Where have you booked to stay? Only we're a bit busy tonight.'

'I just booked a standard room here. Seemed to be all that was left.'

'Oh, I'm sure we can do better than that for a regular visitor. Besides, I suspect Jim would welcome you being close at hand tomorrow. Let me see what I can do to sort things out.'

Tom smiled as Tyler headed behind the reception desk and beavered away on the booking system. He found himself wondering how much Tyler was to an extent a reincarnation of his boss. The attention to detail in this hotel was impressive.

He found himself in a superior sea-view suite with a balcony, if anything a bigger room than before so he was very content. He looked out into the stormy scene outside, and the sea battering the pier and promenade. He could see the theatre lit up in the rain, and tiny figures struggling their way towards it. He looked at his watch. It was coming up to showtime.

He had thought of going down to the theatre later on, but decided to leave well alone. Janet would need time to think things through and might decide that it was all too big a challenge. They were both at a crossroads in their lives, Tom still burning with ambition, while Janet was not. This turn of events might force that decision.

He was becoming peckish, and the room was comfortable and pleasantly warm, in spite of the storm outside. He decided to run a bath and order room service for an hour later. Nothing complicated. A simple medium-rare sirloin steak. As he ran the bath, the seasoned traveller went to his bag, and took out a nice Australian red he'd brought from home, pouring himself a large glass.

He got in the bath and laid back to relax. He was a little drowsy after his drive, but a few minutes later his phone pinged.

'Lunch tomorrow, 1pm? My room in the pier box office. Bring big chequebook. Janet'

He laughed, relieved that she'd got in touch.

*   *   *

In fact, Janet had sent the text message during the first break she had managed since arriving at the pier that evening. They had beefed up security, and she had given each usher a picture of Hannah's husband, with instructions to bring to her attention anyone who looked like the person in the photo. The bag checks were more diligent than usual. She'd also hired two security guards to patrol the backstage area. It was already cramped back there, but it was a necessary precaution. PC Edwards had introduced herself, assuring Janet that they were active in their search.

The show went well again that evening, and Hannah performed flawlessly once more. Amy showed no signs of stage fright and met the audience after the show, developing her self-confidence in doing so. Later on, sat in an empty bar with the audience long gone, Janet finally told Karen of her meeting with Miriam, and of the impending administration.

Karen was delighted. 'Wow! So we finally have the opportunity to buy the whole pier? Well, that's just fantastic, Mum.'

Janet was surprised. 'Oh. Do you think so? I wasn't sure how you'd feel.'

Karen was astonished. 'Feel? Well, it would set me up for life, wouldn't it? What's not to like?'

'But it's a hell of a risk. And we can't possibly raise the money in the time available, anyway.'

Karen looked shocked. 'You sound just like Grandad. There's a darn sight more risk as a tenant, scrimping and saving to pay the rent every year, with Lionel out to trip us up every five minutes.'

'Well, yes,' conceded Janet. 'But we'd have to run the bar

and the restaurant and take care of the pier itself. I wouldn't have a clue.'

'But you'd get people to handle that stuff. It's no big deal.'

Janet wasn't impressed. 'Well, you wouldn't have to do it. It would all fall to me and you're the one telling me to take it easy.'

'Well, true, but we're going to have to restructure to allow that to happen anyway. The bigger enterprise would attract a much wider range of talent to succeed you, and we'd be able to offer a better salary, too. You could job-share until you're ready to step down.'

'I suppose so.'

'Look, I really see this as good news. If Grandad had taken the plunge all those years ago, think where we'd be now.'

'But where on earth would we get the money? And in such a short period of time?'

'Well, it's a hell of a challenge, I'll admit, but loads of people will pitch in. Everyone that Lionel screwed, for a start. Miriam will be up for it for sure. Jim Cameron will most likely come on board because he'll have retired, and as for your boyfriend Mr Stanley, it's right up his alley. He's been raising money for years.'

'Don't keep calling him my boyfriend. He's nothing of the sort.'

'Well, he's taking you to see *Hamilton*, isn't he? And he's a friend that happens to be a boy? So, he's a boyfriend.'

'I haven't said I'll go yet. If he were a real friend, he'd have told me what was going on behind my back.'

Karen was becoming angry. 'No, he couldn't, Mum. You can be so naive sometimes. He was working for the bank on a confidential basis. He couldn't possibly have told you. You're being ridiculous.'

'Well, all I know is that I was with him all day on Sunday and there was no hint of a problem. Now this.'

'There you are, then. I'd get him here bloody quickly if I were you. The clock will start ticking tomorrow.'

'He's already here, Karen. At the Majestic.'

'Ah.'

'I sent him a text earlier. I've arranged to meet him tomorrow. Come along if you want.'

'Ah. Cunning plan. Yes, I'll tag along. We've really got to make this happen, you know, however difficult it is. Come on, let's go. The rain's easing off and Debbie will want to lock up.'

18.

Tuesday

Peter Hodson parked in his reserved space behind the bank, chatted briefly to staff as he entered and went into the branch conference room. He switched on his laptop and logged in, drinking the first coffee of the day as he did so.

He first checked his diary. He was expecting some word on Pemrose later in the day, Jim Cameron having confirmed that a board meeting was now scheduled. Otherwise, it was a fairly light day.

He clicked on his emails, and among the usual head office communications there was one from Lionel Pemrose. Its subject line said Formal complaint. Initially, it didn't faze him. He quite expected a formal email complaining at the decision to withdraw facilities.

But then he saw that he had only been copied in, and the main addressee was the bank's anti-fraud team. Scanning it briefly his eyes were drawn to a particular paragraph. As he read it his blood ran cold.

> *I therefore wish to formally complain at Mr Hodson's handling of our account. Some years ago, he accepted corporate hospitality at my villa in Malaga for both him and his wife, apparently in breach of your corporate policy, and*

used his position to solicit sexual favours from a young and impressionable member of our staff. Whilst we reluctantly decided to overlook his behaviour at the time, it has become clear that since we dealt with the matter, he has become ever more restrictive in his approach towards our banking arrangements, culminating in his recent decision to withdraw facilities altogether. This will directly result in us having to place a profitable business into administration, thus jeopardising local jobs with a long-standing employer, who is also a well-established client of yours.

I look forward to receiving your comments on his conduct as per your procedure. I have also made a formal complaint to the regulator in similar vein.

He then noticed there were a couple of attachments. He clicked on the first one and saw a picture of him sitting on the edge of the swimming pool beside Lizzie. She was wearing a white bikini, and he was in swimming trunks. In the second one he was pictured with her at dinner. As they weren't posed photographs, it was obvious that they were taken without their knowledge. Neither picture really showed anything improper, but the insinuation was clear. The investigation would not change anything, Lionel would know that. This was just revenge.

He had no worries over the corporate hospitality, since it had been formally approved by his then boss. It was just the photographs, although the bank would probably think them irrelevant. With any luck, his wife wouldn't see them anyway. He recovered his equilibrium, although he wasn't completely reassured.

One thing was for certain; he would make Lionel pay for this gratuitous attempt at revenge.

*   *   *

It was at around 11am that two community support officers visited a caravan park in East Runton. They had been on this wild goose chase for a few days and were frankly getting rather bored. One of them ventured into the site office, while the other wandered around the site. The office was empty, so the CSO rang the bell. Minutes later a woman entered through the main door, looking a little flustered.

'Sorry, I was putting fresh soap in the loos. How can I help you?'

'Good morning. We're making enquiries about this individual. I wonder if he's one of your guests. Have you seen him at all, or anyone resembling him?'

The woman was older, mid-sixties at a guess, and she had to put on her glasses to look. She studied the picture carefully, then glanced at the CSO before returning her gaze to the picture. Looking in the register, she turned over the page carefully.

'That would be Mr Lewis. Pitch 23.'

The CSO's face blinked in surprise. 'I'm sorry. Are you sure? Do you want to look at it again?'

'Oh, no, dear. I'm jolly good with faces. He booked in a couple of weeks ago. Paid cash, as I recall. Nice chap.'

The CSO was stunned and took out her radio. 'Well, look, if you're sure, I'll just check in.'

As she did so, a car drove out of the gate at speed. The woman reacted immediately.

'Oh. That was Mr Lewis leaving. That blue Fiesta is his car.'

The other CSO burst in through the door. 'That was him! Castle. He was coming out of his caravan. I wasn't sure he saw me, but he went back in and picked up a laptop, then got in his car and drove off before I could stop him.'

'Caravan 23?' said the woman.

'Yes. How did you guess?'

*   *   *

For Tom it had been a relaxed morning and he dropped in on Jim, who was happy enough to see him.

'Heard from Lionel yet, Jim?' he asked.

'Finally. This morning. Says he'll attend. Didn't want the solicitor, said it was a waste of money. I told him it wasn't negotiable.'

'Good. Absolutely right,' said Tom.

Jim shrugged. 'I feel pretty helpless, to be honest. There's really nothing to do right now.'

'Well, yes, that's pretty much true. Have you decided on the administrators?'

'Well, as I've heard nothing from Lionel, I'm suggesting the firm that you recommended.'

'Decent people. They'll do their job, but not without some sensitivity. Do me a favour and try to make sure they don't screw up and close the pier. I'm probably in enough hot water with Janet Wells as it is.'

Jim smiled. 'Ah. You didn't tell her about things, then? During your house hunt.'

'No. I couldn't really, could I?'

Jim replied, with a slightly impish grin. 'I guess not. Knowing Janet, though, she might not see it that way. She has a very strong if unique view of loyalty. Is there anything I can do to help?'

'Not unless you know how much the pier is worth. I've only got the balance sheet value, which could be way off. Knowing how much we need would be a big help.'

'Now it's funny you should mention that. It seems that Lionel recently commissioned two valuations. They've appended a copy to their bills. I have them here, I think. They won't get paid, though, I imagine…'

Jim extracted them from his case, but merely placed them on the desk.

'If you'll just excuse me, I need the loo. Too much black coffee.'

He headed out of the door and Tom smiled. He took out his phone and took pictures of the two valuations, which were pretty close together in value.

Jim returned a few minutes later and put the valuations away without a word.

Tom broke the silence. 'I'm going to see Janet at lunchtime. I wonder how she'll feel about it all?'

Jim shrugged. 'Well, her father had the chance all those years ago, but was scared of the risk. Janet is her father's daughter. You might have a job on your hands there.'

'Yes. She seems to be thinking more about her retirement, rather than taking on more.'

'Young Karen might see things differently.'

'Karen? I thought she saw herself as more of a creative. But she is a little frustrated by her mother's ways.'

Jim saw things differently, 'Well, that's true as the structure stands today, but there's no reason why a creative can't be the boss, with a strong director in charge of everything else.'

Tom conceded, 'I hadn't really thought of it that way. What happened to Karen's father?'

'Now there's a bit of local scandal. When she was 17, Janet had a brief affair with a tourist and Karen was the result. She doesn't really talk about it, although she's now on good terms with the father and his wife. They come down here from time to time and usually stay here.'

'Ah. That explains things. So, she's never been married then?'

Jim sighed, 'Only to that theatre. It's been her whole life. That's why this is all so difficult for her.'

'Well, we'll soon see how difficult it is.'

Jim looked up, 'It's certainly an awful lot of money to raise in 30 days.'

'Well, I've been in trickier spots. But it's a big number with an asset that you can't get a mortgage on.'

'Well, good luck with it anyway. If I'm unemployed in a day or two, then I'd be happy to help.'

'Really? Lionel would love that, I'm sure. I might well take you up on that.'

They shook hands and went their separate ways.

*   *   *

It had been an eventful morning for Carla Edwards. She'd been doing some administration at Cromer Police Station when one of her CSOs had made contact.

'Hi, Carla. We're in East Runton and we've found Mr Castle. Unfortunately, he spotted us and did a runner. Blue Fiesta. He didn't have time to take much though. I've sealed off the caravan.'

Edwards grabbed her car keys and headed for the car, asking the desk sergeant to contact the relevant backup. On her arrival, one CSO was guarding the caravan, the other was in the office with the site owner. The introductions were brief, Edwards realising that in her haste she'd forgotten to get one obvious detail.

'What was the registration number of the blue Fiesta?' she asked.

The CSO shrugged. 'He left so fast we didn't get it, I'm afraid. Sorry. It all happened so quick. I stuck my head in the caravan, mind, and it's full of his stuff. I didn't touch anything.'

The site owner took out her record card. 'It's on here, love. We always get car details in case of parking problems.'

Edwards took the card and glanced wearily at the CSO, who looked rather sheepish. She phoned the number through to the station immediately. Castle had a head start on them, and in an hour he could be anywhere.

In fact, he was actually getting rather lost in woodland close to Holt. When he'd seen the CSO, he'd panicked. It was all he could do to grab the laptop and his car keys. Heart thumping, he stopped the car in a leafy lay-by and used Google Maps to find out where he was. He needed to lose the car, he realised. They would be looking for it now, so it had to go.

He had no spare clothes and he didn't even have a charger for his phone. Fortunately, he did have his wallet, the phone itself and credit cards. He thought for a few moments, ducking down as a car went by on what was a rather secluded road.

He couldn't risk renting another car, so he needed to stay close to Cromer. Equally, he needed to dump this hire car, and here was as remote a place as he was likely to find. He spotted a track leading further into the wood, clearly not recently used, so he eased the Fiesta down the track and pulled in behind some bushes. He then consulted the phone and realised that he did have one option.

Within a quarter of a mile there was a railway station. A tourist steam railway, the Poppy Line, running between Holt and Sheringham. He could dump the car here, take the train to Sheringham, and then get either the Coast Hopper tourist bus or a scheduled train service to Cromer.

Checking the timetable, he realised that he had just enough time to make the next train, one of only a handful that day. He abandoned the car and took out a rucksack from the boot. He stuffed the laptop and one or two other items in it and headed off at a brisk walk. He checked Google Maps and made his way out of the wood. Picking up the main road, he began to accelerate his stride. He switched his phone off to save the battery, breaking into a run as he neared the station. He reached the ticket office with just enough time to bung some money at the cashier and grab a ticket.

The guard was poised to signal the train to leave, but smiled and waved to him to climb aboard. Out of breath after his sprint, Ian picked an empty carriage and slumped back in his seat, closing his eyes as he recovered. He pondered what he'd left behind. All of his clothes and personal effects, of course. Hannah's mobile, which he'd stolen, and the remaining DVDs. Fortunately, he still had the laptop.

He tried to work out what to do next. He would need somewhere to stay, ideally in Cromer itself. Probably a bed and breakfast of some sort. He still had plenty of cash, but with the police on to him, he was running out of options. He would need to make a move to meet Hannah and get her to see reason as soon as possible. He had a ticket to a show she was headlining, and he was looking forward to seeing her once again.

*   *   *

The board meeting started promptly, with both the solicitor and Lionel dialling in. Jim Cameron took the chair as board secretary. Lionel didn't appear to object. As chair, he asked the solicitor to outline the implications of the letter from the bank and their obligations as directors. Lionel said nothing, so Jim moved the motion to enter administration. Again, Lionel didn't object. The final item was the appointment of an administrator. Lionel said nothing, so Jim put forward the name of the firm on the agenda. The solicitor confirmed that they were a reputable firm with an office in Norwich. Jim expected that Lionel would make a counter-proposal, but he did not. In the absence of any objection, the appointment was carried. The solicitor would provide suitably watertight minutes of the meeting, and that was it. Lionel dialled off without any further comment. The whole meeting had taken a little less than half an hour. Jim sat back, astonished at Lionel's complete lack of engagement. It was as if he'd given up.

Let's get this done, he thought. He picked up the telephone and asked to be put through.

'Collinson,' a voice answered.

'David, it's Jim Cameron of Pemrose Entertainments here. As per our conversation, the board meeting has just ended, and you've been appointed as administrators. I wondered how you wanted to proceed?'

'Thanks, Jim. I'll be along with a team first thing in the morning. Can you just clear a conference room for us to work from and we'll make a start?'

*   *   *

Janet and Karen were at home having an early tea ahead of the show. The meeting with Tom earlier in the day had left Karen fuming, and it was an unusually silent affair, as if neither wanted to break the ice.

Karen was furious at her mother's persistent low-level negativity to the whole idea of trying to secure the pier. They hadn't even begun to do justice to the most difficult topic of all: raising the money to buy it. Instead, Janet seemed to mention every tiny problem and risk that they would encounter if they took it on at all.

It wasn't helped by Janet's attitude to Tom, which seemed rather sulky and distant. Here was a highly skilled professional man, offering his services free of charge to secure the future of the theatre in perpetuity, and all she could ask about was how she'd go about running the bar or getting work done on the boardwalk.

Tom had shown remarkable patience. She wouldn't have blamed him if he'd got in his car and headed straight back to London, such was her mother's attitude. They had travelled back to the house separately, and it seemed that neither of them was in the mood to discuss things further.

Karen finished her tea, put her plate and cutlery in the dishwasher, and headed out of the front door.

'I'm going down early. I'll see you later.'

Arriving at the Pier Theatre, she rang the number of the Majestic, and asked to be put through to Tom Stanley.

'Tom. Hi, it's Karen Wells. I'd like to have a chat with you, to get a few things clearer in my mind. I wondered if I could have breakfast with you tomorrow. I'm busy at a funeral later on, but would 9am be too early?'

19.

Wednesday

Recognising that the conversation might be a little sensitive, Tom had talked briefly to Tyler, who had arranged for them to have breakfast in a small meeting room. After the events of the previous day, Tyler could guess the topic for discussion and was happy to help. With Lionel gone, it was a time for old feuds to end, he reckoned.

Tom met Karen in reception and showed her into the meeting room.

'I figured it was more private here, and it's a perk of having lived here for a while. Order what you like. I'm sorry it's on enemy territory.'

'Thanks Tom. I'll just have coffee and a Danish, please.'

The waiter went away, bringing the coffee and a pot of tea for Tom. A while later a selection of pastries arrived.

'The croissants are good. Almost as good as the French make them.'

'They do look nice. If I stayed here for long, I'd be like a beach ball.'

'Hardly. You still have your dancer's figure if I'm allowed to say that these days.'

'You are. I'll take any compliments I can get at my age.'

'So, you wanted to talk about something?'

She hesitated a little, set down her coffee cup and frowned.

'Well, first I need to apologise for my mum's reaction yesterday. She's just a bit all at sea right now.'

Tom smiled. 'There's nothing to apologise for. It's a huge step, and it's a mountain to climb to raise the money.'

Karen nibbled her Danish and put it down. 'But do you think it can be done?' she said.

Tom demurred a little. 'Well, it won't be easy, but you won't know unless you try. I'm certainly up for it. I like a challenge.'

Karen persisted. 'But what are the odds, do you reckon? Honestly?'

Tom thought for a moment. 'I'd say 80/20 against, given the timescales. That's why I came straight up here when I heard about the administration.'

'So it's worth a shot at least?' she asked.

'Yes, if that's what you and Janet want. I should tell you that I'm a rather bad loser.'

Karen smiled. 'So am I. Mum is too, truth be known. She's just trying to come to terms with what retirement might mean, and this complicates things greatly.'

'Well, I can relate to that, having recently been made redundant from my own business. But let's talk about you. What do you want?'

From her hesitation, it seemed to Tom that Karen hadn't really thought this through.

She finished her pastry, then replied, 'Well, I guess I'm assessing my future, too. I'm over 40 now, and although I love the show, it's all getting very repetitive. I've done it for so many years that it just runs like clockwork now, well, most of the time at least.'

'And Janet's a control freak.'

Karen laughed at his directness. 'Well. Yes, there's Mum's way and there's Mum's way. New technology is passing us by somewhat, and to be honest having the whole pier business to run would give us more opportunities. But Mum just sees it as a bigger workload for her.'

Tom nodded. 'Oh, you often seen this in a family business, generations rubbing up against each other.'

'You do?' she replied.

'Oh, yes. It's inevitable when your mother has no interests outside of her work. She brought you up alone, and then her father died leaving her to run the show. When did she have time for herself?'

Karen shrugged. 'Well, now is her time, I guess. I can do so much more, and we could automate stuff to make things in the back office easier. She's tried to cut her hours, but it's two steps forward and one step back.'

'Well, I offered to take her to see *Hamilton*, and I'm still waiting for some dates.'

'Exactly. Good luck with that. I was a bit surprised when she went house hunting with you, to be honest.'

'So was I. But it was a nice day. I certainly enjoyed it.'

They talked for an hour or so, and Tom was surprised that a mother and daughter who lived under the same roof, and were so close, couldn't actually work things out.

Karen looked at her watch and realised that she needed to go.

Tom laughed. 'I find it funny seeing people looking at their watches, up against the clock, when I've suddenly got all the time in the world.'

Karen was collecting her things. 'Well, it's a really sad day. Our great friend and long-standing Punch and Judy man, Cyril

Brown, died recently and it's his funeral today. The whole cast will be going. It's not until a bit later, but I need to make a move.'

'So what, may I ask, does your father think? Have you spoken to him about it at all? It's OK, I know the story, and not from your mother.'

'Well, Paul says to go for it, but he would, of course. He's a football manager, so with him it's all about finishing first.'

'Well, I agree with him of course, but I mustn't try to talk your mother round. I don't know her well enough, and at the end of the day it's really none of my business.'

'But you came back. You didn't need to.'

Tom admired her directness. 'Well, yes. I do like her, Karen. She's good company and I miss that, after my wife died and someone retired me rather early.'

Karen nodded. 'She likes you too, I think. She had a good time that day. I think she's just about forgiven you for not letting on about things, even though she had no reason to expect you to.'

'Good. But I'll plead not guilty on that. I've built a career based on keeping confidences, and I'm not stopping now,' he said.

'Yes. I know. Look, just let us get today out of the way. Cyril had no immediate family, and Mum was really close to him, actually we all were. We all visited him in his last days. So today we look back, but tomorrow I promise we'll be ready to look forward. Mum's frightened at the moment, but that will pass. If you've time on your hands, could I suggest you write a bit of a plan as to how we'd go about raising the money, and we'll have a council of war on Friday? Miriam needs to be in on it, too. She's well connected to the local money.'

With that, Karen got up to leave and Tom extended his hand. She took it and hugged him briefly.

'Thanks, Tom. Thanks for being there at the right time.'

He saw she was choking back tears as she headed for the door.

*   *   *

The church had filled up nicely. Two cousins were all that were left of Cyril's immediate family, but the extended one included a number of older celebrities, as well as friends from generations of Punch and Judy audiences, and a large local contingent. The Pier Theatre group sat together near the front. Lauren and Les joined them, with hugs all round.

It was around halfway through the service when the rector called on Lauren to speak. She had a single piece of paper in her hand as she reached the lectern. For someone used to singing to huge audiences, she had felt awfully nervous that morning, and Les had offered to read the eulogy for her. But this was something Lauren knew that she had to do herself. Her voice was now recovering, but she was still barred from singing. She steadied herself, put on some reading glasses, cleared her throat and took a sip of water before speaking.

'Good morning, everyone. I'm Lauren Evans. First of all, apologies for my voice, it's just about come back after the tour, although I still can't sing. Doctor's orders. But I simply must pay tribute to my dear friend, Cyril Brown. You see, when I first arrived in Cromer in 2009, I was pretty much washed up and virtually bankrupt. I'd been dropped by my record company and was basically out of work. But although my self- confidence had gone, I still had the airs and graces of a star, and was, forgive my French, a right stuck-up bitch.'

The audience chuckled in response as she continued.

'Cyril was actually the first local I met. He was sitting on the pier in his top hat and tails, every inch the Punch and Judy man. His cheeky smile and old-fashioned courtesy made me feel welcome at a time when I didn't feel I belonged anywhere. Anyway, on my first morning, the director, a complete no-hoper by the way, told me my fortune in no uncertain terms. By the following morning, I'd decided it wasn't for me. So I headed to the railway station to go back to Wales.'

Janet looked across at Les, as Karen giggled.

Lauren continued. 'Now, Cyril arrived out of the blue and sat down on the bench next to me. Frankly, I didn't want to talk to anyone, but the train was late and, without really addressing me, he gave me the pep talk I needed. To this day, I remember his words. He said, "You will recover, you know? The great talents always do."

'Well, thanks to Cyril, and Les, and the Pier Theatre of course, I have recovered. I've lived the dream and I'm the happiest I've been in my life. Rest in peace, Cyril old friend. You simply lovely man. This world is the less for your passing.'

She was shaking and in tears as she walked back down to where Les was waiting for her. He hugged her but he was suppressing tears, too. The congregation broke out in warm applause.

At the end of the service, Janet, Karen, Amy and Hannah walked to the front, and sang *Somewhere Over the Rainbow* in tribute, with Lauren silently mouthing the words. As the congregation left, Miriam Pemrose hugged Janet, before spotting Julia Maitland at the door waiting for her.

'Hi, Julia,' she said, hugging her long-standing friend.

'Beautiful service, Miriam, your luvvies can certainly put on a show.'

'Yes, they certainly can. He affected a lot of lives, did Cyril.

Such a pity he fell out with Lionel, but then he wasn't alone in that. How's retirement?'

'Well, I'm still running my work down this week and next, talking of which I need to meet you and Janet; would Tuesday be all right?'

'Yes. Fine by me. Just send us both an email and we'll confirm it. What's it about?'

'Ah. Now that I can't say right now. It's complicated,' she replied.

*   *   *

It was around 4pm when Jim Cameron left the Majestic, having spent the day with David Collinson. The standard documentation had gone to each location, and an official letter had been sent to the staff. He'd written a separate document to the staff in the hotels group and had sent it to Lionel for approval. In the absence of any comment, he'd shown it to Tyler, who said he'd send it out in his name as chief executive.

Collinson thanked him for his help, but then handed him a notification of redundancy, saying that he would be on garden leave unless summoned to attend work. Cameron took a walk down to the pier, knowing that Debbie would be on duty. They'd worked together for a long time, and he thought he owed her an explanation.

He went in through the door, noticing the administration notice taped to the front. He ordered a pint of Woodforde's from a girl behind the bar he didn't know, but as he sat in the window in the sunshine, pulling off his tie and opening his collar, he heard a voice behind him.

'Bad day at the office?'

He turned to see Debbie smiling sadly.

'Can I get you a drink, Debbie?' he asked.

He got her a white wine and they sat watching the tourists enjoying the sunshine.

'I never thought it would come to this,' she said.

'No, neither did I. A really sad day.'

'Lionel's shot his bolt this time, then. Where is the lecherous old sod now?' she asked.

Jim quaffed his beer and replied, 'Malaga'.

'Bloody typical. Nowhere near when the shit hits the fan. Leaving you to clean up after him.'

'That's about it,' he replied.

Jim was through making excuses for Lionel. Why should he bother now?

Debbie continued. 'Do you know if anyone's interested in buying it? What's happening to you? Do you know anything yet?'

Jim looked up. 'I was given my notice half an hour ago. Not to worry, though, I was going to retire soon anyway.'

Debbie stopped mid-sip. 'That's tough. Mind you, I'm too young to retire.'

Jim shook his head. 'You'll be OK, Debbie; and if not, speak to Tyler. He'll look after you. Good guy, Tyler.'

'Will Mrs Wells make a bid, do you think?'

Jim had expected the question. 'Who knows? They might do, but I'm on the other side, remember.'

'Well, I hope they do. This split arrangement makes no sense.'

'No, it doesn't.'

'But will the pier be sold as a business? Surely they won't shut it in the middle of the season?'

Jim considered how to respond. 'Well, I'd have thought not,

but Mr Collinson is in charge now. He's very businesslike and efficient. Remember that he's done this before many times.'

Debbie sipped her wine. 'No Punch and Judy this year, either. Cyril Brown's funeral today.'

Jim was saddened. 'Oh, I didn't realise with everything that's going on. I'm not sure I'd have been welcomed at the funeral, mind.'

'Well, Miriam was there, and Cyril didn't bear grudges, which is more than can be said for Lionel.'

* * *

Karen got ready to go down for the evening show, which Hannah was headlining. Both mother and daughter had attended the wake, a small affair in town, and were just very quietly going about their business. Karen had a sense that there was a stand-off between them, and someone needed to break the ice. They were standing in the kitchen making tea when she spoke.

'I had breakfast with Tom this morning,' Karen said.

Janet looked at her but said nothing.

Karen continued as she made herself a snack. 'I told him that I wanted him to raise the money to buy the pier.'

Janet stayed silent and was clearly ready for a row.

Karen now addressed her mother directly. 'I'm not prepared to sit idly by as Grandad did and let someone take over who might be worse than Lionel. It's my future I'm fighting for. Join in, or don't join in, but I'm going for it either way.'

Janet stared at her incredulously. 'Oh, so I don't count anymore? Now just suppose Tom's on someone else's side. He's done loads of deals. Suppose he uses you, then grabs the whole lot for himself and his mates?'

Karen set down the knife and stared back at her. 'What? Why would he? I don't understand.'

'He's made lots of money before. He's only in it for the deal. He's another Lionel. Just buys and sells businesses as if they're chattel. No regard for the consequences. He's just another City barrow boy.'

Karen stared at her and stood, hands on hips. 'I can't believe I'm hearing this crap.'

Janet was angry now. 'So why didn't he tell me about clause 3c? Because he didn't want us to know about it. It was Jim who told Miriam, not Tom. He kept quiet about it, didn't he? So that he could buy it on the cheap.'

Karen shook her head. 'That's just a stupid conspiracy theory. He didn't tell you because he was working for the bank.'

Janet nodded. 'Exactly. Working for Peter Hodson, who, may I remind you, screwed us in 2009.'

Karen assessed her mother's logic. There was just the merest shred of evidence to create a doubt.

But Karen decided that she was wrong. 'Are you ever going to trust anyone in this life ever, Mum? So, OK, suppose you're right. What else is there? You weren't exactly successful raising the money in 2009. Miriam saved us. You were going to sell us down the river, remember? Why not see what she thinks now? Because whatever you make of him, Tom Stanley is our only chance of raising the money. I think this is all just a smokescreen because you're just too chicken to take a risk for once.'

Janet slapped her face. It hurt. Karen turned, grabbed her coat and handbag, and opened the front door.

'I'm sorry Karen ... I didn't mean ... I didn't mean to hurt you, love.'

Karen slammed the door. Janet crumpled into a sobbing mess on the settee.

*   *   *

After getting into Cromer on the bus, Castle had been to a supermarket and bought some essentials, then booked into a holiday flat on the outskirts of town, but within walking distance of the pier. He'd paid by credit card online. It was risky, but he just had to chance it as he was running out of options and reckoned that going to a bed and breakfast was a worse idea.

He shaved his facial hair off completely and had his hair cut short at a barber's shop. He chided himself for not doing so before. A schoolboy error, but for most of the time he hadn't seen himself as a fugitive.

He looked at himself in the mirror. Yes, he looked just about different enough. He had a ticket for tonight's show. At least he'd get to see her up close. He'd booked a seat in the fourth row, but well off to one side so she wouldn't see him. Until after the show. He had actually managed to check things out backstage a couple of days before. A closed but unlocked fire door had allowed him in.

The headliner's dressing room was marked as such, and the two clothes rails within it were marked Amy and Hannah. He was going to take more of a look around, but heard someone coming, and decided that he knew enough.

He had weighed up different options. She was still in the hotel, which made gaining access to her there difficult and, in any event, he thought it likely that her policeman lover would be staying over. She was escorted to the pier and back, so the only time she was backstage alone would be after the show.

He bought a large wrench at a DIY store. He didn't want to take the policeman on unless he had to, but, if necessary, he would. He left it until quite late to go down to the theatre and found a waste bin near the fire door behind the pier where he stowed the wrench. He noticed that the door was still as he had left it on his last visit. He then entered the foyer as the audience went in. He smiled at the usher as she looked at his ticket.

'Enjoy the show,' she said as he went in.

'Thanks. I will,' he replied.

He found his seat, on the end of the row, and consulted the programme. He could see what the final tune was, so he understood the running order. He settled back to watch the show.

* * *

Karen was still appalled by what had happened earlier. She recalled the impact on her cheek, and the devastated look on her mother's face afterwards. In her whole life, she couldn't remember her mother laying so much as a finger on her, even as a child. The only time she'd really seen her cry was back in 2009 when she'd told her who her father was.

Karen was distracted and functioning on autopilot that evening. She continued to be amazed at how seamlessly Hannah stood in for Amy to give her a regular break. The fears of a recurrence of Amy's stage fright seemed to have receded, and the show had received great reviews, not only locally but also in the theatrical press.

She noted that one of the two hired security guards had not shown up that evening, but Graham had escorted Hannah down as usual, and would walk her back after the show. They owed him a huge debt of gratitude for all he was doing.

She went backstage and completed the standard pre-performance checklist. She checked in with Gerald as musical director, Judy, the sound engineer, and the beginners in the cast. She then gave the 'go for performance' call, as she had for the last ten years. It was all very routine now. What could possibly go wrong?

*   *   *

Janet had stayed home that evening. She had been completely thrown by Karen's decision to take the initiative. Although she enjoyed Tom's company, the link with Peter Hodson was a painful reminder of his betrayal in 2009, when he had revoked the theatre's overdraft and conspired with Lionel to fund his revamp of the pier. Any friend of Hodson was definitely no friend of hers.

But she had to concede that Karen had a point. Tom had the skills to raise the necessary money, and nobody else that she knew did. And, in truth, she knew she was guilty of not seeing things from Karen's point of view. Janet's single-minded view of life had helped her survive through any number of crises, but now she was becoming tired of fighting. She looked forward to taking more time out from the theatre, but found it so difficult to let go. With hindsight, she hadn't really understood that Karen had ambitions beyond running the show. Perhaps mother and daughter had been too polite to each other, or perhaps she'd been slow on the uptake. Either way, tonight was a watershed, and she'd got the message. Things had to change.

Well, there was one thing she could sort out. They had known each other for years from opposing sides, but when Lionel was being particularly difficult, she had always rung this particular number, and he invariably brokered a solution. Thus, she rang the recently redundant Jim Cameron.

'Janet Wells. Long time, no speak,' he said.

'Yes, Jim. First of all, I'm so sorry about the events of today. A dreadfully sad day all round.'

'Thanks, Janet. Yes, I gather it was Cyril's funeral today. It puts my own wee problems into perspective. A lovely man. Shame he didn't see eye to eye with my former boss, but he's not alone in that.'

'So, how are you this evening, Jim? It must be awful.'

'Well, tonight I feel unemployed. Redundant is the technical term,' he replied, rather flippantly.

'Oh, God. So soon? After all these years? I'm lost for words, Jim.'

'No worries, I was retiring anyway. There's many that I feel sorry for tonight, but I'm not one of them. Now, what can I do for you this fine summer's evening?'

It took her a while to say what was on her mind, but in essence Janet repeated her fears of collusion between Peter Hodson and Lionel Pemrose, and her fears that consequently Tom was simply doing Hodson's bidding.

Cameron thought before replying. 'Well, I haven't known everything that Lionel has got up to recently, and I certainly didn't back in 2009. Was Hodson's decision to pull your overdraft linked to Lionel's plan to get rid of you? It was a big coincidence, wasn't it? And they were close at that time. Balance of probability? Yes, they were in collusion.'

'I certainly thought so.'

'But the second part of your point is way off-beam. Lionel now despises Hodson for pulling the rug from under him, so the idea that the administration is to allow Lionel to somehow restructure the group is plain wrong. He's licking his wounds out in Malaga.'

'But Tom works for Hodson. How can I trust him?' she asked.

Jim laughed. 'Because Tom Stanley is one of the straightest guys I've ever met. He has acted entirely properly towards the bank and towards Pemrose Entertainments as a company. He was an entirely honest broker who did everything he could to keep the business afloat.'

'So, what if he offers to help me to raise the money to buy the pier?'

Jim thought for a moment. 'Then you would be a fool to turn him down. And if you trust me at all, I'll help as well as far as I'm allowed to. I'm through with Lionel now. It would be good if, as I retire, I can help sort this bloody pier situation out once and for all. Lionel said it's the jewel in the crown of the town and he's right. You'll never get a better chance.'

Janet said quietly, 'But I'm scared, Jim.'

Jim was incredulous. 'Janet Wells scared? I never ever thought I'd hear you say that. Now, can I offer you some advice?'

'Of course.'

'Well, you just need to trust people more. Tom will help you, and so will Karen, Miriam and I. You have a lot of friends in this town. Just stop thinking that you have to do it all by yourself.'

'I don't know anything about running a bar and restaurant, or looking after a Victorian pier for that matter, and frankly I'm getting too old to take on new stuff.'

'You've got people like Debbie who do, and we have a system of inspection on the pier structure itself. Qualified contractors who plan and deliver the annual maintenance schedule. All I do is pay the bills. Piece of cake, really.'

'Well, OK. But I don't even know how much we need to raise.'

Jim hesitated for a moment. 'But Tom does. Let's just say that I made sure of that. Look, you have 30 days to prove you have the funds, and nothing to lose in trying. You can't afford to waste time working out who to trust. Ring Tom now and get things moving is my advice. You have to launch a big local publicity campaign to get loads of small donations coming in, while Tom tries to land the big fish. Miriam knows people, too. You have to do this, if not for the town, then for your Karen.'

*   *   *

The finale song was underway. It would soon be time to make his move. He knew that the cast signed autographs afterwards, so he could watch from outside until she went back through to the dressing room.

As the show ended, he slipped out ahead of the crowd, and checked that the fire door was still wedged slightly ajar. He then took up his position outside. He could see her posing for photographs in the foyer in her electric-blue stage costume. Her policeman friend stood by as she laughed and joked. The big Polish guy was there too. Ian waited until the crowd slackened a little, then went down to the side of the pier, finding the wrench he had hidden, in spite of the semi-darkness.

He slipped into the darkened backstage area and could hear female voices. The dancers, he concluded. He slipped into the headliner's room and waited, crammed into a corner of the room. He could hear people leaving through the rear exit. The fewer people around, the better. Then he recognised a female voice.

'See you later, Lech. I'll see you outside, Graham.'

Then the door opened and a smiling Hannah came through the door.

'Hi, Hannah. Long time, no see. Enjoyed the show,' he said calmly.

She turned to face him and wanted to scream, but no sound would come out.

'We don't have much time. I love you and miss you so much. I need you to come home now. The life I built for you is crumbling around my ears. Whatever problems we had we can work out. Let's just run away from it all right now. Please.'

Hannah could hardly recognise him, but could see he was in a highly unstable state, and saw the wrench in his right hand. She could try to scream, but knew that she'd never make it out of the door.

Somehow, she found her voice. 'Well ... of course ... I've been missing you too, darling. Let me get dressed and we'll slip out of the side door. Just give me a minute or two.'

He seemed placated by the statement. Then she heard Lech's voice outside.

'Hey, Hannah, I'm getting drinks in the bar. Do you want your usual?'

She saw the fear in Ian's eyes, and needed to hold it together.

'Yes, please, Lech, and get a pint for Graham, will you? He's outside. A pint for Graham, OK? I'll see you both in the bar.'

'A pint for Graham? Oh ... yes, OK. Will do.'

Ian seemed a little calmer now. She needed to stay in control.

'Let me get my clothes on and we'll get going. They'll all be in the foyer.'

He smiled, then moved to hug her, but she pushed him off as she unzipped her stage costume.

'Plenty of time for that later, darling. Not now.'

She grabbed her top and put her jeans on as he listened at the door. She took as much time as she could.

'Come on. We don't have much time,' he said.

'OK. I'm ready now. Oh, sorry, forgot my handbag. Now, where is it?'

She tried to buy more time, but he grabbed the handbag and gave it to her.

'OK, I'm ready now,' she said. 'You go out first, check that the coast is clear.'

He slowly opened the door and leaned out into the darkened corridor. As he did so, she shoved her foot against his backside, and as he fell forwards she slammed the door shut behind him. She then held the door closed with all the strength she could muster.

Outside in the darkened corridor, the waiting Graham leapt on him, pushing him to the floor as Karen switched the light on. Ian somehow rolled Graham around as they fell, so that Graham was actually underneath him. He raised the wrench to strike but Lech, moving from behind, grabbed his arm and pulled it to one side. In one movement, he dragged him off Graham. Using his superior height, he pinned Castle to the floor, then used his left knee to pin his right arm. Graham then pinned the other arm with his left knee.

'It's all over now, sunshine. Just you hold it right there,' said Graham, a little out of breath.

Castle tried to wrestle free, but the combined weight of the two men was too much.

'You not get the message first time, pal. We don't treat women bad,' said Lech, picking up the wrench, just in case.

The security guard came through to help them roll Castle

over onto his front. Then they yanked his arms back and restrained him, using a pair of handcuffs that Graham had hung on to, just in case. Minutes went by as they waited for the police. In the meantime, Karen edged her way through and knocked on the door to the dressing room. Hannah let her in, then sat down, staring blankly ahead.

'It's OK, Hannah. They've got him secured outside. Just stay in here. The police will be here soon.'

She held a quietly sobbing Hannah for several minutes as they waited; then they heard the sound of a police car in the distance. After what seemed an eternity, she could hear voices outside. Eventually there was a knock at the door and Lech appeared.

'Is all OK. All done. They take him away now,' he said.

Karen led the still-shaking Hannah out into the foyer, while Debbie brought some coffee. Hannah said nothing, simply staring straight ahead. Carla Edwards came in and sat down in front of her.

'It's OK, Hannah. He's in custody now and he'll stay there. He's shown a propensity to violence and he's a flight risk. We'll leave things for tonight as you've had one hell of an evening, but I'll come down to take a statement from you and your colleagues tomorrow. Will that be OK?'

Hannah nodded and got herself together. Carla retrieved and bagged the wrench, then spoke briefly to Graham and Lech before leaving.

Lech picked up his pint of beer and sat down. Graham joined them shortly afterwards.

'Enjoying your pint, Graham?' Lech asked.

Hannah managed a smile.

Graham looked reprovingly at her. 'I'm teetotal of course, but mercifully Mr Castle didn't know that.'

Hannah shrugged. 'I didn't know what else to do, so when Lech shouted asking if I wanted a drink, I figured if I asked for a beer for you, he might just smell a rat. A pretty feeble effort but it worked, thank God.'

Lech shrugged. 'You sounded very strange, and the door was closed too. You normally leave it slightly ajar.'

Hannah spoke quietly. 'He was in front of the door, so I couldn't get away in any case, and he was holding that wrench as if he might use it. I didn't want to risk it.'

Karen nodded. 'One of the girls told me she thought she saw someone leave the show right at the end and go down the side. When Lech came through looking puzzled, I wasn't taking any chances, so I rang 999.'

Graham was sipping a coffee. 'He was bloody strong, I'll give him that. When Hannah shoved him, I thought I could get him pinned down, but he pretty much threw me sideways. Thank you, Mr Wojiek. I think that wrench might have done me some damage.'

'Well done to both of you. The two of you were very brave,' said Karen. 'Anyway, I think we'd better get Hannah home now, guys. Have you recovered a bit now, love?'

Hannah nodded. 'Yes. A bit. It was such a shock to see him sitting there when I came through the door.'

'My fault, really,' said Graham, 'I should have checked your dressing room first. I just didn't want to invade your space.'

Lech laughed. 'As they say here, Graham, you don't want to go there. They're so messy and they throw hairbrushes at you sometimes.'

With that, Karen helped Hannah on with her coat, and leaving Lech with his pint, the other three walked back up the pier together. Even now, there was a faint hint of light left in the western sky of high summer. As they reached the hotel, Hannah kissed Graham on the cheek and he took his leave. Karen went in with Hannah.

They had a glass of wine together, as Karen sensed that Hannah wasn't quite ready to be alone.

Karen took the initiative, 'You've been to hell and back these last few weeks. Why not take a few days off? I'm sure Amy won't mind, and Mel will understudy for you after your ordeal. You need to take some time.'

Hannah sipped the wine and weighed it up in her mind.

'Thanks, Karen. You've all been so kind to me, and you're probably being very sensible, but if I do that I'll just dwell on things that have happened. I'd rather get on with the job, I think. It's that buzz that's kept me going these last few weeks. I've loved headlining, too. It's just so great to be back.'

'You've done incredibly well. Why not think about it? Let me know in the morning. Just take some time to reach a decision. Are you OK on your own tonight? I can stay if you don't feel safe.'

Hannah shook her head. 'I'm fine now he's not out there, so there's nothing for me to be afraid of, is there? I'm just so glad that it's done. Graham's been just wonderful, you all have.'

Karen hugged her and headed for home herself. She was rather hoping that her mother would be asleep when she got home. But as she opened the door, Janet got out of her chair to welcome her.

'You're really late, love. Whatever's happened?'

'Oh, hell, where do I start, Mum? Pour me a whisky, will you? Actually, make it a double.'

It took a while for her to recount the story, Janet becoming more shocked by the minute.

'How on earth did you cope? I don't think we've ever summoned the police to a show before. It must have been terrifying.'

'Well, Graham and Lech did so well, and as for Hannah, well, I don't know where she gets her guts from. To stay calm and draw him into thinking she was going along with him? That was simply amazing. I'd have screamed my head off. She won't even take the day off. Says this is the best things she's done in years.'

'Well, she has performed incredibly well, love, hasn't she? Understudying Amy can't be easy.'

As they talked and drank their whisky, Karen began to relax. It had certainly been one hell of a day.

Finally, they seemed to have talked enough and Karen looked at her watch. It was gone midnight.

'Gosh. Time for bed, I think, Mum.'

'Yes. I think so, Karen. But I just need to update you on my evening.'

Karen had almost forgotten. 'Oh … yes. Sorry. I've rather monopolised things.'

Janet sighed, 'I lost it this evening and I hurt you. I'm so sorry. I just don't know what happened.'

'Yes.'

'Well, I spoke with both Jim Cameron and Miriam Pemrose earlier, and then I rang Tom Stanley. We've agreed to meet tomorrow to discuss a fundraising plan to buy the pier. You're right. It's your future and I need to finish the job before I retire.'

20.

The Following Week

Miriam and Janet were sitting in a smart conference room, ahead of their meeting with Julia Maitland. The fundraising had started the previous Friday, and the JustGiving page had exploded into life, generating hundreds of small donations, triggered mainly by reactions on social media.

Miriam was feeling positive. 'Clever of you, getting Karen to be the media contact, Janet. Young, passionate and a local girl, too. Donations are rolling in.'

'Well, someone has to take on the media interviews, and I didn't think I'd give the right impression. It will take up a lot of time, but it's going to be crucial in building momentum. I've spoken to our PR people and told them to give it all they've got.'

'But what about the show?'

Janet explained, 'Well, I've spoken to Les Westley, and we'll look after the matinees between us for the next month, so Karen is free in the daytime to focus on it. It's fortunate that he's at home right now.'

'I gather Lauren wants to help, too,' Miriam replied.

'Yes. She'd sing on the beach today if she hadn't been banned from singing. Her donation on JustGiving nearly gave me heart failure.'

Miriam nodded. 'She loved Cyril Brown. That speech she

made at his funeral. Hardly a dry eye in the church. But as wonderful as it all is, we both know that we've hardly scratched the surface. Let's hope Jim and Tom have found some big spenders.'

'Yes, I know. But I'm not saying that to Karen. She's so fired up you wouldn't believe. I can't bear the idea of us failing, but we're going to need a miracle, that's for sure.'

Miriam nodded, 'Well, those extra performances will help. I gather Lech rounded up the cast.'

'Yes. It's a great gesture. They don't get much time off as it is. Bucket collections at every performance, and Lech's even doing Cyril's Punch and Judy Show in the church to raise money.'

Julia Maitland came in at that moment, and they all hugged each other warmly. She had Cyril Brown's file in her hand.

'So, Julia, how's retirement?' asked Miriam.

'Early days. Still handing things over to people. But Cyril was a little bit special, so I wasn't about to hand this one over,' she said.

'A bit personal to you too, Julia; he told me he'd been a client of yours for years,' said Janet.

'Yes. He had. Well, that's why we're here, of course. It's been a little complicated to sort out, but I think we're there now.'

'I guess there's the house to empty, a bit of a mess as I recall,' said Janet.

'Well, no. That's quite easy, really. He's left that to his cousins to sort out. It's the rest of his estate that's been the problem.'

'The rest?' said Miriam.

Julia looked at the file, and then smiled at both of them.

'Yes. Now, tell me, I assume you've both heard of the author Celia Braun?'

Janet spoke first. 'Well, yes. Who hasn't? I've read a few myself. Women's fiction.'

Julia smiled. 'Well, suppose I told you that Cyril Brown was in fact Celia Braun?'

Janet and Miriam looked at each other. 'You're not serious? Celia Braun is not a woman?' said Miriam.

Julia shrugged, 'Which is why Cyril never disclosed who he was. He couldn't do book signings, and in the early days he wasn't comfortable performing in public after his stage fright, unless you were a child, of course.'

Miriam looked at Janet. 'Good lord. So, for all those years he was writing, and none of us knew.'

Julia nodded. 'Yes, he completed his last novel only days before he died. It's now with his editors.'

Janet realised. It now made sense. 'Well, thinking about it, when I visited him he always had that old laptop on the desk that he'd brought from home. I just thought he wrote stuff for television and radio. I had no idea.'

Julia continued, 'Cyril instructed me to sell the rights to his work, but more recently he was approached about a TV series and the film rights. It's a specialist area, and it only got resolved last week.'

Miriam and Janet looked at each other as Julia slipped a document out of the folder.

'So, as per Cyril's will I'm instructed to hand over this cheque, which I think will be well-timed given your current fundraising efforts.'

She slid the cheque across the table. Miriam and Janet looked at it.

'Oh, my God,' said Miriam.

'Is that nought in the right place?' asked Janet.

Julia smiled. 'Congratulations. I thought you'd be pleased. I wanted to tell you last week, but I couldn't.'

Janet was dumbstruck. 'It's, well, a complete game-changer. Thank you so very much,' she said, taking out a tissue from her handbag.

'Well, it's obviously Cyril who you should thank. Apparently, when he saw his books in the nursing home, he surreptitiously signed them all, the old devil.'

Janet shook her head. 'That doesn't surprise me at all.'

Julia slid an envelope across the table, addressed to Janet in Cyril's handwriting.

'Cyril asked me to hand this over to you as well, Janet. I suggest you open it later.'

'Have you got any more surprises up your sleeve, Julia?' asked Miriam.

Julia laughed. 'Only two more cheques, I'm afraid, one from the firm and one from me.'

*   *   *

It was late in the evening by the time Janet and Karen had an opportunity to catch up on the events of the day. Karen had done any number of media interviews and filmed a video for social media. Janet and Les had covered the matinee show, which had gone very well.

The cheque from Cyril was the largest by far, but only one of many that they had started to receive. Janet showed Karen one of the letters she'd received, on Majestic Hotel headed paper.

Dear Janet
If you don't mind, I'd rather keep this donation secret, for obvious reasons!

Good luck!
Jim Tyler

Amongst the others there were cheques from Jim Cameron and from Tom, while the comments on the online donations were just as touching. Karen was busily cashing up the day's bucket collections, too.

Janet showed her the letter from Cyril.

Dear Janet
Hopefully, my little donation to the theatre will be of some use. It had always been my hope that one day you would succeed where your father didn't and acquire the pier in its totality. Alas not in my lifetime, but hopefully in yours. I'm sure Celia Braun would approve.

My sincere thanks to you all for visiting me while I was in the nursing home. It made the days much more pleasurable and gave me a valuable break from my writing.

I hope my chat with Amy was useful to her. Stage fright is all in the mind, of course, but as I know only too well, the mind can play tricks which are sometimes difficult to unravel. From what I saw that day she is a wonderful talent and wouldn't be the first headliner we have seen to be riddled with self-doubt!

Thanks to Lech also, for giving Felix back his voice. It meant a lot to me. You are indeed fortunate to have such a talented compère.

But most of all my thanks to you for being such a dear friend over the years, in particular since my wife passed away. It is clear that you too will soon face that most difficult of decisions; when to retire. Karen is a talented lady who must have her day in the sun, and you have earned a long and enjoyable retirement. Don't be afraid to let go, Janet.

The pier was my second home, and I loved it very dearly. I hope that you find a new Punch and Judy man to replace me. Entertaining people, particularly children, has got to be the best job in the world, as we both know.

All my love
Cyril xx

'What a special guy,' she said, handing it back.

Janet took it and spoke as she read it once again. 'He's right, of course. About letting go. It's not easy, but I'm trying.'

'Yes, Mum, of course you are. Talking of which, will you do the prize-giving at Miriam's golf day? I'm on the BBC that day.'

'Yes, of course. It'll raise a few grand, for sure. Do you want to go to the ball at the Majestic? I'll cover the evening show if you and Bryn want a night out. I'll do Amy's gig instead.'

'Oh. Well, if you're sure you don't mind. That would be lovely. We've got some great raffle prizes coming in. Dad's dug up some football memorabilia, and some Wembley tickets. These raffles raise a fortune.'

'I expect Lauren's private musical evening will top the lot,' said Janet.

'I'd fancy Lech's kids' tea party if I had kids, it'll be hilarious. He's got the Felix voice off to a T.'

Janet sipped her tea. 'Yes, they're all rallying around. Great to feel the love, isn't it?'

'How about Tom? Has he had any luck?'

'Bit early for some of the big fish he's courting. But we've had some nice personal donations.'

'Oh, and you'll do the secondary school gig next week will you, Mum?'

'Yep. Might have to sing too, although Hannah said she'd come. It's going to be a school concert on steroids. Talking of which, Les is seeing what the record company will allow Lauren to do. She can't sing until the autumn, but Les wants to do a posh-frock fundraiser in London when she can.'

Karen frowned. 'The problem with all this is we don't have enough time to actually get it all in the bank, do we? Lots of events taking place later in the year, but I can't help think that in spite of everything we're doing, we're still a long way short of what we need in the 30 days.'

Janet was philosophical. 'Well, you said to trust in Tom, so that's what we'll have to do.'

'Are you going to *Hamilton* with him?'

'Yes. When this is all done and dusted. I'll probably stay over in London. Make a weekend of it.'

'Ooh! Mummy's going on a dirty weekend with Tommy!'

Janet looked at her reprovingly. 'Don't push your luck. I'm sure you and Bryn had separate rooms.'

'You're ... simply good friends, then?' smiled Karen.

'Well, that depends on whether he comes up with the cash.'

'I see ... I didn't know you were that expensive. At one time, all it took was a bag of chips and a bottle of cider.'

'You know what I mean, Karen.'

* * *

The following day started fine, so Amy Raven got up earlier than usual for the morning after a show. Hannah was headlining the matinee, so she thought she'd do something that she hadn't done for many years.

Picking her old guitar from the top of the wardrobe, she tuned it, then rehearsed five of her old songs, together with her latest single. It took an hour or so, but she was content. Her father helped her to load the gear in his car and ran her into Cromer. She took her battered old hat from the top of the wardrobe with her.

She took up her position in front of the pier, as her father erected a pasting table full of CDs and merchandise. The visitors wandered by, curious as to who this was.

'Just like old times,' said her father.

'Yep. I just hope I can do this. I'm really nervous, Dad. Strangers spook me,' said Amy.

'Well, you're under no pressure, love. Besides, look who's here. Hi, guys.'

Hannah and her daughter Gwen had arrived just in time. Hannah was dressed in her show costume, but with a coat over the top.

'We thought you might need some backup to collect the cash and keep the hordes at bay,' said Hannah.

It was Hannah who took the microphone by way of intro-duction, removing her coat to reveal her electric-blue show costume.

'Ladies and gentlemen, boys and girls. Welcome to Cromer Pier. You will doubtless have heard of the Cromer Buy our Pier campaign, so we've come down this morning to sing a few songs and relieve you of some cash. Please give generously. We've got signed souvenirs and CDs for you to buy, too. So, without further ado please give a big Cromer welcome to the star of the Summertime Special, the sensational ... Miss Amy Raven!'

Amy's father was relieved as his daughter cut seamlessly into her opening song, while Hannah and Gwen rattled the buckets.

The crowd gradually filled the ramparts along the promenade, and Amy's father was soon busy with the merchandise. The applause after each number grew and grew, along with Amy's self-confidence, and she wrapped up the set with her latest single. Hannah took over as Amy signed merchandise and posed for selfies. They finished with one of Amy's biggest hits sung as a duet.

Karen and Janet headed down for the matinee and were incredulous at the sight of the huge audience filling the front of the pier. They grabbed a bucket each to make sure those watching from the promenade didn't escape, either.

Amy eventually headed off with her father, while Hannah headed for the theatre for the matinee. Gwen had finished university, and was with her mother in the Cromer house that they had now moved back into.

'Wow, that was the best, Mum. What a great crowd,' said Gwen.

'Yes. I was worried Amy might struggle today, but she's a real talent.'

'Those buckets were full of money, and plenty of fivers, too. It raised a tidy sum,' said Gwen.

'We need every penny. It's great you were able to get down. I've missed you.'

'You should have told me about things, Mum. I'd have come down right away.'

'I didn't want to worry you. You've been through enough with your father as it is. It was time I stood up to him. I don't know what took me so long.'

'Well, at least you have done now. It's not a nice thing to say about my dad, but he's better off in prison. He needs sorting out.'

'Yes. He does. But at least we can live our lives in freedom now, and you can see me headline today. Who'd have thought it 12 months ago?'

'Not me, Mum. I'm looking forward to it.'

21.

The Deadline Approaches

'Well, that's great news, Jason. I'm so glad that your late father's foundation is providing such a generous donation. With you on board, we've nearly pulled it off. I'm so grateful, and I know Karen and the team will be, too.'

Tom put the phone down and sighed. He refreshed the JustGiving page, and keyed the updated total into the spreadsheet, along with the Kerslake Foundation donation.

The updated figures took them beyond the figure required. He breathed a huge sigh of relief. It had taken all of his ingenuity and contacts to get it done. He had called in every favour, and fortunately he had a fair few of those. In a worst-case scenario, he was the Grim Reaper, but on many occasions, he had salvaged bits of businesses or whole entities.

Mike Kerslake had been one such client. He was a brilliant engineer obsessed with an invention that had simply ran out of money, until Tom Stanley had stepped in and developed a business plan which raised the capital necessary to see the project through. When Kerslake died a multi-millionaire two years ago, Tom had attended the funeral, at which Mike's son Jason announced the establishment of a foundation in his father's memory. There had been a number of other ex-clients happy to repay a favour.

Tom was relieved since the deadline was so close, and he could now provide the necessary proof of funds to get the purchase done. He was relying on future fundraising events in the pipeline to provide the reserves necessary for the bigger business that it was about to become and meet the ongoing maintenance costs of a listed Victorian pier.

He was about to tell Janet the good news when his phone rang.

'Hi, Tom. It's David Collinson from the administrators.'

'Hi, David. I was going to ring you later. What can I do for you?'

'Well, it concerns the purchase price for the pier, I'm afraid. You see, our quoted price to you was based on two market valuations obtained by Pemrose management. However, we've now received an offer around 15% higher than that, and as you will know, given our obligations to creditors, it puts me in a difficult position.'

Tom groaned. This was a disaster. They just didn't have any time left. He pondered a little before responding. Let's meet fire with fire he thought.

'Well, given that, as of this afternoon, we're in a position to provide proof of funds to meet your original offer, I would of course expect you to honour it as a legally binding contract. I find it suspicious that this offer arrived only two days before a deadline that only you, the bank and Pemrose knew about. Forgive me, but It feels like a Lionel Pemrose scam to me. Have they even provided proof of funds?'

'Tom, this is really difficult for us both. I've asked for proof of funds from the consortium concerned, but I rang you soonest to try to work out how we can get around it. I'm really sorry, I know you guys have moved heaven and earth, but can you see it from my angle?'

Tom decided to play along. 'All right David. I do understand, although I believe that if we sued, we'd win. I think a conversation with Peter Hodson is called for.'

'I agree. Peter's expecting your call. He knows the consortium involved, but of course I can't reveal that information.'

Tom rang off, and immediately briefed Jim Cameron, who wasn't exactly surprised.

'It explains why Lionel got the two valuations, doesn't it? He knew that the administrator would use them to quote a figure to us, then he makes a late bid largely using other people's money that he knows we can't match. He knows it drops both us and Peter Hodson in it and screws his ex-wife and Janet Wells into the bargain. You've got to hand to him, Tom, he's a cunning bastard.'

'Well, I'm not a good loser. Is there anything that you can do to find out who's in this consortium? To find out who we're up against? They still have to provide proof of funds, and I've still got another couple of days.'

Cameron thought for a moment. 'Well, sadly there isn't, short of burgling the administrator's office at the Majestic.'

'OK. Let's see what Mr Hodson has to say about it. Frankly, I can't see how Lionel would convince investors to buy it. The results haven't been particularly good, have they?'

*   *   *

Lionel Pemrose sat contentedly on his lounger by the pool, looking at his telephone and the email from David Collinson acknowledging his consortium's offer. He'd left it as late as he dared, and even Tom Stanley would now be in a tailspin. Hodson would have to take his offer, if he hadn't already been suspended for misconduct. He would have to do anything to reduce the bank's losses.

He'd heard about Miriam and Janet's attempts to raise the hideous amount of money required of them in an impossible timescale, knowing, as he did, that he was part of the new consortium which would buy the pier and completely ignore the terms of the lease. His consortium would simply occupy the theatre and run one-night shows, while Miriam and Janet ran out of money in pursuing legal action. He couldn't work out why he hadn't simply starved her out before. It had been Freya's idea, actually.

She was lying topless on the lounger next to him, and he turned to kiss her between the shoulder blades. She stirred, but simply murmured contentedly and then ignored him completely.

* * *

It was early the following morning when Peter Hodson showed Tom into his office. Neither was in a particularly good mood. Tom had still said nothing to Janet because she couldn't do anything to help. It was his job to sort this problem out.

For his part, Hodson was due to meet an investigating officer that afternoon, looking into Lionel's complaint, so this latest twist of the knife was something he could do without.

'I'm sorry about this Tom, I really am. I can't say too much, but we both know who's behind this don't we? So, we need to find a way out of this that satisfies us both.'

'Well, I'd be pleased to, Peter, but my legal advice is that the offer letter from the administrators is legally binding, and we can successfully sue them if they take Lionel's .... I mean the consortium's offer.'

Peter shook his head. 'And we both know you wouldn't have the resources to see it through, so let's ignore that. I need something I can defend. If you can come up with 5% more I'm free and clear.'

'I'm sure you are, Peter, but you've seen the mountain we've had to climb already. Surprisingly, we don't have another 5% to lob in the pot, and I've no chance of raising it in the next 48 hours.'

'That's what banks are for aren't they?'

'Not in 48 hours, Peter. Oh, unless you'd give it to us, of course.'

Hodson smiled. 'Well, I can, as a matter of fact. It's within my delegated lending limit, so I don't even need credit approval to do it. I don't want you to have to pay any more than the letter said, but if you can't come up with a good reason for me to reject the consortium's offer, then it's a backup. Janet gets her pier, at least. I know it's a pretty crappy scenario, but it's the best I can do.'

Tom followed his logic. In life, sometimes you have to suck it up and accept that what you want comes at a price. He didn't like the idea of selling this solution to Miriam or Janet, but if that was the only option …

'That's a win/win from your point of view though isn't it? And how can I discredit their bid if I don't know who the members of this consortium are? Come on. You've got to help me out here.'

'Well, I can see that. They even played at Miriam's golf day recently. I really can't say any more. To use a golfing term, I can't be nearer the pin than that, if you read me, but I'm sure Jim can help.'

'OK. I'll do my best.'

*   *   *

They met at Miriam's within the hour.

'It's not much to go on. There were 30-odd four balls that day, and more fat cats than you could shake a stick at,' said Miriam.

'I agree,' said Jim. 'They travelled in from other clubs too. I didn't know all of them myself. Was that all he said? Nothing else at all?'

Tom thought for a moment. 'Well, he did say something like, "I couldn't be nearer the pin than that." I'm not a golfer. Does that mean anything to you?'

Miriam thought for a moment, then smiled. 'Ah. He means the Harlequin group. They were playing the fourth hole, Tom, which is very short. We had a prize for the player who hit their drive nearest to the pin. The Harlequin group won it.'

Jim nodded. 'Oh, yes. I remember. One of them hit a cracking shot. His ball stopped not more than three feet from the flag.'

'So?' said Tom, somewhat perplexed about a game he just about understood, but had never played.

Miriam explained. 'Well, three of those guys are business associates of Lionel's, based in Great Yarmouth. They've all got access to some money, but the only one with any real clout is Lawrence Middleton. If we get to him, then the house of cards falls over.'

'So how do we get to him?' asked Tom.

Miriam smiled. 'One for you I think, Jim?'

Jim laughed. 'Oh, I do think so, Miriam. Leave him to me.'

*   *   *

As she entered the Majestic that evening, Janet couldn't help thinking that holding a fundraiser for the Cromer Pier Theatre Trust in the personal fiefdom of Lionel Pemrose was rather ironic. But Miriam had insisted that it was the right venue, and she was a director of Pemrose Hotels, too. Tyler took the view that his job was to generate profit for his employers, and he was not about to turn away a booking.

For Tom's part, he hated black-tie events, but as Janet had invited him it seemed churlish to refuse. Maggie had often chided him for being anti-social, and as the evening involved a rather nice dinner, with good company, followed by an intimate acoustic Amy Raven set, it seemed worth donning the hired penguin suit for.

As seemed to be the case throughout their brief association though, he was again keeping a secret from Janet. He could only hope that Jim would weave some magic, and that the matter in question would melt into history.

He kissed Janet on the cheek as they met. She was wearing a stunning dress in deep crimson, and really looked radiant tonight. She was in her element, knowing virtually everyone there, while he knew hardly anybody at all.

Pete Hodson had a table, he noticed, presumably a bank table, and he saw that Janet skilfully avoided that particular gathering. Instead, she headed for a table near the front, where Miriam stood talking to Julia Maitland, and he noticed Jim Cameron and his wife. Well, at least I won't be talking to strangers, Tom thought.

'Where are Lauren and Les?' asked Janet.

Miriam looked at her watch. 'Come on, Janet, have you ever known Lauren to be on time?'

'Only onstage,' murmured Janet.

'How's Amy?' asked Miriam.

Janet understood. 'Ah, *that's* where Les and Lauren will be. Soothing Amy's pre-match nerves. Big step tonight.'

Tom was puzzled. 'Why is that? This must be easier than doing the Summertime Special every night.'

Janet looked at him reprovingly. 'I'll tell you later.'

The meal followed, and Tom found Jim's wife good company. Les told a number of stories about Lauren's tour, which, although very funny, got him some good-natured looks of admonishment from Lauren. There was a pause before the cabaret, and during this break, Jim took Tom to one side.

'Don't worry about Middleton, it's in the bag. I spoke to him earlier,' he said.

'Thank God for that. I didn't want to have the Hodson conversation with Janet.'

Jim laughed. 'A swift way of ending a beautiful friendship, I suspect.'

Even then, Tom took nothing at face value. Things changed quickly, so he would wait until the administrator contacted him before doing anything. It would be a long and nervous wait.

As the guests started to settle, it was evident that there was some sort of delay. Les had gone behind to do the introduction, and Lauren followed a while later. Tom could see that Janet was becoming nervous.

When Lauren arrived backstage, Amy was sobbing, and Les had his arm around her.

'Whatever's the matter?' asked Lauren.

Amy said nothing.

Les looked at Lauren. 'Says she can't do it. The stage fright's back.'

Lauren was unimpressed, 'Well, that's no bloody excuse, is

it? I don't think Cyril would be happy, and that's a fact. Now you get your fat arse on that stage, Lesley. Amy's audience is waiting.'

Les shrugged, knowing better than to argue, and went out front.

Lauren pulled Amy to her feet, stuck a tissue in her hand, and passed her the guitar. She kissed her on the cheek. 'You gotta do this, princess. It destroyed Cyril but it's not destroying you now, is it?'

They could hear Les doing a few warm-up gags, but then he cut to the introduction.

'Over the years, the Summertime Special show has seen some stars born and reborn. Back in 2009, we were blessed to have Lauren Evans, but we also have a local girl who I first saw busking on the pier. Now she's a big star, ladies and gentlemen, Cromer's very own Amy Raven!'

With Lauren's hand on her shoulder Amy took the faltering step through the curtain, smiled and embraced Les, before plugging in the guitar, and playing a couple of chords to herself.

'Thanks, Les. Great to see my friends all out tonight. I'd like to dedicate this set to our late, great friend Cyril Brown.'

22.

Decisions. Decisions

It had been a long wait. The bank had sent across the documents for the loan agreement and Tom had sent them on to Miriam, hoping that they wouldn't be needed. He couldn't tell the administrators that they would match the consortium's offer, of course. He just had to hold that card in reserve.

It was around 4pm that his phone rang as he sat in his room looking out to sea.

'Tom, it's David Collinson. It appears that the consortium has been forced to withdraw their offer because they can't provide proof of funds. As such, after a conversation with the bank, I can confirm that we are ready to proceed with the sale of the pier to the Cromer Pier Theatre Trust based on your offer.'

Tom put the phone down a few minutes later and smiled. He opened the door, went out on to the balcony and looked down at the pier, bathed in warm afternoon sun and festooned with fluttering flags.

He rang Miriam to give her the good news, and then Janet, who was with Karen at the theatre, at the end of the matinee. He also arranged to meet Jim Cameron for a beer.

He thought about Maggie and what she might have thought of the events of the last few months. He reckoned she'd have been pleased, and probably proud. He still missed her, and had felt guilty when he went to bed the previous evening and realised that he had not thought about her that day. She would doubtless say that he was being ridiculous.

He whispered to himself as he took in the picture-perfect scene.

'If this is my last hurrah, Maggie, then I think I've done good for once.'

*   *   *

Sitting outside on the pier, Jim Cameron was in fine form as he and Tom nursed their pints and toasted their success. The audience was slowly arriving for the evening show.

Tom set down his glass. 'So, go on, Mr Cameron. What did you have on our friend Middleton?'

Cameron spread his arms in mock defensiveness.

'Perish the thought, Tom. I simply made sure that he saw the planning officer's verdict on Lionel's 2009 redevelopment plan for the pier, while of course assuring him that his civil engineering concern could bid for the pier maintenance contract.'

Tom smiled, 'Yes. But that isn't all, is it?'

Cameron looked and him with a somewhat furtive smile. 'I don't know what you mean, old boy.'

Tom shook his head. 'I know a masonic handshake when I get one, Jim. I got one from you, but not from Lionel.'

Cameron considered carefully. 'Well, he wanted to join, but then he'd have wanted to control it, as he did all of his business dealings. You cannae do that with the masons.'

The show started, and Janet emerged from the foyer with a white wine in her hand.

'Is this a boys' club or can a mere girlie join?' she asked.

Tom stood and kissed her as she sat down. 'Cheers, guys. Good job, methinks,' she said brightly.

'Team effort,' said Tom, as they clinked glasses.

Jim was enjoying the conspiracy. 'An enjoyable gig the other night too, Janet. I gather Peter Hodson was well impressed.'

Janet glared and Tom laughed.

Jim continued. 'In fact, he gave me this to give to you.'

He handed over the envelope, and she dropped a piece of paper as she opened it. Tom stooped to pick it up as she read the enclosed note.

Dear Janet

My heartiest congratulations on your fantastic fundraising efforts. I'm delighted that the pier will be under your ownership in the years to come, as it should be.

Wishing you every success, I enclose my own donation.

Yours sincerely
Peter Hodson

Tom handed over the cheque and thought for a moment that she was going to tear it up.

He stopped her. 'Move on, Janet. Peter Hodson helped in ways you can't imagine. Why not bury the hatchet, love? We're too old for feuding.'

She pondered, then smiled, and leaned across to kiss him again.

*   *   *

It was a couple of weeks later when Janet finally got to see *Hamilton*. They had dinner at Balthazar's before the show. Afterwards, they travelled back to Tom's flat in Docklands on the Thames Clipper, the lights of Canary Wharf illuminating the skyline. She shivered slightly as the vessel picked up speed, and Tom put her arm around her shoulder. She turned and kissed him.

'Thanks, Tom, that was just fantastic.'

'I'm amazed you haven't been here more often.'

'I've never had the time. But hopefully from now on … well, who knows?'

They reached the flat, and Tom made tea. As he brought it in to the lounge, she was looking at two paintings.

'Maggie, I assume? She's beautiful, Tom.'

'Yes. I had them painted just before she was diagnosed. A local artist. A great piece of work.'

She looked at the other picture of a young girl, not more than eight or nine.

'But who is this, Tom?'

'That's our daughter, Sophie.'

'You never said …'

Tom paused. 'Well, I don't really talk about it. It's been a long time now.'

'What happened?' Janet whispered.

'Meningitis. Maggie always blamed herself, of course, but it wasn't so easily diagnosed back then. I was in Newcastle. By the time I got back, it was too late.'

'Oh my God, no. I'm so sorry Tom. That's just awful. So young,' she said.

'Yes, it was, but, hey, it's your evening, Janet; let's not dwell on the past. I do that a lot.'

She could see he was close to tears. She put her arms on his shoulders, so that she was facing him.

'But you will have so many memories of happy times. You must never stop telling me about them. You've travelled the world together. It's completely fine, please, really it is.'

'OK. I just get morbid from time to time, that's all,' he said.

'Well, that's perfectly natural, I should think. As for me, I feel like I'm playing truant from school, having fun while leaving Karen to mind the shop.'

'She needs to have the space to fly, and you need the space to have a good time. Bringing up a young child single-handed while running a theatre? You've bloody earned it.'

'Yes, I guess. Tonight, well, it was so special.'

'I'm sorry I didn't book somewhere posh like the Savoy, but time was a little short and frankly I find them all a bit pretentious.'

'Compared to Cromer, Balthazar's is positively upmarket.'

'Oh, I think the Majestic's jolly good, all things considered, if you don't think of it as enemy territory.'

Janet considered this. 'Well, as long as Lionel isn't in residence it's OK. They should put a flag up when he's there, like they do for the Queen.'

'He'll lick his wounds in Malaga for a while with his lady friend. He's a coward at heart. All that's left of his empire is the hotels, and Tyler runs those. If he's got any sense he'll retire, like Jim has. You need to know when to quit, Janet.'

'What, like you did? Don't make me laugh. I can't see you retiring any time soon.'

'Well, I'm not sure that anybody wants me now. Peter Hodson did me a favour when he rang, nobody else seemed to want me.'

'Well, if that was your last gig, it wasn't half bad. You won't find me complaining. But what will you do?'

'Well, I might still buy that place in Weybourne, if the locals will grant me asylum.'

'I think we might just allow that, but I'll need to check up on your whereabouts once in a while.'

'That would be a pleasure, Mrs Wells.'

23.

Finale

Janet dozed by the pool. It was still sunny and warm for late September, and the dressing gown she had on made her feel very comfortable and relaxed indeed. The infinity pool looked out over Lake Como, and she never tired of the view, even after five days. Venice had been simply beautiful, especially when you got up early and stayed up late to dodge the crowds. Then to come here, to soak up the scenery, take the boat everywhere instead of driving, shop in stylish shops, eat and drink indulgent Italian food, or simply lie in the sun with a trashy novel... It was all quite idyllic. Oh, and as for the opera in the arena in Verona, well, words failed her.

Reality would return soon of course, although now it would be a different sort of reality. She suddenly had someone she trusted, who was intelligent and cultured, and who shared her interests. Tom had bought the house in Weybourne, meaning Karen and Bryn had the house in Cromer virtually to themselves.

They needed to go home so that Karen could take her much-deserved holiday, joining Bryn in Nashville. The season was over, and the planning for the Christmas show had already started. Karen was now creative director, while her mother was executive director, but only until interviews found a replacement, and certainly by the spring she would retire for good.

Hannah was already booked to do the Christmas show, and most likely next year's Summertime Special. Amy was back in the West End, and Tom had lined up tickets for her opening night. Lech was on cruise ships in the Caribbean all winter, but would be back next summer, with Felix of course.

They had left things pretty much as they were with the bar and restaurant. Debbie was perfectly content with her promotion, but Karen's bigger plans would be for the next executive director to implement. Miriam would make sure that the trust was professionally managed, with Jim Cameron joining the board of trustees.

She was also looking forward to Lauren's three nights at the Albert Hall. The proceeds from one night would give the trust the reserves that both Tom and Jim had insisted on.

Peter Hodson had taken early retirement the previous month. He'd been officially exonerated by the inquiry into Lionel's complaint, but when offered voluntary redundancy he'd decided to take it.

As for Lionel? Well, he had not returned from Malaga, apparently staying with Freya in the sunshine of southern Spain.

Janet sensed movement, and a shadow closed out the sun momentarily as she felt a light kiss on her forehead. She declined to open her eyes.

'So, you've finally woken up then, Tom. What time is it?'

'Only 4pm. We've plenty of time. Time isn't important to either of us anymore.'

'I only got up because you were snoring.'

'That's what happens after you have a bottle and of red wine with lunch.'

'Oh, yes? You didn't exactly fall asleep immediately though, did you?'

'Well, that would have been discourteous. Besides, It's always nicer in the afternoon.'

'It is, is it? Well, I suppose there won't be many siestas when we get home, Tom, and certainly no skinny dipping in a pool.'

'Perhaps not. I'm not sure what the neighbours would say.'

The End